MINSTRELS' COVENANT

Book II

of

The Minstrels' Tale Mystery

Nance Bulow Morgan

Dreamer Books

Marston, NC

This is a work of fiction. The events and characters described herein are imaginary and are not intended to refer to specific places or living persons. The opinions expressed in this manuscript are solely the opinions of the author and do not necessarily represent the opinions of the publisher. The author has represented and warranted full ownership and/or legal right to publish the materials in this book.

Dreamer Books
www.dreamerdesigns.net
Nance'sOffical Website
www.nancebulowmorgan.com

ISBN: 978-0-9915625-1-0
Library of Congress Control Number: 2014937801

Nance Bulow-Morgan

Nance Bulow-Morgan and the Dreamer Books Logo are trademarks belonging to Nance Bulow-Morgan

CREATED AND PRINTED IN THE UNITED STATES OF AMERICA

Dedication

To my dear friend and cohort, Dennis Jindrich, for sharing some great adventures, both real and imagined, and making me understand that there is a place for mysteries in the fantasy genre.

To Carolyn Jindrich, for allowing our imagined adventures to play out in your home for years and still finding a way to love us. We love you too!

·~·Foreword·~·

After a harrowing adventure through the gates of Hell our heroes have settled down in the beautiful and cultured city of Mareese. They have just put to music their tribute to the forgotten race of dwarfs and the sacrifice they made to keep all Mankind from the evil that lies behind those gates to hell. Their reputation as minstrels has grown and they are asked to perform at a reception for a visiting ambassador.

As they play for the gathered guests, the ambassador is murdered in front of them all. Known for their skills at investigation the two minstrels are caught up in the events surrounding the murder.

Join us now as we check in on our intrepid heroes as they prepare for the evenings festivities…

·~·Table of Contents·~·

·~·Chapter One·~·

I was feeling well recovered from my greatest adventure. I had been to the ninth level of Hell and it left me with no small melancholy. The deep curse that had been laid on me had never completely left me and I still bear the deep chill of it, but I have learned to cope. In that adventure I found my long lost mother and released her from the bonds of The Dark One. In long nights since she has written to me the events of my life that she had hidden from me.

I learned that The Dark One, whose name is Malisgalar is my father. In human form he seduced my mother, a witch, so that he might sire a child of great power. He would be very disappointed in me. My mother had discovered his true nature and knew that he was a devil when he came to her again on the day I was born. He stayed only long enough to see if his spawn survived, then he went away again to wreak his havoc elsewhere, intent on coming back for me when I came of age.

He did return and found my mother alone in our forest hovel. She had been sent away. I always thought she sent me away to learn the martial arts, but I learned that she had done it to hide me away from him. When he returned she would not tell him where I was. He took her captive and returned with her to his hell to torture her for the information. When he could not get it from her he cut out her tongue, but did not release her from his hell. He found a way to set in motion the events that would reveal me to him and bring me to his realm instead.

Malisgalar and his dark armies did battle with many righteous armies of men. Montar was triumphant in the end, and with great strength, and the aid of magic he put the devil back into his hell and bound him there. Even though the devil was ensnared he still had minions who were not and they cast about the lands in search of the means to release him from his chains and to find me.

As with all things, even magic can be undone. His minions stumbled upon the means, but the keys they needed to unlock his binds were cast across the lands. They were defeated for a time by the safeties that Montar and his magicians and clerics had put into place. Their triumph was that I became one of the people caught up in the efforts to keep him imprisoned.

Time passed and life seemed to go on in its steady way for me. I searched for my mother where ever I went, not knowing what had happened to her. I met my partner Andreas during this time and we travelled together from then on. It is at that junction of my life that my time caught up with itself and I was thrown into events that would destroy Malisgalar, recover my mother, and reveal my dark heritage. After the events played out I was worn of body and spirit and I needed rest. But first, I needed to see to the well-being of my dear Mam who raised me with much love even when persecuted for being a witch.

My partner Andreas and I had been acquainted with the new governor of Mareese when she gave aid to our quest to defeat Malisgalar once and for all. She offered my mother a place in that great city. They were in need of an apothecary and my mother had a vast talent for it. She had no worldly possessions, and I had only what I could carry on my back or in a portion of a carpet bag that I shared with Andreas. So a deal was made and with the wealth I had accumulated I set her up in a small shop with a kitchen in back and a small apartment above.

I spent the better part of a year at rest, only working to compose a Bard Song, The Lament of the Mountain King, with Andreas. When we were satisfied with it we took ourselves to an open overlook within the city and began to play. A crowd gathered as we performed the Bard song, and our fame as minstrels began to grow ,and our pockets became full again. It was a good life and for the first time we both felt as if we had a home.

The continent of Crystalier and the city of Mareese were at peace, but, remnant hordes still roamed throughout other lands causing pain and havoc. There was still evil, but there were always those who stood up to fight against it.

On the continent of Ahnges they had a history of war that went back through all generations for as far back as history was recorded. Even while routing the hordes from their lands they could not come together. There are seven cities on Ahnges all of them ancient and ruled by kings of ancient blood lines. All but one of them was greedy for control. King Frahn was hungry for unity, but the other kings clung to old ways and would not unite behind him. After the events that brought down Malisgalar he became very interested in the emerging powers spread out across the sea. He sent spies to evaluate Crystalier and Dinar and report back to him. After hearing their reports he sent an ambassador to visit the various realms and fashion a treaty that would increase trade and open diplomatic channels. His hope was that then the other kings would see his city, Nagrom as a base of influence, a port city and capitol from which they could all prosper.

The Ambassador was a likeable man named Esporanza. Eight years senior to King Frahn. He arrived on Crystalier and made Mareese his first stop there. He and Governor Diony Vin Heile have gotten along well. She is anxious to improve her city since the rebellion that brought down the overlord two years ago. The city thrived under her loving leadership, but revenues were hard to come by since the overlord overtaxed, and kept the money for his personal coffers. What money was regained in the rebellion had to be used to reinforce defenses during the Horde Wars that developed while Andreas and I and our Paladin comrades moved on the gates of Hell and Malisgalar himself. There was no dispute about the treaty from Mareese. Diony saw it as a way to regain wealth and gain a powerful ally. She planned a reception in Esporanza's honor and together they would announce the treaty details to the nobles of Crystalier.

Tourabain, the Duke of Ge and his wife Modglyn were in attendance with their adopted son Web, his young wife, and a small entourage. Soros and Jen who had been key to the success of the Mareesian Rebellion had returned from their woodland holdings for the first time since. They came along with a few men and women who made their life in the solitude that the woods afford. They meant to see their interests protected. Mayor Brohaugh from the southern city of Jour was in attendance. This was his first meeting with Governor Vin Heile, but they had a common cause to better the lives of their citizens and their first encounter was mutually beneficial. The fishing town of Coastello sent their mayor and several representatives of the fishing trade. The Elders from the Mystics Academy were all in attendance as were several heads of trade guilds throughout the cities of Jour, Coastello, and Mareese.

The event promised to be a great event and Andreas and I had been asked to entertain. I was delighted by the prospects and fought back the chill and the haunting memories of my last adventure. We had lost one of our dear companions by my hand while under the possession of one of Malisgalar's minions. I shudder from the pain of it still, the utter dread that I felt that night came back to me in full each time I remembered Wallace. I had just begun to dare to love him when the minion took us both in his control and when he was done

4

with us Wallace lay dead by my hand. I fought back the memory and struggled to put on a glad face.

I spent the early part of the day assisting Mam in her shop. An agitated young man was one of our last customers. I had to calm him while Mam mixed the ingredients for his pregnant wife's ailment. He feared for the life of his wife and unborn child. I put my hand on his shoulder and calmed him the best I could.

"Be calm Phyla, my mother is very good at what she does. It is just that the ingredients you require are back in the kitchen. She is preparing the potion right now. I will check on her for you. I'll be right back. We will have your lovely wife and your unborn babe as right as rain, you'll see."

The young man calmed at my words, but the look of concern did not leave his face.

I crossed the shop and pulled back the curtain just as the bell above the door jingled and another customer entered the shop. This was a young woman about fourteen years of age. She was well dressed and carried herself proudly.

"Someone will be with you in a moment, Miss," I announced and went behind the curtain.

My petite white haired mam was spooning a mix of herbs from a mortar into a silk sack. When it was nearly full she held the poultice close to her heart with her eyes closed tight. Then she placed the sack against her forehead. With her eyes still closed she moved her lips in the words of an incantation. No words were heard, but instead soft grunts as she whispered across her tongue-less mouth.

I stood in silence with my back to the closed curtain waiting for the breath of magic that would fill the pouch. When it did, mother pulled the pouch down and still incanting tied a tight prim bow around the opening. She smiled at me and gave the poultice a loving pat, then came around the table with it.

"I must prepare to leave for the Manor," I announced. "You have another customer waiting. I will see you in the morning. I'm sure it will be a late night."

Mam patted my throat and looked me in the eye. With the hand that held the poultice she made a motion against her own throat as if releasing some sound from there. It meant sing beautifully.

"I will Mam."

Mam patted my cheek, drew back the curtain and went into the shop. I watched as the young male customer took the poultice eagerly, paid his coin and turned to go, but Mam grabbed his arm to stop him. She took a slip of vellum from the sash of her apron and unfolded it for him to read. He did read and said, "Thank you, Pria," before rushing out the door, and running up the street.

Mam turned to the young woman customer with a welcoming smile. A slight tilt of her head and a practiced slant to her eyes said, "What can I do for you?"

It took the young woman a moment to realize Mam was a mute. It embarrassed her and she stammered a bit before she recovered her composure. Mam just stood by patiently and smiled in an attempt to sooth the girl.

"My father needs something for a blinding headache. He is Ambassador Esporanza, the guest of honor at tonight's festivities at the Governor's' manor and he is currently indisposed. He needs something that will make him right quickly."

Mam knew just the thing and went about the shop gathering fresh herbs from plants in the window or dry from jars, boxes, or drying racks. Mam was meticulous about her shop and everything was exactly placed in categories and labeled in bold letters on parchment glued to the containers or tied by string to the stems of plants.

I smiled as I watched her. She hummed as she worked. It was good to see her so happy. All she had ever wanted was to help

6

people. In Mareese they held no animosity toward her. She thrived and the help she gave brought her peace. I watched a while longer cherishing her.

She took her gathered ingredients back to a counter and took down a glass vial and a bit of wax. Next she pulled down a short stout candle and a round disk on a rack that she placed above the candle. She lit the candle and moved to a cabinet from which she retrieved a flagon of oil. She poured enough oil to fill the disk to one of the marks she had scratched on the surface. She let the oil heat as she crushed fresh leaves into it and then added a pinch each of two finely ground powders. When the fresh leaves were properly wilted, she pressed them down hard into the oil to extract any remaining essence from them. She plucked the leaves out with a silver tweezers then crushed two dried leaves into a dust using a stone mortar and pestle. This she added to the hot oil and whisked it gently with a straw brush. When the ingredients were blended and the heat was right, the oil turned from a light amber to nearly clear. She poured it slowly into the brown glass vial so as not to bruise it and stopped it with a pinch of wax down the bottle neck and three drops of wax dropped individually to drip and dry across the lip and down the outside of the neck. She set that aside and went to a small writing desk to write out the prescription instructions.

The vellum Pria handed the young woman was crisply folded, but she unfolded it to reveal the writing to her. She pointed out the headline. "Take only as instructed."

"And that will cure his headache?"

Mam nodded her white haired head and pointed again at the directions she had written. The young woman who had come on the ambassador's behalf looked down but did not read. "He has been under a great deal of stress. The negotiations in Behlanna went poorly. Now he turns to your young Governor. She is gaining a very

7

shrewd reputation. I cannot tell you the hoops she has him jumping through. He has not been well since we arrived here, the poor devil."

Mam gave a sympathetic shrug to her shoulders.

"Well, thank you," the girl said and took the vial from Mam. "I should run this right to him." Mam tapped the paper one last time as the girl turned from her toward the door, but the girl did not look at it. The bell on the sash rang and the girl waved the paper as she shouted, "Thank you," and skipped off down the street. Mam watched after her with a concerned look on her face.

I turned and went through the kitchen up to my room to prepare for the evening's event.

***

Harp and flute music lilted out to the streets through the open entry doors of Governor Diony Vin Heile's home. Children danced along the board walks and an old man spun his good wife who kicked up her heels before they walked off hand in hand. In the Manor House, guests were milling in from their estates, or lodgings in town, or quarters within the manor. Serving staff milled about with earthenware demijohns of mead and wine to fill the revelers cups.

I sat crossed legged on the edge of a dais set near the large hearth to the side of the great hall. Andreas stood softly plucking the strings of his mandolin. We would play softly until the meal was served then eat at a small table set aside for us next to the dais, nearer the hearth. When the meal was over the Governor, at her discretion would request entertainment and we would play a few songs singing harmony on them all.

Several young courtesans stood nearby considering Andreas's good looks. Standing on the dais beside his seated partner he seemed taller than his natural six foot six inches. His tailored black silks lay softly against his lean musculature. His green eyes were piercing against his dark brown skin and his facial features were fine, square, and masculine. His hair fell black as ink in wild ringlets to his shoulders. He noticed the attention and smiled a great grin of white. The girls flustered, and moved away as one embarrassed group. I laughed aloud from my place beside him, but the sound was lost among all of the activity.

It wasn't long before the attention of a young knight found me. I wore a light blue gown that highlighted my olive skin gone darker from our afternoons playing on the streets. He was handsome and I noticed that our eyes were nearly the same color blue. His eyes did not meet mine as they scanned down from my newly cut auburn hair that accentuated my long neck. He had stopped his gaze on me as he entered in with the Jourian entourage. The entourage passed around him and still he stood enthralled. At one time a man as handsome and as stationed as he would have peaked my interest, but since the adventure that took a lover away from me in the realm of darkness, and the cold dark that sits in my soul I have stayed very much to myself. Only Andreas and my mother know how I ache inside. I socialize, and go through my daily tasks at Mother's store, but inside I struggle with it. I gave the knight a nod as I played, happy that I did not have to smile while playing the flute.

Diony Vin Hiele made her entrance with her man and protector, Brynal. She was a young but shrewd governor of the city state of Mareese. Her youth was confounded by her long hair gone prematurely white. Still she was beautiful and her violet eyes almost always had a serene cast to them She was earning respect among the elder nobility across many lands. The guest of honor, Ambassador Esporanza followed with a young woman on his arm. I presumed she was his daughter, I knew her as the young woman who had visited Mam's shop for a headache cure. Two Ahngesian soldiers accompanied them in, but moved aside of the door and took a post there. The rest of the procession made their way through the guests to the head table. Esporanza was from the city of Nagrom on the large continent of Ahnges. He carried himself erect but was not overly proud as Ahngesians were known to be. He smiled and greeted people warmly as Diony introduced them. The young woman was indeed his daughter, Mya. She clung to his arm and nodded shyly during the introductions.

Dinner was delectable, and the governor talked at length with the ambassador during and after the meal. When the meal was cleared Diony made introductions of the ambassador to the dignitaries and guests and explained the details of the peacetime treaty. There were very few rules and the cities would be in control of their own enterprises, there would be a list made of what each city from both continents needed and what they had to trade for it. There was to be a great conference at a location, yet to be determined as soon as Esporanza had all parties signed on to accept the invitation. The location would be somewhere mutually acceptable All of the Ahngesian kings would be invited so that the individual cities could come together and negotiate. Nagrom and its broadminded king, Frahn, were offering all sort of incentives to agree to a treaty including small contingents of men at arms. The proposals were well accepted and after a brief session of questions and answers, Diony signed the treaty and put her seal to it. She called for us to play and then she and Esporanza carried the treaty document to the visiting Crystalier nobles for their signatures. Mareese was the first to sign. The document was not yet binding, but conveyed a unanimous interest in negotiating further.

We played a medley of country folk ballads but when the treaty was rolled up and delivered to Esporanza's lead guard for safe keeping we switched to a reel and Andreas began to sing. His tenor voice skipped playfully across the bawdry lyrics of Rudolf's Feud. A few young folks came to the floor to dance. Next I sang an ancient ballad that highlighted my range between alto and high soprano. We were into the first few stanzas of our first duet when the ambassador suddenly clutched his belly and lurched forward with a moan. Governor Vin Heile stood and leaned over him. He spoke something to her while others of the governor's and ambassador's circles ran over to assist. We watched attentively but continued to play soft calming music.

After a long time he sat back, pale, and sweating. He was encouraged to retire to his room, but after taking some water he refused and waved to the gathering. "Sorry, folks. That's what diplomatic missions will get you; a sour belly. I'm fine, really. Please go back to the festivity."

Andreas and I conferred a moment to agree on a piece that would calm the anxious crowd and began anew with an instrumental rendition of The Fairies Dream. Half way through Esporanza grabbed at his belly again and then his heart before he was thrown into violent convulsions that overturned his heavy chair and threw him to the floor before anyone could stop it. He hit his head on the chair and was out cold, but his body continued to thrash about. Mya screamed and Diony called for her physician who was already running across the room.

It was an awful scene. The poor ambassador slowed in his convulsions and regained consciousness after being held down by two of Diony's strongest men. He grabbed for his daughter. The looks on both faces were sheer terror. Thea the court physician could only speak soothing words to the man. She could do nothing to calm his continued thrashing. Diony's man Brynal and her security chief Ray Vin Wholfe did what they could to keep the anxious crowd back. They were for the most part cooperative but words like treachery and conspiracy were already being whispered in the crowd. Suddenly the convulsions stopped. Thea checked his eyes, his throat, his heart, and his breathing. She cautioned him to rest a moment before they saw him to his room. When it seemed that Esporanza would recover and he pulled his daughter close to whisper in her ear and give her a hug his body lurched again. His words to his daughter went unsaid. He arched the full length of his body while more shaking moved him across the floor on his side, knocking over chairs and serving tables before his attendants could stop him. Then he stopped, coughed up a clot of blood and died.

"Looks like the parties over, hey?" Andreas whispered in my ear.

"You are a cold bastard, Andy. Yes, Brynal and Ray are beginning to usher people out. Shall we play something?"

"What would be appropriate? Anything too happy seems disrespectful anything too heavy, a dirge played too soon."

"Your right. Let's pack up then and see if we can be of any help?"

"Right."

It didn't take us long to have our things packed away and join Diony at the table where she watched as Thea and one of Esporanza's men prepared to carry Esporanza to his quarters upstairs. Mya sat in a chair near Diony staring at the contorted body of her father. She was in shock and needed to be tended. Andreas knelt before her and cupped his hand under her chin to turn her head until she saw him. I did not see the other of Esporanza's guards and assumed he had run off on some errand related to the Ambassador's death.

"Come child, let me get you some brandy. It will calm you. Diony is there somewhere quiet we can take her?"

"There is an empty suite near theirs. I'll see it is made ready." She motioned to a servant standing at the perimeter of the room. The middle aged woman came over and Diony made her request. The old girl trotted off gathering two more maid servants as she went.

Meanwhile Brynal continued to talk to the girl, who only stared at him. "What is your name child? I am Andreas and my friend here is Saeede. Let us take you away from this. It has been a shock and we want to take care of you. Shock can be dangerous if not looked after. Come now." He held his hand to her and she took it, but did not stand. It was as if she had two minds, one that wanted to be away and another that could not bear to leave her father.

"They are taking him," she said, and that was all.

Thea and the guards were lifting him. Diony joined and we followed with Mya. We were escorted by two palace guards. When we came to the ambassador's suite I entered and saw that no one was there. Andreas stayed outside with Mya. Diony told me which door led to his room. I held the door as they moved in and placed him on his bed. Thea began to work on his tightened muscles so that she could lay him properly. I went into the other bedroom, assuming correctly that it belonged to Mya and gathered up the things I knew a young girl would need for the night. I stopped at the bed on my way out and gathered up two beautifully crafted rag dolls. I left the others tending to Esporanza. I knew that Diony would find us if we were needed.

The small suite was already prepared and a boy was running up with a flask of brandy just as we came to the door that Diony had directed me to. I opened the door and Mya moved in stiffly. Andreas took the brandy from the boy who ran off again. Once we were all inside he closed and locked the door behind us.

The servants had started a fire and I led Mya to the chair nearest it and wrapped her in a fur from the foot of the bed. Andreas found three glasses in a credenza and poured three fingers of brandy for each of us and one for the girl. "Sip this," he said. She did so and the warming liquid lifted a bit of her stunned pallor. Then the tears came and I moved to console her. Kneeling before her I reached up and hugged her to me. I let her cry for a long time, before encouraging her to sleep. She went to the only bed room in the suite. When she assured us that she needed no help we told her that we would stay in the parlor for the night, so if she did need for anything we would see to it.

It was quite late when a soft knock came upon the door. It was Brynal and the old servant woman. "Saeede, you had better come with me," Brynal said.

"We are watching over the girl."

"I know. Sel will take over for you. There has been a — development. I'll explain along the way."

Andreas and I followed and Sel took her place in the chair by the fire.

"Your mother has been arrested," he said, putting a hand on my arm to steady me.

"What?" The idea was incomprehensible. "About the ambassador? Why?"

"She sold the daughter a tonic for him this very afternoon. Thea has determined that he was poisoned. Y our mother has a great knowledge of such things. Diony and Ray are questioning her now, along with two of Esporanza's men."

"This is a mistake. There is no way my mother would ever do such a thing. Why would she? She hasn't a political bone in her body. There cannot possibly be a reasonable motive. She doesn't even know the man." I was nearly shouting and Brynal warned me to take control of myself. "She would not do this," I whispered.

***

Mam was on her knees on the floor in front of Diony's large desk. Her hands were bound behind her. Two men who I knew to be the ambassador's guards from the reception stood behind her with their arms crossed at their chests. Diony stood between her desk and my

14

mam. Ray Vin Wholfe was beside Diony. All eyes turned to us as we entered. I began to speak but Diony's look and words stopped me.

"Ah, here is the translator now."

"A minstrel?" One of the men said incredulously.

"Yes, is that so odd? Our Sade has many talents." My eyes were on my mother's and hers on mine. She was frightened and pleading for my help with her expressive eyes. The voices around me were a blur. Andreas nudged my arm and I became aware of Diony saying… "conspiracy to murder. Sade will translate." Diony motioned me forward.

The questioning began. Ray Vin Wholfe started, "Pria tell us where you were between three and nine hours last night."

The pathetic sounds of my mutilated mam came softly, shakily from her tongue-less mouth. Understanding her was as much about watching her lips form the sounds she could no longer make and matching them with those she could. Her mouth would open and reveal her stub of a tongue trying to form S's, L's, and T's for instance.

"H-pah."

"Shop" I repeated.

"Can anyone verify that?" Ray continued.

Mam shook her head no. "C-o-d"

"Closed," I said.

"When did you close?"

She shrugged her shoulders and held up three fingers to say she thought it was around three but she was uncertain. I translated that even though it was obvious.

"Did you sell a tonic to Ambassador Esporanza's daughter today?"

Mam shook her head yes. She looked at me, wondering why I didn't say more. I tried to implore her with my eyes to be patient.

15

Her eyes widened. I could not communicate in a way that had become common for us, as I faced the accusers who stood behind her.

"What was in that tonic?"

"Boo Err-I, Paperahit Oi, Eh-er eef," she began.

"Blue Vermine, Peppermint Oil, and Silver Leaf" I translated.

"Bar of Whi Wiow, Buer oom, and Ier."

"Bark of White Willow, Butcher's Broom, and Ginger."

"Are any of these ingredients toxic or deadly?"

"Ah ee ha mi."

"Not in that mix."

"Did you administer the tonic to the ambassador?"

She shook her head no.

"No," I said.

"Who then?"

She shrugged her shoulders.

"She doesn't know."

"Who did you sell the tonic to?"

One of the men behind mother spoke up. "This is insane she has told you that already!"

"Yes, so she has. Please remain quiet." Ray was annoyed. He had been trying to trip Mam up to see if she was lying. He was good at his job, but to have him use it on my mam angered me even more.

Being told to be quiet annoyed the man, but he seemed to realize his error and was silent for a time.

"I'll repeat the question. Pria, who did you sell the tonic to?"

"Ambahor auher."

"Ambassador's daughter."

"Are you certain? How do you know it as her?"

She shook her head, yes she was certain, and said, "He iro-u her-ef."

"Yes she is certain, because she introduced herself."

16

"Can you describe this person?"

She began by holding up ten fingers and then four while shrugging her shoulders.

"Around fourteen years old."

She took both hands and held them close together.

"Thin," I translated.

Then she held out a strand of her hair. She looked around but no one had the color she was looking for, "Bah-e"

"Blonde."

She made a circular motion around her face and then another that imitated a flower blooming.

"Beautiful," I said

"He wah…," she made a motion with her hands on either side of her face while wiggling her fingers.

"She was…," I began. "Nervous, Anxious?" I asked.

Mam shook her head no.

"Crazy?"

No.

"Scatterbrained?"

Yes, she shook her head yes emphatically.

"Why did she come to buy the tonic?" Ray continued.

"Ambahor ha hea ahe."

"The Ambassador had a headache."

"How did you give her instructions if you cannot speak?" Of course Ray knew the answer, he had been a customer.

Mam motioned as if writing with one hand while the other was a sheet of parchment.

"She wrote it down," I was saying, as Ray was asking; "You wrote it down?"

Yes, again that emphatic shake of the head.

"Do you do business here at the manor house often?"

"Nah offeh"

"Not Often."

"When was the last time you were here?"

"Ma a-oh."

"Months ago."

Ray hesitated a moment thinking of his next question, but never asked it.

"We need to speak to the daughter," he said instead.

"I hate to wake her, after such a shock," Diony said.

"Time is of the essence in such matters," Ray replied.

"Yes, I suppose you are right. Andreas, bring her," Diony ordered. Andreas nodded and left.

I knelt down by my mother and helped her up. The two men objected. "She is an old woman!" I said and led her to a chair, but I dared not unbind her hands.

I took a spot next to her and stood there with my hands crossed at my chest in imitation of the two men. The defensive stance did not go unnoticed by them or Diony, who gave me a withering look, but I shrugged slightly and did not rearrange my stance.

"While we are waiting I suppose introductions are in order," Diony said. "As you gentlemen know this is Sade a court minstrel." She used my common name and not the formal Saeede in an attempt to protect my identity. It seemed to work for there was no contradiction to it. The men simply nodded. "Sade this is Garthe and Gebha. They are Esporanza's guardians. They brought Pria to us with these accusations."

"Not Vin Wholfe?" I wondered.

"No," Diony replied. She was annoyed by that, I could tell, but she did well enough to hide it from the two men who did not know her well.

I would ask about it later. For whatever reason Diony was protecting my identity, or my connection to my mother, I was not about to call her on it with those two men present.

A long uncomfortable length of time had gone by when Andreas finally returned with Mya. She was sleepy and a bit disoriented, so Ray and Diony spoke to her gently prodding her to see what she remembered about the last evening's events before Ray took control again and began asking questions in his commanding manner.

"Mya did you go into town yesterday afternoon, before the reception?"

"Yes."

"Why?"

"To buy flowers for my hair."

"Oh yes, were they the flowers you wore in your hair last night?"

"Yes."

"Very Pretty. You looked quite lovely." Ray was putting her at ease.

"Thank you."

"Did you stop anywhere else?"

"Yes."

"Tell me where."

"I had a meat stick at a vendor near the Cause District and I also bought some embroidered slippers from a cobbler near there."

"Are those the slippers you are wearing now?"

She looked down at her feet, surprised to see them there. "Why, yes they are," she giggled nervously.

"You stopped nowhere else?"

"I was running out of time, the hour of the reception was drawing near, but Garthe had ordered me to stop at the apothecary for a headache cure."

"Is that true Garthe?"

"Yes. The ambassador had reported to Gebha that he wasn't feeling well. Gebha reported to me and since I knew Mya was going into town I tasked her with the errand."

"Did your father ever mention that he had a headache to you, Mya?"

"No, but he has been getting them often lately. He was complaining of being tired. The travelling was getting to his old body and I don't think he was sleeping well. There are a lot of pressures to what he does. Sleeping in a different bed every few days doesn't help him. He never mentioned a headache, but maybe he had one. It wouldn't surprise me. He tried to be strong about those types of things. Why?"

"We are not certain just yet. Have you ever met or seen this woman?" He asked indicating my mother.

Mya looked her over suspiciously, "Yes, she is the apothecary."

Ray leaned back against the desk weighing what he had learned. "Anybody else?"

"Did your father have any visitors during the day?" Diony asked.

"We would have known that," Garthe said, "and we have already told you he saw only Mya, and you, and your household servants. The servants brought him food and his bath in the afternoon. Mya was in and out, and you came, as you know, to go over the evening's agenda."

"When was the last time you saw Mya with her father?" Ray asked.

"Shortly after the third hour of evening."

"What did they do?"

"She brought him the potion and then went off to make ready for the evening," Garthe said.

"Went off? Do they not share a suite?" Ray asked with confusion.

20

"They do, but you wouldn't expect a young lady to make ready with the door open, would you?"

"Who administered the potion to Esporanza?"

"Well, he must have."

"Must have? You don't know?"

Garthe was suddenly angry. "We are not with the man every second. Had I known Mareese would be the cause of his death I certainly would not have left him. There was no indication he was in any danger."

Ray was silent again for a moment and he stared at Garthe in amazement, no doubt weighing him against his outburst. Diony clenched her jaw at the obvious slight Garthe had just leveled at her city and at her ability to keep it safe.

Garthe shifted under her gaze but no apology came.

"The old woman must be lying," Gebha interrupted the silence with a shrill voice. He was a young man, and his voice obviously was not done changing. He cleared his throat and continued "What is your hesitation?"

"I am not an impulsive man Gebha. This matter weighs heavily. I have before me a respected proprietor who has compassionately seen to the hurts and ills of this cities citizens. She is loved and respected here. I am searching for any question that will give me the answers we all want."

"What answers are those?" Gebha asked.

"Well, who of course. How and why. I really wish you would have come to me before you dragged this woman from her bed and accused her of this murder. It seems there was a span of time when anyone could have slipped in and administered an overdose. Perhaps Mya herself who was just in the next room."

Mya cried out. "No! I would never."

"Your own physician cries poison, who else would have that knowledge, but your apothecary?" Garthe shouted.

"Who indeed, how and why?"

"You do not believe that she did it?"

"I did not say that. And I will not say it until I am certain of it. I will question the household staff. We will ask if anyone saw Pria in the palace yesterday. Could anyone have tampered with Esporanza's food? Who handled his food? That sort of thing."

Mya gave a little whimper.

Diony said, "I am sorry Mya, I know this must be hard for you. It will not be easy on any of us. Hard questions will be asked and they must be answered. You can return to your room for now —Andreas."

Andreas moved to assist Mya and they were soon out of the room.

"What is your plan for the old woman then?" Gebha wanted to know.

"I see no other option but to hold her until we have more evidence. If she is guilty she will stand accused in front of a trial."

I could hold my decorum no longer, "What!" I knew I was about to blow whatever cover Diony was offering me and recovered. "Surely you can make some concession for her age. Those damp cells of yours will surely make her sick. You can keep her safe while investigating I'm sure."

Diony jumped in but leveled that cautious look at me again. "I will see what we can do for her. I will need extra guards. I think we can put her in the east tower."

I knew the east tower. It had been our home while we closed the deal on the apothecary shop.

"If you think that would suffice," I said, and let her see the relief in my eyes.

"I do. Brynal will you see to that?"

He nodded and went out.

22

Mother looked up at me from the corner of her eye. She did not know why I was not acknowledging her or why Ray was not asking if I had witnessed the purchase, but she had good instincts about it and gave no reaction that would connect us.

Brynal returned after a short time with two guards and escorted Mam away. She gave me one last conflicted look over her shoulder as the door closed and she was led away.

"I believe that is all for now," Diony said to us all. "Sade, keep yourself available to us. I am sure we will need your services." She emphasized services slightly, and I was certain she would be asking Andreas and I to begin our own investigation. "Garthe, Gebha, we will keep you informed. You are welcome to stay as long as you like. Mya will be happy for your familiar faces. Get some rest before the sun rises."

With that we all filed out and left Diony and Ray behind the closed door of her office.

***

Andreas slept in the chair close to the fire. Sel had gone back to her own room after we returned from the interrogation in Diony's office. I could not sleep from the anger and the worry. I became more and more angry about the situation the longer I dwelled on it. The look in my mother's eyes as they took her away broke my heart.

What was Diony thinking allowing her to be locked up? She knew my Mam. Then I was angry at being made a party to it. My anger was excusable, yet irrational and my loyalties were strained equally with lucid reasoning and trust; hot disdain and confusion. I paced the balcony in the chill of the morning and watched as the shadows of Mareese diminished to pink, then orange, then white as one sun, then the other moved up the arc in the sky. Through the space between buildings I caught a twinkle of the sea reflecting them

23

back. I took a deep breath to brace myself for a long day, and turned to go wake Andreas.

Diony stood in the arched doorway looking out at the same scene. She met my eyes as I turned. "Sorry, I did not mean to disturb you."

"How long have you been there?" I looked passed her to see Andreas still sleeping in the chair.

"Only just arrived. Have you slept at all?"

"Couldn't"

"Neither could I. Ray and I had a long talk about Esporanza and his death. Then I woke Thea and talked to her at length. I have only just left her."

"And?"

"And—it is a certainty that he was poisoned. How, when, why, who; all remain unanswered. There are hundreds of suspects."

"So you don't believe Mam did it then?"

"I don't know ,Saeede. I hope not, but right now she seems a good suspect."

"What?" I yelled and Andreas woke with a start. His hand went to his staff sword leaning against the chair. He quickly assessed the situation and stretched his long body to begin waking up.

"Someone, somehow got poison into Esporanza. Right now the only person we know of with the knowledge of such things is your mother. Have you spoken to your mother at all about the treaty?"

"Of course, it is the talk of the town."

"How does she feel about it?"

"Is this an interrogation?"

"I had hoped you would see it as a conversation between two people who want to get to the bottom of this and protect your mother. I love her too you know."

I had to turn away from the gaze Diony met me with. She was doing her job, and she had been more than kind to me. Still I was angry with her and yet I was ashamed that I was. I walked back to the low wall at the edge of the balcony to look out across the roofs of the tiered city and watch the fishing boats casting out to sea from the wharf until I could answer her. "I know you do," I said at last.

"How does she feel about it then?"

"I don't know really." That sounded like a ruse so I went on. "Mam is not a person to involve herself in the ways of political intrigues. She is happier with simple pleasures."

"Is it possible that she could have made a mistake? A miscalculated measurement, a mistaken herb perhaps."

"She is too meticulous for that to happen. You've seen her shop. It is immaculate, she works methodically. Nothing is ever removed from its spot until it is needed. She gathers it all on a tray then moves to the appropriate work area and blends it all together. When she has finished she returns everything exactly to its designated spot."

"I have seen her work. She does not always use a recipe; surely you can see that it is possible that she could miscalculate."

"Possible, but improbable."

"Alright, let me move away from that then."

"Please do," I grumbled.

"We have at least a hundred people who were guests last night and another twenty-five or so who cooked and served. Ray and two of his trusted men are going to split the task of visiting each one. I have given an order that no one who was present here yesterday leave this city until they have spoken to one of them. I am sure that there will be some complaints and I will have to do some damage control if that comes from any of our visiting nobles, but it can't be helped."

She looked weary. I was suddenly reminded that this young woman was not much more than a girl and yet in a few short years she had lead a rebellion, rebuilt a city, trained an effective militia, and had been a chief ally in our battles with the underworld. I wondered aloud if she had used her great powers of perception in any way since Esporanza's death.

"I have, I know that your mother is not lying about the girl or the ingredients. Yet Mya is not lying either. Garthe is just angry at the world and Gebha just seems removed as if he has no stake in any of this.

"Thea is convinced from the color of Esporanza's mouth and the smell of his spittle that he was poisoned. If Ray and Brynal become suspicious of anyone than I will join them at the questioning, but..." She shrugged her shoulders. She was as lost as I was.

Andreas moved around Diony in the doorway and joined me on the balcony. He sat upon the low wall and rolled his neck to loosen the kinks he had acquired from an odd position in the chair.

I turned my back on them both and walked the length of the balcony. I stood at the end and looked across another view of the city. I didn't really enjoy cities, but Mareese was an exception. I rehashed all that Diony had told me. Suddenly it hit me. "By the Gods I am such a zombie-headed dolt at times!" I spun in my excitement and had to sit down hard to avoid toppling myself over the wall. "All night long I couldn't stop the events from churning over and over inside out and backwards at times, but now I see it. The girl—"

"Mya?" Andreas interrupted.

"Yes. I watched Mam mix that potion. There was no mistake. If there was one its more likely the girl made it. She had no interest in Mam's written instructions, even though Mam tried to get her to read them three times. Maybe she didn't need to read it. Maybe she just needed people to know she bought a potion from Mam."

"You think she deliberately gave him too much? She killed her own father?"

"I smell a plot," Andreas said. "If that's true than she may have never even used Mam's potion, switched it, but Esporanza needed to think it was medicinal so that he would take it willingly."

"Yes!" I said. "It makes sense. Now we have two suspects: Mya and my mam. She is smart to have us chasing false leads and false suspects."

"Are you sure you aren't just grasping at some way to clear Pria of this?"

"Of course I am, but think about it. She wouldn't be the first child to kill a parent. We don't know anything about their relationship do we?"

"Young girls aren't normally taught how to kill someone with poison, Saeede."

"True, but what if she didn't use poison, but used an overdose instead?"

"*If* she did it."

"Yes, if. Let us start our own investigation. It is my mother. I owe it to her to do all I can."

"The fact that it is your mother is the very reason I should not allow it."

"Why?"

"Impartiality."

"You think that I cannot maintain perspective?" My voice was tense, but Andreas jumped in to save me.

"I will keep her honest Diony. I know her. She will want the right answer no matter how much it may hurt. If she gets confused we will work it out together."

"Yes," I said.

Diony was quiet while she looked into us with her mind. She was gentle, but thorough. "Alright then, I will allow it. I know that no matter what I say you will conduct an investigation of your own anyway. I find that prospect hopeful and dreadful all at once."

"Is this why you kept me unconnected to my mother? You and your damn perceptions."

She smiled, "It is. I thought it best to not have Esporanza's people connecting you to your mother. This way I can say I do not know of your investigation, because I will have to deny knowledge of it if you are caught at it. I can just say that as one of my court I felt it best to protect you until more was known. We did need your interpreting after all.

"We have been friends and I hope that as my friends you can appreciate the tender position this murder puts us in." She searched deep into our eyes again, but I did not feel her soft touch on my mind. She waited for our nods of acknowledgement before continuing.

"I expect you to share information directly with me or Ray Vin Wholfe before you haul someone in and drop them unexpectedly at my feet as those rogues did last night with your mother. I expect, no I insist that you give reason and warning before doing so. The reputation of this city is just recovering from its dark days. I want the world to see that we are moving beyond that. Your means of investigating cannot be sanctioned publically. We must act within the law, but you can move in ways that we cannot."

"Will you allow us full access to his rooms, witnesses, and any other leads that we may follow up on?" Andreas asked. I decided it was best to let him do the talking for a while to show Diony I could be reasonable.

"Garthe is anxious to return the ambassador to his king. I have already arranged to have his body anointed and sent back to his country. His ship will sail tomorrow. For now his rooms are locked, and guarded by his two men, as it should be. The window has been left open to let in fresh air. If you go soon you should be able to get in through the window."

I looked across the balcony to the window of Esporanza's room. It would not be easy especially at this time of day. She was aware of my gaze. "I'm sorry, Sade. There is nothing more I can do without breaking protocols and risking suspicion on my house."

I nodded my understanding.

"Can you clear the courtyard at least?" Andreas asked.

"I believe I can arrange something."

"Thanks. I'll grab our bag." Andreas went to prepare our things.

Now was my time to speak for myself. "What of mother in the meantime, surely you do not mean to hold her while this goes on? It could take weeks. Her reputation will suffer. I never told you how we were run out of a city because they thought she was a witch. Well, she is actually, but in all things there are good and bad. With Witchcraft the black magic gets all the attention. White witches do good through blessings and cantrips, potions and the like. They are often unknown and living their lives amongst the people in caring giving ways as is my mam.

She once brewed a potion that healed a man on his death bed. The physician who had tried unsuccessfully to cure him called her witch. He was an influential man and had no trouble stirring up superstitions. The next time we were in town for supplies they chased us through the streets. One man tried to steal me from Mam's arms. She muttered something, I know now was a curse, and he wobbled and became ill. I was but a child. Mam tried to keep my eyes from it, but I saw what she could do. She only did it to protect us and get away. I saw the man again when I was older, he was fine. She was doing good and was punished for it so the physician could save face. It was then that we moved away from the cities protective influence and into the woods. We did the best that a small woman and a child could to build a house hidden away amongst the trees. I don't want her to have to relive that, exiled in your tower for wanting to help a sick man. Please let her return to her shop and home."

"I will take it into consideration, but she may be safer here. The population already knows of Esporanza's death."

"Yes, but the people trust you. You have shown them that you are good and honest. If you place Mam back into her life they will trust your judgment and she will not be persecuted. Even if anyone does find out she was arrested, it could easily be passed off as rumor or caution on your part.

Diony thought about that a moment, then said, "Alright, but I cannot expend more than an extra patrol circuit around her place. You will be involved in your own investigation and will not be able to protect her."

"Fine, just get her home before anyone here knows better."

"I'll have Ray make the arrangements. I will find someone to remain here with Mya, while I have a meeting with my staff, to keep them out of the yard. I'll talk to Ray then."

·~·Chapter Two·~·

We knew our way around the Governor's Manor. It was more of a sanctuary really with towers and manor houses surrounded by gardens. The home had belonged to the cities founder long ago, before the cluster of homes, businesses, guild houses, and warehouses had built up around it. It had been used more recently as housing for the many– too many guards that had been activated during the reign of the Overlord, Kaedl until he was overthrown in the rebellion. Diony had given the Overlord's palace over to the citizens and it was being converted to apartments to accommodate the poor and homeless. The newly renamed Governor's Manor was a group of stout buildings surrounded by a low wall with a tower on each corner. It was humble enough for Diony's tastes, but the Main House was grand and fit for guests and entertaining.

The courtyard was empty of people. Diony had called a meeting of her household to explain what was expected of them during Ray Vin Wholfe 's investigation. We made our way to the promenade that ran from the Main House to the green house. At the far end was a stone stairway that led to the balcony that ran back along the top of the promenade. At the end of the balcony the roof swept down off the floors above. The roof was tile which made the task delicate. It was a tricky climb up onto the balcony wall to reach out and grab the edge of the overhanging corner.

I was small and light so I went first. I still wore the gown from the last night's reception so I stripped down to my underthings. If I got caught it would be very embarrassing to have to stand before

Diony and Ray unclothed. Andreas had to lift me to the edge of the roof. I swung side to side until I could get one leg over and found a groove in the tiles to brace myself. I rolled my body up awkwardly to sit upon the roof. Andreas tossed me the carpet bag and I moved across the roof with it until I was above the Ambassador's room. Andreas pulled his long form up onto the roof easily and joined me. We took a length of silk rope from the bag and Andreas tied it around a chimney at the peak of the roof. We let it down just to one side of the window to a length that ended just below the window.

This time Andreas went first. The rope held and he shimmied down to peek into the window. I watched from the roof as he gave me the thumbs up sign then moved over and pulled himself in. I waited, listening a moment, when I heard nothing I followed.

We crouched together just inside the window. The door across the room was closed. We could see the shadows of the guard's feet below it. The ambassador lay upon the bed in the position given to the dead who would be anointed. Coins served to keep his eyelids closed, but his face was sunken and his lips were slightly drawn back. The rest of the room was neat and orderly.

I moved to the ambassador's bedside. He was already beginning to stink and I covered my mouth and nose. His lips were still discolored from the poison. Andreas moved across from me and together we folded back the crisp linen sheets that covered all but the man's head. We undid his buttons and ties and examined his exposed body rolling him in and out of sleeves and leggings so we missed nothing. There were no marks or bruises, except what would be expected from his convulsions and the early stages of decomposition. We redressed, repositioned and recovered him. A table and chair were arranged together near the bed. An empty cup remained there with the residue from the drunk contents. It smelled distinctly like ovate seeds.

"Dark Berry Root," I whispered to Andreas. "Mam won't allow it in her shop, she says it is too delicate to work with and very expensive. It is basically harmless as a dash added to tea for sweetness. It has a very distinct smell though. I'm surprised that Diony allows it in her kitchen. Since it is so expensive. I have found her to be very thrifty." I held the cup out for Andreas to smell it. He dabbed a bit of the residue onto a corner of a handkerchief. He wrapped it up and gave it to me. I placed it in my bustier. I would bring it to Mam and have her confirm it for Dark Berry Root.

We heard the guards talking outside and stopped to listen. There had only been one a moment ago. If they entered we were in serious trouble. We did not move as they spoke. They were bored and anxious for Thea and the priest to arrive to anoint Esporanza. The second shadow soon moved on while the other remained. When we were certain he would not enter we went to check Esporanza's belongings. The dressers and chests had been emptied and packed into his bags in preparation for his trip home.

We found nothing that would indict Mam. There was no list of instructions, or empty vial of any type. Perhaps Ray had them. We would ask. We searched under the bed and mattresses and found nothing. Andreas went about the room casting his magic to lift and move furniture so that we could look behind furniture under tables and candles, behind drawers and remain silent. We found nothing else, until I searched the ash bin. There were some tiny charred pieces of Mam's list. I could just make out her letters on two of the pieces. I removed them carefully and wrapped them in Andreas's handkerchief. There was nothing else to uncover. We slid out of the window and up the rope while the courtyard remained empty. Andreas untied the rope and placed it in the carpet bag. I leapt from the roof to the balcony rolling to a stand to catch the carpet bag from Andreas. He leapt and landed in a bent knee crouch. I removed my dress from the carpetbag and dressed quickly. We made our way from there and across the courtyard to the Kitchen House.

The person in charge was a pert young woman no more than thirty years old. She had worked for Kaedel, the conquered overlord, and begged to stay on with Diony to repay her for setting the city free. She lived rent free in the Kitchen House and as a member of the household she wanted for nothing. Diony made it perfectly clear that she could not pay her with the people's money, so she sold pies in the village markets on Adara's Day.

Her name is Sar and she greeted us warmly, "To what do I owe the honor of a visit from the city's finest minstrels?"

"We came on business, to arrange entertainment for the dignitaries forced to stay until Ray Vin Wholfe and Diony agree to let them leave," I said.

"Yes, of course. What a tragedy. Poison I hear."

"So it seems, but how? His own people were always around him."

Andreas was wandering about the kitchen under the rouse of smelling and tasting. He got his hand slapped with a wooden spoon by one of Sar's bakers for putting a finger in the batter. What he was really doing was investigating.

"I don't know. Maybe it was one of them?"

"Ssshhh. Don't say that too loud. Dignitaries and their nobles are so sensitive. If anyone heard you say a comment like that it could put Diony in a diplomatic jam." Of course I had the same suspicions, but we didn't want word getting around just yet.

"Were there any unfamiliar faces down here during the day of the reception?"

"Oh no, I only use people that I am familiar with. Wait, you don't think it was in his food do you?"

I ignored the question for now. "What about waiters?"

34

"No. Some of the nobles have tasters. But the food is brought out and the taster does their chore right at the table."

"I wonder if Ambassador Esporanza had a taster."

"No, not that I was made aware of. Are you investigating?"

"No, no. Just an interesting topic. It is sad of course, but it is hard not to get caught up in it.

"We really came for a cup of tea and to see if you had a schedule for the next few days. We thought we'd help out and play an evening or two. Try to smooth some ruffled feathers."

She spoke as she moved about the kitchen preparing tea for us. "We normally serve dinner around the fifth hour of suns' downing. With guests Diony will roll out some extra spirits and things will run later into the evening. I'd say at least until eight hours."

She delivered our tea.

"You wouldn't happen to have some Dark Berry Root would you?"

"Oh no. That stuff is wonderfully sweet isn't it? But, it can be dangerous if improperly used. Not safe to have around a kitchen. What if someone should be experimenting with a recipe and not know the danger?"

"Oh," was all I said.

We drank our tea and were preparing to leave when Andreas moved ahead of me to take a garbage bin from a scullery boy. "That is very helpful Sar, thanks for your kindness and the tea," I was saying.

"You are welcome. I hope I get to hear you play."

"We will save a song for you," I said, and then to Andreas, "Andreas, If you are done harassing everyone."

"Just helping out. Thought I'd take the garbage out for them, since we are leaving anyway."

"Oh no, that is too much bother," Sar said.

35

"Not at all," Andreas replied.

"But you will have to sort the meat and bones for the hounds from the greens for the garden. If there are any sacks or glass…No, Siggy do your job."

"I was, Sar but he insisted."

"I don't think you can take back an insist, Sar," I said. "Let him do it. It will make him feel useful. He is just a slug otherwise," I teased.

She sighed and gave a disconcerted look to Siggy and Andreas. "I suppose then," she laughed. "Siggy you can go fetch some wood and keep these ovens going."

We left and trotted out to the garbage heaps behind the kitchen garden.

"Good thinking Andy. This has to be trash from last night."

He set the bin on top of the low rail fence that divided the refuse types. We went about getting dirty and sorting it out. We found nothing in the kitchen trash, but that did not prevent us from searching deeper into the bins. Very near the bottom of the rotting vegetable bin was a brown vial from my mother's shop. The wax seal was broken and had been re-stoppered. There were still contents inside. It was not near the top, or in the glass bin. Someone had deliberately buried it deep to hide it. This did not conclusively prove that my poor old mam was innocent but it certainly lent credibility to the theory that the purchase of the headache cure was just a ruse to throw suspicion onto her.

I wrapped the vial in the kerchief and tucked it in my bustier. We returned the bin to the kitchen, washed up at the pump and went to see Ray Vin Wholfe.

He knew about the poison from Thea, but they had not determined the type. He was surprised by the charred pieces of my Mam's instructions. When I showed him the vial he recognized it as one of my mam's. He looked dubious, no doubt realizing that had I wanted to I could have produced a liquid filled vial and planted it just about anywhere. We read each other's body language. It was tense, but he relented.

"The hearth was clean and wood set in, when we inspected it. It is the way the staff would have worked, preparing the room while the ambassador was at dinner. There were no ashes. It must have been done after we left the room," he said.

"Hadn't you restricted access to the room by then?"

"Yes, we had." Ray began thinking, but he didn't share his thoughts.

"Why would you light a fire for a dead man?" I asked.

"Good question. His guards split their duty, and they are quartered down the hall. No need for a fire."

"Well the hearth is clean now. There is no wood and plenty of ashes. The household staff would have lain in new wood if they had emptied the ashes. Unless they were asked not to. Who ever has killed Esporanza is likely still here and trying to cover their tracks."

"I will find out who put the wood in for the fire and who cleaned the hearth after. I will let you know what I find out.

"Diony caught up with me before her meeting. I was just going up to have Pria moved. Would you like to accompany her?"

"Of course."

***

The guard at Mam's door saw Ray and unlocked the door for us. When he opened it Mam was up and pacing her room. I could tell she had very little if any sleep and the look she leveled at me was full of anger and confusion.

Once we were inside the guard locked the door behind us. I pulled the handkerchief with the Dark Berry Root on it and asked Mam to smell it.

"Tell me what that is Mam."

She was hesitant. As if she thought I was actually trying to indict her. She looked at Ray and back at me with questioning eyes.

"It's okay Mam. We are trying to help. I wiped this from residue in the bottom of the ambassador's tea cup."

"Ar erry roo"

"Dark Berry Root?"

She shook her head to affirm. But her eyes were fearful.

"Don't worry Mam; we will get to the bottom of this. Diony has arranged for you to go home until we do, Okay?"

"Yeh, Yeh!"

"Ray is here to see that it is done."

"Show her the scraps first."

So I did.

"Show her the vial," Ray said.

So I did.

Her eyes grew very wide and she frantically motioned for something to write with.

Ray went to the door and knocked. When the guard there opened he was ordered to bring parchment, ink, and quill. "Be quick," Ray said, and the guard ran off.

It was only a few minutes, during which Mam paced and wrung her hands. She took the items from the guard and began to write quickly at a stool beside the cot.

I read over her shoulder, "Dark Berry Root and Silver Leaf create a slow acting deadly poison when combined."

"So?" I asked.

She wrote and I read, "Dark Berry Root is difficult to distill. It would take a very knowledgeable person to do that. It is not dangerous alone." She looked up at me. I had not made a connection and shrugged. She wasn't telling me anything I hadn't learned from being at her elbow as a child and again for the last year. She wrote again and again I read, "Silver Leaf is a mild sedative. It relieves anxiety. I used a bit in the ambassador's headache cure."

"Are you saying this could have been an accident, Pria?" Ray said.

She wrote, I read, "Or a very insidious plan by a very knowledgeable person. Silver Leaf is a common ingredient in any apothecary shop. It can be used for many things but most commonly in headache cures because it is very effective for that. Dark Berry Root is not used in many shops, because it is expensive and because a good apothecary would know the dangers of it and choose to stock an alternative. I don't keep it on my shelves."

"What is it used for normally?" Ray asked.

I read, "It is often used as a sweetener in tea. In large doses, alone, it can be used to better circulation, but the person must be watched for signs of internal bleeding. I would not want to administer such a thing. Too nervous."

"Damn!" Ray said. "I had thought you solved this. We better talk to Thea again. I had much rather it was an accident. Perhaps it still is." He was quiet a moment while he thought. "I believe you are innocent Pria," he said. "I was doubtful of the vial at first, but I have been well aware of your daughter's movements since last night. She has not been home to retrieve one, and I knew she had gone to the Kitchen House. That and her good reputation as well as yours have convinced me.

"No strong evidence is pointing to you, so unless it does somehow we will release you to your own custody. Still until this is resolved you will be watched, and protected, at home. Saeede and Andreas will accompany you along with two of my most discreet men, just in case there is any trouble in route."

"We have to go though. I will see you there shortly."

39

She kissed each of us then. She knew we were on the case, and that made her happy.

***

We got Mam home in time to open the shop. It would be a long day for her. Andreas and I had work to do. We stayed only long enough to freshen up and change into clean clothes. We promised to be back as soon as possible and then we would watch the store for her and she could sleep.

Ray's men looked about the place. We gave them full access. No doubt they were looking for Dark Berry Root. Once they completed their search they left, but stayed in the neighborhood, browsing, shopping, eating, blending in, and watching the shop until we returned.

We made our way back to the Manor. We wanted to talk to Thea the physician, Mya, and the ambassadors guards Garthe and Gebha, as well as whoever had prepared the ambassadors room. As I was going over these people of interest in my head a flaw in our thinking came to mind.

"You know Andreas…"

"I know me well!" He puffed himself up in mock pride.

"Be serious, I have uncovered a flaw in our thinking."

"Do tell."

"If a chambermaid had gone in to prepare the room and laid in wood for a fire, wouldn't she have also tidied up and taken away the tea cup?"

"You're right! So what gives?"

"I'm not sure. If they didn't go in to tidy up, why not?"

"Yes, why? Diony is too fine a hostess and her staff admire her for it. They would be sure to have the ambassador's room ready if only to please her."

"I suppose it may have been early, maybe they just hadn't gotten around to it."

"Perhaps. We will talk to the principle of the house."

"Should we ask to see Diony first?" I asked.

"No they know us well enough, let's just wander about. We can always say we are just checking to see when it would be best for us to play. I still have our bag. We can set up anytime, anywhere. Perhaps we can even play a song for the dearly departed—a tribute of sorts at the behest of our thoughtful governor."

"You are a sly one."

"Yep, but that's what you like about me."

"Yep."

***

We were allowed entrance to the Manor without question. Our carpet bag had become an entrance pass in most places around town. What people didn't know was that we carried more than our instruments in it. Sometimes, if we carried our armor or weapons it was ungodly heavy. Fortunately today was not one of those days.

We found Diony with Brynal in the hall on their way to breakfast. "What brings you back so soon?" she asked.

"We thought perhaps we could play for your disgruntled guests; maybe rub elbows with the elite."

"I see. Brynal and I were just discussing how you were going to go about your task."

"We thought perhaps a song of tribute over the body of the ambassador might be appropriate. At your suggestion of course."

"Of course. We were just going to breakfast. Will you join us? I can think about your musical arrangements in more detail while we eat."

"You know, I am hungry," Andreas said.

"Saeede?"

41

"Yes of course, gov'ner. Thank you."

"Will there be others there?" Andreas asked.

"Oh, yes. Soros and Jen, the acting Mayor of Coastello, Mayor Brohaugh from southern Jour, Tourabain and his family are expected. Perhaps Thea, she has a busy morning but we were going to meet right after the meal to see to Esporanza's anointing. We will await Master Eble of the Seers and a local cleric from Esporanza's faith."

"Good, very good," Andreas and I spoke as one. The opportunity to listen and watch people converse about what would no doubt be the topic of the day would be a great help to us. If we could join the conversation without breaking protocols it would be that much better. These were not kings and there did not seem to be any political intrigue amongst the guests Diony had named. We were of nearly equal status given our recent rise in prestige.

When we arrived in the dining room several guests were already seated and others were still arriving. The atmosphere was casual, but moods were somber. We sat away from Diony and Brynal as fit our station and our purpose. Once everyone had arrived Diony asked a serving maid standing nearby to serve the meal. It did not escape us that neither of Esporanza's men, or Mya was present. They were in mourning, but I suspected Diony had somehow kept them away from what could be a delicate situation for her.

We took seats at a corner of adjoining perpendicular tables. We were joined there by Mayor Brohaugh and two of his sons. We introduced ourselves and found the Mayor to be polite, but guarded. Of course that made us wonder if he had something to hide. He complimented our music and we offered to play for his house if ever we found ourselves in Jour. That broke the ice a bit and his sons who had been quiet joined in.

When that line of conversation ran out Andreas turned the topic to murder. "Terrible about the ambassador, aye? Was it a stroke?"

The look that passed between Brohaugh and his boys did not escape us. They didn't seem worried, just guarded. They didn't know how much they should tell the governor's minstrels if they didn't already know a thing. We would have to try a different tactic.

"That didn't look like a stroke to me Andy," I said, as if I knew what a stroke looked like.

"What else would do that to a person?" Andreas asked.

"I don't know; epilepsy, poison maybe?"

"What do you think ,Sir Mayor?"

"I really don't like to speculate about such things."

"Ya, you are probably right. You're a better man than me."

One of the boys spoke up then. "I heard they arrested someone," he said. His father shot him a stern look and his brother kicked him under the table. We pretended not to notice.

"For the ambassador's death?" Andreas asked faking incredulous. "Well definitely not a stroke then."

"What else did you hear?"

"We really shouldn't be discussing this," Brohaugh said.

"O, come on Sir. What do you think everyone else is discussing?" Andreas asked with a flourish of his hand to indicate our fellows. "Help an aspiring bard out, Sir. The more we know the better our tale, the better our song." Andreas was very good at manipulating people. He would be a very good asset in this investigation.

"Well, I don't know."

"Alright," The dejected Andreas spoke. "I don't want to make you uncomfortable. Did you know the ambassador well?"

"No. I only just met him yesterday afternoon at an introduction gathering."

"Such a shame. I wonder if the treaty will be completed without him."

"I'm sure it will. We will discuss a representative to go to his King. Something will be worked out in the proper time."

"We will leave that to you office-bearers," I said. "I have no head for that sort of thing. give me a flute and a harp and I'm content."

"Flute, harp, and sword are your reputation," Brohaugh said.

"There is no contentment at the end of a sword, Sir," I countered.

The conversation ended on that awkward exchange. We had not gotten any information from Brohaugh. He was not so stupid as to give two people he did not know any information. We finished our meal and sat back. Andreas flirted with a serving maid, but when she moved on I was surprised to have him put his arm around my shoulders.

We exchanged a look. "Hard nut to crack; that one," he whispered and smiled, but did not remove his arm. Covering his whisper with an affectionate gesture I guessed, but I never knew where we stood about each other. It was a topic we mutually avoided.

Lord Tourabain's family was seated on the other side of the table from Brohaugh but down a bit, spaced out as families often do in public. Tourabain was Lord of the strong hold of Ge. He was accompanied by his lady wife, their son, and his new bride. We knew of him. He had been supportive of the rebellion against the overlord. His son, Web was a refuge of that conflict and had been warmly accepted in exile and subsequently adopted by the lord and lady. Web had been key to removing Diony from the city when the overlord had put a price on her head.

Tourabain entered our conversation cautiously. "Mayor Brohaugh, it is good to see you again; boys." He nodded to each of them in turn. To us he said, "I have not met my friend Diony's friends, and minstrels. I am Tourabain." We each stood to reach across and shake his hand.

"Your reputation precedes you M'lord," I said.

"And yours you. How is it that Diony's own minstrels do not know the latest news? You were here last night were you not?"

"We were, but we tended the ambassador's daughter only as long as replacement could be found and we went home to our rest. We are only minstrels here; with only a minstrel's jurisdiction," I lied.

The look Tourabain gave me indicated he suspected otherwise.

"Diony promised a full report this morning. I had hoped it would be at this meal where she can update us all at once," I said smoothing over the topic.

"Perhaps," he said.

The meal was finished and mulled cider was served. Diony cleared her throat and tapped a spoon against her cup. She leaned forward but did not stand to address the gathering.

"My dear friends and keepers of Crystalier, greetings. I am so very sorry that we have had a tragedy here in Mareese, in my own house. Ambassador Esporanza was very kind to me and approached us here in Mareese about a treaty with King Frahn and his province in Ahnges. We had some intelligence on both men and the treaty would be beneficial to us all. That is why I invited you all here and last night we all signed it. Shortly after, our new friend died right before our eyes. Last night was long, and complicated, and busy. This morning we have very good reason, based on evidence gathered, to believe that he was indeed murdered — poisoned in fact.

"I am afraid that I must follow protocols and reluctantly extend the order that you all remain in the city until we can speak with each of you. My people assure me it should only be a day or two longer. We will interview all those present last night. It has already begun with my own household, even I was questioned by Ray Vin Wholfe my chief of security. He is not here now because he has gone out into the city with a list of last night's attendees and will try to speak with them all today and begin with you tonight. He hopes to finish that process tomorrow or the next day. I hope you can find it in yourselves to be patient. I know that you all have business waiting at home, but I'm sure you left your holdings in trusted hands. We need to know what you may have seen at last night's activities. Even seemingly unrelated events to you may be a missing detail to Ray."

When she leaned back Brohaugh was the first to speak. "How can you guarantee our safety? How do you know this won't happen again?"

Diony was hurt by this question; her emotion flashed across her face, but was gone as she quickly regained composure. "I cannot. There is no indication that this was anything more than an attack on Esporanza. If it is my house that you distrust then there are several fine inns in town. They have been discreetly alerted that we may need extra rooms for our guests. All you must do is choose one and we will see you are taken care of. But, I am not able to extend my security that far. Here at least I can offer increased vigilance. I understand your reluctance sir, it pains me to have my house so tarnished, but I understand. These arrangements can be made for you all if it is what you desire."

"Tell us what you know so far," Soros from Coastello said.

"Well, we had a person of interest in custody last night, but that arrest was made in haste by vigilantes who were present here last night. The arrest was made without the knowledge of anyone officially investigating the incident. Our investigation led us a very different way and that person has been released."

Now I knew why Esporanza's men and daughter were not present.

Diony continued, "They are still under the watch of Ray's men in hopes that they may be of further value to our investigation. Our physician has called the cause of death poisoning. We have an expert who has confirmed the type of poison, but that matter is still part of the investigation so I should not discuss it at length.

"Ray Vin Wholfe has my full support and we are both utilizing all of our resources."

"Does that include your keen extra-sensory skills?" Soros asked.

"It does."

"Then we should have a quick resolution to this crime. Jen and I will stay."

"Tourabains will stay."

All heads turned to Brohaugh. "You have the confidence of your friends, one of which I hold close in Lord Tourabain. I will put my trust in that. We will stay."

"Good then. I am sorry but I must tend to business as regards Esporanza. I have asked my minstrels here today to record events, but also to pay homage to the man with song. His body will be moved to the chapel on the grounds here and he will be properly anointed and laid in state in preparation for returning him home to Ahnges. We only await Master Eble and Stern from the Massif's Church. You are welcome to attend. In fact I am asking that you do so, to show Esporanza's people respects. So adieu until then, you may go there straight from here. The officiates should be along if they are not here already.

"Minstrel's if you would come with me please." She and her man Brynal rose and walked out leaving their guests. We followed quickly and joined them in the hall.

"Good work Diony," Andreas said quietly. "You have a subtle way about you."

"I'm sorry?"

"You lie flawlessly."

"I don't lie."

"Well, okay, but you don't always tell the truth."

"Some parts of the truth are revealed in their own time. I have decided to let time play out in this."

47

"That is always wise in cases such as this."

"You did lie though."

"Andreas!" I said. He was crossing a line.

He grinned. I hated it when he got impish with dignitaries. I never knew how it was going to end. Brynal was already tensing up.

"You said you invited us here."

Diony smiled and Brynal relaxed.

"You have an open invitation here as you well know. There was no lie."

"But it was our idea to sing and you did not ask us to record events."

"Still no lie. You granted me discretion over the musical tribute and as my minstrels it is your job to record these things. So you see—no lie."

"Okay I give, but when did we become *your* minstrel's?"

"Why on the very day I fell in love with you both. I remember you played for us after the Horde Wars. I hugged you each and said, *'My minstrels.'* Don't you remember?"

"I do, but I thought it was just an emotional response."

Diony was grinning and shook her head no. She took Brynal's arm and began walking away. "Minstrels," was all she said and winked. Brynal threw back his head and laughed.

Andreas and I stood a moment looking at each other. She had bested him. That rarely happened. We laughed then too and trotted to catch up.

We followed them to Esporanza's room. The door was open and the guards were together talking in the hall. Mya was not present. The guards stopped talking quickly when we approached.

"It is about time," Garthe snapped.

We were all taken back by his temper. We had not even spoken a word and Diony warranted respect for her position and in her own home.

"Hold your tongue, Garthe. Diony has been tending to business on Esporanza's behalf all night. You have no reason to set upon her so," Brynal said. He was a man of few words but he took the task of protecting Diony seriously as both her lover and Lord Protector.

"Haven't I?" Garthe spit back. "My lord was murdered in her house. We brought you a suspect and when Gebha went to question her early this morning he found she had been released. Then when preparations for my lord should be made you all tarry over breakfast with your mates."

"We hardly tarried, Garthe," Diony said. "I had a meal with the visiting dignitaries after leaving our investigation to tell my guests they would be staying even longer during this investigation. They aren't exactly happy, but they are cooperative. I left them directly after to come here. Thea will be along shortly I'm sure, and the officiates are scheduled to be here at any moment. Your matters are well in hand and a priority. Where others are investigating this tragedy, I must avail myself to that as well as your arrangements and other affairs of state. Snap at me like that again, sir, and I will have you detained as a hostile influence in this investigation."

"What!?!"

"I believe I was quite clear."

Garthe was red in the face and his breath came in huffs. Gebha stood to the side and behind him. He looked at the ground. I thought that odd under the circumstances, even for a quiet lad. I wondered what he was thinking. I nudged Andreas who had not noticed and nodded toward Gebha. The cock of Andreas's head told me he also thought it odd. We would have to find a way to talk to him before their ship sailed on the morrow.

"What of that old woman?"

"There is no strong evidence against her. There have been developments and we acted accordingly."

"Without my consent?"

Thea joined us at this time. It did not take her long to sense the mood and she moved into the room to tend to Esporanza without a word.

"Consent? You have no authority here. I intend to keep you informed, but I do not answer to you. Where is Mya? I had actually intended to give her the respect of telling her these things first."

Garthe was beginning to look as if he might explode. "No authority? I am the man's protector just as much as Brynal is yours."

"Good job," Brynal said directly to Garthe.

I was beginning to get nervous. Both men had a hand on sword hilts. Whether that was a conscious intent or just an angry impulse I couldn't tell, but either was just a twitch away from assault.

"Now you can hold *your* tongue, Lap Dog."

Brynal took a step forward.

"Gentlemen! Enough!" Diony's raised voice resounded in the close quarters of the corridor.

"We will discuss everyone's conduct after the rituals. For now let us tend to Esporanza. Go fetch Mya."

"I may not have authority here, but I don't take orders from you either."

"Fine then she can miss the ceremony and I will inform her that her father's own man was the cause of that."

"She won't believe you."

"Do you care to test that?"

He thought about it. He was backed into a corner. "Fine!" he said at last and wanting more to be away from us than anything else; he turned to fetch Mya. "Let's go Geb."

They left together. When they were out of earshot Diony said, "There is something not right with that man."

"Hard to miss," Brynal answered.

"Not him—Gebha."

"What?"

"He has some extra-sensory perceptions. He is blocking his mind. I noticed he seemed unconcerned about the quarrel. I thought that was strange so I probed him, but he was already blocking. I don't know him from the Academy and we are about the same age. It is possible he knows of my abilities and was on guard. He did it without much effort, but he did have to concentrate."

"Hiding something?"

"Well I can't tell that if I can't reach his mind, but I'd say it was suspicious under the circumstances wouldn't you?"

"I would," Brynal answered.

"And I," I said.

"Me too," Andreas joined.

I will tell Ray when I see him. If you two get a chance…"

"Already in the plans," Andreas said.

"Good. Then for now all we can do is tend to this business. I want you two to go into the room, find a good corner where you will be able to see everyone and begin to play."

"As you wish," I said. Andreas followed me in and we took a spot near the hearth. I noted that the ash bucket had been emptied. We pulled flute and harp from the bag and began to play softly. That had the effect of background music and would still allow us to hear what was being said.

Brynal and Diony waited until Mya arrived and then entered behind her and Esporanza's men. Moments later two old men entered. I did not know either of them personally but knew them to be Eble, Master of the Seers Academy, and Stern from the Massif's Church.

Greetings and introductions were made. When Eble hugged Diony she whispered something in his ear and he shot a glance at Gebha. She had asked him to try to read his mind.

The anointing ceremony began. Esporanza was cleansed and wrapped by Thea and Eble as Stern chanted over him. At one point oil was placed on his forehead and wrists, then a aspergillum was shaken over his body and consecrated water rained down on him. Stern asked that we quit playing and he led us in a prayer. The whole while Mya stood a little aside from everyone hugging her arms around herself. She was strong and cried silently, but did not wipe her tears away.

Stern instructed Garthe, Gebha, Brynal, and Andreas on how to roll the sheet up tight to Esporanza's body and lift him. They led the procession from the room and out of the Manor House to the chapel where Diony's guests were already gathered. I packed Andrea's harp in our bag and had Thea carry it for me while I played a soft lament at the rear of the procession.

The ceremony was short as was the custom for Massifs. Another custom was for a trusted family member or friend to stand watch over the deceased to protect them from evil spirits. It was believed that if the guardian was of good heart and good faith that evil spirits would not be able to harass the rising spirit of the dead. Mya insisted it be her and her alone. Garthe wanted the honor, but Mya would not relent and it was her right so Garthe had no choice but to give in. Diony would see that food and water was brought to her. The congregation milled about a little longer, speaking condolences and then dispersed their separate ways.

Garthe and Gebha seemed to be in a heated debate as they walked back toward the manor. They were quiet, but very animated as they moved to the entrance nearest their room. We found ourselves with Diony, Brynal, and Eble watching after them. I broke away from the group and retrieved our carpetbag from where Thea had placed it. That caused the others to break off their gaze, all except Eble. We stood around him talking quietly amongst ourselves. If the two guards turned to see us we would just look like stragglers with Eble seeming to be part of our conversation. They never did turn and Eble was quiet for a few moments after they were out of sight. When he had assessed the two guards fully he gave us a report.

"Garthe is an open book. He is tired and aggravated. He did not want the assignment given to him by his King; that of watching over Esporanza on this trip, but he is loyal to his king. He worries more about his reputation back at home for failing to protect the Ambassador than he does about Mya. He considers her an annoyance especially now that he has to act as if he cares about her well-being. He is furious at you, for many things, Diony. Right now it is for supporting Mya's claim to the protection of her father's spirit. He sees it as a breach of protocol, an insult to his duty.

"Gebha is indeed guarded, but not impenetrable. I tried to reach him during the procession, but he was guarding. I got through a little just now. He is wary of Garthe and doesn't trust him for some reason. He is anxious to leave and be back home. He doesn't really care about Mya either, but I sensed no animosity toward her from him either.

"That is really all I got. I hope it does you some good."

"It will do Eble, thanks," Diony said. "What good it does remains to be seen. We have until tomorrow. If we can't link them to this then we have to let them go home with Esporanza."

"What about Mya?" I asked.

"What about her?" Diony asked.

"Well, she could still be a suspect. We haven't really looked at her very hard, or any of them really, but let's not forget about her."

"You're right. I guess I just feel sympathy for her. It hasn't been so long since I lost my mother."

"We can't afford for our sympathies to blind us right now," Brynal said.

"Yes, I will be more careful," Diony said.

At that we turned to go back to the house.

·~·Chapter Three·~·

Ray was still in the city interviewing guests from the last night's reception. He had already interviewed a few of Diony's household, but we wanted to conduct our own. Mya and Esporanza's men were looking more and more suspect and we wanted to get a better feel for their activities leading up to and just after the ambassador's murder. We would gather this information first by speaking with Diony's staff and then we would approach the suspects and see if their stories matched. We conducted ourselves as neutral and identified Mam only by her, description, profession, or name. We started with the young men, mostly volunteers who acted as guards at the Manor House in exchange for room, board, and martial training. None of them had seen Mam alone on the Manor grounds that night or since she had left her rooms there a year ago. One however walked passed Mam's place the afternoon of the reception and saw a young woman fitting Mya's description leave the shop and run off toward the manor.

We moved on to the chambermaids next. We needed to know who had prepared the ambassador's room for his return from the reception that evening. The simple answer was: Gebha. He had gone out to the kitchen very late on the night after the reception and got an armload of firewood. One of the scullery boys surprised him when he went to throw out the dish water. Gebha said he hadn't wanted to bother anyone, but Garthe had sent him out for the wood so they could stand vigil over Esporanza in the ambassador's room. None of the maids had yet gone to tidy up before the ambassador was inflicted.

After that they had been forbidden to go there. None of the chamber staff that we talked to knew anything about who might have cleaned up the hearth or dumped the ashes.

Next we went back to the kitchen. Sar was still there and we made her believe we were gathering information so that as minstrels we would have an accurate telling of the tale when all was said and done. She made her staff available to us, but aside from Mya coming to get tea for her father in the late afternoon there was nothing they could tell us that seemed relative to the case. It was odd though, normally Mya would not go to the kitchen herself. The request would have been sent through Garthe or Gebha, to the chamberlain, to the kitchen who would have sent it over. Perhaps she had gone straight from Mam's shop to expedite the headache cure for her father. Whatever the case the detail had not been revealed during Mya's questioning in Diony's office.

We desperately wanted to interview Mya, Garthe, and Gebha separately. Mya would be easy. We had only to visit her at the chapel. We hoped that she could give us some clue to Garthe and Gebha's routines so that we could separate them. We left the kitchen and walked to the chapel. We found Mya draped over her father's body. She looked up when she heard us enter. She looked awful. Her whole face was red , puffy, and tear stained. Her eyes were mere slits.

She tried to be proud and composed, but it just wasn't working. At that moment I no longer believed that she could kill her father. "What do you want?" she said.

"Sorry, mi' lady," Andreas said. "We thought perhaps you could use a couple of friends. If you'll pardon me saying so you don't seem all that fond of your father's men."

She looked shocked and was quiet a rather long time before saying: "I am lonely. Garthe and Gebha have no real duty to me.

56

Garthe sees me as an annoying incident on a normal day; a loose end since Papa's death. He will see me safely home, but will be glad to wash his hands of me when that is done. Gebha is not so bad, but he is new to Frahn's Service. Garthe is to report back about him when we return. So Gebha does everything Garthe tells him to do. He teases me, and lets me tease back, but never when Garthe is around."

"We came to see if you needed anything, but I see by the empty tray that Diony has had food sent out," Andreas said.

"Yes."

"Still, if there is anything, I could run for it. Sade could keep you company until I return."

"I could use some water."

"Done," he said and ran out.

Our sympathy worked and she warmed to us. She sat down on a stool near her father and gave me her attention. She was a young girl without a mother or a father now and so no real social station. Her situation back home would only be good if Frahn showed her some sympathy, but he was not bound to do so. She seemed to know that. She looked thoroughly dejected, but I had a question that needed an answer.

"When you went to get the tea for your father, was he alone?"

"I didn't get the tea. Someone brought it up for him."

If she was not lying; and I didn't believe that she was, why had Sar said she had come for it?

"Did you see who?"

"No I was getting ready for the reception in the other room."

"Certainly your father said something to the person. Did you hear any voices?"

"I heard him say, 'delicious,' and then I heard the door close after the person left."

"The person never spoke?"

"I didn't hear them, but I wasn't really listening either. Do you think that person killed my father?"

I wanted to give her some comfort, but there was none at that time. I said, "I don't know, Mya, but it seems likely."

"What will I do now?" She asked and looked deep into my eyes.

"Be strong. Life hits us with great losses at times. We must be strong and carry on. Do you have any family; uncles, or aunts, perhaps, that you could go to?

"My mother had a sister, but I don't know her. I heard from her once after Mama died, but she never responded to my letters after that."

"If you told her your situation, surely…"

"I don't even know if she is still alive. She was older than my mother."

"Is there no one else? A cousin perhaps."

"No I am the last and only child in either line."

"Have you told Diony this? She could send someone ahead. Maybe find your aunt."

"Do you think she would?"

"She has very limited resources by which to run this city, but I know she would do all she could to attempt it."

"Can you speak to her for me? I don't want to leave Father and I should give her time to see what she can do?"

I saw Andreas returning across the courtyard. "I will go now if you'd like."

"Yes, please, and thank you so much."

I curtsied and backed away before turning to run out and tell Andreas where I was or rather, wasn't with our questioning.

I ran off to find Diony and hoped to return quickly.

Diony was in her office with Ray. Brynal was at the door and opened it to announce me. I was let in and was apprised of Ray's investigation of the guests who had returned to town last night. Several saw Mya shopping that afternoon. Only the florist where she bought the flowers for her hair actually spoke with her. The florist was a member of the agriculture guild and had been one of three representing that guild at the reception. She found the girl to be polite, perhaps shy, but not anxious or jumpy. She bought the flowers and left and headed up the way toward the Manor which was coincidentally in the same direction as Mam's shop from there. No one saw Mam anywhere near the Manor or the grounds.

I shared with them what we had learned from our interviews with the chamber and kitchen staff. I told them that we were visiting with Mya now and that Mya had been seen in the kitchen before the reception to order some tea for her father and that she had waited to bring it to him herself. I added that Mya claimed she was in her room preparing for the reception and had not gone to the kitchen at all.

Ray said he had gotten the same story when he questioned the kitchen staff but had not yet questioned Mya about it. He was glad that I had.

I changed the subject to Mya's request for assistance to find her family in Ahnges.

"That isn't really my responsibility. Frahn should be the one," Diony said.

"Yes, but I get the feeling she doesn't trust him. She is a cast away in the sea of nobility now."

"Poetic," Ray said. "Did you just think of that?" He smiled.

"Yes, actually," I said and returned the smile.

"Might want to work on that."

"Well, anyway, " I said turning my attention back to Diony. "She asked me to make the request so she didn't have to leave her father and to give you time to see what you could do about it."

"Did you have anything to do with this request?"

"Well, I may have slipped up. I know how compassionate you are and she seems so small and alone. It was killing me. I'm not good at that sort of thing, and I don't have the authority, but maybe you do."

The look that Diony gave me was unreadable. Her words were not so unclear. "Go, tell her I will consider it. Thanks for the report."

I bowed and left quickly.

I arrived back at the chapel and told Mya that Diony would consider her request, and left with Andreas.

"What did you find out."

"Not much, I'm convinced she didn't do it, but that someone used her as a pawn. She feels it too. She said so. I do know that Garthe and Gebha change their shift in the middle of the day. Gebha goes to the kitchen for lunch and then goes to relieve Garthe who then goes to the kitchen for lunch before returning to their room for some sleep. If we could be in the kitchen at mid-day we have a very good opportunity to see them both. It is mid-day now."

"Let's go. I am hungry."

Mya was right Gebha was in the kitchen. Sar was serving him at the large community table at the far end of the building. Gebha paid us little mind as he began to eat a venison sandwich. Sar was excited to see us though.

"Have you come to play for the kitchen?"

"No Dear," Andreas said. "We've come for something to eat."

"Aye Me," she said. "I will be glad when things return to normal around here. People in and out at odd times all day."

"I could get it if you just tell me where things are," I said.

"No, No. Quicker if I do it. Have a seat at the table."

We sat across from Gebha who looked up and gave an acknowledging nod as he chewed. Andreas put our bag under our bench.

"Morning," we both said.

"Afternoon rather," Andreas corrected. "It has been a long night and yet it still feels like morning."

Gebha nodded again.

"How are you all holding up after last night's tragedy?" Andreas asked, getting to the interview while seeming to make small talk. He was good with people and I envied that. My job was to watch Gebha's reactions. He was a young man, but he seemed calm so far.

"As well as anyone could expect I suppose."

"We just paid Mya a visit. She is a wreck."

"Yes, well her father did just die unexpectedly."

"Yes, Right."

"I'm sorry. We have never been properly introduced. I am Andy, this is Sade. We are sorry for your loss. It must be hard to swallow."

"What's that?"

"Well here you are a young man. This must be one of your first offshore assignments; and a very important one at that, and now you will return with the body of the man you were meant to protect. I'm just saying that it must be a hard pill to swallow."

"Yes, very hard. I'm just glad it was Garthe's watch and not mine."

"Oh? Where were you when it happened then?"

"I was asleep in my room."

Mya brought our sandwiches and two mugs of cider, and left without a word. We owed her a song. We would play after our interviews.

"All the better for you then. I would hate to be in Garthe's shoes," Andreas said.

"Yes," Gebha said and returned to eating his lunch.

The questioning couldn't end there, so I entered it myself. "Didn't you want to join the party?" I asked. We knew that he had escorted Esporanza and Mya to the reception along with Garthe, but was not seen after Esporanza had been stricken.

"I did for a while. Garthe and I accompanied the ambassador and his daughter to the reception as was our duty. I had been on watch all day because Garthe had been busy with the business of Esporanza's schedule and meeting people, that sort of thing. The reception extended my shift. Normally Garthe does the overnight shift so he can be present for meetings and events with the ambassador. After everyone was seated for dinner Garthe excused me and I went up to bed."

"Did you see anyone in or around the ambassador's room then?"

He seemed to be thinking, but answered quickly, "No."

We weren't really getting much out of him, so I changed to a more direct tactic.

"Such a tragedy, on the eve of a successful treaty. I hear he was a lovely man. Hard to imagine someone so dedicated and loved having enemies."

A flash of something went across Gebha's face. When he answered his voice cracked and he had to take a swallow of cider before continuing. "I didn't know him as well as Garthe did, but he was kind to me. He never raised his voice or was demanding. We could have been friends had this not taken place."

"Who was it that delivered Esporanza's tea?"

"I never saw. They must have come while I was changing for the reception."

"Wouldn't Garthe have taken your spot for that time?"

"It didn't really seem necessary." That indiscernible flash changed in him for a split second. It put my senses on alert, but whatever it was was gone as soon as it came.

He was about to finish his sandwich. We needed more from him. I felt it, but there were no other questions that came to mind. He pushed his plate away and stood to leave.

"Sorry for your loss," I said.

He only nodded. When he was gone we ate a little sandwich and discussed in low tones our feelings about Gebha. He seemed sad, but awkward, as if he was nervous. He was young though and young men often have trouble with emotion. He had easy access to Esporanza all day, but did he have the means and a motive? If we were to conduct this investigation without letting those we were investigating know it, it would be hard to get alibi's and motives. We would have to keep conferring with Ray and Diony. We did not like that. It was hindering and inefficient.

Sar came over with another sandwich and a mug of cider. "For the other one," she said. "He'll be along shortly."

"We owe a song, Sar. Can we play for you after we eat?"

That raised her spirit. "You don't owe me, but we would all love to have you play for us."

"Well consider it done then. Just a song or two. Diony is expecting us to play in the common hall."

"Thank you, that will be such a treat!" She ran off to tell her staff.

Garthe came in, stopped short when he saw us sitting opposite his plate, recovered and then moved in. He nodded at us, a gesture of greeting. What was it about those two soldiers that they couldn't just say hello?

"Greetings," Andreas said.

Garthe nodded again to Andreas but gave me a sideways look. Apparently he didn't like me. So of course I said, "Fine day isn't it?"

I believe he had wanted to say yes but it sounded very much like "humph."

I ignored his short temper and pushed ahead. "I'm sorry that we all met under these tragic circumstances. We haven't had the proper opportunity to give you our condolences. This must be very hard on you."

He looked up from his meal and met my eyes, but still his only response was a nod.

Andreas took over then knowing that I wasn't going to get anywhere with this man. "My name is Andy, this is Sade."

"I know who you are," Garthe growled.

"Oh. I don't remember us being introduced."

"You and I weren't. She and I were. When you went to get Mya during the questioning of the alchemist." He looked at me when he said alchemist, he knew who I was to her. I read it in his eyes. I was curious why he didn't acknowledge that openly. He called her alchemist not apothecary. Alchemy was considered to be more sinister than black magic in some cultures. I had a feeling Ahnges was one of them. I didn't like his insinuation.

"Why did you arrest Pria without alerting Diony or Ray Vin Wholfe?" I asked.

"It seemed expedient. I knew that Mya had purchased from her that day and that the potion would have been put in Esporanza's tea. I was busy with Diony off and on all day making sure schedules and arrangements were met. After he died Diony and Ray were taken back. They had so much to think about that I just went on an obvious theory and brought the woman in."

Andreas felt me tighten up and put his hand on my leg as a warning. "You mean a hunch? So you had no evidence against her?"

"Just the potion. She had the means for such an act."

"Perhaps, but she is an old woman who can't speak. How would she get by the guards to administer the poison?"

"She didn't have to. She used us."

"What motive would an old shop keeper across the sea from Ahnges have to kill a king's ambassador?"

With that question Garthe looked a bit contrite, and answered slowly, "I haven't figured that out yet, but I will."

"No you won't," I said, "because there is none." I threw the remains of my sandwich onto the plate. "I've suddenly lost my appetite." The man was just looking for someone to pin this on so he could go home and call it case solved. I second guessed my words almost immediately, but then calming I was glad that he knew who I was and that I had defended my mam.

"I don't know what you two are playing at, but I suspect that wench Diony is behind it."

I jumped back in. It angered me that he had such disregard for Diony, but it was important that he not believe we worked for her. "No sir! She knows nothing of this. My mam is innocent and I intend to prove it, no matter who the culprit is."

"So you question me?" Garthe's tone was a hushed shout. "Do you find me suspect?"

"Shouldn't I? You have been uncooperative from the start. Did you jump to a conclusion and arrest my mam, or were you looking for a convenient scapegoat?"

"I don't have to take this from you."

"No, you don't, but others are going to ask these questions of you if they haven't already and your reluctance to answer doesn't make you look good in this. Perhaps you didn't poison him, but maybe you turned a blind eye, and that is still murder in Mareese."

"You have no authority here as you have just admitted. I will answer no more of your questions!" He took up his plate and cup, stood, and went out of the room.

"Nice going, Sade. We got nothing from him."

65

Garthe was right. I had lost perspective and there would be no talking to him again. Worse, he would probably tell Gebha of this and that would lock him out too.

"Let's think about it," I said, trying to put a positive light on the situation. "Gebha claims he was in his room asleep at the time of Esporanza's death.

"That doesn't mean he didn't do it. He could have placed the Dark Berry Root in the tea, at any time after Mya brought it into the room, knowing that Mya or Esporanza would add the headache remedy from your mam. He stated that he left his post to change for the reception. Did he? Is that just a simple alibi that can't be proven or disproved. Maybe he served the lethal dose just before or just after that. He was also on duty during the time before the reception, while Garthe was busy with the details of that and Mya was in her room getting ready. It gives him opportunity. Mya said she heard her father say 'delicious', assuming he was sipping the tea that had just been delivered, but there was no response."

"Yes, I don't think we can rule him out yet. We don't really know much about either of Esporanza's men. But who is this false Mya? You aren't saying that it is Gebha are you?"

"No, I don't know that, yet. His attitude is casual, not like a man who has just killed someone. Still I also don't want to rule him out yet. So many things are beginning to point to him. He was awfully glad to point out it was Garthe's watch, but although Garthe is in charge they are both charged with the same task. And then there is the ability to block his mind. Why does he feel it is necessary to do that?

"Did you notice when we asked about his relationship with Esporanza that his demeanor changed? Just for a very brief moment but he seemed to—falter for lack of a better description. It happened again when I asked who delivered the tea."

"I did notice. I couldn't determine if it was fear or sorrow. His voice cracked a little when he answered and he had to take a swallow of cider before continuing. I thought he seemed genuine though when he said they could have been friends had this not taken place. I don't know Sade, If there is a false Mya it seems more likely of the two that he would be better to pull it off than the older and bulkier Garthe."

"I don't know, but anything seems possible at this point.

"Garthe then; he seems intent on pinning this on my mam. He as much admitted that. Is he guilty or protecting someone? Maybe Gebha. He also had plenty of opportunity to put the Dark Berry Root into the tea himself, perhaps more. He is the one that tasked Mya with stopping at the shop to purchase the headache cure."

"How can we determine which of the two of them has the knowledge of Dark Berry Root, as well as Silver Root being a common headache cure and a deadly mix with Dark Berry Root?"

"We'd have to trip them up somehow."

"We'll have to talk to Ray and Diony about that now though. You really put us in a bind here, Sade."

"I'm sorry. I used to be better at this."

"Is that devil cold getting to you again?" Andreas had taken to calling the cold chill Malisgalar's minion had cursed me with 'the devil's cold'. It made it easier to discern his meaning in certain conversations.

"It is always there, though at times I think it might be subsiding. This time I admit, I just lost my temper. This is my mother we're talking about. I've been fighting the cold pretty well, until you mentioned it."

"Sorry."

"No worries, it was a legitimate question. But back on topic; if Ray can ask about the herbs maybe Diony can read something in their thoughts."

"No harm in asking."

"What about Mya?"

"I believe she is innocent, but that the evidence will seem to point to her. She was used somehow, I'm sure of that. It will be hard for her to take when she learns it is true, but she believes it already."

"I agree. Esporanza was her whole world. I fear for her well-being when she returns home. She has no status unless Frahn grants her his protection. I can see no reason she would want her father dead."

We noticed Sar lingering around us and knew we would not get away without a song this time. We pulled out mandolin and harp and pushed our plates away so we could sit on the table. After a quick check on the tuning of our instruments I began on the harp and Andreas joined on the mandolin in a soft rendition of Nomarast's Dilemma. I sang lead and Andreas filled in on the chorus. The song is about a noble lord who morn's the death of his wife while suspecting his beloved daughter of killing her. It seemed appropriate for the time.

We followed up with a heartening ballad about a prince in love with a scullery maid. The tune was quick and light and the lyric's were easy to pick up. As we ended the entire kitchen staff was swaying or tapping their feet and some actually sang along. We left them with smiles on their faces and as we crossed the court yard on our way to find Diony we could hear The Prince and The Maid being sung from the kitchen.

***

As we approached Diony's office we saw Garthe leaving from the door just beyond the office. That door led to Diony and Brynal's private chambers. That could not be good. Diony rarely took business into her home. Garthe did not see us but Brynal came through the same door soon after and turned toward us. He stopped when he saw us and wagged a hooked finger at us to indicate we should approach. We felt like children being summoned for punishment. Judging from our interview with Garthe and his being with Diony so soon after we probably were.

Diony was in her bedclothes, covered by a long robe. She sat in a chair near a window that looked out over the city. On a little table beside her were a flagon of wine and two half empty wine glasses. She was leaning back in the chair, rubbing her temples.

"Di?" Brynal said.

"What?" she snapped, not turning or opening her eyes.

"Sade and Andy are here."

"Oh, that was fast."

"They came to us."

"Convenient," she rubbed her head a bit more and then said, "Come in. Sit down."

There was no where to sit except one chair on the other side of the little table so we moved in and took our seats on the window sill. Brynal followed and flopped into the open chair.

"Have either of you slept yet?" She asked.

"No," we said together.

"You should. Do you know how I know?"

"Because you haven't slept yet either?" Andreas asked. We both knew that wasn't why, but we felt compelled to even act like children facing punishment.

"No, I know because you obviously are not thinking straight. Imagine how I felt when Garthe was pounding on my door only moments after I sat down to relax. I thought a bit of wine and then bed before having to deal with the dignitaries at the evening meal was well called for. But no, apparently my minstrels are off asking questions of the ambassador's guards. Not just any questions, but stupid questions. Garthe is threatening to leave on this evening's high tide. I could stop him, and I've tried to convince him but I risk a diplomatic situation if I force him. If he goes, how do you think the other lords and ladies will take that? If he goes our investigation falls apart.

Further he is demanding your mother return with him to Ahnges to face trial there. You assured me you knew what you were doing. That you could keep perspective. I trusted you. The very reason I hesitated has come back to haunt me."

She stopped speaking and glared at us. I couldn't speak. The words I had spoken to Garthe in defense of my mam had created an international incident with Mam's life in the balance.

"I had hoped to send the two of you as an answer to Mya's request, but now that cannot be done. I want the two of you out of here now before Garthe sees you again. Go home and get some sleep. When I come to some solution I will send for you."

"But I…"

"No, Saeede. I don't want to hear explanations or anything from you right now. You have cost me my sleep and now I must think through this with a tired mind."

"Perhaps we…"

"No, not now. Go."

Andreas was standing and pulling me up by one arm. "Come on Sade," he whispered.

I made some nonsensical sounds; half thoughts strung together. Brynal led us out and shut the door a bit loudly behind us.

"Gods, Andy, what have I done? I never considered this."

"Nor I. Lets go, we could use some sleep. After, we will put our heads together and find a way around this."

I let myself be led away. Time and space seemed distorted. I couldn't wait to be home and dreaded it all at once.

"Don't say anything to Mam until we know what Diony decides," Andreas said.

"Right. Smart," I said.

·~·Chapter Four·~·

When we arrived Mam was just turning the painted sign in her window to the "open" side. It was a bit late in the day for that, but she had gotten sleep and didn't want to stay closed any longer. She was only called upon to blend teas that afternoon. That was fortunate because she worried about the false accusations, which made her worry about making a mistake.

Andreas went to his apartment and I went up to bed. I found it difficult to sleep and after a couple of hours of dozing and waking I got up, bathed, found fresh clothing and after dressing sat awhile trying to decide how I would tell Mam about our failed investigation. I wasn't sure I'd be able to hold my tongue until Diony called for us again. I don't think anything ever weighed so heavily on my heart, not even the death of my beloved friend, Wallace. I took a deep breath to steady myself and went downstairs.

Mam was asleep in her bed. I thought that was odd, I was sure I'd only slept a couple of hours. I pulled the door shut quietly as I passed her room and went downstairs to the kitchen.

The kitchen was full of the savory aroma of chicken stew. Andreas was cooking. He did not hear me as I padded to the bottom stair. "Nothing more sensual than a man who can cook," I said.

"Don't let anyone tell you otherwise," he said, turning to acknowledge.

"Smells great."

"Thanks, it will be ready soon. I brewed some of your mother's Smart Tea. I thought it might help us figure out how to go about finding Esporanza's killer."

"I'll get some mugs. I hope you brewed a large pot, I'm feeling pretty dull right now."

"You'll be better after a good meal."

I gathered three mugs so when Mam woke she'd know we were thinking of her. We let her sleep and drank our tea while the vegetables cooked in the stew.

"I have something to tell you."

I sat forward to listen.

"While we were up at the Manor House, someone broke into my apartment. They were careful. I didn't notice at first, but then certain things were not in my familiar reach as I always leave them. I checked my chest where I keep my important things. Everything had been very carefully returned as if nothing had been removed, but I went to the bottom where I keep that ledger we took from Eindal's room in Behlanna. Do you remember it?"

"Of course how could I forget. Was it there?"

"No. As far as I can tell it is the only thing missing."

"Had you ever deciphered it?"

"I was working on it."

"Where are your notes?"

"I kept them separate, and they did not find them wedged behind a board in the ceiling. The ledger didn't fit there so I locked it up in the chest. The notes don't amount to much. They are just preliminary thoughts, but I'm glad to have them. Still, I can't do much with them without the ledger. Aside from the front door and two windows the chest is the only other thing that locks in that place.

"What are your thoughts?"

"That who ever broke in is somehow related to Esporanza's murder and that they were looking for something to indicate what we knew about it, or they will try to indict us with it. They found the ledger instead, perhaps they recognized the arcane language. Maybe they know its value.

"I spent a torturous couple of hours in the place so as not to let anyone who might be watching know that I had discovered the break in. They were good, Sade. I checked the keyhole trap you set just like you showed me and it is still intact. After the time passed I left and walked as casually as I could here. The shop was still open but Mam was looking weary. I sent her to bed and watched the place about another hour before I closed up. No one came in, but I noticed a young man walk by several times very slowly."

"Did you know him?"

"Never saw him before, but I'd recognize him."

"I'm going to check my room. I don't have anything important there, but I'd like to know if anyone was fiddling about in there."

Andreas stirred the stew and followed me up.

When I had gone to my room earlier I just flopped down on the bed and paid no attention to anything else, but the thoughts in my head. Now when I looked around it was as Andreas had described. My mirror had been moved aside on my dressing table and the hair brush was too close to the edge. The contents of my drawers were all there, but things had been returned just a little too neatly.

Andreas stayed in the doorway as I went through things. When I was done I announced to him that they had been there. "We should check the shop. No, we need to wake Mam and have her check the shop and her room. If something is out of place in the shop she will know it."

"They were here with Mam unprotected just downstairs, or while she was sleeping here before opening the shop; and with Ray's men

75

watching the place" A thought hit me, an impulse, and those often proved correct. I told Andreas, "After we angered Garthe he went to Diony and threatened to leave and take Mam with him. I think we may have been skirting around the wrong conspiracy. What if Garthe and Gebha are in this together? While we were playing in the kitchen Garthe went to Diony, but where was Gebha? We assume he was asleep, but perhaps he was here or in your place."

The thought excited Andreas. "Yes, and if it was Gebha we could have tipped him off before Garthe, giving him more time to go through our places, and that could even mean he works alone."

I was moving to Mam's door as Andreas finished his thought. I knocked and heard the creak of the bed as she got out of it and came to answer the door. She was befuddled from all of the interrupted sleep of the last day.

"I need you to take stock of the shop."

"What? Now? Why?" The words came broken to her mutilated tongue, but I understood them.

"It's important. Andreas's apartment and my room have been carefully gone through. Whoever it was is looking for something. They had plenty of time and opportunity. Please just come..." I stopped speaking when Mam turned from me and went to the small chest she kept beneath her bed. It was locked and she seemed relieved, but once opened she became excited.

"Gaw. Eh Gaw!"

"What's gone?" I asked.

"Ur-eh. Carip, Ree."

"Shit!" I whispered.

Andreas didn't understand so I translated Mam's speech for him. "Journal, Cantrips, Recipes."

"Shit!" he whispered. "Down to the shop. Let's get this over with."

We followed him down but he stopped in the kitchen. "Give me a minute to get around along the walls and shelves and get to a window. Remember I saw that young man pass by several times. I want to see if anyone is watching. There is still plenty of daylight. I'll whisper to you when I think its okay, if I don't it's not and I'll come back here." Without waiting for a response he lay on the floor and crawled under the curtains. I held the cloth so the two panels would not separate and alert someone who might be watching for movement in the shop. We waited in silence then we heard Andres just outside the curtain. "I'm back," he whispered.

I held the curtains again. "Come on," I whispered back.

He crawled under and jumped to his feet. "Definitely someone in the alley across the street and down two storefronts. Care to see who that might be?"

"Of course, but what plan?"

"Well, I was thinking. You can go out the back and slip into the alley nearly opposite that one. I will leave and head toward home. If he follows me you follow him. If he comes to the shop we will both move on him but let him enter first. If he goes somewhere else we will follow and see where. Mam, you should wait here with the doors locked. I made some stew. Eat and go about your normal tasks. Do the inventory."

"What if he doesn't move?"

"Then I'll circle back up the alley and we will watch him until he does."

I ran upstairs to put on my mail and strap on two swords. Back downstairs I went out the back door and waited to hear the click of the door locking behind me. I moved through the back alley of the neighboring businesses until I came to the intersection of the alley that was nearly across from the one that Andreas indicated. I was careful and moved until I could see the culprit that was lurking there.

Loitering is a more accurate description. He was a young man, dark hair and complexion. He stood at the end of the alley, just off the boardwalk on that side. He rolled a dragon stick then lit it and smoked it. Dragon was a stimulant drug. One stick could boost a person's stamina well beyond normal limits. He appeared innocent enough to be a passerby; just someone resting, or waiting for someone in one of the nearby shops. I crouched low and when he glanced up the street I moved closer and took a place behind some raw planks, leaning against the porch of the limners shop. I could see him well through the spaces in the planks and the open risers of the porch steps. I watched as his motions stopped for just a split second. I heard the distant bell from over the door of Mam's shop. The man shifted and slipped back in the shadows a bit to hide from Andreas, but he was still in my sight. Andreas passed between us but the man did not move. He was anxious though and turned his head from the shop to the street in Andreas's direction to the other direction, back and forth several times before moving into the street. He stood and for a moment he watched the alley where I hid. I thought I had been discovered and he intended to come in, but he turned and moved toward the high side of town and away from Andreas.

I moved up the alley and watched as he passed Mam's shop. I turned around and ran back down the alley. I turned left, ran passed the back door of the shop and up to the next intersecting alley. I moved into the shadows cast by the buildings, getting as close as I dared to the street, and waited for my target to pass. When he did I climbed the lean-to attached to the next building and using a window sill as a ladder I boosted myself up onto the low peaked roof. I moved up just below the cap of thatch at the peak and trotted along it, to the end. There I crouched low as my target made a turn and then another to move up higher into the tiered city. I lost sight of him momentarily and looked for Andreas, but did not see him yet. I jumped down to the roof of an attached building and then across a thin alley to another building that was on the corner of an intersection. The street was busy, so I stayed on the low side of the roof away from the street and climbed down a wooden gutter to another alley. I was very near the street here and moved out casually to make my way across that street to the one my target had turned on to. I saw Andreas then working his way quickly through the pedestrians on the boardwalk and coming my way.

I moved up the street. It curved gradually up and around the natural slope of the mountain upon which Mareese had been built. I could not see the man and so I picked up speed a little at a time until I could make him out ahead of me. When I did, I moved to the inside of the curve and stayed near the buildings keeping him in my sight just at the edge of the apex in the curve. If he turned I could just stop and take a step back to be out of his view.

I glanced behind me and saw Andreas in much the same situation. He was following me, following our target.

If the man turned left in two streets I would be convinced that he was heading to the Manor House. I followed and when he did I motioned discreetly to Andreas to meet up with me, but continued on in the pursuit.

When he joined me I instructed him to take to the roofs and wait across from the Manor House. I would continue, just in case the man turned off, but I expected we would join up at the Manor entrance. Andreas slipped into a nearby alley. I trotted up to the road and crossed it to get a look and see the target. He was no where in sight. We only had our eyes off him for a moment. When I looked back to Andreas he was no where in sight. I turned up the boardwalk on the other side and increased my speed so that I was nearly running which was not appreciated by the other pedestrians. I moved just off the walkway onto the cobbled street and looked both ways and in shop windows as I began up the street again. The Manor House was just ahead and I had to admit to myself that I had lost the man. I glanced up, but I did not see Andreas. I had not expected to, but I was hopeful. I continued on my way, but stopped short and turned to gaze into a window when I saw Mya emerge from a millinery shop. I watched her reflection as she looked up and down the street and then skipped her way to the Manor House gate.

That was odd. When we left the Manor Mya was standing vigil over her father's body. That ritual should have lasted until the body was to be moved to a ship, and Esporanza's small entourage would accompany him home. Perhaps Garthe had succeeded in moving his departure time up to one of the evening tides. But, Mya had been distraught over her father's death and worried about her status when she returned home to King Strahn's court. Skipping was not a thing she would do, not today.

I went across to the millinery shop and asked the proprietor if she had seen a swarthy young man enter. She had not. She had just been busy in the back pulling some bolts of cloth down for an order. She had heard the jingle of her entry bell. I described Mya to her. She had not seen her. I wanted to search the place but was pressed for time. I told her that if she found anything odd or unusual about the store that she should call on me at the Manor House or leave a message at the Apothecary's Shop. She was troubled by my request, but agreed.

I went out and made my way quickly to the Manor House. I went up to the guard whom I knew and inquired about the comings and goings of the day. Gebha and Garthe had not left. "They are busy making arrangements to depart. Only Mya had come that way and had been in town all afternoon and had just returned. Andreas joined us and asked about any dark haired boys who worked at the manor who may have come through the gate.

"I've told you all I know. I've been here my entire shift. You could check at the postern gate."

"Thanks, we will."

We went around the outside of the low wall surrounding the manor. It wasn't a fortified wall and the grounds were in full view to anyone walking along and looking over. The postern gate was also guarded and we asked the same questions of the man there. He knew less than my friend at the main gate. We asked for entrance and he obliged us, even though our carpet bag was back at my room.

We knew we were on thin ice with Diony but we had to make her aware of these developments. Rather than risk angering her further and being denied; we went to find Ray Vin Wholfe. He was alone in his small office next to Diony's. He was surprised to see us knowing of Diony's distress about us, but he did not send us away and listened attentively to our story.

"So you never did check your mother's shop then?"

"No, it seemed more important to flush out a possible connection to the ambassador's murder," Andreas said.

"Are you certain it was this false Mya we have been theorizing?"

"I am," I said. "Someone is posing as Mya."

Ray sat back, thinking. We let him and after some time he shared his thoughts with us. "Disguise. The only people who have the ability to do that well are actors and assassins. There are no troupes in town at this time; so assassin." He rose from his chair and lumbered his aging body over to the door. Looking out over the courtyard toward the chapel he said, "Andreas please go and check on Mya. Saeede wait here while I go get Diony. She needs to hear this."

Andreas and Ray left the room together. I went to the window and watched as Andreas ran across the courtyard to the chapel. He went in just as Ray returned with Diony. Brynal was not at her side. I turned back to the window and saw him running toward the chapel.

81

I turned my attention to Diony and did not see anything that happened in the courtyard after that.

I stood with my back to the window and waited for the governor and her sheriff to be seated. Diony did not look pleased with me, but her attitude softened as my story unfolded.

Brynal and Andreas entered together about half way through my telling. I trusted that Andreas had brought Brynal up to date on the latest events. Neither of them seemed unduly anxious so I concluded that Mya was safe. I finished my story and they told theirs.

Gebha had gone to Mya at the chapel after he had eaten his lunch. He had asked her if she needed anything and she had said no. He told her that he admired her for taking a stand and winning her right to stand vigil for her father's spirit. She was happy that he had acknowledged her and was determined to stay the whole night to prove herself to him. Gebha encouraged her not to step one foot out of the chapel; that a true vigil meant to stand beside the departed at all times so that no one could disturb the spirit.

"Go and bring him back here immediately," Ray ordered. Brynal turned to go.

"Mind if we tag along?" Andreas asked.

Brynal looked to Diony who nodded her approval.

We went at a trot to the room Garthe and Gebha shared. Garthe answered Brynal's knock. He was annoyed at seeing Andreas and me.

"What do you want, Brynal? Why have you brought these two to my door?"

"Diony sent us for Gebha. Is he here?"

"Tell me why she wants him. I am in charge of the Ambassador's affairs. Not that she cares."

Brynal hesitated, weighing his next move before he spoke. "Perhaps you should come too then. Where is he?"

"Not here. He was going into town for some things he wanted for the voyage home. I haven't seen him since he relieved me for lunch. I hope he doesn't expect me to pack his things. He'll find himself wanting aboard ship."

"You better come now, Garthe."

"Tell me why."

I interrupted. "You're a smart man Garthe, figure it out. Come with us or consider this courtesy call over." I couldn't resist and I knew if I angered him once more he'd be anxious to tattle to Diony. I was right. He glared at me a moment then moved out into the hall and closed the door behind him. We gave him room as he turned back to lock it and we all moved briskly to Ray's office.

We let Garthe lead and he had barely opened the door when he was demanding explanations from the governor. She countered wanting an explanation of Gebha's failure to comply with her demand that he attend this meeting. The explanation was accepted, for the time being. Ray went out to order some of his men into the city to search for Gebha. While he was gone Diony relayed both stories to Garthe and included her opinion of why Gebha had encouraged Mya not to step one foot out of the chapel.

Garthe had been standing or pacing during all of this and at the end of the telling he flopped down in the chair next to Diony. "Played for a fool. Damn it! Why could I not see it?"

"You were more concerned for your reputation and that closed your mind. You owed Esporanza and King Frahn to be open to all possibilities. You only trusted what was familiar to you. I suppose that is natural in times like these, but as servants of the better good we must always be aware, and even wary. Perhaps this lesson will serve you well in your future service to Frahn."

"If he'll still have me."

"Help us now and I will speak to Frahn on your behalf."

83

"You would do that? I have not been as kind."

"We have not captured Gebha or proven beyond doubt that he is the killer. Help us to do that and be right about it and we can salvage what diplomacy we have between us."

"I will. He has not come for his things yet. Come with me and we can search them together."

We all went, except Brynal who stayed behind to inform Ray when he returned.

Garthe unlocked the door and moved toward Gebha's bed, but stopped before he got there. "It's gone. It was just here when you came for him."

"It was," Andreas said, "I saw it there."

"He must be close," Diony said. "Spread out and see if you can catch him. I will tell Brynal and Ray. Someone go get Mya, she maybe in danger!"

"I'll go," Andreas volunteered.

Diony and Andreas were already moving down the hall.

"I don't know the city. I've been sheltered here the whole time," Garthe said.

"You can come with me if you'd like," I offered. "I'm going to check on my Mam," I said.

Garthe hesitated, aware of the magnitude of trust coming from me.

"Decide now," I said.

"Yes."

We were off at a run. I did not take to the boardwalks but ran along side them on the street, or we took alley shortcuts and arrived at the backdoor of the kitchen in short time. Garthe was nimble and kept up well. I produced my key from the chain around my neck and let us in, locking the door again behind us.

Mam heard us and came in from the shop with a wicked looking club that she kept behind a counter. She did not put it down and even wagged it a bit when she caught sight of Garthe.

"It's okay, Mam. He has come to help. We have reason to believe that Gebha is the killer. Garthe has as much interest in catching him as we do. We came to see you safe."

She lowered the club and then wagged her finger for us to follow her into the shop.

I could see that she had been taking inventory of the stock. On the table where she mixed teas was a clear unlabeled vial and in it a dark root. She held it up for us to see.

"Dark Berry Root?" I asked.

Mam nodded, yes.

I asked Garthe to look around the shop. "Do you see any other clear vials here?" He searched well and in the end he acknowledged there were none.

"Will you show us where you found it?" Garthe asked.

Mam looked to me for permission and I gave it.

She led us to a shelf up high. She needed a step ladder to reach it and she placed the vial of Dark Berry Root in the spot that she had found it. Next to one of her own vials labeled Brick Tree Root.

I asked Garthe to look around the shop. "Do you see any other unlabeled vials here?"

He seemed reluctant, but he did search again. "I saw nothing unlabeled. I trust that this is not from your shop."

Mam humphed and removed the vial from the shelf, stepped off the ladder and returned the vial to the table.

"Madame, I am sorry. I suppose that is little comfort, but we do not know if you are safe here right now. Gebha has eluded us and if he is the killer." Garthe let his thought trail off. "Will you please come back with us to the Manor House until this matter is put to rest?

85

I have made many errors in judgment. I would not be able to live with myself if one of them became the cause of harm to you."

Mam looked to me for some guidance again.

"How can you say no to that?" I said. "Go gather somethings for a few days stay. I'll see if we can make arrangements for your protection here during the day. I know you'll want to keep the shop open. Keeps suspicion off of you until this blows over. The money is pretty decent too."

She turned to Garthe then, but could not resist one more derisive humph before giving him a quick little curtsey. Then went upstairs to gather her things.

"That curtsey was her way of accepting your apology."

"I figured that. Listen, do you mind if I go inspect that alley where you first saw Gebha?"

"No." I took him to the window and pointed it out. "It is just there. I'll watch from here."

Garthe gave me a disapproving look.

"I have your back partner," I said.

He turned without another word and went to the alley. I watched as he moved up it a bit and out of sight. I still didn't trust him completely and was about to go find him when he re-emerged. He stood in the very spot Gebha had stood and surveyed his surroundings. When he was satisfied with that he stooped, picked up something from the ground, and then returned to the shop.

He held out his hand and revealed several smoked dragon ends. "These could be Gebha's dragon nub ends. He is fond of the smoke and rolls them well, like this. This is not looking good for him."

Mam came down just then with a small bundle under her arm and we left by the front door; locking it of course. Garthe and I fell in behind Mam letting her pace us and kept her close.

The sky was beginning to darken. I would be glad to have Mam safely at the Manor House before full dark. We saw many of the sheriff's men talking with citizens along our way. The responses citizens gave all seemed negative. When we arrived at the front gate we were told to report immediately to Diony's office.

Ray was there with two of his men. Brynal was there again and took his usual spot, leaning against the wall behind Diony. His arms were crossed and he was looking stoic. Diony was looking tired. They were both attentive to the conversation taking place between Ray and his men. Andreas was not present. I assumed that he had chosen to watch over Mya.

Ray's men had been sent to the millinery shop. Under an ugly hat displayed atop its wooden box they found a black wig and a rag covered with brown grease paint makeup. Gebha must have sensed things moving in on him and knew he could not be caught with it. Once he returned to the manor as Mya he must have quickly changed to himself again. The manor and the grounds were being turned upside down but nothing had turned up so far.

Ray had a report from another of his men who was not present. He and another man had gone to the docks. No one there saw anyone fitting Gebha's description. Of course, if he was out of uniform he would look like many of the men who worked the docks or came from the ships there. The two men went to the harbor master and asked to see all the manifests of the day, paying special attention to any ships having left upon the first evening tide, or scheduled to leave upon the second. They paid special attention to the Grace which was the ship that had been arranged for Garthe and company to leave that evening. They had gone aboard to question the captain and search the ship. Gebha was not found. It appeared that Esporanza's killer had successfully given us the slip.

What they did not find was the stowaway hiding on the Errant a small ship bound for Nagrom. Under questioning of that crew no one had seen anyone fitting Gebha's or Mya's or the swarthy young man's description. Either Gebha had help, was just plain lucky, or very good at his work. Unfortunately for us; I thought it was a combination of luck and skill.

·~·Chapter Five·~·

"So it is decided then," Diony declared. "Saeede and Andreas will play for the dignitaries at supper tonight and I will thank them for their cooperation. Eble and I will search their minds for any hints of complicity in the murder. Though I doubt there will be any. If Gebha is an assassin it is more likely he is from Ahnges. Perhaps one of Frahn's adversaries."

"I have arranged another ship to depart at second tide tonight. She is called the Wind Dancer and is dressed out well. Saeede and Andreas will join you as advocates for Mya and emissaries for me. I will produce a letter for you, Garthe that will set you right with King Frahn. I hope that he will see it is proper to continue this investigation from there."

"I am sure he will, M'Lady. Thank you for that."

"You are welcome. I only wish we had all seen it sooner."

That night at dinner Diony announced progress in the case of Ambassador Esporanza's murder. She did not reveal our suspect, even when asked. Truth was we didn't really know. Gebha may also have been an assumed identity.

Diony clarified that the issue was not fully resolved and that led to her next matter: "In the course of the investigation and while Esporanza's man Garthe was packing to leave it was discovered that the treaty document that had been in his possession only hours before was also missing. We felt early on that the killing was a political move aimed at undoing the treaty. It was the only reasonable motive. We are certain of that now. I propose, if you are willing, that we author a letter to King Frahn expressing our interest in the treaty and that once those responsible for the death of Esporanza are found and dealt with that we revisit the issue with him personally at a location of his choosing. We would sign the letter and send it on with Garthe and his people. I am sending two of my own people as emissaries and they would hold the letter until they are met by Frahn. What say you?"

There was some heated discussion. With political intrigue at play no one felt like jumping back in without first being sure they would be protected. In the end the letter that was written conveyed their trepidation to convene treaty talks. Diony worded it with well measured amity. When the murder was solved and justice was done the leaders of Crystalier were willing to reconvene.

All the leaders present signed the letter but only after knowing who was carrying it on their behalf. Only Mayor Brohaugh of Jour was hesitant. Jour had been miraculously unscathed by the Horde War and so the people there were not as involved with the events or the players involved in it. When it was pointed out that we were the key to avoiding a full scale invasion from Hell's gates he knew about that and agreed to let us carry the letter to Frahn. Being cursed by a minion of the dark one sometimes has its rewards.

We were to leave at second tide. We played four songs after dinner as agreed upon with Diony and then she excused us to prepare for our voyage. We went together to find Mam put up in a nice suite between Ray and his wife and Diony and Brynal. She would certainly be protected there. We had little concern that she was at risk if Gebha left the city, but as a precaution she agreed to stay until the matter was resolved. She gave me instructions on where to find the green bark that would minimize my sea sickness and we said our goodbyes.

She kissed my cheek then and looked deep into my eyes. A shadow of sorrow crossed behind her gaze. A lump came to my throat. We had both known a day would come that I would go back out into the world. We had never thought her life might be at stake when I did. She hugged me long and hard and I returned the same. Her strength surprised me. She shared a long look with Andreas. She said nothing, but he understood her expressive eyes and responded; "I will." She hugged him then for the first time ever. I thought he would cry, but he fought it. I kissed her check and we left.

We went together to Andreas's apartment and gathered what he needed, including weapons and armor. The carpet bag was in my room so we gathered everything in a blanket and tied it together as one big bundle that we carried between us. The land lord lived downstairs and Andreas paid him six months in advance. "If I am not back by then send a bill to Diony herself for the next six months. If I haven't returned in a year you can sell whatever you want or rent a furnished apartment after that." The land lord agreed and we hurried on our way to Mam's.

"Diony is not going to like that."

"I'm good for it. Besides if he thinks she is involved he won't be tempted to cheat me. We'll be back before that anyway."

"I hope so, the last time we went off chasing a murderer it ended up being a devil's game. We were gone nearly a year."

"You dwell on that too much. Where is your sense of adventure?"

I sighed and said, "Lost."

"Well maybe we will find it along the way. I don't have a care about that treaty one way or the other. I want the killer for Mya's sake. She's a good kid. I want to see she will be cared for, but after that my priority is that ledger. I haven't given you details, because I'm not sure yet, but one of the things Eindal was going after maybe a great relic, possibly forged by a god, maybe even The All God Himself."

As he spoke I unconsciously slowed my steps. I found myself staring at him slack jawed barely able to keep moving. He stopped, laughed, and reached over to push my mouth shut. His laughter made me think he might be making fun.

"Seriously?"

"Yes."

Slack jawed again I looked for words but found none. We continued and as we neared Mam's shop I found words. "We have to get that back; in the wrong hands... gads!"

"That was pretty much my thoughts, but they sounded so much more intelligent in my head."

"Shut up."

We went around by the alley and let ourselves in through the kitchen. Andreas followed me up and watched as I gathered my gear, removed my mail and swords and placed it in the carpetbag.

"What protection did Diony agree to give to your mother if you are away?"

"She and Mother will see to her protection within these walls. Diony has offered to have her patrols keep an eye on things in the neighborhood. I trust her to have Mam's interests at heart."

We un-wrapped his bundle and packed his things into the carpetbag. It was bulging now and took us both to pull it tight and do the clasps.

We sat up in my room awhile talking, nothing important; just old stories. The prospect of adventure was beginning to excite us.

"I think my sense of adventure has come back to me."

"Good, so not lost, just misplaced."

We went to bed after that to catch a bit of sleep. Andreas took Mam's bed. I heard him tossing and turning as I laid awake going over things in my head. I decided there was nothing we had missed. Still I was restless. I got up and double checked our gear and repacked, consolidating what I could. I wanted to be ready for any turn of events. I assured myself we were well equipped. Andreas must have heard me moving about and came to knock on my door. I opened it and he came in.

"I can't sleep either."

"Too much has happened and is about to. I can't seem to put it to rest."

"Ya, I could think of something we could do to pass the time," he said and patted the bed.

"Don't say it unless you mean it."

"Oh, I mean it."

"Well, then don't say it unless you are willing to commit."

"I'm willing if you are."

He called my bluff. I had only been teasing. Usually he was too. I loved him, that was true enough, but he had caught me off guard. Was he actually willing to commit to a lover's relationship? Was I? Did I love him like that? I didn't know. He looked serious.

He saw my hesitation and let me off the hook. "Some other time then."

Damn, I hoped I hadn't lost my chance. "Andy?"

"Yes?"

"Ask me again when this is over?"

"Well, you may have to remind me," he said in his usual teasing way.

"I will."

He smiled and came to hug me. The urge was there in both of us. He kissed me long and hard. Then he looked down into my eyes, reading them as I read his. I read confusion and I know he did too.

"Shall we go to the ship? Maybe we can sleep there. We won't worry about oversleeping here," he said.

"Yes, an excellent idea. One less thing to worry about. Maybe the night air will clear our heads."

"I hope so. I'm exhausted."

"Ya, I thought I was too."

He picked up the carpetbag and we went downstairs. I took a vial and crammed it full of green bark and jammed that into the top of the carpetbag. After one last look around we left through the alley door, locking it before turning to make our way to the ship.

The Wind Dancer sat high in the water. The boson sat on a barrel at the bottom of the gangplank. He checked our names from his list and gave us directions to our berth. We went through a door under the forecastle and found a very well appointed berth. We claimed our beds, stowed the carpetbag in a small closet, opened the porthole to the warm night air, and stretched out on the beds. The slow rhythm of the swaying ship and the creek of the moorings soon lulled us to sleep.

When I woke I could tell that the ship was underway. I put a pinch of green bark under my tongue before the sea sickness could claim me. Andreas was not in his bed so I went to find him.

I saw him on the quarter deck standing with his legs wide apart and his arms crossed at his chest. He was facing the wind and held his chin high. He looked marvelous; reveling in the magnificence of the great ship as it cut through the surf. I strode out to cross the main deck and join him, but I had no sea legs and staggered toward the rail. A sailor caught me and pushed me to the capstan where I could grab on. I thanked him and he nodded before going back to his duties. I looked up at Andreas who was smiling down at me now. Oh how I envied him his lust for the sea. I moved awkwardly to the manrope atop the rail and struggled along toward the companionway to the quarter deck. Andreas at least had the decency to come to the top and assist me from there.

"No sea legs, hey?"

I had no words for how annoyed I was at him for pointing out something that was not only embarrassing, but obvious. My weakness at sea angered me greatly.

He led me to the transom rail where I turned around to watch our progress. The sails were tight and we slid through calm waters, scudding along in the earliest hours of morning. The last moon was on the western horizon and the first sun was just peeking up over the east. I enjoyed the voyage while I could, but even with Mam's green bark pressed under my tongue I spent two more barely tolerable days on ship.

On that third day the sky was kissed with the first purple light of morning and we could see the pale edge of a land mass ahead of us. Within an hour we could see the city of Nagrom. It sprawled out from the port toward a crescent of foothills that separated it from the rest of the continent on three landward sides. A thick fog rolled back from the docks so vigorously that it seemed as if the mountains beyond the foothills inhaled it.

We sailed in under a northern span of the Sea Bridge. I watched as the maze of buildings that was Nagrom were revealed as we approached. The streets and alleys meandered through the city, with no apparent plan. Buildings had simply been built wherever there had been space available and the streets wound their way through on whatever course that had created. The only thing that looked planned was a boardwalk that led straight from the wharf to a castle situated at the crest of the centermost hill. The boardwalk was a continuation of the central pier belonging to the docks. As the docks ended and the city proper began two tall walls spanned out at right angles from either side of the boardwalk heading to the northwest and southeast. They rolled over the hills on either side, until they turned toward the sea and became the sea bridges. At the end of each bridge was a square stout building. The buildings served as the Harbor Masters' office and lookout.

The crew lowered the sails and maneuvered into a slip at the Harbor Master's Pier. Two sailors let out the walkway and two others were soon over it to tie off to the pier bollards. The captain followed and all five men climbed the stairs together to the Harbor Master's building. The remaining crew secured the foresails. They would maneuver out of the slip and into their dock at the main wharf under power of the mizzen sails which were now at half mast. The captain and his men returned shortly. "Three" he called out and the men went to work. We were soon smartly moored to pier three.

Mya and Garthe came out to the main deck then and we went down to join them. The cargo in the hold below included the coffin of Ambassador Esporanza. We stood aside as the task of emptying the hold began. It was short work unloading with the help of the dock crew. The captain had arranged a wagon with two ponies to transport Esporanza. The coffin was hoisted and then lowered to the deck where eight sailors lifted it and carried it to the waiting wagon. Garthe drove the wagon with Mya at his side. We walked behind. We were standing at the gates of Frahn's castle before both suns were up.

Garthe was saluted at the gate and he stopped to converse with one of the men there. We had beaten the message sent ahead by Diony. Perhaps this was Gebha's doing as well. The meeting with Frahn would be even more intense than we had anticipated. We made our way through one gatehouse, an outer courtyard where livestock grazed, under a barbican, through another gatehouse, into an inner courtyard. We stopped at a wide porch before the thick wood entrance door of the castle stronghold. Upon seeing the coffin a door sentry ran into the house while the other came forward to greet Garthe.

Garthe was relaying the woeful circumstances of his trip to Mareese when the sentry returned followed quickly by a tall robust man of about thirty years of age. He wore a simple silver circlet raked to one side upon his head of flowing white hair. His countenance was weary, aged before his time. This was King Frahn and the look upon his face was unreadable, so many emotions seemed present all at once. When he spoke his voice was strained, but controlled.

"What the hell happened, Garthe? Who the hell are these people? Where are Esporanza and Gebha? Who rides in the coffin?"

"M'lord," Gebha began and gave a military salute; fist over heart. "The Ambassador has been murdered." The king was visibly shaken and seemed not to see Garthe as he continued, "This is his coffin graciously provided by the Governor of Mareese. She sent a message ahead, but somehow we beat it here. You'll remember the young lady; Mya, Esporanza's daughter."

"Yes, of course. Mya," Frahn's acknowledgment was dismissive. I could see why the girl was concerned about her future. She moved closer to Andreas.

"It appears that Gebha is not who he presented himself to be. We believe that he is the killer."

"What? How?"

"Poison, M'lord. An investigation was conducted and the evidence does point to Gebha, although we have reason to believe Gebha is not Gebha and may well be an assassin proficient in the use of poison and the art of disguise."

"And who are these people?" Frahn asked, motioning toward us.

"Emissaries sent by Diony Vin Hiele They were responsible for unravelling the case. Let me present Saeede and Andreas."

We bowed appropriately and Andreas spoke for us. "If your highness would allow it we would very much like to present you with our findings, but here in the courtyard doesn't seem the proper place. If we could go somewhere more private?"

"Of course, yes. Please excuse me it is just that I am taken back."

"Perfectly understandable, Sir."

Frahn spoke with his sentries then, ordering the body be removed to the chapel in the outer courtyard. "See to it that Boroth lays him properly, and anoints him for a prolonged state. Many will want to pay respects. Have him come to me when this is done, and notify Sion that we have guests and will be having many more." The sentries saluted and conferred together before going off in opposite directions. One jumped up in the wagon and turned it around. "And see this door is manned," Frahn shouted out after them.

"Aye, sir!" They both shouted back without stopping.

"Follow me."

Mya hesitated and looked after the wagon. Andreas put his arm around her shoulder steering her toward the door and whispered, "Stay with us now. It is important that you represent as your father's heir."

We followed Frahn through an entry hall and another set of massive doors to the great hall. The room was arranged with tables lined along either side of the room. A raised dais was at the far end. On the dais were several large chairs in a line. The central most was for Frahn. It was not ornate as some thrones are, but looked comfortable. He went to it, but did not sit and turned to face us, below him on the main floor. I wondered if he had contrived that position to make us acknowledge his station. It was the way of kings, contrived or not. Two sentries stood at either end of the dais. He ordered them out, to post at the door. He waited until they left the room and closed the door.

"Tell me then."

Andreas began, leaving nothing out, not even my relation to the apothecary. He presented Garthe in a better light than he had performed, but diplomacy called for it. We needed to convince Frahn of our loyalty and dedication to his best interests and right now Garthe was one of his interests. At one point the two letters from Diony were mentioned. Garthe presented his, and Frahn seemed pleased. I presented the treaty letter and the king relaxed a bit for the first time.

After the telling we moved ahead to our current strategy of continuing the investigation in Nagrom and asked for his cooperation. He had become more reasonable during Andreas's narrative and eagerly complied with our request, even offering us rooms at the castle. We had talked about this possibility and graciously declined for ourselves, feeling it was better to distance ourselves from him for now as the investigation moved ahead. We did ask for a place for Mya while the affairs of the funeral were going on and until he could find a place for her in his court. He looked upon us with a wary eye, but agreed, concluding with the statement; "For now." We took that arrangement with as much grace as we could muster. We would re-address the matter when the investigation was successful, in hopes that it would give us some leverage.

Garthe was assigned to his regular duties as a captain of the guard, and given additional assignments as liaison between us and his king, and as protector to Mya. His face read like a book. He was not happy with the extra duty, he was a soldier, not a pageboy or nanny. We were glad of it. Garthe might not like it, but he would perform at a high level. He would be being watched more closely by his king now. We explained to him that Frahn had trust in him or he wouldn't give him such important assignments. He was better for it, but still grumbled about the extra work. We recognized that he was tired too and promised to call on him only if absolutely necessary. Andreas advised him to work on keeping his emotions off his face.

Frahn seemed a hard man to know and although he was cordial, he seemed not to trust easily. We were sure our actions would be watched as well.

He dismissed us and we left the hall. Mya was a nervous wreck, and was not happy that we would not be lodging at the castle. Garthe promised she would not be harassed if she kept to herself, but was courteous to everyone she did have to interact with. She accepted that, although somewhat dubiously. We said goodbye and left.

***

We arranged rooms at an inn called the Tumbling Highlands. The great tavern room spanned nearly the entire width and length of the stone and timber structure. At one end a huge stone hearth filled the wall, the stone chimney climbed that wall beyond the high timbers and out through the roof. At the other end, the bar spanned into the room then curved back twice until it finally met with the back wall just below the stair landing creating an L shaped work area for the bartender. The stairway led up along the back wall above the bar to a balcony that led to the rented rooms. Huge trestle tables were arranged between the bar and the fireplace and round tables surrounded them at the edges of the room. People lounged about visiting with friends or workmates.

After seeing to our rooms, we went to the attached stable run by the inn's owners. We would need horses if our investigation took us out of Nagrom. We purchased two very nice mares. These horses were raised from a good stock, but they were not as nice as Grey Daria or Dark Corydon. We had been unable to bring our loyal beasts aboard ship and left them boarded in the town stable in Mareese.

From there we went back to the docks and began asking about ships that had come in recently from Mareese. There were only two beside ours. Both were traders, but only one originated in Mareese and came directly. It was called the Errant. That coincided with what we had learned from Ray's men and their investigation on the wharf back in Mareese. When we asked a dock worker if there had been anything unusual about the Errant we were told of a sailor that had ridden up from the hold by hanging onto the cargo net and when the net was swung over the dock he leapt down and ran off into the city. The captain had determined after a quick attendance of his crew that they had missed a stowaway.

"The Captain was furious; his perfect record gone."

"Did anyone recognize the sailor?"

"No, but some even said it was a women. That made the captain even more angry. He is one of those thinks a women on board is bad luck. No offense."

"None taken," I said.

"Did anyone see where he – she went?"

"Well, I watched him – her go until I lost sight some where near the City Stables. Ran like the wind that one, moved with grace through the people like a leaf caught in that wind."

"Is the Errant still in dock?"

"No, she went out again the same day. The captain had a perishable cargo bound for Plano."

We thanked the man and offered to buy him a drink if we ever saw him at the Tumbling Highlands. He shook our hands and we went back into town. Our destination was the City Stable.

The stable master was a young man about twenty five or so. He came to us when we asked for him. We asked about anyone coming to the stable that might have been in a rush to acquire a horse.

"Who wants to know and why?"

"No need to worry, friend. We are from Mareese and on the governor's business. We just need to know if this person came through Nagrom and how. You are not in any trouble here," Andreas said.

"Well, I get my horses from people sometimes and maybe they didn't get their horse in a legal way. I've had trouble that way before. I get suspicious when strangers come around asking questions."

"We aren't asking about someone wanting to sell a horse. We need to know about a purchase, or maybe someone left a horse but returned to pick it up and was in a great hurry. It would have been in the last couple of days."

"Not while I was here."

"Maybe one of your stable men?"

He looked around and then seeing one of them called out. A teenage boy about sixteen years old came over and the stable master posed our question to him.

"Old Sam said something like that, day before last."

"Go fetch him for me."

The boy ran off and soon a man smelling of manure came through the doors leading to the paddock. When the question was posed to him he laughed and told us the story.

"Yes indeed. She was a fright. Might have been a pretty thing but she looked like she hadn't slept. Her clothes were those of a man and they were untidy. She needed a bath to be sure. She came in here barkin' orders. Well I may be just a stable man, but I don't take to being mistreated. She said she had a horse here. I had to check the logs. She was kind of fidgety while I checked and demanded to saddle up while I did. I didn't see no harm. I was pretty sure what horse was hers and she went right to it. I confirmed it and when I got to the stall she was already mounting up. She threw the coins at me and galloped right out."

"Any idea which way she headed." Andreas asked.

"Not for certain, but she made a sharp turn right outside here. That way would take her toward the north gate."

"What lies beyond the gate?" I asked.

"Nothin' but the whole continent of Ahnges. A whole lot of wilderness, speckled with a town here and there."

"Did the girl have any identifying marks or signets, a livery perhaps?" I asked.

"No but I remember the brand on the horse."

"Yes?" Andreas and I both asked at once.

"It was Harald's mark."

"King Harald?" the Stable Master asked.

"Aye. A round swirl surrounding an ocean wave." Old Sam answered.

"Where is King Harald?"

"He resides in Breen," Old Sam said.

We thanked them and made the same offer of a beer if we ever saw them at the Tumbling Highland Inn. Information was coming to us cheaply in Nagrom. We went on our way quickly. We stopped at the inn stables and asked to have our horses saddled and ready. Andreas went up to get our bag and I settled our bill even though we had not stayed. It wouldn't hurt to have the proprietors good relations if we need a place or information later.

We rode quickly along the boardwalk that led to Frahn's gate and we were let in without question. Garthe was not hard to find in the outer courtyard with Mya. They were speaking with a clergyman on the chapel stairs. At seeing us he excused himself and came down to meet us. We told him of our findings and wanted him to get us in to speak directly with Frahn. He called for Mya and she came immediately. Andreas helped her up behind him and Garthe climbed up behind me. We rode over the bridge into the inner courtyard at a trot. Garthe slid off the back of my horse even before we had stopped and was running up the steps as we dismounted. We followed and stopped just inside the door of the great hall. Garthe had interrupted some other business and merchants looked rather annoyed by it. Frahn was leaning over while Garthe whispered in his ear. He looked up at us and waited while Garthe finished then he turned his head to speak into Garthe's ear a moment. Garthe came back to us, "Follow me," he said. Frahn returned to his interrupted business, but did not take his eyes from us as we left the room.

Garthe led us through a series of rooms and an inner courtyard surrounded by rooms and buildings dedicated to the running of the place. A kitchen garden and well filled most of the open space. We cut across to an entrance near one of the towers. A few rooms later we were sitting in the parlor of the king's own quarters. We sat in awkward silence until Frahn joined us a few moments later.

Frahn's eyes went to Mya. "Is this news suitable for the girl?" he asked with a tone of disdain.

"It does concern her father, Sir," I said.

"Very well then. What have you discovered that takes me from my duties?"

Andreas spoke for us again. We felt that until we knew Frahn better that it was better man to man. He told them of our conversations on the docks and with the city stablemen. Frahn questioned the fact that it might be a woman when Gebha was a man.

"We told you of someone skilled in the art of disguise. Who is to say that it cannot be a woman. Or perhaps it was Gebha, a man disguised as a woman to protect his true identity. We do not find it that hard to believe and ask that you consider it as a possibility."

"I can do that."

"Good, I will continue then with that in mind." Andreas continued the story and Frahn was sitting forward in his chair listening intently.

104

When Andreas came to the end and the implication of King Harald possibly being involved, Frahn fell back in his chair and looked up at the ceiling. The rest of us sat in silence waiting for his response.

When he spoke his tone was soft but malicious. "That bastard! I always knew he could not be trusted. He must have a spy amongst us. If that is true they will know you are here. Who has left the castle since your arrival, Garthe?"

"No one that I know of M'lord. I will check on it though."

"Do it now."

Garthe bowed to his king and left quickly.

"What do you plan to do?" he asked us.

"Well, Sir it seems to be expedient to follow quickly and apprehend the man, but we have no real description. Unless of course he is truly Gebha. We can not act on a matter so delicate as calling another King's man murderer without your blessing. I can promise you our loyalty in this matter. We are determined to find the culprit who laid this murder on our governor on the very eve that the treaty was signed. We have sworn a covenant to Saeede's mother and my dear friend, to clear her name with no room for challenge. For Mya's sake we swear covenant to bring this person to you for justice."

"You seem quite passionate about this."

"We are sir."

"Can you do this with out bringing the wrath of Harald's people to my gates?"

"We will do what we can, but a matter at this level of political intrigue often has a life of its own. What we would like to do, is determine who exactly Gebha is, who he— or she works for and how closely. We would like to have physical evidence of that. When we have that and we can connect that person to our evidence then we would like to capture that person, away from Harald and bring him— or her here to you. If Harald is involved he should be alarmed that his assassin is missing. If we are successful Harald will not know who took Gebha, nor will he know where or why. What you determine to do with the person at that point is then up to you."

"That sounds like solid thinking, but can you do it?"

"We have some experience in matters such as these. We know how to conduct ourselves at court, if that become necessary. Our biggest disadvantage is that we do not know who Gebha actually is or what he looks like. He however will recognize us easily. What can you tell us about him? How did he come to be one of your trusted men?"

"He became known to us about a year ago. About the same time I began formulating the conditions of a treaty. He presented himself as a Shepard's son. One of seven as his story goes, and the youngest. He saw no future as an heir to that and wanted to make soldiering his life. He showed great promise early. All of his training went so well that my swordsman suggested I put him into service. Six months ago I did just that. He was a friendly sort and with his skills I felt he would be a good match to accompany Esporanza. Esporanza knew of the boy and approved. Garthe was not so happy. Garthe is a good soldier, smart and loyal, but sometimes his ego gets in the way of him always wanting to impress me. I am trying to train him for work that will bring him closer to my inner circle. I want him to have these experiences. I am glad that he performed well in Mareese."

We did not correct Frahn's misguided assumptions of his trusted man.

"He felt that he could keep Esporanza safe by himself. I took his reaction as jealousy and gave my orders.

"The treaty is very important to me. I am fortunate to sit on a predominant piece of Ahnges. Trade with Crystalier would boost our economy as well as theirs, though we do quite well here in Nagrom already. I wanted to be the first king from Ahnges to forge a friendship with Crystalier. It could serve to mend broken alliances here as well with the upcoming power of Crystalier at my back. The increased moneys that would come from the calculated trade would enforce our defenses.

"I have been getting news from Crystalier for a long time. The last few years have been very interesting. I know of the troubles in Mareese and of the young woman who rose up against a tyrant and now sits as their governor. I know about the two of you as well. I bet you thought I didn't recognize your names. I sent my own spies to Crystalier and Dinar when I began to hear about the Hordes.

"Frustrating, that I should know so much of this far away place, and yet miss what is right under my nose."

"That is often the case I'm sorry to say," Andreas said. "Perhaps we have moved quickly enough that you can halt any bad effects to you and your kingdom."

"I am tempted to let this matter go. To see what Harald's next move will be."

"I would caution you not to, Sir."

"Why is that?"

"Do not give Harald time to turn the other kings against you and your treaty."

Frahn sat still, considering Andreas's last statement.

"He could have done that already. If he is behind this assassination as we suspect he is, then he has previous knowledge. He could have been working the kings up even before Esporanza set sail. I have no word of that though."

"Then the time is now for you to shore up your alliances. The funeral will offer you that opportunity."

"I think I see where you are going. Esporanza was well known and liked by many of the kings, even though they did not agree that we needed a treaty. There are seven kings in all including me. I could let it slip that Harald was behind his death. I could tell them that the purpose of Esporanza's trip was to test the waters about a possible treaty."

"That may not be wise. Don't forget that Gebha has also stolen the treaty document. No doubt to wave it in the face of the other kings to turn them against you."

"Clever. I don't see what it is that we can do then. The tides are swelled against me and you are too recognizable."

"Actually our being recognized is the least of your worries. We will just have to not be seen."

Frahn's eyes lit up. "Do you really think you can avoid it?"

"I know we can."

Just then Garthe returned to report that no one aside from us had left the castle grounds since our arrival. If there was a spy they were watching from somewhere. We would have to be careful of our movements. Frahn thanked Garthe, and asked him to stay. He turned his attention back to the matter at hand.

"You don't say much, Saeede. How do you feel about it?"

"We have the skills, Sir. I believe we can go unseen." *Just not sure how yet*, I thought to myself.

"Do it then. Bring me Gebha and the treaty document."

"As you wish, Sir."

We left taking Mya with us. We sent her to her room and instructed her to stay to herself and not to talk with strangers. She was to be courteous and polite of course, but by no means was she to mention the treaty or anything about her trip to Mareese to anyone. She would be watchful and report any unusual conversations or events directly to Garthe. We promised that when we returned we would pin Frahn down about her station in his court.

We went to the kitchen for a meal. There was nothing unusual in that. The kitchen was was busy with the midday meal and preparations for the evening meal. We were served a bowl of stew and a chunk of bread. While the poor old cooking maid had to shout her orders over the bustle of the workers, we were able to pilfer a few items to bolster our stores for the road. We were glad to have them, it sped up our departure from the city. We didn't want to ask and tip our hands to a spy who might ask around later.

We could not afford to dally at the castle any longer, even if our sudden departure called attention to us. It could not be helped, our suspected murderer already had a great lead on us. We felt we knew where Gebha was heading, but the time was to his advantage to secure a safe place of hiding.

When we were ready we rode out through the postern gate of the inner courtyard and made our way to the north gate of the city. There we asked for directions to Breen. It was a winding way up out of the valley bowl and through the mountains that surrounded Nagrom on three sides. The way was well travelled and the pass through the mountains was an easy go of it. On the northern side of the pass the mountains quickly gave way to rolling foothills. The woodlands that covered them were dense, but the road cut through straight as an arrow. We rode on as the suns moved down toward the horizon. Under the canopy of trees night fell before the suns did, still we rode on.

All through the night we travelled. The horses carried us well but by morning we were all in great need of rest. We came upon a shelter a little way up the road. It was a small barn on the roadside with a small money box nailed to a stump near the door. Here people could rest and if they had money and were generous they would drop a coin or two into the slot of the locked box. When we approached we saw only one horse tied to the rail outside.

I dismounted and handed Andreas the reins to my horse before approaching the horse and barn. I cut an apple from what we had pilfered from Frahn's cook and moved onto the road. Perhaps this one horse belonged to Gebha. I intended to find out before we moved on the building.

I ran along the far side of the road across from the barn to a point near the horse, then I angled toward it. It caught sight of me and moved as far away as its tether would allow.

"Sssh, Sssh now," I whispered. "No harm beast, no harm. Are you marked? I just want to see your mark." I spoke in hushed tones all the way up to her. I let her smell me and reached up slowly to stroke her nose. She fixed on the apple and I gave it to her. While she munched I went to find the brand mark. It did not match the description of a round swirl surrounding a stylized ocean wave. There was no need for us to disturb whoever it was that slept inside.

I went back to Andreas and mounted up. We walked the horses slowly passed the barn and a far distance beyond that. We looked back at the barn often and there was no sign of anyone about. We remained unseen. We were glad of our success and urged the horses to a gallop letting them find their pace. When they tired we dismounted and lead them off the road into the trees.

We walked about an hour more following a thin creek until it widened to a stream and ran fast enough to drink from safely. The suns were high enough to seep light into the woods by then so we made camp. We would rest by day and travel at night as long as was possible.

The horses watered themselves from the stream. I unburdened them of our packs and saddles and let them graze freely of the grasses beneath the trees. Andreas rolled out our bed rolls and we were soon asleep with our heads upon our packs. We trusted the horses to put up enough fuss to wake us if danger came near.

Danger did not disturb us and the suns were high in the sky and moving toward evening when we woke. We took time for ablutions but we shared food as we lead the horses back to the road. We shared the last of the half apple we had split for the horse along the roadside. We split another apple between the horses; a reward for the good ride. When we reached the road we mounted and urged the horses to a gallop again. The road fell behind us the rest of the day and into another night.

Around midnight the road began to slope down toward a curve ahead. The trees became sparse and the road lit by the light of both moons shone like a ghost river over the land. We slowed the horses and moved on.

The smell of the sea was in the air and the thinning trees were distorted from the salt and wind. The curve brought us to the tip of an inlet. Below us a great bay opened up. We could not see across the bay to know what was out there, but we could sense the of vastness of it. The light of the moons showed us the cliffs and the beach below. The coast ran ragged and rocky to the west and north. Above us the land sloped down to that point above the bay and a stream bed passed under a wooden bridge. The bed was dry, but in a good rain it would make a fall onto the beach below and flow into the sea. We walked the horses one at a time across the bridge and mounted again. We let the horses choose their pace as the road curved back again to a northern route. The land dipped down toward the sea on our left and up into denser woods on our right. Fishing shanties with small boats dotted the shore for a few miles.

We road on until the land began to rise again to our north. Breen would be at the top of that rise and we did not wish to be seen yet. We turned the horses back toward Nagrom and chased them still in full tack. They were fine horses and would find there way home. We were sad to have to let them go, but they no longer fit our needs We took to the trees and moved away from the road, continuing in a northeasterly direction until the sky began to brighten.

We estimated that if we ran we were still a half a day from Breen. We took time to equip ourselves for any possibility. Our intent was only to survey the area, but we would not leave anything to chance. We left no armor or weapons in our bag, only our instruments remained. We could not use our musical talents to ply for information this time. New minstrels in town would be sure to raise Gebha's suspicions and make him wary and harder to catch.

We moved through the trees toward Breen until we found a place up in the trees where we could watch the intersection of road that met outside Breen's gate. From there we could see over the wall of the stronghold and realized that there were actually two strong holds.

The city of Breen was built mostly inside a stone stronghold on one side of a tidal inlet. That was the side nearest to us There was nothing unusual about the business of the place that we could see. It was well guarded and the largest building within those walls was a barracks. The others were the shops and homes of the tradesmen that supported the city. A blacksmith, wainwrights, and cooper shared two buildings near the barracks. Several other residences inside the wall; housed those who worked for the King in the fortress across the inlet. Several more were nestled up close just outside the wall. One large home served as a boardinghouse for passing travelers and was the only business establishment outside the wall.

Across the inlet from the large community stronghold was another smaller fortress built upon a hill that looked out over the sea on one side and the community of Breen on the other. It was a square stone building two stories tall encircled by a thick stone wall. This was King Harald's place. On the city side a wide causeway led from the wall, down the hill side, to a gate house and drawbridge that could be lowered to join with the mainland and the rear gatehouse of the community stronghold. Getting to Harald's fortress across the inlet would be difficult, but not impossible.

The drawbridge remained open throughout the day. Late in the evening several people left the fortress and made their way into homes within the stronghold of Breen. Shortly after that a contingent of soldiers left Breen for the king's fortress, and a like contingent emerged from the fortress and went to the barracks in Breen. The drawbridge was drawn up then and all of Breen dimmed down as activities ended and her citizens went to bed. Atop the four corners of Harald's fortress large braziers were lit. We could see the shadow of sentries pass between the fires and our line of sight. Perhaps the fortress would not be so easy to get to as we first thought.

We lashed each other to the tree and took turns sleeping while the other watched. Nothing remarkable happened and in the morning we climbed down and made our way to town.

I pulled on an old cap, down low on my head and wrapped my cloak loosely around my form. I was to be Andreas's younger brother if anyone asked. We were borrowing a page from Gebha's book. I was extremely nervous. We had never gone deep into disguise. I changed my walk until it met Andreas's approval and kept my head down. I was to be fifteen years old so my size fit the disguise and if I should forget and use my normal voice I could claim the cracking voice of adolescence and forge ahead with a deeper voice that Andreas had also approved.

Andreas for his part tied back his unruly hair and had not shaved since we had boarded the ship from Mareese. He detached the blades from his staff swords and used the staff as a staff. The swords went into the carpetbag and we walked to the town on foot from the road that ran east out of Breen. Posing as a farmer's sons we sought for work to supplement the income of a large family.

We walked through the farmsteads and houses outside the wall, passed the boarding house, and announced ourselves to the gate guards. They accepted our story so well that they gave us leads on who might be looking for help, and we entered Breen. The courtyard was busy. Livestock were being lead through the gate to graze in the grass outside. Sheep were gathered into pens and were being sorted for shearing. Chickens ranged freely, pecking at the ground throughout the courtyard. Women gathered at the well to tote water for the days chores while children ran about in play. Several merchant stalls along the outer wall were just opening. The smith and cooper worked together to fire up the forges while the wainwright was already removing the hub from a wagon wheel.

It was to the smithy that we went. They were in need of workhands. Andreas spoke for us and introduced himself as Sig, (his father's name), and I was his little brother Helm. They eyed us warily. My chainmail armor and Andreas's studded leather gave them pause.

Andreas pressed ahead, "Pardon our appearance. We have travelled far and the road is not always safe. We are just seeing to our protection." That seemed to appease them. Andreas answered all of their questions with an ease that caused me some concern. I did not know how effortlessly he could lie. Before the interview was over I was small for my age because I'd been sick as a baby and that had left me slow in the brain. I could talk of course, but I had trouble communicating my own needs sometimes. Oh sure I was strong enough. Farm life had made me that way, but the farm couldn't fix my addled head. I usually hated it when Andreas went off script like that, but this time I could see the way of it. This gave everything a reason. I could keep my head down and not speak and Andreas had to make all the decisions, so if we failed it was all his fault. I smiled broadly and even with my head down it could be seen. I think the smiths thought it was part of my addled personality. In the end Andreas convinced them that we could do the work. They agreed to pay us each one copper a day, plus a loft to sleep in and meals with the condition that I be able to pull my weight.

They gave us time to stow our gear in the loft. I removed my cloak and chain mail and bloused my tunic out over my belt. I am petite but I needed to be careful not to reveal my true gender. After we got settled in, the smithies put us straight to work. We hauled water, ore, and wood and manned the bellows.

Andreas engaged the wainwright in some conversation when he was helping him refit the hub he had repaired. Later that night when we were in the loft and the smiths had gone to their homes he told me what was said.

"I asked him about available women in town. If Gebha is a girl then why not ask? I told him I wanted to court a woman of noble blood, to raise my status in the world. He told me all about the young women of the servant class instead."

I laughed, "What did he say?"

"He laughed much as you just did, but I played starry eyed bumpkin and he said, *'Nothin' wrong with settin'your self up high I s'pose.'* Then he told me about three young women at court. Of the three one often travels for the king, and only just returned yesterday. She is the daughter of the king's dead sister. Her name is Lily."

"Why does she travel?"

"I asked him that, but he wasn't certain. He figures it just keeps her out of the way."

"So now what?"

"One of us has to get up there and see this Lily."

"If Gebha is Lily he—she will pick us out in a second."

"I thought of that. If we are on an errand no one will pay us much mind. We go and do the errand, and while we are there we ask some young buck about the fair Lily. Men are pigs Sade, haven't you learned that yet? Any man who thinks I am after her will happily point her out just to see me fail."

"So when you say one of us needs to go you mean you."

"Well it does seem safer."

"What if she sees you while she is being pointed out?"

"I won't let her see my face. That would lessen the mystery of the pursuit and I'll tell that to anyone who questions me about it."

"Okay. So now how do we get you sent on an errand?"

"Simo finished the hub today. The wagon belongs to the fortress. I'll offer to deliver it, and use my pursuit of a noble woman as an incentive to get him to allow it."

"That sounds like it will work."

"I'm sure it will. Now, tomorrow go over to the tailor and buy four men's shirts get two for you but buy them large and two for me to fit. Get yourself some trousers too and stuff the front with something."

"I hate this."

"I know but it is working so far. I will make my trip to the fortress as quick as possible."

·~·Chapter Six·~·

Andreas's plan went even better than we had hoped. Simo agreed to let him go to the fortress, but Simo would go with him. When the time came late in the afternoon Simo invited me as well. "You've worked hard lad, let me show around."

I was nervous about that. Sending Andreas was risk enough. If Gebha saw us together it might be even more of one. I stammered looking for an excuse, when Andreas said; "My brother is awkward around people, sir. Perhaps it is better that he stay here."

"Nonsense. People at the palace need to know the two of you. I'll introduce you to those you'll be more likely to have business with."

We saw no way out of it.

"Jump in back there little frog," Andreas told me.

I shot him a look from under my cap. But I did as big brother said and put my back to the wagon seat and kept my head down.

Sure enough my name became Frog from that point on and when we got up to the fortress Andreas was introduced as Sig, and I was his little brother Frog. We drove in around the greensward between the wall and the palace house to the wagoner's barn. The wagoner was out in the yard unloading a wagon of goods. Simo and Andreas jumped down to greet him, but I only moved to the edge of the wagon and dangled my feet over and swung them alternately back and forth. This allowed me to play the fool Andreas had made me and keep my head down. When we were introduced again Simo mentioned that I was a little addle brained, but a good worker.

The wagoner checked the hub and paid Simo.

"Come lads, you can meet my wife. She works in the kitchen."

He and Andreas started off but I remained in the wagon until Simo called for me. I followed then but kept my distance. If Gebha, or Lily was about I thought it was less likely he—she would recognize us if we were separated. I heard Andreas say, "I warned you, he is awkward around people."

When we entered the front of the palace I pulled my cap down lower and raised my head enough to get a look around. A wide hall went straight ahead of us to a wide open doorway. To our left and right it ran along the outside wall of the entire place. The hall was the height of both floors of the building. Simo lead us around to the left where the hall turned again following the outside wall of the palace. A terrace lined the upper floor of the building proper so that anyone upon it could look down at those walking in the hall. It was supported by the rooms of the first floor.

"Ever been inside a place so grand before, lads?"

"No Sir," Andreas answered, "but I could easily get used to this."

"Well maybe you will someday. If you meet the right girl," Simo said and laughed so loud it echoed in the tall hall.

I stayed a good twenty paces behind Simo and Andreas. I noted the position of all doors, and the fact that there were no footholds up to the terrace, and that we had not seen another sentry since leaving the front entrance.

I heard Simo say, "Here we are. Ah, Frog maybe wants to marry a noble girl too huh, he is enthralled with the majesty of the place. Well, maybe I can take you to the inner palace, but just for a peek."

"Come on Frog," Andreas ordered.

I trotted up and the smell of freshly baked bread filled my nose.

The place was bustling so near dinner time. Simo waved and his wife ran over. If she was not many years younger than Simo then she was very healthy. He kissed her cheek and she hugged him tight.

"Who have we here?" she asked, and stood waiting introduction.

"These are the boys I told you that we hired; Sig and the little one there is Helm. I kind of like to call him Frog as Sig does, because he is so jumpy."

Andreas was bowing politely while I just tried to look stupid. That is hard for me, you know. "That is exactly why he got the name!" Andreas said. Simo and his wife laughed.

"This is my wife Nia."

"Glad to meet you, Ma'am."

"I'm just showing the lads around a bit, so they can run errands if we need 'em to. Bero paid me for the wagon, so we can eat this week.

"Very, good. I should get back to work. We are very close to serving." She kissed Simo on the cheek and ran off.

"Well then, I have one more stop and we can go."

"Will we see any girls?" Andreas asked.

"Ah youth, only one thing on your mind. If you continue to conduct yourself as well as you have so far, maybe I'll take you through the palace garden. You can get a peek of the place where the young ladies often gather. No introductions though, that would be frowned on."

"No," I blurted out.

"Oh stop it Frog," Andreas admonished. "If you don't want to go you can just go back to the wagon. They are just girls, you'll have to learn to be around them sooner or later."

"Later," I said and turned on my heels right there and stomped like a spoiled child for about ten steps, then I just hung my head and trudged back down the hall.

Andreas had played that exactly right and I was glad to be away from them. It separated us and gave me the chance to do some snooping. I dared not venture down the central hall, but I stopped to survey it. A balcony over hung the open door and looked over the hall. There was a large wooden door on the balcony that would gain entrance to the room beyond. A guard took notice of me and ushered me out. I said nothing and returned to the wagon.

Andreas's order had been advantageous. The wagon had been pulled in so I wandered along the shelters and barns on the green until I came to a stable. The individual stalls each had a spilt-door with the top half open to the air. I wandered up and looked inside the first one and saw a great beautiful war horse. He was spirited and bobbed his head as he came over to me. I let him smell me and then I rubbed his nose. I saw no one, but heard voices a few stalls away. I strained to hear but I could make nothing out. So I scratched the horse's neck to look innocent if the people came by and caught me there. The horse turned into it and I could see his rump. I got a good look at the king's brand for the first time. I would always recognize it from here on out.

The voices from the stall came closer. They were moving down the central alley and I heard one say. "There is nothing he will do about it. Lily can do no wrong in his eyes. That is the second horse she has ruined in as many years. That fetlock looks real bad."

"Give the poultice time to work," I heard another say. They never turned to see me there and moved out of earshot. I patted the war horse one more time before moving down the stable looking into each stall. When I saw one lying down in the stall with a poultice wrapped around the right front fetlock I knew it was the horse Lily Gebha had ridden out of Nagrom. The horse was gray-colored with spots of black and white. This was an unusual coloring and I was sure I would know this horse anywhere. The stall was freshly cleaned and laid with straw. Oats and water filled the troughs, but there was nothing that would connect a person to this particular horse.

I pulled myself up on the half door and held myself there on my elbows with my feet dangling just above the ground. I talked softly to the horse and she raised her head turning her muzzle toward me. I let her get my scent and continued to talk to her. She blew at me and turned back to lay her head down. She was not interested.

Andreas and Simo found me leaning over the stall like a kid. I confess being able to act like a child was growing on me.

"Time to go, Frog," Andreas called.

I waved but turned back to the horse and said; "Bye Horse. Smell ya later." I jumped down then and raced passed Andreas and Simo, across the causeway and drawbridge, and back to the smithy's shop. The cooper whom everyone called Coop was just closing up for the night.

"So there you are, Helm. Simo kept you long at the palace. I waited but supper calls. Where are your brother and Simo? I pointed toward the gate house and he stood looking until he saw them emerge. "Well I guess you are okay then. I'll be going now. See you in the morning." He went to ruffle the cap on my head but I flinched; afraid that he would uncover my feeble disguise "Sorry, boy didn't mean to scare you. I mean no harm to you." I turned aside and ducked my head, playing the role Andreas had invented for me. Coop sighed and left me.

Simo and Andreas were there soon after. "Come for dinner lads," Simo offered. "I make a mean bacon stew."

We followed Simo home. The place was small and dark. He lit a fire and I sat away from it at the far end of a timber table. He fed us and Andreas smoothly changed the subject when Simo started asking about our family. We had just dad and five boys and a sister. The farm was failing which was why Sig had decided he needed to marry a girl above his station, so he could care for his family. "How do you think I should go about that Simo?" Andreas asked.

The rest of the meal was full of Simo's fatherly advice about women and women of nobility in particular. Nia arrived home from work and Simo ladled a bowl of stew for her and she joined in. I was tired of avoiding eye contact, and my neck was sore from keeping my head down all the time, so I feigned sleep. Andreas took the cue and we went back to our loft above the smithy.

I was anxious to exchange information with him, but waited until we were settled into our bed rolls before comparing notes on the fortress itself and sharing my findings at the stable.

"I'm sure I will recognize that horse again. I don't think the stable master is willing to risk another into Lily's hands. If that horse is ridden again it will be by her and then we can identify her."

"I saw her. Simo took me into the garden. She wasn't with the other girls. She was reading, studying something very intently. She never even looked up. I don't think she was aware of anything else. I saw her well and she never even knew I was there."

"Excellent! Could you see what she was reading?"

He sighed heavily, before saying; "I couldn't be sure, but I jumped when I thought it might be Eindal's ledger. Simo thought I was just stricken by love at first sight. He dared me to approach her. Even though protocol forbids it. He was teasing, of course and I don't think he really would have allowed it. I was tempted you know, just to see if it was the ledger, but I couldn't risk it. He loved teasing me about it. It made his day. I like him. I am sorry that we must deceive him. I told him I would wait until I could meet her on my own ground."

"Good thing he doesn't know what that means. Let's look again about what we know of the place. Tell me again what you saw after I left you."

"The hall that we were in goes all the way around the inner building. We went down and around and back up in the opposite hall. There is a single door on that side, a thick metal clad monstrosity. It is guarded by the only other guards I saw inside. Four of them, two in the hall and two inside. It is a treasury. Simo told me that all of the citizens keep their money there. He went to a man at a desk and said he wanted to make a deposit. The man led him to another room with another metal clad door and two more guards. I was told to wait, but I could see through the door that they had left open. The man paged through a thick book and when he found his place Simo wrote something there; his name and amount I assume. The man then counted the money and checked what Simo had written. After that they moved out of sight. They came out together and the door remained open.

We left the treasury and went back to the front of the building and down that center hallway through those doors under the balcony. There is a barbican and portcullis as you walk through a short hallway, but then there is the garden when you first walk in. It is open to the sky. All around it are archways that lead to rooms or halls that lead further into the palace. Doors can shut them off from inside, but they were all open. The second floor is the same except for a veranda that looks over the entire garden. At the back of the garden a set of stairs comes down off the back of the veranda. There are several seating arrangements throughout the garden, but there is one under the stairs that seemed more formal, with cushions and tables by the chairs."

"So if we can get up over the outer portion of the building we could drop down into the central garden?"

"I believe so."

"Did you see any guards in the garden? What to do about the roof guards?"

"I saw guards in the inner halls of the building, but I didn't go in so I doubt I have an accurate count of them. I saw six. Are you sleepy?"

"Not now."

"Lets go lay on the barn roof here and see what more we can see over at the fortress. Maybe we can time the pattern of the roof guards. Places like that always seem to have one."

We watched together for a couple of hours, but then Andreas watched while I slept and I relieved him before dawn so he could sleep. We could determine nothing about the grounds around the fortress greensward from our perspective but we studied the pattern of the guards upon the fortress wall until we could establish a countdown between rotations. We also determined the patterns of the guards within the city and felt comfortable with the combined knowledge. We went back to the loft just before daybreak so the smithies could wake us when they opened shop.

Vance, the blacksmith brought us bread and apples for breakfast. We went about our tasks with a watching eye to the fortress bridge and anyone coming or going there. We also watched the guards atop the walls. In the daylight they were stationary having the advantage of distance sight. There were no errands that took us to the fortress that day. When the smithy closed we went to buy some bread and salted meat so that we didn't have to eat with the smithies every night. Then we went back and prepared to infiltrate the palace.

When night fell we opened the barn door just enough to slip out and closed it behind us. We made our way through the shops and houses to the west wall. It was the shortest climb, and offered us attached roofs that gave direct access to the top of the wall. It was also the wall with the longest span between guard towers and the closest to the cliffs.

We were afraid to use our rope or hooks because they might reveal us so we climbed using the narrow holds of the hewn stone and mason joints. We climbed side by side as quickly as we could in the shadow of the wall. At the top we checked the guards before walking across the footway atop the wall and climbing down on the outside. We were on the moonlit side of the wall then and well visible to anyone who might look down. No alarm was called and we ran along the bottom of the wall to the stone buttress that would support the drawbridge at this side. We made it there undetected and tucked ourselves into the shadow underneath it. We waited for the fortress guards to pass on their circuit and then we stuck our heads out to look above us to the two towers of the stronghold's back gate.

There were no guards visible to us so we ran full speed to the trees some distance from the north side of the city. Once safe within the cover of the trees, and satisfied that we had not been seen we made our way to the narrow of the inlet. We skirted the cliffs around to the fortress side of the land and moved to the edge of the trees there. We lay on our stomachs beside two trees and watched. When the guards performed their circuit and moved away toward the towers we began our count and ran to a point at the bottom of the north wall that was roughly center. The north side was deep in shadow. We could not see the guards now but they would not see us. We continued to silently mark the circuit of the guards. When the time was right we nodded to confirm the time to each other and made another climb, side by side.

We gained the top and crossed the wall unseen. Below us the greensward was empty We climbed carefully down gripping with just the tips of our fingers and toes. After a quick look and listen we padded across the distance to the stronghold wall. The shadow between the walls was pitch black. We caught our breath and finished our count of the guard rotation and climbed again. This time we were at the greatest risk for discovery because we would be crossing between guard posts..

At the top we crawled quickly across to the inner side of the wall and peered over. A slate roof slanted down toward the garden. We hadn't considered this properly in our plan. We had thought we could drop straight down off the thick wall and onto the veranda. Making our way across a roof was problematic; leaving us vulnerable to detection and attack or capture.

A quick look into the garden revealed no visible guard. We communicated through hand signals and quickly decided to slide down the roof and jump down into the garden below. There was plenty of cover there and if we failed to be silent; being still might protect us.

We went together; one sound at landing was better than two. We took the shock in our knees and landed in simultaneous rolls for cover. My chain mail rustled and sounded like the clank of plate mail to my ears, but there was no response from any direction. That seemed peculiar to me. The place should have been on full alert after one of their own fled here for protection after committing murder. Perhaps it was not politically motivated after all. Maybe Lily Gebha acted alone, but under what motivation? Maybe she was that sure that she had gotten away with it. Maybe Harald was reluctant to reveal himself even to his own men. All of my uncertainties would have to wait. Andreas tugged at my sleeve and we moved to the stairs that led up to the balcony from the garden.

We saw no guards anywhere within the garden courtyard. All the doors to the interior rooms of the palace were closed. The portcullis Andreas had mentioned was down at the garden side of a short hallway. The doors that led to the main hall were closed at the other end and barred from the garden side within that short hall. At that moment it appeared that our best way out was back the way we had come.

We moved along the wall side of the stairs where they were less likely to squeak and stopped before landing on the balcony. It was near time for the guards to pass on their circuit. From our vantage point, crouched low in the shadows of the stairwell we waited. Two guards approached each other from one of two towers at the front corners of the fortress. Two more were visible leaving those same towers and heading toward the back towers; one along each of the east and west walls. From our peripheral two more emerged, one along each north and south wall moving toward the approaching guards. The guards met in the middle of each wall for a brief time to exchange reports. As they talked one would face the garden and scan the area while the other watched over the outer wall. To have guards watching over a secured inner courtyard seemed to indicate that Harald was being more cautious than we first thought. That simple order would not have raised much suspicion in the minds of the sentries. When they were satisfied they moved on. We did not move, nor I think did we breathe until they were all out of sight and back in their towers.

We had no knowledge of who resided where within the building. It seemed most likely though that the king would be furthest from any entries so that he was well protected. That reasoning led us to believe that the door that was nearest to our position would access his residence.

I moved onto the balcony and took a few steps to the door. Andreas remained where he was. I listened but at the late hour I heard nothing. I checked the door for trips and triggers, but there were none. When I checked the latch I found the door was unlocked. That simple act triggered a reaction from the guard just inside. I think he expected someone he knew and he faltered when he stopped to get a look at me. I lunged at his neck and pulled him down. When we turned in our struggle Andreas clubbed him in the back of the head. He went out cold. The action took only a few seconds and made less sound than our landing in the garden, but we moved him inside and closed the door quickly. We bound him there behind a couch with his tunic shoved in his mouth. We would have to move quickly now.

We were in an opulent parlor. Each wall had one door in its center, all were closed. Each one would have to be checked and that would take time. There was nothing to do but go for it. I moved left and Andreas followed. This door was locked. It was nothing I hadn't seen before and I made quick work of it. We slipped into a bedroom and shut the door. The bed was occupied. I started to move toward the bed, but Andreas held up one finger and began to channel the elements. In a moment the even breathing of the sleeping occupant went silent and I knew we were safe in Andreas's Utter Silence. Between us and the bed was a small sitting area with a table and two chairs. Upon the table were several documents, pen and ink, a seal and sealing wax. We had chosen well. This was the kings chamber.

I sorted quickly through five separate documents and found the signed treaty among them. I folded it quickly and put it into my blouse. I moved to other surfaces and even got down to look under the bed and into a small chest I found there, but I did not find Eindal's ledger, Mam's journal or any other incriminating documents. I saw no reason to dally there. We left the room and I locked it once again.

I moved to the door directly across from the king's chamber. Andreas followed, but slowly as he concentrated on keeping us in silence. This door was likewise locked, but the trap upon it was complicated. I was able to bypass a scything blade that would have lost me a finger or two, but there was another internal trap that confounded me. My heart quickened. I was certain this must be the room of our assassin to have such skills as this trap would need. I could not out maneuver it. So I unlocked the door. Andreas stood back against the wall along one side of it and I on the other, pushed the door open. A conflagration burst silently through the door way and singed my right side. Andreas was far enough away not to be affected and the silence held to absorb the blast and my cry of pain.

Pain or not I had to act. Even in silence the blast had set off a percussion that I felt with a strong impact. Anyone inside would have felt it as well. I was closest to the door and jumped in. A young woman was rising from her bed and reaching for daggers laid upon her bedside table. I rushed in, but did not reach her before she threw deftly. I dove and rolled but the dagger caught Andreas in the shoulder. He clutched at the wound, but had enough sense to close the door behind him. The silence faltered as I jumped up and faced the woman. I could see Gebha in her face, but this was not Gebha. This was Lily. She brandished the knife and opened her mouth to call an alarm, but Andreas had mustered the elements once again and the silence enveloped her. A second of surprise caused her hesitation and I slugged her hard in the chin. She went down hard. I left her there and went to check on Andreas.

He let the silence go again while I pulled the knife as he bit down on the collar of his armor. I bandaged it well enough for the time being and he cleaned up the drops of blood and the dagger while I bound Lily to a chair and gagged her with a pillow shoved into her mouth and tied around her head. Then I carefully sacked the room. I truly sacked it, by placing all interesting and useful items into a pillow sack. Among those items I found Eindal's ledger and Mam's journal in a trapped box hidden at the bottom of a wardrobe. I spoke in a whisper to Andreas. "Search this place for a secret passage. I'm going to bring that guard in here. It won't be good if someone passes by and finds him."

"Good. Watch for the circuit. It should be soon; just incase the interior guards rotate as well."

I nodded and went out. At the door to the balcony I stopped and opened it just enough to watch the top of the wall for the circuit. Andreas was a bit behind in his timing. The circuit was in progress. I watched as each set of guards met, spoke, and then moved on When they were in their towers I closed the door, locking it this time. No guard approached or entered the room. I began the count in my head.

The jostling I gave the guard as I drug his bulk across the floor woke him and I had to hit him again, twice before he obliged me and blacked out again.

Back in Lily's room again. I locked us all in. Andreas's search had been successful. The stones at the back of the hearth were not mortared as tightly along one side as might be expected for a fireplace. I asked Andreas to make us silent again and went about examining the hearth and the wall around it. It was not trapped, that I could tell, but feeling that Lily had more expertise than I in that skill did not ease my mind. I was nervous as I triggered the opening mechanism; a loose stone at the side of the mantle. The entire back wall of the hearth swung out onto a narrow landing. I peered around the opening and found the stone landing was at the top of stone stairs that lead steeply down within the wall of the palace. The closing mechanism was also a pressure plate but this one was located high up on the wall inside the stairwell. My fear of Lily's abilities was unnecessary; she had chosen to keep her secret escape route untrapped. I suspected that was practical, in case she ever needed to run in a hurry.

I took the guard back to his post and laid him on the ground just inside the door. I untied and ungagged him and left him there. I had taken Lily's dagger from Andreas and tossed it under a chair a little away from the guard just enough so that the pommel could be seen.

130

Now we just had to get Lily out of there. With all of her items gone with her, it would seem as if she had left of her own accord. Since the guard had only ever seen me, a women, with Lily gone and us undetected the guard might convince himself that it was Lily who attacked him. It would look like she entered into the king's chamber, stole the treaty, and ran.

I returned and made the bed to make it seem as if she had not slept there. We left the pillow in Lily's mouth tied around her head and untied her from the chair. Andreas helped me to lift her and drape her over my shoulders and then he slung the sack over his shoulder. We stopped long enough to give the room our approval of its tidy appearance and stepped into the passage.

Andreas triggered the closing mechanism and were pitched into complete dark. He lit a candle he kept in his belt pouch and led us down carefully, holding the candle between us. We did not speak until we had travelled beyond the palace grounds.

We could hear the crash of the sea ahead of us and knew that we would exit outside. Soon after we saw a shift in the light and knew the exit was just ahead. A low opening was situated in the cliff wall about twenty feet from the cliff tops at the narrowest tip of the inlet. It was hidden by rocks and grasses sprung up in the cracks of the earth. Rough holds had been gouged out of the dirt, well hidden amongst the rocks and grass. A spill of dirt and rock was below us. It looked as if it was a natural condition, but at a second look it occurred to me that this was the remnants of a careful tunnel excavation. It was not overgrown as was the cliffside so it was a recent thing. I pointed it out to Andreas.

"I've been thinking on what to do next. If we turn up missing from the smithy we will implicate ourselves and the search will be on. We can't take her to the trees and tie her there. They will find her if they search the woods."

"We fell short on our planning didn't we?"

"I did not expect this to go so well. This time though we may not be able to bluff through."

"Well we did okay so far. We could leave her here. It's a gamble, but I'll bet no one else in the palace knows of this passage, not even the king."

"They could find it if they search hard enough, but I like it. Can you hide it with some trick of the elements?"

"I think I can. Wait here."

He was gone for a long time. I searched for a protruding root in the passage wall. When I found one thick enough to suit to my needs I dug around it so that it was a loop in the wall and tied Lily to it. After that I sat and watched the palace for any signs of alarm and waited for Andreas to return.

He made no guarantee of his work but proclaimed that we were safe from discovery from that access for a good while at least.

The climb out of the tunnel was made difficult by Andreas's wounded shoulder. I had to take the sack and assisted him several times, but we made it to the cliff top and into the trees at the top. We stumbled about a bit in the dark under the trees, but when we found a safe place we stopped to properly tend Andreas's wound. This was something he had been teaching me and I knew he needed to be stitched, but I had never attempted such a thing before. With his instruction and the assistance of his good hand we accomplished a reasonable mend. I laid on some unguent and bandaged him well.

We ran along the edge between the woods and the road, until we could see Breen in the intersection ahead. We crossed the roads at a distance then and cut through the woods to come out to the south of the town. The moons had passed across the western sky toward the north and that would cause the south wall of the city to be in shadow. We crossed back over the road again to be back on the side of the city. There was a farm stead nearby the southern wall and we used the buildings there for as much cover as we could gain moving up, but there was clear land between the barns and the wall.

We had lost track of the timing of the circuit of the city guards so we had to wait for one to occur in order to time our movements. We watched the fortress guards and they were lax in their duties late in their shift. As we watched I fashioned a harness for the sack so that I could wear it on my back and climb hands free. When the time was right we ran to the wall.

Our climb back over was highly anxious as Andreas struggled with the climb. He fell onto the roof of a shop, but at the early hour no one was inside. The noise caused a dog to bark though so we jumped down quickly and made our way through shadows, back to the smithy where we locked up and went up to the loft.

Andreas went right to sleep, but I hid the sack within the straw and stowed our armor and weapons beneath it before lying down myself.

We were awakened by Simo yelling up at us from the bottom of the ladder. "Wake up sleepy heads. Day has broken. Plenty to do."

Andreas answered sleepily and we dressed in our work clothes and went down. Coop provided the morning meal and gave us a list of duties to start the day.

We needed to fetch water at the well, bring in wood for the forge fire, stock the bins with raw ore and polish the finished copper pots. I knew Andreas would struggle with the lifting so I did the heavy work and set him to the polishing. I hauled the wood and built the fires then fetched the water. I kept my eye to the fortress as much as I could. The changing of the guard went as usual as far as I could tell, but soon after three guards rode down the causeway, across the bridge and out of Breen at a gallop. At the intersection they split off each following a different road. I reported this to Andreas as I stocked the bins with ore before the smiths were done talking and ready to work. When that was done I pitched in with the polishing. We worked quietly with our ears perked up for any sounds of guards or gossip from the fortress.

We took our lunch at the benches around the well hoping again for some word of news from the fortress, but none came to us about last nights events. Half whispered gossip told us that there was a small faction already wary of Harald and his declarations that ate away at the well being of his citizens. That bit of information might prove useful to Frahn.

Simo invited us again for dinner and we accepted certain that his wife would have something to say about our foray, but we were disappointed. We went back to our loft not knowing whether to be anxious or relieved. I changed the bandage on Andreas's injured shoulder, swabbing it again with more healing unguent. The wound looked good and we agreed that it would heal well in time.

I woke after midnight and left Andreas in the loft to rest and heal while I went over the wall and made my way through shadows of the waning moons to the tip of the inlet. I had with me a water skin and a package of bread and cheese to feed Lily with. I climbed down and into the tunnel. I could smell urine as I approached. It was inevitable that it would happen. We had left her for a very long time. I would remember to bring a change of clothing for her the next time. She had squirmed enough to fray the rope a bit against the root. When I approached she kicked at me and would not settle down for me to feed her. I hog tied her and tied her neck to the root with a knot that would tighten the rope and eventually strangle her if she continued to squirm. I left the food and water out of her reach. It was cruel, but I had to teach her to obey me. I went back to Breen and slept again until Andreas woke me for the day.

There was a presence of fortress guards milling about all day. Two of them came and spoke with Vance. They were curious about us, as they put it, it was Harald's policy to know about everyone in his protection. There was no mention of an assault of a fortress guard or the robbery of the king's chamber. They seemed relieved when Vance described us as a farm kid and his idiot brother. They stood around making friendly small talk for awhile after that before moving on.

After the guards left the smithies gathered together. They all agreed that it was odd to have the guards come about checking on workers.

"Something is happening," Simo said. "Harald has already taken more than his share of our labors for his own. What now? Will he tax us for taking on laborers as well?"

"I wouldn't put it passed that greedy bastard!" Vance said.

"Nor I," said Coop. "I guess we will have to wait to see what happens."

"I will ask Nia to have her ears open," Simo said.

"You'll tell us if she hears anything?" Coop asked.

"Of course, don't I always?" Simo replied.

So, Harald's citizens were not as carefree as they first seemed. They did not like or even trust their king. For whatever reason Harald was keeping the events of two nights ago quiet. Over the next few days the guards that had ridden out returned and rode straight up to the palace. Each night I went to tend to Lily. Each night I was more fearful of being caught.

Lily had become more relaxed and on the fifth day of her capture as I fed her she asked, "What do you intend to do with me?"

I lied to her. "We are holding you for ransom. You in exchange for the treaty document."

"Harald will never agree to that."

135

"We will see." I said no more on the matter. Her eyes searched mine for some hint of my thinking. I searched her eyes in return. She was doubtful that Harald would comply. She was expendable to him. The realization that a skilled assassin was expendable alarmed me. Harald was beginning to emerge in my mind as being very cold and calculating. He did have his men searching, but were they searching for her or the treaty document? I wondered what the orders were if they found her. I held on to the hope that our plan had mislead the king and that he looked for her as a thief and traitor. I let her see the hope in my eyes. I gagged her again and tied her by the neck to the root once more.

We were getting nervous and looking for a way to escape with Lily when the smithies gave it to us. They needed supplies from Nagrom. A wagon was packed with trade goods and instructions on who to deliver to. They gave us a list of supplies to purchase, a letter of introduction, and an IOU. Simo's wife, Nia prepared a basket of food from the fortress kitchen and it was tucked away under the seat of the wagon. I went in and put my chain mail on under my clothes. That made room for the sack of Lily's things. It was a struggle to carry and make it seem light but I think I managed. I got it stuffed under the wagon seat next to the basket without comment.

"You've worked hard laddies," Simo said. "You deserve a little adventure. It will be work, but an adventure as well. Young men as you should have some adventure before they go off and marry bossy noble women." He found himself very funny and laughed that hearty laugh of his. I liked Simo. He was good to us. I hoped we could find a way to return his order to him. We did not expect to be coming back.

Andreas promised not to let them down. We waved good bye and Andreas drove the horse and wagon out of Breen. We turned south onto the road but drove only until we were out of sight in the slope of land that took us down toward the sea. We pulled the wagon well away from the road and hid it in some trees, covering it with branches both felled and gathered.

We were exhausted and slept under the wagon, happy to sleep without feeling the need to listen for sounds of approach. It was late afternoon when we woke. We made a meal from the delectable leftovers Nia had gathered for us and waited for the nearest fishing shanty to close up for the night. When the lights went out we began our approach.

The owner had two boats one was a small lugger for fishing with large nets tossed out into the sea. The other was a row-boat for quiet personal fishing with a pole. We slipped the knot that held the row-boat to the pier and got in. Andreas sat upon the bow tip, I took the seat by the oarlocks I pushed us hand over hand down the length of the pier until we were clear of it then I slid the oars into the oarlocks, steered us around, and rowed north along the shore toward the inlet where Lily was hidden.

The night was dark but cloudless. The two moons were in their waning phases. As the cliffs rose above us and we gained the mouth of the inlet the air temperature dropped suddenly and we slipped into complete darkness. If Harald knew what advantage this gave to marauders he would be sure to reinforce his defenses. We would be sure not to tell him.

Navigation was difficult, but as the cliff walls closed in I took in the oars and we propelled ourselves by pushing along the walls until the bow hit the fall of debris below the tunnel. Andreas would stay below and tend the boat to keep it from banging on the rocks.

I went up with more rope to wrap around Lily. I left her hog tied and tied her neck ropes to the extra rope. I would lower her down but if she fought me I could control her. I only knocked her against the walls a few times, unintentionally and the clatter of rock was lost in the sound of the surf. I could barely see Andreas as he stood up in the boat and reached up to guide her in. When she was secure I tossed the rope down and made the climb down slowly, finding my holds by touch alone.

We made our way easily and undetected back to the fisherman's shanty. We tied his boat as we had found it and pulled Lily from it. She fought us and the boat slammed hard up against the pier. A dog barked vigorously from inside the shanty. At that point we no longer cared about stealth or noise. Flight was of the utmost importance. We could not be seen and risk being reported to Breen. We drug Lily out nearly capsizing the boat. She hit the water and we all splashed about until we gained the ropes and drug her out.

A lantern was lit in the shanty.

We pulled up on the hog ropes and carried her between us at the fastest speed we could gain with the extra rope trailing behind us.

We heard a door open behind us.

I glanced over my shoulder again and again to see a dog snuffling about on the ground trying to get a scent. The fisherman went to the boat and saw the marks of a scuffle in the sand. The dog went with him and snuffled frantically at the end of the pier.

I could see no more after that. I had to keep my eyes forward to avoid stumbling in that awkward run through the dark night. We made the trees and dropped Lily hard upon the ground. Andreas held her while I checked and tightened knots.

The fisherman took a dagger from his belt and called his dog to him. They went together to check on his lugger. We waited until he emerged again. The dog went again to the end of the pier and picked up our trail. He began to follow it and the fisherman looked out over the land with his lantern held high. We held Lily down beneath us and watched for a long time, until at last the fisherman called his dog to him. He was afraid and went inside, but the lantern did not go out.

We caught our breath in that time and after coiling the extra rope and slinging it over my shoulder we walked the rest of the way back to the wagon. I uncovered the wagon and rearranged the load to make room for Lily along one side. Andreas untied her enough to let her stretch her arms and legs but we gave her no time to get comfortable. We lashed her down like cargo with her back to the side boards. She fought and we could not be gentle. When she was lashed tight and she could not move we filled in around her with the crates and pots that the smithies had charged us with. When we were satisfied that the Nagrom revenuers would not see her if they checked our cargo we lashed the canvas cover down tight.

We rode out of the woods and Andreas urged the horse to a gallop. Lily was in for one hell of a ride. The horse was spirited and large enough for such a haul. He seemed to enjoy the run. We covered ground quickly and by morning we had come to the bridge over the dried stream bed. We took the bridge by foot. I lead the horse and Andreas made sure the wheels stayed on the narrow way calling out to me as corrections were needed.

We rode on again until night fall, making it to where we felt we should have been if we would not have had to go back for Lily. The wayside refuge house was still ahead of us but for now we found a track wide enough to maneuver the wagon into the trees. We released Lily from her cargo cocoon and untied her feet. I led her into the woods to relieve herself while Andreas put together a meal from Nia's basket. When I assisted Lily with her clothes she kicked me hard in the groin. Perhaps I looked like an idiot boy to her as well. It still hurt and I went down. She tried to run, but I scrambled quickly enough to grab the trailing rope that was still tied around her neck. I yanked hard and she fell backward with her feet coming out from under her. She slammed the ground with her back and I could hear the air escape her lungs in one great rush. As she lay helpless gasping for air I hobbled her feet.

When at last I returned her to camp Andreas looked at me skeptically. "She tried to run. We had a scuffle. Now its your turn to watch her while I take care of my own business."

When I returned Andreas had her tied to a tree and was feeding her. "Eat, then get some sleep," he told me. "I'll take watch. When you wake up we'll start out again. I can sleep while you drive," he said. After tending to the horse I did as I was told.

When I woke it was still dark. We got underway as quickly as Lily's struggling would allow. I had a brief moment of sympathy for her, but that passed quickly when I thought of what she had try to do to my mam. When Andreas had finished lashing her to the wagon I found myself wanting to pull the ropes even tighter, but I refrained. The discomfort her position in the wagon afforded her fit my need for retaliation, for now.

Andreas and I had to man handle the wagon to get it turned around, then I took us out of the woods carefully. When we hit the road I snapped the reins and that good strong horse lurched forward at a gallop. The wagon was loaded and the weight kept it from bouncing, as much as I would have liked. Punishing Lily in that way seemed futile. We were making good time though and I did not let up until the horse was ready. We would be in Nagrom that night.

We arrived several hours after dark. The gate was closed when we arrived, but the guard there had instructions to let us pass no matter when it was that we arrived. We road straight to the postern gate of the inner yard and we were passed through quickly there as well. A runner was sent ahead to announce our arrival to Frahn. We rode through to the inner courtyard and parked the wagon at the porch. Frahn trotted out to greet us.

"Were you successful?"

Andreas threw back the tarp, moved the concealing cargo away and revealed Lily strapped to the sidewall. I climbed in to undo the lashing.

"You are certain? You have evidence?"

"All that we need. Sir."

"Good, good. You have arrived just in time to present it to the visiting kings, as I had hoped. I was running out of ways to detain them." He turned to the sentries at his door, "See this murderer to the hole."

"Sir," I began. "If it is all the same to you. I'd like to see her properly incarcerated myself. Andy can begin the report without me. I'll be along right after."

"Of course, yes, yes." Then to his guards: "See to it."

I allowed the sentries to wrestle Lily out of the wagon. I had grown tired of her kicking. They made quick work of it, but she refused to walk on her hobbled feet and they had to drag her.

Her prison was in the Northeast tower. The only tower without windows or arrow slits in the lower floors to allow light in. I opened the door and the sentries let Lily fall to the floor. I shut the door. The room was nearly barren. The only features were a stairway that wrapped up along the wall to the floors above and a pulley laced with a rope. The rope had a hook at one end and the whole contraption was mounted to the beams above a heavy open beamed trapdoor in the floor. A sentry pushed back the heavy iron bolt and heaved the door open. He reached in to retrieve a leather harness. The other sentry was untying Lily. I drew my sword and aimed it at her belly to stop her struggling. She was lifted to her feet by the two sentries and fitted into the harness that pinned her arms to her sides. I had never seen such a thing and asked about it.

"We call it The Forgotten Room. This is a punishment worse than being held for ransom, or locked in a tower room. I've only known it to be used once before, by Frahn's grandfather, on a traitor."

They drug Lily to the open trapdoor and attached the hook to a loop on the back of the harness. Lily and I looked inside at the same time.

Ungagged now she shrieked, "O no. You can't. This is not humane."

"You forfeited humane, girly, when you messed with Mareese and my mother."

Her eyes widened in surprise. Was it possible she had not made that connection, even with Garthe so angry about it? Maybe she was just surprised that I knew and only thought we had been after the ledger. I did not question her on it.

The forgotten room was a deep vertical shaft which was only wide enough for a person to stand up in. Lily wouldn't be able to crouch down, kneel, or sit. I doubted that she could even turn around in it. The shaft was so deep that there would be no way to reach up to the trap-door even if she did manage to get her arms free of the harness. Lily would be forced to remain standing, in the dark, until she was released. I wondered if Frahn would release her after he heard the evidence against her.

Once we got her feet in I saw terror in her eyes. "You can't do this!" she cried. "Will I not be heard?"

"That is up to the kings now."

"The kings will see that I am released."

"I wouldn't be so sure, Lily Gebha. Frahn called the kings to council after Esporanza's funeral. We have arrived just in time to present evidence to them before they depart for their homelands. For my part I cannot think of a more fitting punishment for you, for now. We will see what the council rules."

It was easy to lower her into the shaft using the winch overhead. Once Lily reached the bottom, a flick of the rope released the hook and the rope was taken up. The trap-door fell back with a solid thud and the bolt was pushed through with a satisfying clank.

The sentries decided which of them would now stand guard there until morning when arrangements could be made for a permanent post. I was led back by the other and found my way to Frahn's Great Room. Frahn was in his throne and Andreas sat beside him in one of the lesser chairs. They leaned in close together and I could see that they were talking, but their whispers did not reach my ears.

I moved forward to join them, but chose to sit upon the steps at their feet.

"Satisfied?" Frahn asked me, with a bit of evil eye in his gaze.

"Much," I said

"Andreas has presented me with the events and the treaty document. I have agreed to pursue the treaty further after a council of the Crystalier leaders. I will avoid presenting it to the kings, unless Harald brings it up."

"Harald is not here," Andreas spoke, half question, half statement. If he was, then who was that in the king's chamber back in Breen and when had he left that city?

"No, he has not responded to my invitation to council.

"I had hoped to bring the kings on board after they saw the benefits of a working treaty. They are a suspicious bunch. We still clash amongst each other. I don't expect them to be happy about another out of country power in the mix. If I had cobbled together a treaty with Crystalier and increased my power base I believe I could have swayed them to look at Nagrom as the capitol. Harald may have succeeded in destroying that vision. The kings will see me now as an underhanded player. Perhaps I was, but it was with good intentions."

"Your intentions are yours to explain, Lord Frahn. We represent Crystalier and especially Mareese. We will follow your lead as long as it seems prudent. Our concern remains justice for Esporanza and Mya," I said. "How is she?"

"I barely know she is here. She stays to herself."

"She is frightened for her life. She has no one to care for her. Her only living relative was Esporanza."

"Yes, I've looked into that. Esporanza mentioned a sister in law, but she died shortly after his wife. I have asked the other kings, but no one knows of any other family for her. I can put her to work here, but she has no status. I cannot simply elevate her. She would have my protection here, but I don't believe she would be happy."

"Can you not just declare her status?"

"I could, but a life at court, without being noble born would put her in a tight spot. Nobles would look down on her, and servants would despise her luck. She would not be welcomed."

"But she is an ambassador's daughter."

"Esporanza was my choice. He was not a man of station. He was a friend to me from a young age. He once worked here in the scullery. I trusted him more than anyone." The king's voice cracked and he hesitated to gain composure. "We had a common dream, to unite Ahnges. He was my best friend.

"I took a lot of grief from my nobles and advisors here. I fought hard to get him recognized. He spent his life preparing for the job; as I said we had a common dream and we talked of it our whole lives. I promised that when I became king I would find him a place in my kingship. His position was not well received and his work here was difficult for him. He was a very likable man. Even though he failed to gain the interest of a trade treaty amongst the kings he was liked and respected. That is the thing that caused us to look outside of Ahnges for a way to unite the kings. I thought I could bring him some peace and notoriety by sending him away. Instead I brought him death.

"I don't see a peaceful existence for Mya here, unless it is as a servant. I'm sorry."

"We didn't realize Esporanza's situation. Thank you for sharing it with us. Perhaps there is some other way. We will think on it," I said. "When is the council?" I asked changing the subject.

"The last king arrived here six days ago. Once they were all here we had a wake and then the funeral was the next day. Many came only for the council, but there are those who came to honor Esporanza. Normally the council would be after a two day mourning period. It has been four and the kings are getting anxious. I have told them I was waiting for a messenger with news about Esporanza's death. They do not care enough about that to wait much longer. I am extremely glad that you have come. I have been on pins and needles waiting for some thing to happen when word did not come right away."

"We regret your stress, Sir, but these things take time."

"Yes, so they do. I think that now you should stay in quarters here. That will show that you are important to me. I will introduce you as Emissaries from Crystalier. That will play well when I explain things."

We spoke more of our place and duties for the following days, but the night grew long and Frahn himself showed us to our rooms.

***

Mya found us at breakfast. We had been discussing her future and decided to bring her home with us. She could have the attic of the shop. Mam could use the help and company and I could then do as I pleased. She sat across from me and next to Andreas. I believe she

145

had a bit of a young girl's infatuation with him. I waited until she was settled and well into her meal before addressing the topic.

"Mya?"

"What?"

"Andreas and I had a long talk with Frahn last night. He is concerned about you. He and your father were very good friends, were they not?"

"They were, but they were fighting a lot lately."

"Oh, about what?"

"Kingly things; affairs of court and diplomacy."

"Did they disagree about the treaty?"

"No not exactly. My father and I were not really accepted at court. Frahn sent us to do the treaty. Father thought it was too early, that the other kings should know of it first."

"That is pretty much what Frahn told us too. He feels responsible for your father's death. He was trying to protect him from the stresses of this court."

"I suppose that's right."

"Well because of the way his court has treated you and would continue to do, Frahn feels you would be happier somewhere else. How would you feel about coming back to Mareese with us? My mam has a small room in the attic and she could use help around the shop. It wouldn't be like being a servant girl here. You would earn a small wage and once your chores were done you could go about town. We could introduce you to children your age."

"I am not a child."

"Of course not. I just think of people younger than me as children."

"You aren't very old either you know."

146

"No need to be sharp, Mya," Andreas said. "Saeede is offering to take you into her home. A place where you will be treated well and you won't be a servant."

"But I'll have to work."

"Yes," he said. "but, you will be free to do otherwise if you hate it, though I would advise you to take her offer. I don't think a better one will be coming anytime soon. You'll have a roof over your bed and food in your belly."

"Will you be there?"

Andreas looked at me with that question in his eyes. This was the second time in recent history that he seemed interested in more than our friendship. I was not yet ready to commit. We had agreed to wait until this business of the murder and the treaty were solved. As way of response I simply said: "Aren't you always?"

"Well not *always*, though that would be nice." His look was puzzling. He seemed a bit hurt but he smiled. "Yes, Mya. I'll be there."

"Where do you live? Couldn't I stay there?"

"No, Mya that would not be appropriate. I'm old enough to be— your brother, and I only have a small apartment. There is barely room for me."

"O well, I guess I should. I don't really fancy staying here."

"Good!" I said, and I was a little surprised to find how excited the idea made me. "You will move your things into my rooms for the rest of our stay here. From now until we get to Mareese you are my ward. That means you fall under my protection, as the ward of an Emissary it gives you a bit of status, but just a bit. Don't go getting too big for your boots."

"I won't" She finished her meal and pushed her plate aside. "Should we move my things now or after the council?"

"Now."

147

We all went together to her room. She didn't have many belongings and we had her moved in just a few minutes. I stopped a passing chambermaid and told her of the new arrangements. Andreas was in the room next to ours. He left us and we prepared for an extended stay.

***

We met the five of the remaining seven kings throughout the day. Harald never did show, neither had he responded. He was too busy trying to track down his traitorous assassin.

Frahn held the council off one more day giving us time to rest, and the opportunity to be acquainted with the kings. There was an air of displeasure about the visiting kings. Mya was quiet and polite, the perfect lady. She held her head high as the daughter of an ambassador should, even when she was treated with disdain by the kings or others amongst the gathering and household staff. Andreas was her chosen stalwart companion. He was exhausted by her constant need of him by the end of the day and she was bored by the whole affair. I put them both to bed and promised Andreas I'd wake him if anything interesting developed.

Nothing did develop. I woke my two charges in time to freshen up for the evening meal. Frahn invited us to sit near him, just below his wife, the bishop, and his mother. When the plates were being cleared, sweets were offered, and more ale poured; conversation turned to the council and was directed at Frahn.

"Surely you could have buried Esporanza without the Kings' Council present. What has been the long delay? Here are your messengers. Let's have it. What do you have up your sleeve, Frahn?" Elys of Kirsh called out from across the room. His kingdom was high up in the eastern mountains. He had a reputation for being unreasonable.

"Yes, what Frahn?" Thome Kelt of central Kelton joined. "I liked Esporanza fine, but his mourning was over days ago."

"I had hoped my hospitality would be enough to bring us together until this evening could happen. I know you have waited longer than you, or I intended, but this is a delicate matter and what I needed took a bit longer than I thought. Only Harald has not responded to my invitation, and there is much about this that involves him."

"He has broken protocol by not responding. Let's get on with it."

"Since when do you put stock in protocol, Elys?" Narhan of Yer joined in.

Laughter went up among all the kings except for Frahn who could not afford to distance anyone.

"Since I've come to know you all as cheats and scoundrels." Elys fired back.

Disorder ensued, and Frahn sat stoically, allowing it to go on for a long moment, but when hands went to weapons he stood and his voice boomed throughout the hall.

"Cease! Now! Have I ever come to a council in any of your halls and raised chaos?"

Frahn was putting his reputation on the line. The visiting Kings and their followers fell silent.

"Of course not." Frahn said. "I only ask the same respect in my own hall." There was some further grumbling and final shoving, but everyone returned to their seats. "It is true that Harald has broken protocol, but I have much to say about him and I had hoped that he would have the courage to stand before you and tell his side. I yield to your common sense and good graces. He has had plenty of time now to avail himself. If you all agree; and I mean all; then we can proceed. What say you?"

There was much talk and Frahn sat back down to give them time. He sent his servers around to top off the ale in his guests' cups.

"Does Harald know why you have called this council?"

"He does, without a doubt. He is well aware of events that have led me to convene it."

There were a few more moments of discussion among the kings and their advisors and then August from the furthest city of Hoarfrost said, "Lets put it to a vote. I vote to have the council now. If I can drag my old bones here from the Hoarfrost then Harald, who is closest, and has the most to lose, most certainly can."

"What say you all?" Frahn asked.

Each King raised his hand and a collective "Aye" echoed in the rafters.

"Are your historians ready to record the council?"

Another collective, "Aye."

"Then let me begin by telling you how Esporanza died. This time with details."

Frahn was an excellent story teller. He left no facts out and embellished just enough to draw those present into the details. Even Mya, Andreas, and I enjoyed the telling. I looked out at the faces of the kings and their companies and they were enthralled. In this telling Esporanza was merely assessing interest in the treaty while in Crystalier. Afterward he circulated the letter that had been written by Diony and the other Mareesian leaders expressing further interest after the matter of Esporanza's death was cleared away, but that they would not act without a face to face meeting. Frahn had once said he would not reveal the letter, but the tactic would help Frahn to smooth over his previous miscalculated actions with no one the wiser.

"How do you know that it was Harald's assassin?"

"Before I answer allow me to formally introduce the two emissaries sent from Crystalier. They were key in investigating the murder; Saeede and Andreas. I will let them answer that for you."

Andreas did not hesitate to take the floor. "Good Kings," he began, "My partner, Saeede and I, having some experience in these matters, were asked to investigate. Here are the facts as we uncovered them. Many have already been revealed to you through Frahn's narrative. I will lay them out in a more objective manner.

"Our initial suspect, the apothecary is well known in the city of Mareese. She has cured the ills of many there and is known to be of a kind and nurturing nature. She was not seen in or around the palace in days. For a time we had two suspects, the apothecary who brewed a potion for the ambassador and his daughter, Mya, who sits here at my side now. Preliminary questions caused us to think she might have some cause to see her father killed. It was she who went to the apothecary and purchased the potion that we thought killed him. Garthe had asked the girl to go as part of her errands and purchase a remedy for her father's sick head. She did as she was asked and returned with it, delivering it to her father and then went to make ready for the reception in her father's honor. But how then was he killed if Mya did not do it? Could it have been an accident: an overdose perhaps? Could Garthe who ordered the potion have wanted him dead? Keep those questions in mind as I proceed. We learned that while Mya was preparing for the party, closed up in her room, someone resembling Mya went to the kitchen and ordered tea for the Ambassador. That person waited for the tea and then delivered it to the Ambassador themselves. Her father was served the tea that eventually killed him while she was in her room putting flowers in her hair. This additional person that looked like Mya confused us at first, there was no one present who fit the part, except Mya.

151

"Saeede and I went to investigate the Ambassador's room in the governor's manor house. We found and collected a bit of residue in the bottom of the cup still sitting on his side table. That residue turned out to be Dark Berry Root. We also found the charred remains of the handwritten instructions for the headache cure in the ash bin in the room. On further questioning of the apothecary we learned that the potion she brewed and sold to Mya had an ingredient called Silver Leaf distilled into it, a very common ingredient in headache cures. She explained to us that Dark Berry Root and Silver Leaf create a slow acting deadly poison when combined. The symptoms are exactly as Frahn had described in Esporanza. Maybe you have even brewed Dark Berry Root in your own tea as a sweetener." Some of those present shook their heads, yes.

"You may want to reconsider that."

Andreas continued. "We wanted to see if the perpetrator had disposed of any evidence and went to the garbage heaps to see what if anything we could find. Hidden in the compost pile was a brown vial like that used in the apothecary's shop. The wax seal was broken and stoppered but there was still a bit of liquid inside. The vial was not near the top of the heap, or in the glass bin, where it should have been. Someone had deliberately buried it deep to hide it. That action seemed to point to the apothecary again, but she had not been seen at the manor house.

"Upon further investigation with Esporanza's man Garthe present we determined that the apothecary uses brown vials like the one found in the trash heap. She uses brown glass, to protect the contents from sun light. We also found an immaculate shop with all items clearly and accurately labeled; everything except one clear vial containing Dark Berry Root, unlabeled. It was found during an inventory done at our request. We believe it had been planted there to cast suspicion on the woman. The apothecary never denied that she had served Mya the afternoon before the reception. The girl had said she came for a headache remedy for her father the ambassador. The girl was not at all interested in the instructions provided by the apothecary and ran off without reading them. Mya said she brought the potion directly to her father and then went to dress for the reception. The apothecary said she had not been to the manor house in months. Through a bit of mysticism by one of Mareese's most talented mind readers it was determined that both the apothecary and Mya were telling the truth.

"So who was talented enough to disguise them self so well as to fool a household of people, Esporanza's guards, and Esporanza himself? Who would also have the knowledge of the Silver Leaf and Dark Berry Root?" We knew only one type of person—assassin. The Governor of Mareese ordered all the dignitaries present remain in Mareese until they could be questioned. That task fell to her sheriff and when we conferred with him we could see no reason to suspect any of them. There was no means, no opportunity, and most importantly —no motive. None of them had a huge entourage, but each and every person was questioned to the same conclusion. The governor and her entire household were questioned both by us and the sheriff; there we found no means, some opportunity among the staff opportunity, but no motive there either.

"For a while we suspected Garthe. He did not appreciate our questioning. He was protecting the honor of his charge and his king, but as the investigation proceeded he allowed us access and even assisted.

"At one point I discovered my rooms had been gone through. The murderer was trying to see what we knew. My partner's room was also ransacked, but nothing was taken, as there was nothing of importance to our criminal there. But the apothecary had a journal of notes stolen from her private rooms around the same time. A man had been seen stalking outside of the apothecary's shop. It was then

153

that we requested a full inventory. We saw him and so we had the shop closed and watched him. He left and we followed. We had him nearly all the way to the manor until he made a turn. Saeede was trying to pick him out of the crowd when she saw Mya emerge from a millinery shop. Mya skipped off straight to the Manor House of the Governor. We knew Mya to be distraught about her father's death so skipping was an odd behavior. We also knew Mya to be sitting vigil over her father's body in the manor's chapel. I went to check on her personally and found her there just as I had expected to. She told me that her father's man, Gebha had come to talk to her. He praised her for staying with her father and educated her on the protocols of that ritual, one of which was to not leave the chapel for any reason.

"From there Saeede, myself and the governor's man went to check on Gebha in the room he shared with Garthe. Garthe was there preparing for the voyage that would bring Esporanza home for his funeral. Gebha was missing. A short time later Garthe discovered that the letter the Crystalier leaders had entrusted to him to bring to Frahn was also missing. Gebha was never seen leaving the Manor House, The dark skinned man who fit the description of the one we had been following had not been seen coming or going. Only the false Mya had left by either gate. Everyone else was involved in preparations for the evenings farewell gathering.

Saeede and I refocused our investigation at the Manor House. The Sheriff sent some of his men out into the city in search for Gebha. Two of them found a dark wig and a rag full of dark makeup hidden under an ugly hat at the millinery shop. The dock master was questioned and ships were searched but no one had seen Gebha. He had given us the slip.

"We learned that Gebha had enlisted in Frahn's army and that his training went so well that he was recommended for more important duties. Frahn was already considering the possibility of an offshore treaty that would bring wealth to Ahnges. He needed another man to escort Esporanza to Crystalier and ordered Garthe to take him on. The idea was to test his loyalty and see how he did in matters of court. We found out the hard way.

"We knew that Gebha originated from here. So the leaders of Crystalier asked us to accompany Garthe and Mya back here to continue our investigation. We soon learned that there had been a stowaway on a ship originating in Mareese. The stowaway escaped capture at the dock, but was described as both a young man and a young woman. Quite curious, but believable since we were dealing with a master of disguise. We also learned that a horse had been boarded and that a young women in quite a hurry had come to claim the horse and she was not at all polite about it. This occurred at about the same time the stowaway had run from the docks. The horse had Harald's brand and was seen leaving the northern gate with a female rider charging up the road toward Breen.

"Saeede and I went under disguise ourselves then and obtained employment in Breen. Our jobs gave us the opportunity to enter the palace and I, under the guise of looking for a noble women to marry had a girl called Lily pointed out to me. I was told she was favored by the king, a niece of a dead sister. She had the face of Gebha and I knew it was the culprit we were after. A few days later when the time was right we stole into the fortress of King Harald. In the king's chamber we found several paper's one of them was the treaty proposal that Esporanza had carried to Crystalier. We retrieved it. Though this indicated that Harald ordered the assassination he was not the person we were after, not yet. That is a matter for kings. We were charged with finding Esporanza's killer and bringing that person to justice.

"If Lily and Gebha was the same person we knew she would be close by and we were right. We found the apothecary's journal and an item of mine amongst her things. We were certain now that we had the killer. We stole her right out of her chamber and brought her here to face justice. I believe the reason Harald is not here now is that he believes Lily has stolen the treaty that he had intended to use against Frahn. He believes that she has betrayed him and that regaining that document is more important than this council."

Andreas sat back in his chair then and waited for the questions to come. Elys was first.

"If you have this woman where is she now?"

Frahn answered, "I have her in custody where she cannot possibly escape. If it is the wish of this council I can produce her."

"I believe that would be appropriate. Let us see her and have her speak to these accusations," Tanath of Calibe said.

The other kings responded in kind.

Frahn motioned to the sentry behind him. The man leaned forward to hear his order. "Go to the forgotten room. Tell the sentry there to bring the prisoner, but clean her up first. Stay and help him. Be quick, let's not leave the kings waiting."

Next Frahn ordered more drinks and nibbles be served. This took the king's minds off the wait. Frahn knew how to keep the kings in control. Perhaps he would be a uniting force after all.

I leaned over to Andreas. "You handled the shady elements of this very well. I don't think you missed a thing."

"Thank you. We are getting good at this aren't we?"

"Too good perhaps. If this thing goes foul, and Lily contradicts you, or worse Frahn, then we are complicit in a conspiracy against kings."

"I know. I wonder if it will go well for us that we have no allegiance to any here."

"Our allegiance to Frahn is implied right now."

"Let us not think on these things. Have some cheese and enjoy the fine ale from Frahn's stock."

"I suppose I should. Maybe if I'm drunk I won't mind so much if they turn on us. I'll die quickly at the end of a sword."

Our fears were warranted. The moment when Lily would speak could turn this all back on us. How well Frahn and Andreas had covered the treaty document and turned it into a polite query of Crystalier leaders was yet to be seen.

The impatience of waiting was beginning to rise when a commotion was heard in the hall. Soon after Lily was brought in kicking and struggling to pull free of the strong grip of the sentries. When she realized where she was and who was present she stopped a moment. Our presence at the council of kings did not bode well for her and she knew it.

"Bring her," Frahn ordered, and the sentries drug her to a place at his feet. Frahn stood to address her. "You are called Lily. I will call you Lily Gebha as those who brought you to me do. Lily Gebha, I accuse you of the murder of my ambassador, Esporanza. That he was on a diplomatic mission when you killed him increases the charge to assassination. I believe you were ordered by your king, Harald, to commit this crime and that brings a charge of conspiracy. All of these come with a punishment of death. Harald has breached protocol and has not responded to my request to attend this council. The kings have voted to continue without him. The evidence has been presented against you. What have you to say for yourself so that evidence may be weighed?"

Lily stood at the foot of Frahn's dais. She turned aside of him so that she could see all of the kings and those of us on the dais with just a turn of her head. She shifted nervously as she gathered her words and the shackles that bound her hands and feet chimed in the anticipating silence.

When at last she spoke it was with a question. "Does Harald know that you hold me here?"

This one question spelled disaster for Frahn. He had implied as much under questioning from the kings. Frahn's reply put the matter down.

"Harald knows that I called him to council on the matter of Esporanza's murder. If he chooses not to attend for what ever his reasoning then I am not obligated to reveal my findings to him outside of council." He looked then to the kings. "What say you all?"

The kings turned to their historians whose jobs it was to weigh such matters against the councils of the past. Some historians conferred together before returning a ruling to their kings.

They answered in turn; all in agreement to Frahn. Lily hung her head and shifted nervously taking time to assess what she would say next.

"What I did I did for my king. Would you put to death one of your own loyalists for satisfying your command? What you choose to do with me bears on all future decisions of this council in like matters. You know that well."

"Then you do not deny that you killed Esporanza?"

"I do not."

Mya gasped and all eyes turned to her. When Lily met her eyes she could not bear the child's gaze and hung her head. Frahn saw an opportunity to play on the sympathy of the kings.

"Do you have no remorse for you actions—no remorse for causing a child to be fatherless?"

"What I did I did for my king. I can not allow myself to feel remorse. If I did I would be ineffective."

"And yet I watched as you hung your head under the child's gaze. I call you assassin and yet you are no more than a misguided tool of a king's selfish desire."

Lily met Frahn's eyes with a fire in hers. "And what was Esporanza to you? King," she spat.

Frahn nearly lurched at her, but in the next second remembered himself. Every muscle in his jaw was tight as he checked his action. "Harald knew of my discussions with Esporanza. He had his spy here, maybe he still does. He came to me about it himself. He could not see the ability to trade openly with out taxes and would reduce smuggling and encourage open trade. I only want to bring wealth to us all. I am tired of fighting with my brethren kings. I seek a life where we can live together, protect each other if the need arises, trade goods together without worry of intrigue. Crystalier has a long history of unity, but they were not strong. In the last few years they have fought for the life of a great enlightened people in Mareese and they have helped and succeeded in the quelling of demons from hell. My desire was not a selfish one, Lily Gebha. My desire was to better us all, even Harald, but he wants everything for himself and so he sent you to undo that—to undo Esporanza. Esporanza was a dear friend to me. We desired the same things for Ahnges—unity."

"Yes, unity. With you in control of the treaty!" Lily shouted back.

I looked over the faces of the kings as all sat engrossed in the proceedings. They were listening intently to the exchange. Elys, the most outspoken of them leaned forward in his chair, his elbows on the table in front of him, his chin in hands. I could not read their feelings on their faces. I wished I had Diony's gift to enter into the minds and thoughts of others.

Frahn's shoulders sagged and he returned to his chair. A murmur went through the companies of the kings. Frahn sighed and leaned forward. He looked into the eyes of each king as he spoke. "Perhaps I moved too quickly. I know the animosities that exist amongst us; long bred suspicions. I wanted to present to you a firmly negotiated treaty that I could present in full; a gift, a boon not a bane. You all know me. I have spoken to each of you separately and at other councils seeking support for a united Ahnges. Elys, what was it you said to me when I approached you with the idea?"

"I thought we spoke in confidence," Elys said as he stood up.

"We did. So instead tell the kings what was my purpose of that conversation."

"To unite Ahnges."

"Thank you, Elys." Elys returned to his seat.

"Narhan, we spoke at your daughter's wedding. Will you share with the kings?"

Narhan rose and cleared his throat. "I have no doubt of your aspirations to unite us, Frahn. I told you that I did not think it could be done with the kings alone. I had no idea that you would turn those words into a large-scale incident."

"What else did you tell me?"

"That if you found a way you would have to prove it to get the attention of the council of kings."

"Can any of you deny my intent, even if my tactics may have been wrong?"

None stood.

"Do you care to cast more accusations on me, Lily Gebha?"

"Ask the kings about your desire to create one king to rule over them all. Do they know about that?"

"I don't even know about that. It is a hope, yes. Would it be possible? Would it be me? I would be lying if I did not say I aspired to both. I think all the kings would. My position on the sea seems to allow greater access to outside trade.

"Our people deserve better than we give them now. We all feel that way about our clans and cities. Each has something the others need, but we have old ways that we must shed. We don't need to fight to obtain them. We choose to fight. We can not see the

160

advantages of free trade. I hope that bringing rich wares to our shores help us to see the benefits and open our eyes to a new way of living. Crystalier has a more inventive way of life. They can bring us crafted goods that we do not produce. We could trade or sell them goods that they do not have. That is what I know for now.

"Elys, they can craft great receptacles of all kinds from the ore in your mountains."

"The Smithy in Breen can do that."

"Those are ordinary things. The artisans on Crystalier will create works of art."

"I don't need art to store my grain or cook my food."

"Perhaps not, but you will want them when you see them."

"Have you seen them?"

"Not first hand, but I have had them described to me in great detail. Other things as well. They have weavers there that produce the finest cloth. Look at the clothes of the emissaries; how soft and comfortable. You could cast off that scratchy wool and look like kings rather than rumpled warriors. They have delicacies that do not grow here, juicy and abundant."

"If they have so much that is extra ordinary what can we offer them from our ordinary?" Thome Kelt asked.

"There is the ore, and you Kelt have great strong Iron Wood Trees. Narhan, I don't believe that spice, Paradise Seeds that you have up there grows anywhere else in the world. The people of Crystalier would be amazed at the aromatic scent and the hot spicy flavor. Their cuisine is rather bland compared to ours, I am told. Tanath I am also told that the dragon leaf in your territory is superior to any that they grow. Hoarfrost has Cauldron. We use it for jewelry here, but as beautiful as it is, it is fragile and breaks easily. The glassblowers in Crystalier could crush it and make a very unique icy blue glass. Breen has delicate shell fish that are unrivaled here or in

Crystalier, though Crystalier has beds of fish that we have never seen. As for Nagrom in our mountains grows the kaff plant from which we brew that dark black tea we all love so well. They have certain teas in Crystalier, but nothing so robust as our Kaffee. Nagrom is also well situated to accept ships and transport goods in and out. Breen and Hoarfrost are also well situated, but not equipped for accepting ships right now."

"You presume too much, Frahn!" Elys said.

"How so, Elys?"

"You should have asked us to be a part of this, before representing us."

"Would you have taken the steps to be involved, without first seeing the possibilities?"

Elys was thinking on that, when Narhan spoke. "No Elys, you wouldn't. You are too lazy and content with things as they are." There was a bit of laughter amongst some of the company, but Narhan continued. "We have become too accustomed to things as they are. I have my lands, greater than all others. I have need of nothing. But, here is Frahn, young and insightful. He came to us and we shunned his thinking feeling it was impossible to have better and not having the energy to find out more. So he took it on himself and here now when he tries to prove it has value he is thwarted by one of the most stubborn amongst us, Harald."

Thome Kelt joined, "Harald may be stubborn, but you are an arrogant bastard, Narhan. You; in that isolated ice land you call a country. Harald was protecting his interest as he saw it. I for one will not fault the man for that."

"Was he protecting his interest when he had not even fully heard what those interests were, or was he acting out of fear? Fear that Frahn might actually become more influential than he himself had been, or ever could be," Narhan countered.

"I say we set aside this business of the treaty for now and treat it as a circumstance to Esporanza's death. This woman before us could well have created an act of war with the Crystalians. Instead, they seem to have put their interests into justice for a murder committed on their soil by one of our citizens. I dare say we would not have been so calm about such a thing. I say that Harald acted with intent to slander Frahn and undermine his good actions. He also acted with the blessing of the council and refuses to speak to it now. Frahn has called the council and humbly admitted his error in judgment," Tanath said.

Heads nodded affirming Tanath's words. Narhan sat back and the room was a murmur again as the kings conferred with their councilors. They finally agreed to proceed with the matter of justice. They could not agree on death simply because some of them also employed assassins, though they called them spies. Spies were a necessary means of communication and news and they did not want to set a precedent that might tie their hands later.

Lily was found guilty of crimes against Ahnges, a crime punishable by death but it was Narhan who proposed a plan. He offered his dungeon, as a neutral ground to hold Lily. "Not Harald's territory; not Frahn's," he said. The other kings felt she should not be transported so far and it was agreed on that Tanath would hold Lily in Calibe until Harald came to council to explain himself. If that happened the matter of Lily's final sentence would be reconvened. If Harald chose not to appear within the month he would be deemed a despot and the council would become a council of six kings. Lily would then be executed for committing traitorous acts on behalf of a despot king.

We were satisfied that Lily remained imprisoned, even though the foundation of her actions remained unchallenged. If Harald chose not to appear and lost his seat on the council there was no action decided on how to depose him. If the treaty was approved then he had no say in it and his city would not benefit from it. He would be in effect exiled.

Still the whole process left me aggravated. As a council they were ineffective and lacked substantial guidelines. This was something we would be able to tell the leaders of Crystalier before they agreed to sign a binding treaty.

We agreed to stay two more days. As minstrels we are used to being asked to sing for our supper; as the saying goes. Several of the kings stayed behind as well, but Elys and Tanath who travelled for awhile on the same road left together to see Lily properly escorted to her prison cell in Calibe. We had a wonderful time at Frahn's. He was a good host and we wanted for nothing. He danced with his demure wife and the visiting Kings joined in. We got to know them some, so when we returned to Mareese we had a very good impression of who the chiefs of Ahnges were and how they might react to treaty negotiations. Mya seemed satisfied with the justice handed down on Lily and began to prepare for a life in Crystalier. We felt good about our part in the events and looked forward to a warm reception back home in Mareese.

·~·Chapter Seven·~·

The day we chose to leave dawned damp and foggy. There had been a hard rain the night before. The courtyard was slick with mud and we were splattered with it after loading a pony cart with Mya's worldly possessions for transport to our waiting ship. Many of the items were things of her father's that Frahn saw to it she had. Among them was her father's writing desk and stool. I had just finished lashing things down. Andreas was going over final arrangements with two of Frahn's men to deliver the of goods and profits to the Breen Smithies, that we would not be able to. They would return them along with their horse and wagon. Frahn included a well worded letter that alluded to recent events , but gave no mention of us by name. The shipment was a grace by Frahn. Frahn had taken Mya aside and was talking with her just inside the castle door when two of Frahn's gate guards and twelve men from Elys's and Tanath's troops came galloping into the courtyard.

It was immediately obvious that they had been in a skirmish. Frahn ran forward with the rest of us as we assisted the men down from their mounts and brought them into the great hall near the fire. Andreas assessed their injuries while we awaited Frahn's physician. No injuries was life threatening but only after they were being tended did Frahn ask for their report.

It was Tanath's captain who gave it. "We were pushing on through the storm to get to the refuge house for the night. It was not yet dark and we only had a few more miles to go. Our visibility and travel were impaired by the rain and one supply wagon. We were suddenly set upon by brigands. Arrows filled the air. They targeted only the kings. Elys and Tanath both went down before we could rally around them. We are the only ones to survive. We were twenty eight in all when we left here. We lost sixteen in the defense. They are strapped to their horses and wait in your outer courtyard. The brigands were excited to find the girl and were satisfied to take her and the wagon and go after slaughtering most of our party. I felt no duty to protect her thinking that they would treat her more cruelly than she would get in prison. A poetic justice for her crime against you, Lord Frahn, but then as we were seeing to our dead and wounded I found this upon the ground." He opened his hand and there was a cloak clasp fashioned with the round swirl surrounding an ocean wave – Harald's mark. We had seen that same design before on the fortress guards in Breen. "What we thought was brigands appear to be something else."

The room went quiet as the implications sank in. Harald had committed an act of war. It seemed insane. All of the kings had become amicable to Frahn's attempt at treaty with Crystalier. They were not wholly convinced, but they had agreed to send delegations from their cities to travel together to Crystalier to assess the possibilities. It was not likely that one or more of them were in legion with Harald, certainly Elys, the most outspoken and belligerent of the kings was not.

The remaining kings were Frahn of Nagrom, August of far north Hoarfrost, Thome Kelt of central Kelton, Narhan of Yer. August was an aging king, he was capable, but he would not endure war well. His terrain in the Icy Mountains kept him well and well protected. He had no need of war. Thome Kelt would find his city in the center of the fighting if there was a war of all the realms. His people were loggers and farmers more than soldiers. They would suffer the most. Narhan of Yer had a kingdom of lush temperate rainforest on the northern coast of Ahnges. His people were sturdy and accustomed to hardship they would make good allies, but of all the kings he and Frahn seemed the most like-minded. Narhan was self-important, and greedy. That caused him to be interested in bringing riches to his kingdom. Harald's actions made no sense. How did he expect to survive against the other six kingdoms? It was a question we could not answer at that time.

Frahn ordered wagons be made ready to carry the dead and wounded. He called up a full platoon of fifty men to escort the bodies of Elys, Tanath, and their people home. That left him fifty trained men in his stronghold. He called for his citizen soldiers to prepare themselves and standby for further instructions.

Frahn held our ship and we stayed in Nagrom. If there was to be a war we wanted information to relay home. Mya was still a concern and we wanted her back in Mareese where she would be safe, she had been through enough already.

By the afternoon all was ready, but Frahn would not send the troops out until the break of day. We were asked to stay on to discover who among us was Frahn's spy. Andreas would go with the troop and I would stay behind. If the spy was still in Frahn's employ then we promised to find them either way. But, we had made a promise to Mya as well. Frahn asked his wife, Queen Sion, to go along with Mya and see that our arrangement's for Mya were carried out. His wife agreed, she knew her own protection would ease Frahn's mind to concentrate on these new developments. Her ladies would stay behind in case one of them was the spy. She would seek out Diony and pursue an alliance. We had prepared letters to Diony to explain the developments, to go along with those written by Frahn. Sion carried the letters personally. Nothing was spoken to anyone else. Frahn and Sion, Mya and I went down to the ship in the late hours of the night.

It was Frahn's own ship with Frahn's handpicked man as captain. The ship was small and sleek, not a merchanteer at all. It would be swift. The crew was only three men, the captain, and two crewmen. The small berth that served as Frahn's quarters while aboard would have to serve the women. We searched the ship meticulously for hours until the tide came in. We found nothing amiss. The ship cast off before the suns peeked over the horizon and we watched as she slipped swiftly away toward the approach of morning. Mya's treasures would have to wait to sail home with us.

Back at the castle the escort was about to pull out. Andreas went ahead of the column riding with Tanath's captain. He played a slow tune upon his flute and nodded to me but continued to play. In that moment, when he would be out of touch and in harm's way I knew my love for him. I blew him a kiss and hoped he would know the meaning. I knew that when this was all over I would be able to bring down the barriers between us. I hoped he would still feel the same about me then and bring down his walls too.

Frahn and I stayed and watched the procession pass. He was surrounded by members of his house and citizens at large. I stood a step behind him, wary of an attack as we stood outside the protective walls of his stronghold. He was showing himself to be a good and kind king. If he needed protection I would not hesitate to give it. When the procession passed he stayed and looked after it, until every last man had made the turn toward the Northgate out of the city. I followed him as we entered the castle walls. Frahn walked a little ahead of me lost in his own thoughts and I kept watch over him as we moved into the castle. He lumbered into his great empty hall and slumped into his throne. I sat nearby on a stool with my back to one of the large trestle tables. He was aware of me, but he did not speak.

"Do you wish to be alone, Lord Frahn?"

"No Saeede, I wish your council, but I have no right to ask it."

"You are a king. What more right do you need?"

"Yes, a king, right born, by the grace of God. What right does my birth give me over Man?"

"If God put you here as you believe He did, than your right comes from Him. I am not a person who is sure about gods, but I have seen demons with my own eyes. I have seen forces I cannot explain. I have never seen a god. In Mareese they believe that everyone has a predetermined destiny, that destiny will find you, and once known it is up to you to act in order to fulfill it. Perhaps these events pre-tell your destiny."

"What if my destiny has found me and it is the destruction of Ahnges?"

"You are overwhelmed. I think. Your vision to bring prosperity and unity here is a good one. I think that it is more likely that Harald is leading a misguided destiny. His actions make no sense. When I think of all I have learned about your country and its kings he seems destined for disaster. The unity of Ahnges may have been given a boon. Tanath's and Elys's people will turn on Harald. Narhan seems loyal to you, even if it be for his own gain. August and Thome seem impartial but they may yet be swayed as events unfold. You have allies. Lead them."

"Into war? I have no heart for that."

"No, lead them away from it."

We sat a long moment in silence. He could not believe my words and searched my eyes for some deeper meaning, but there was none. I did not look away from his penetrating gaze.

"That may prove more difficult."

"It is strange, isn't it? When Men seek vengeance they see first the prospects of retribution, to cause the same pain that has been brought upon them. Harald stands in the way of your destiny to bring peace and prosperity to Ahnges. For that he may well have to die, but

169

if you could spare him that and still bring prosperity and peace would that not show you to be the kind and merciful king that you desire to me? A king of Man."

"He has caused the deaths of three important people. Elys was a hothead and often committed crimes against the other kings. His realm is a harsh wilderness, when he was in need, if others could not give he would take. His people are like barbarians. I think he only opposed me because he saw prosperity in the spoils gained from war. I am glad that he softened some by the end of council. Tanath was more reasonable, but he liked a good fight. If one presented itself, he would fight with the side more likely to win. Tanath would have likely joined with Elys and been a united front. Their people have become like their kings. Harald's people are simple miners and craftsmen, but he has provided for them in times of need and has developed a strong military; even his civilians are well trained. If Harald had gained their trust then Kelton would have been a simple victory. They would have cut me off. Yer might have given them trouble and Hoarfrost can survive a prolonged siege. I do not understand his game.

"It is possible that in light of his actions the surviving kings will band together, but it is more likely they will see it as my problem and will only join if and when they are threatened."

"I do not envy you, Sir. I am sorry to say this *is* your problem for now. When you have means to resolve it I will do what I can for you. For now you have tasked me to find your spy. If he or she has not gone out with your troops I will find them. I promise you that. For now it is all that I can do for you."

"You have been of some small help, already. You have pulled my mind from the strategies of war, though I cannot neglect them, you have put me onto finding a strategy for peace. Now I want to be alone to reflect. Thank you."

"I go then, Sir. I will be making music about the place. I am first a minstrel, and it serves me well to observe and watch the comings and goings of people. It will be my first step to finding this spy of Harald's. Of course I will say it is at your command; to calm the household after these stressful events."

Frahn understood and gave his blessing. "Of course it is," he said.

***

I played in all areas of Frahn's castle for three days. I would perch myself in some out of the way corner or up on a window ledge. I truly enjoyed the time to play my music. I began to diddle about with a tune to lay behind lyrics for a ballad I was working on. I called it Frahn's Quandary. I would play a few hours in one spot watching the timetable of the palace unfold, break for a bite to eat, converse with the household workers, or take a short nap. Then I would move to another area, like the paddocks or the garden or the hall outside of chambers.

The second day I went to each place at a different time. On that day I was able to learn in my conversation with a domicile steward that one of his maids had taken on a new suitor. He was frustrated with her for bringing the man into her cottage. I played up dismay on my part and was able to get the name of the maid. Some discreet questioning of others gave me the location of her cottage. It was one of many in the outer courtyard.

I had not played in the outer courtyard yet and so I went straight to it. I took a stool from the kitchen and sat myself down where I could watch the cottage but still be in a spot central to the courtyard. I played there the rest of the day and into the evening. It was wonderful. Mother's danced with their children and husbands with wives. I could look up at the walls and watch the guards there swaying to the music as they looked out over the yard and the city. I located a spot atop the chapel that would give me a view of the cottage and let me see over the walls into the city. I would be spotted by the wall guards of course, but if I was there to entertain, as was the deception, then I could play, be out of the way of the guards and watch the cottage from a better perspective.

I stopped my recital in the yard and went into the chapel to speak with the cleric there. He was delighted to help me find my way up to the chapel roof for the sake of the men. He complimented me on my unselfish charity, giving of my talents and thereby my love; blobbitty blobbitty blah blah blah. He went on and on. I don't think he would have appreciated my duplicity. I would have to speak to Frahn, apparently his people didn't do kind things for one another very often.

It was near dusk. One sun had already set and the other kissed the horizon. I was hungry, but the time seemed right for me to get a view of the maid's new man. A squire went about the courtyard lighting the torches in sconces around the wall and on posts placed in the ground along the path between the gates. I gave him a distant, unspoken thank you as I situated myself and called a guard over to me.

"I have come to play just for those of you here on the wall, compliments of King Frahn. So you will hear me as you go about your duties. I will take requests if there are any, and if I know them, as I can fit them in."

The guard thanked me and passed the word.

I began upon the mandolin. I played soothing melodies to not disturb those going to their evening rest below. I watched as the maid came home. The cottages in the courtyard slowly went to sleep one by one. Only the torches lit the courtyard. I switched to the flute and played a few requests. Hours went by and then a lantern was lit in the maids cottage. I kept playing and watched as the lantern went out. A guard had come to watch as well when the lantern lit, but a few minutes after it went out he moved on. When he did I saw a shadow move between two cottages toward the wall near the stable, in the direction of the yard's postern gate.

I said goodnight to the next passing guard and made my way down off the roof, out of the chapel, and hurried up the path to the moat house gate. The bridge was down and I was known so I passed through. I had a passing view of the outer courtyard's postern gate, but saw no one there. I turned when I crossed the bridge and went straight to the tower that overlooked the postern gate and that side of the city.

The guard there was attentive and I asked did he see anyone leave by that postern gate. He had not, so I craned to see into the outer court yard between the postern gate and the stable. There I barely made out the shadows of what looked like two men. I pointed and the guard saw them too.

"Do not call the alarm just yet," I said. "Let me get closer and see what they are up to. If you see three shadows and a fight, then I will take what help you can give me."

I left the carpetbag with him and belted on my swords. I ran down the tower steps and did not stop running until I came to the first cottage in the outer court yard. I could see the guard and he me. I moved passed the cottage and into the shadows slowly to not make a sound as I moved toward the stable where I had seen the shadows. I could hear whispers and moved closer still to hear the words.

"Let Harald make of it what he will. He wants Frahn disgraced. I tell you he has sent the queen away. I know not where, but she has not been seen since the troops left. He keeps close company with that emissary from Crystalier now and her play thing has been sent away at the head of the troop. I'm sure Harald can make some fiery rumor of that. Couple it with the underhanded way that he handles his

173

diplomacy and it should not be hard to cast the name of upstart upon him."

"I will leave with the market errands. No one will count it as odd. I doubt another lackey in the mix will gather any attention at all. I will miss Lorey, she is a sweet lover. Move in on her quickly. She is weak and will fall for you quickly in my absence. Look for me at the Tumbling Highlands in about eight days. You can report to me what she tells you then."

"Did you leave a note?"

"Aye. I told her I was a wandering man when we met and I was a wandering man now. I said she deserved better than me, so use that when you talk with her. She is unbelievably gullible. Show her some sympathy and she will be yours before you know it. Go home now. I will rest here until I see the market group head to town."

No more was said and I heard the soft padding of one man running off. I waited to hear a door but the sound did not travel to my ears. A moment later I heard some soft scuffling from the spot where the conversation had taken place, then a yawn and pleased moan as the spy made himself comfortable for the remainder of the night.

I moved back toward the main path but meandered carefully through the shadows of the cottages until I had a perspective that allowed me to see one end and side of the stable. I crouched in the darkest shadow between two cottages, and strained my eyes into the shadows around the stable. It was difficult, but when the man shifted his position I located him and made my way to him. He did not hear me and I raised the pommel of my sword to come down upon his temple. He made no move against me so I knew my success. I threw him over my shoulder, picked up the bundle that had lain under his head and ran as fast as his bulk would allow.

The guards had orders to let me pass freely, but this was unusual and I was stopped at the gate. Rather than explain I asked for escort to the king. My request was granted. We were joined by the tower guard and we all ran together to the castle doors. The sentries there had taken defensive stands as we approached, but upon recognizing us opened the door.

I chose one guard to accompany me. "The rest of you go back to your posts. Say nothing of this." Once inside I ordered my chosen guard to run ahead and wake the king. "Tell him I am coming with a captive."

I was nearly to the king's chamber when he ran out and met me in the hall. He led me to another chamber, one without windows and ordered the guard to stand outside. "Let no one in, No one. Do you understand?"

"Yes, Sir, of course. No one will enter."

"Good."

I dropped the unconscious spy on the floor and Frahn locked us all in. He walked slowly over and knelt down to see the man's face.

"I don't know him."

"Nor should you."

"He has been posing as a lover to one of your maids who live in the outer court yard. I learned of him from various conversations with your staff. He has been here only a few months, stays to himself except to please the maid. Her name is Lorey. I spied him from the chapel roof as I played for your soldiers there. They were very grateful to you by the way. It was very late and all the other cottages had gone to sleep. I left the chapel and went to the moat tower across from the outer court yard's postern gate. I and one of the guards there saw the shadows of two men near the stable. I snuck down and got near enough to hear the end of their conversation, but it was enough."

"Tell me."

"Harald means to defame you to the other kings. Lorey is concerned that you have suddenly sent your queen away. You should know that sending Andreas away and keeping me close has caused Lorey's mind to wander to distasteful things between us. This man intended to use Lorey's pillow talk to fuel Harald's plan. Coupled with what he called underhanded diplomacy; sorry, they intended to cast you as an upstart. It seems that Harald's war will be one of words—his against yours.

"He planned to leave with the market errands, he did not say for where, but I assume Breen. He left a note for Lorey breaking it off. The other man who I could not see or follow is to work his way in and become Lorey's next love. He will move in on her quickly. Her lover called her weak and unbelievably gullible. He expects her to fall for the other quickly when he is gone. They set a meeting at the Tumbling Highlands in eight days to exchange reports.

"You have a window of opportunity now. Lorey thinks he has gone as does this other man. I believe Lorey is just stupid and needy. I know now who she is and I will watch her for you. When this new man showers her with attention we can catch not one, but two of Harald's spies."

"You have done well, Saeede. I thank you."

"One of the easiest jobs I have ever had to do, Sir. Happy to do it. How will you keep word of this from getting out?"

He thought a moment. "The forgotten room for now. When he is conscious I will pull him out and question him there. Come, let's take him now, before the house wakes up."

I hoisted the weight over my shoulders again and the man moaned. I told Frahn, "If he wakes up knock him out again."

"Aye," Frahn opened the door, and told the guard to follow us. We were only seen by the guards at the castle door and along the wall. They recognized their king and though they must have wondered at this odd activity they did not question or stop us.

The spy was in the shaft of the forgotten room and still did not wakeup. I worried that I may have hit him too hard. Our accompanying guard remained in the tower of the forgotten room with orders to wake us both if the man stirred.

I returned to my room, happy for the rest and fell asleep quickly. It was late in the morning when a knock came upon my door to wake me. The spy was awake.

Frahn was already on his way to the tower and asked that I come as quickly as possible. I was surprised, but pleased to find that my carpetbag had made it back to my room as I slept. I washed and dressed in a most ordinary dress and tucked a dagger into the sash. I walked casually through the halls, trying not to call undue attention to myself. I was conscious of Frahn's reputation now and chose to take the long way around through the palace rather than to cut through the gardens of the inner court yard. If I was seen to follow him directly more people would begin to talk. Still I knew if it seemed I was following him at all they would talk. I did what I could to avoid people, but it was not entirely possible in the light of day. I hoped that prying eyes would at least reason that the prison tower was no place for a romantic tryst.

I arrived at the tower and the spy was being hoisted out. His expletives were vile and threatening. He was pulled down in front of Frahn but he was not unharnessed. I moved in and took a place where Frahn could see me, but when the spy tried to turn to see me his tethers prevented it.

Frahn built his questioning slowly. He asked where he came from, his name, and his reason for coming to Nagrom. The man had quick answers. Frahn turned his questions to the man's affair with Lorey. Frahn acted concerned for her welfare. He told the spy that as she was one of his house he felt a fatherly obligation to her. The man began to stumble over his answers. If he did not say he was leaving her Frahn might make him go back to her. If he said he was leaving then maybe Frahn would put him back in the forgotten room. While the man struggled to explain Frahn interrupted and caught the man off guard. "And what of these late night meetings in the shadows of the stable?" Frahn said and leaned in to gaze into the man's eyes. Harald's spy feigned innocence but his body language gave him away.

Frahn paraphrased what I told him of the conversation I had overheard.

The spy went silent.

Frahn told him how it was going to be; either he gave his partner up, or we would catch him when he moved in on Lorey. If that failed we would catch him at The Tumbling Highland when he began asking about his missing friend, or when he left Lorey and went back to Breen. Frahn was nice enough to give him time to decide. The man decided on silence. Frahn gave him time to think about that decision; time in the shaft of the forgotten room. Frahn stood to go. "Let me know if he relents," he said to the spy's keeper.

Frahn moved straight for the door and I joined him. Once outside I asked, "What do you think? I could not see his face. Will he relent?"

"The shaft has had that effect before. It does not matter. I know that my wife is safe and that is a great deal off my mind. In four days it will be eight since the troop left, counting today. They should arrive at Kirsh today or tomorrow. I hope that Andreas is able to convince them to hold. If not I will be honor bound to support them. Tanath's people will join then too."

"Don't worry. Andreas has a certain charm. It is very hard to say no to him. He will bring you back the envoys you asked for."

"I hope you are right."

I hoped so too.

The next day I sat upon the chapel steps playing on my mandolin. I found a spot in a corner of the top step that gave me a view of Lorey's cottage. I got there early and watched as she walked through the yard on her way to work. The village in the yard came to life. The busy people tended their work and children came out to play. I walked to the cottage and knocked. No one came to the door. A quick glance around showed me I was unnoticed. I tested the door and finding it unlocked I let myself in.

It was a one room cottage. I saw no signs of male habitation at this time. So the second spy had not made a move yet as far as I could tell. I searched and found nothing to influence me against Lorey. I left and went to breakfast. I placed myself in areas that Lorey was tasked with. She was emotional from time to time and confided in another maid. I could not hear all of what was said, but what I did was typical of a supportive friend.

After dinner I went back to the chapel steps and played. Some of the villagers came and gathered around me. They were mostly children so I played music that they could dance to, or songs that told stories a child could appreciate. I watched as the workers from the castle made their way to their cottages in the yard.

Lorey was stopped by a man about her age. I took notice. They talked a few minutes. I could only imagine the conversation, but the body language told me this was a sad woman telling a man her pain. He listened quietly but touched her arm or rubbed her shoulder several times during her speech. She was crying in the end. He said something and she kissed his cheek, then she turned and ran to her cabin. He watched her go; then I watched him go. He had a cottage near the main gate. I did not see where he worked, but I would be back.

I spent the next day milling about in the outer courtyard. I did not always play. Sometimes I told the children stories, or talked with the women as they worked their gardens or hauled water from the common well. I strolled about looking for the man and saw him working at a grinding wheel in a yard beside his cottage. He was busy sharpening the villagers tools and did not notice me there. He was skilled and efficient in his work. Tools of all sorts leaned against a rack. I saw no knifes or swords, but imagined this man had filled this position because he knew how to care for weapons. He was of sturdy build, bigger than the first spy. I supposed he could be a soldier. I could think of no good reason to talk with him so I went back to the castle and looked for Frahn so I could report.

My next days found me spending a great deal of time at The Tumbling Highland Inn. The bartenders name was Auffie. He supplied the liquid spirits for Frahn's house. I was sent with an order from Frahn as a way of introduction. I explained my true purpose for being there and we agreed upon a signal. I would signal him when our second spy walked in; he would signal me when he began asking about the first spy.

I played for Auffie's customers and he allowed me to put out a hat for tips. It took six days for my mark to appear. When he did I transitioned the song I was playing into a tune called The Keepers Wife. Auffie had chosen the song as my signal to him. Auffie looked up from behind the bar to find the new arrival and we both watched as the man took the table I would have chosen. He put his back against a corner and had a view of the whole room and the balcony that ran above the bar to the rooms upstairs.

I finished the tune, announced a break to wet my throat, took my earnings from my hat and went to the bar.

Auffie drew a large draught and delivered it to me. "His name is Tige as far as I know. He has lived in the city for several months; a year maybe, then got in at the castle doing some work up there. The man you are holding is most likely called Ajia. They come here often. They don't mingle much just drink and talk with their heads close together. Ajia stayed here when he first came to town about three months ago, until he made his way with that pretty maid Lorey and she invited him to stay with her."

"Thank you." I paid for and drank my beer slowly. Tige drank two beers and ordered a third in that time. I went back to my little stage; a table in the corner near a great hearth. I sat upon the table with my hat upon a stool a little bit away from me.

The dinner hour came and went. My tips grew as the evening went on and Tige was becoming drunk. I was about to call it a day when Lorey came in. She looked over the room until she saw Tige and then she went to him. Auffie snapped his bar rag twice against the bar; his signal to me. I had left this part of the story out for him. I shrugged my shoulders as if I did not understand it myself.

I played until Tige and Lorey went off together. The hour was near closing time. I hurried to pack my things and took up the loaded carpetbag. I stopped long enough to thank Auffie and give him a few coins from my hat then I went to follow Tige and Lorey.

I trotted up the board walk until I could make them out up ahead. The man was leaning on her as she steadied him for the walk. I heard them laugh as he staggered and tripped. I had an opportunity to get close to them; I could offer help and maybe put some distance between them at the same time. I quickened my pace and caught up to them before we reached the castle gate.

"You look like you could use some help," I said and before they could respond I had Tige's other arm wrapped over my shoulder. "I've seen you around the castle," I said, leaning back and catching Lorey's eye over Tige's sagging shoulders. She did not look happy with my interference. "We haven't been properly introduced. I am called Sade,"

"Lorey," she said.

"Is this your husband?" I asked, although I knew better.

"Oh no," she said. "This is just our first date. I am just taking him home."

We were at the castle gate then, but once we were all identified the gate was opened and we were allowed to enter.

"Some first date," I said.

"Yes, well he is a good man though. The drink takes some of them worse than others."

"I'm not judging. Thankfully my man holds his liquor well." I took the opportunity to begin damage repairs on Frahn's reputation regarding me.

"Your man, but I ..." She stopped herself from what would have been an awkward accusation. I took it another way.

"Yes, he was sent off with troop. It is lonely here without him. I pass the time as best I can with my music."

She was steering us passed what I knew to be Tige's cottage. I had hoped to keep him from her, and get a look inside his place. I would have to settle for a look later.

"I have heard. You play beautifully."

"Thank you, my mother encouraged me from a very young age. It has given me an interesting life and enough money to survive on."

"Why did you have out a hat tonight? Aren't you a guest of Frahn's?"

"He has been kind enough to extend his hospitality, but I am really here at the bequest of others. I still need to make money to see to my extra needs. A woman needs certain things a king cannot provide."

"Certainly King Frahn would see to every need a pretty thing like you could ever desire." She was teasing me. I had managed to make her feel friendly toward me quickly. She was indeed gullible as Ajia had said.

I took the high road and another step toward repairing Frahn's reputation. "Oh no. He is so in love with the queen. I have had some opportunity to get to know him on my business here. He longs for her, and only her, as much as I pine for my man. Loneliness throws people together, but true love is something worth waiting for."

She skipped a step at that. I was taking a stab at her then but she could not be sure of it. We went on. We were very near her cottage. We did not speak the rest of the way.

"I can take him from here," she said.

"I don't mind. Let me help you get him inside, and I'll go then."

"Well, alright then."

It did not take long for us to flop him into bed and stretch him out.

"Good night then," she said curtly.

I bowed and left. Tige was grabbing for her even before I had the door open. She giggled and I heard the bed creak as she added her weight to it. I passed her window on my way toward the castle, but doubled back in shadow to Tige's cottage.

It was locked, but I found the key amongst those I had pilfered from Tige while we put him to bed. This cottage had one room and a loft for sleeping. There was nothing downstairs out of the ordinary, but the loft was another story.

A feather mattress was on the floor under the peak of the roof. Two chests like those issued to soldiers were placed side by side against the outside wall and served as a headboard to the mattress. I cleared an ink well and pen and a glass of water from the top of one chest and set them aside carefully. Both chests were locked, but the keys were with the others. Inside the first were various weapons and one full set of chain mail armor complete with greaves, cowl, and a tabard. Upon the tabard was Harald's crest! I carefully folded the items back and replaced them the way I had found them. I opened the second chest. In it were many ordinary items of a man's daily ablutions. Below an empty water basin and towel I found correspondences from Harald and Ajia. I read a few until I was sure of what I had.

I replaced all as I had found it and locked the chests. I went out the door and locked that too. Under cover of the dark and shadows I returned to Lorey's door. I could hear them inside, both in the throes of love making. I wrestled with what to do with the keys, but reasoned that it was most incriminating if Tige remained in possession of them. It was risky, but I quietly checked and found the door still unlocked. I lifted the latch slowly and let the door swing in enough to reach in with the full length of my arm. I slid the keys across the floor and pulled the door closed. The sounds of lovemaking continued and I was safe. I let the latch slide into place slowly with just a whisper of a click. Then I ran to the stable and stopped to rest upon the ground with the carpetbag supporting my back. My heart was pounding from the excitement of my discovery. I caught enough breath to serve me and picking up the carpet bag I walked out into the main path and hurried to the castle. No guard stopped me. They were accustomed to me by now.

Frahn was not in his great hall, so I went by myself to his rooms and knocked upon the door. The sound was louder than I had anticipated, my excitement was making me stronger or perhaps just more aware. Frahn answered and I pushed in with out a word or invite. He could see I was breathless and showed me to a chair. He poured water from a pitcher on his table and I drank greedily before speaking.

"It is a man called Tige; your tool tender. He has a cottage in the outer courtyard. He is with Lorey now so I went to his cottage. In his chests by the bed in his loft are letters from Harald and another called Ajia. Auffie says Tige's partner is most likely a man called Ajia. I also found weapons, a suit of armor, and a tabard with Harald's crest upon it! I put it all back so that you can catch him red-handed with it. The keys are on the floor inside Lorey's door. You should wait for him, have someone there watching so when he returns you can search the place yourself. Tell him that Ajia gave him up."

"You are quite good at this type of thing aren't you? I won't ask you how you accomplished this."

"Probably better that you don't know."

He scrutinized me with his eyes. "Yes. Quite right."

"You should go to bed."

"I won't sleep."

"Then go to your room and wait. Go about a normal routine. I will come for you when there is something to tell you."

I stood and bowed. When I got to the door Frahn said my name and I turned back.

"Thank you."

I nodded, bowed again, and left the room.

·~·Chapter Eight·~·

I wish I could have been there when Frahn went after Tige. He told me the story over celebratory brandy in the garden.

After I had given him my report and left him to go to my room it took him only a moment to decide what to do. He dressed and strapped on a sword. I had not seen him armed during my two week stay. He took two of his captains and they went to Lorey's. He said they were there within a half hour of my report.

Frahn himself pounded on the door until Lorey, wrapped in bed clothes opened it and peeked around the door. *"M'Lord, whatever is the matter?"*

"Step aside Lorey," he said. "My interest is in Tige for now. I will deal with you next." He was really enjoying himself. Frahn was smiling as he repeated the exchange.

"She must have been quite confused," I said.

"She was, and terrified. Silly girl. I have her under arrest. I've put here in a tower room for now. I may have to let her go. I have to be able to trust those who work for me."

"That's a shame. What if she learns a lesson?"

"How will I know?

Not having an answer I shrugged. We sipped our brandy and he continued his story.

"I picked up the keys from the floor where you said they'd be and knowing they were his I asked Lorey instead if they belonged to her. *'No sir, I've never seen them before.'* Then realizing that she had probably implicated Tige she tried to blame you for dropping them. It was amusing knowing that you actually had. She is so weak, so desperate for love she just acts without thinking.

"By this time the captains had rousted Tige from the bed. The man was still drunk and they had to help him into his pants. *'We'll see who they belong to,'* I told her."

"I ordered the captains to bring them both and led the way to Tige's Cottage. About half way there he began to struggle. I had to take Lorey so the captains could control him. He must have begun to realize what was happening.

"I dangled the key ring for all to see it. I found the door key, opened it, and held it open for Lorey. She obeyed without a word, but she was hesitant. The look she gave me was full of frightened tears. The captains shoved Tige in and we entered behind him letting the door close with a slam. I placed Lorey in a spot where she could see into the loft. Tige stood in the center of the room like a frightened cat. He was ready to pounce if we made a move at him. It was then I did as you said and told him that Ajia had been caught and had given him up as his partner. 'To prove it I will tell you what I know,' I said, and I did. He said nothing, but when I told my man to search the loft his expression changed. I think he was contriving a story.

"The lockers were handed down and my captain rejoined us. I dangled the keys again for all to see and then threw them to the captain. He found the proper keys and unlocked but did not open them. I gave that command to Tige. He did not want to do it. He actually shook his head no and backed away. At first I feared a trap, but remembering that you had opened them I went and did it myself. 'What have we here?' I said when I saw the tabard. It was the most immediately incriminating thing and I wanted him to know that we had him absolutely.

"I found the letters then and sat in a chair to unfold them. It was like torture to Tige. I was so calm that he did not know how to react.

After I read a few and knew what we had I refolded them and put them back in the trunk. I had the captains take Tige to the tower and place him in irons. I told them to send four men for the trunks. I waited for them with Lorey and spoke to her while we waited. I don't think she was complicit in any of this but I must punish her for what she has caused to happen."

"She is as much a victim as you are, Lord Frahn."

My directness took him back, but to his credit he had heard me. "That is so. But I must teach her a lesson."

"Yes, I suppose you must."

"Are you always so direct in matters with Kings?"

"I have never had a matter such as this before, but I would not be good to you if I were not."

"That is also so. Do you have any suggestions?"

"I wish I did, Sir."

We were on our second brandy and had been sitting quietly trying to think of an appropriate punishment when he gave up. "Let's leave it for now. She is safe in the tower and I am curious to see how Tige reacts when we raise Ajia from the pit. Are you curious to see it?"

"O, yes I am, but I think it is better that I not be a part of that. I have been careful not to seem involved. I don't want to bring any of Harald's rage upon the people of Crystalier."

"That is wise, I suppose. Well, I've just enough drink in me to make it even more interesting," he stood. "Take the rest of the brandy with you. You've earned it." Then he walked across the garden to enter the tower.

I finished my drink as I watched after him. I liked the man, but I was still uncertain what kind of king he would be. He had equal measure of compassion and callousness. I filled my glass and took it and the bottle back to my room. I *had* earned it.

189

My window overlooked the outer courtyard. I crawled onto the wide sill and sat there sipping my brandy. I thought of Andreas and even though I had felt a confused love for him for several years the depth of feeling now surprised me. We had promised to talk after Esporanza's murder was solved. He had conveyed his interest in me. I believed I was ready to love him back, but for the curse that was on me.

The curse—I had not felt the chill for days! How many I could not be sure. I had become so used to it that when it left me I had not known it. Was it a curse at all then? Perhaps it had been a long malaise after all. What excuse then did I have left not to love Andreas?

I had long thought that our business of investigating was too dangerous to support a love relationship. I knew that I had just been using that as an excuse. It was an excuse I was comfortable with. It was time now though. If I wanted him to love me back I would have to claim him, or he would go to someone else. You would think acknowledging that I was in love and being nearly certain that he loved me back would make me happy. I think I was more terrified than anything.

I sat in the window for a good part of the day in a state of melancholy. Terror and brandy have that effect on me. As the day waned I moved to my bed. The soft breeze through the window and the effects of the brandy lulled me into a pleasant sleep.

The next few days I wandered the castle and Nagrom. One day I brought only my flute with me and played a tune or two here and there, but I was bored with it all. I was bored with people, the city, Frahn's hospitality, Frahn, spies, politics of kings. I wanted to go home. I was homesick. That was another first for me. Love and homesick all at once, that was just too much for me. I tromped back to my room at the castle. I was going soft!

Sleep was what I needed. I thought that I was just too tired and unable to think straight. If nothing else sleep would block out what I was feeling. I slept the entire afternoon and would have slept longer but I was awakened in the dark of night to shouts from the outer courtyard and the sounds of several horses. I went to the window and saw Andreas and the troop returning. I pulled on a robe over my linen frock and ran shoeless to the yard to greet them. Others of the house and town were gathering as well. I stopped on the castle porch where Frahn stood and waited for the men to dismount. The soldiers were released, but Andreas and the captains came forward with four strangers. Andreas introduced them to Frahn. He had brought the diplomats from Kirsh and Calibe. Frahn was excited and welcomed then enthusiastically. The group moved into the great hall and Frahn called for servants to tote bags and bring food while rooms were made ready.

Andreas came to me at the door and held me back as the others entered. "Do you think we would be missed if we didn't go in?"

"Frahn will want to hear what you have to say."

"I have nearly completed the decipher of Eindal's ledger!"

"What did you find?"

"You won't believe me."

"Andy, what did you find?"

"Not here. It's too precious to risk."

"Let's get this over with then so you can tell me."

"Yes, what a drudge this all is. I just want to go home."

"Me too."

"You better go change. You look..." His look said it all.

I appreciated that look. I raised my eyebrows and teased, "Do you think so?"

"I know so. Now go change or you will be a distraction to these men."

I did as I was told, but I wanted Andreas to look at me that way again. I wore a dress that would speak to my station and be proper, but still get his attention. So much of what I owned was plain and wrinkled from being stuffed in that old carpetbag. I chose a thin linen chemise that was soft and fluid against my skin. Over that I wore a simple dress and my favorite suede bodice corset dressed it up just enough. I pulled the front lacings of the bodice tight. The rolled edges were wrapped in ribbon and accented my form nicely. The long sleeves also laced and I pulled them tight enough so that just a bit of the chemise sleeve showed through. I like what I saw in the mirror. Not bad for a crumpled heap.

I slipped into the great hall as discreetly as I could, but the man speaking to Frahn faltered and watched me as I took my seat next to Andreas who did not stop looking at me. I smiled at him and he wiggled his eyebrows at me.

I made my apologies for my late attendance. Frahn introduced me as the other emissary from Crystalier and the conversation continued. They were discussing arrangements to include the other cities in an offensive against Breen. Frahn was against it, but if they insisted he would offer support of supplies and money, but not men, not yet. If they flushed Harald out then it would be over and he felt having his army present might make Harald more determined.

The night went on into morning and a plan was at last being hammered out. As part of that plan Andreas saw no problem volunteering us to ride to Kelton, Hoarfrost, and Yer to carry the message of a war council against King Harald and Breen. We agreed to do this one last thing for them, but then we were going home. We were excused and told to prepare for an extended trip. Extended trip—the phrase just aggravated me. I'd say the trip had already been extended beyond our expectations. We went to the kitchen and told the baker there what we needed for food supplies for the journey. She promised it all by the next morning.

Andreas pulled me along by the arm. I anticipated of his news about the ledger. I kept my pace with him and found myself reveling in his excitement. Once inside his room he grabbed me to him and hugged me long. I did not fight him and returned the hug.

"Did you miss me?"

"It surprised me, but yes, I did."

"Ah Sade, I was not surprised by how much I missed you."

"Truly?"

"Yes."

I kissed him. "We still have a talk."

"Okay here is the talk. I love you. I have for quite sometime and I think you have love for me too. So as is the custom I am asking for your hand. A one year commitment and if then we still love each other we get married. Say yay or nay."

I was dumbfounded. All my window sitting and soul searching would come to this. He had been more romantic with that traitor bitch Sardon. Still, this was an actual proposal, and he knew me well, very well, good and bad.

"I say, yay, but you owe me some romance when we get home."

"Yes, yes quite right. I have it all planned. You will be impressed."

"Humph . You are a cad you know. I will be counting down the year. Expect a retraction."

"Oh, Poor Sade," he said and kissed me. It was a sweet, tender, arousing kiss. "Just so you know what you'll be missing if you do. Now the ledger."

"No, later. Now us." I kissed him a sweet, tender, arousing kiss.

We spent the rest of that night and the next day in bed. We spoke of many things, made love and spoke again. I told him of my chill diminishing. We set some parameters to our relationship. I told him of my little adventure at capturing the spies. He finally got to tell me about the ledger. His findings were incomplete but promised an exiting ending. That was all he told me, deciding instead to save it for a later time when he was absolutely sure of his translation When it was near evening and there was nothing left to discuss we got up and packed.

"Why are we doing this Andy?"

"So that I can have you to myself. Once we are back in Mareese there will be your mother and now Mya, not to mention Diony and resolving all of this with her."

"Oh, good then. I thought you were feeling loyal to Frahn or something. We really owe him nothing. We could leave now and not go directly to Mareese."

"Yes, well, where is the excitement in that?"

I stood close and let my body touch his. "You don't know?"

We did not appear for the evening meal, but Frahn sent for us.

"Dammit. Well, Love, duty calls," I said.

We bathed and dressed as quickly as we could. All of Frahn's advisors were present at the head table. Frahn gave us a disappointed look, but said, "Have you made your preparations?"

"We have. If you have horses for us we leave at first light."

"I have letters here penned by me, dictated and signed by the emissaries of Kirsh and Calibe. I have letters of introduction signed by us all. You are to deliver each document to the three kings: Thome Kelt of central Kelton, August of northern Hoarfrost, and Narhan of Yer Hoarfrost's closest neighbor. I have drawn you a map. Go to Kelton first. That should take you four days. Then Yer or Hoarfrost next it does not matter, but stay wide of Breen. You know yourself, Andreas that there are Breen forces about. I have already sent to Diony in Mareese to explain your delay. The representatives from

Kirsh and Calibe will deliver this same letter to their rulers. Once you are on your way we will put into action our common defenses. There is one more letter that will get you through that on your return. Do not lose it."

Frahn passed a leather scroll down through his advisors to us. Andreas untied it and spread it on the table between us. We read over the letters together.

Frahn spoke as we read. "Keep yourselves hidden. Avoid Harald's troops at all cost."

"And if we can't? What if we are captured?" Andreas asked.

"I trust that you will not be, but if that happens we should know. Breen has called for her citizen's to come into the city and defend. We have our own men amongst them to watch activities there. If you are brought to Breen we will know."

I had not spoken at any of Frahn's councils preferring Andreas speak for me as was the custom of men, but I could not abide by these arrangements. "Sir, Frahn, I must speak directly."

"As is your way. Please Saeede say your mind that we may all know."

I took a deep breath and began, "Andreas and I owe none of you any loyalty. We are here on behalf of Crystalier. As I see it our work here is rightfully done. If we are attacked and killed in the wilderness what alert will there be then? What benefit to you if that happens?"

"It will not happen. You won't let it. You have faced more dire enemies than Harald. You will find a way, of that I am tremendously confident."

"We are good at we do sir, but you are all asking us to take a great deal of risk on your behalves."

"Containing Harald must happen before the treaty can go forward. The leaders of your country have a declared interest in that treaty going forward. You came here with that in mind. See it through,

195

woman, and improve the lives of people in two countries. Go home a hero."

"I am already a hero, in many more ways than you know. I do not need this assignment to feed my ego. I don't think we are asking too much for you to declare your protection if we are captured. Surely we will avoid it at all cost, but none of us know how far Harald has gone, or what alliances he has made outside of your cities. If we are captured I am asking, no, I must say it right. I am demanding a promise of rescue."

Andreas was tugging at my skirt. I leaned in to hear what he had to say.

"Don't blow this. We will be as kings ourselves just for this service."

"You promised me a marriage. I mean to see it and it will not happen if we are separated and languishing in some dark rooms in Harald's cellars."

No one spoke as we whispered. I straightened and stood as tall as my small frame allowed. "We have lives to get back to good sirs. We would gladly do you this service. We are asking no expenses but what supplies you would provide your own messengers. You would send them, but for the skills we have that they lack. There should be a price, but we ask for protection instead. If you are not willing to give it for the risk we take, then we have to withdraw. Would not the taking of a king's messenger be an act of aggression at least, if not an act of war?"

"Normally that would be so," A man from Kirsh yelled out as he stood, "but normally the messenger is not carrying a message of potential war against the captor. Harald would be within his rights to deal with you as he saw fit. You must not be caught."

"Still," a man from Calibe chimed in, "I believe my people would want you to be rescued and so I will commit to at least attempting such a thing in the event that it should be needed."

The man from Kirsh countered. "My people are few and we will need all of them for defenses."

"I am reluctant in all of this, but it was my treaty that brought us to this point. I will pledge to join men to Calibe's if there is need of a rescue," Frahn said.

"Good then, and great thanks to you. I hope that we will be so successful that a rescue will not be necessary. We wish to get this done without linking Crystalier any further." I bowed and took my seat.

"I didn't know you could be so diplomatic," Andreas said.

"It is only right that they provide it. I only sought what I saw as right."

"And a wedding."

"Yes, and that."

He laughed and took my hand under the table.

Dinner ended and the representatives came over to us two at a time with a list of fine points they wanted the other kings to be told. Some were in the letters others were not. We listened patiently and asked questions when necessary, but mostly we just wanted to get on with it so we could get it done and go home.

·~·Chapter Nine·~·

The morning we left marked forty-eight days since we had sailed from Mareese. This mission would take seventeen at the very least, if all went smoothly. Frahn saw that we were well supplied and we rode out of Nagrom by the eastern gate with two horses for riding and two to pack our gear. They were all fine strong horses and even packed they would be able to move swiftly.

Once we cleared the mountains around Nagrom we stayed off the road. We navigated down to the shore and rode as fast as the horses could take us. Rocks rolled in and rolled back with the surf but a stripe of hard sand ran between them and the rolling cliffs above us. A fog lay just above us until the suns raised high enough to burn it off. The season was moving toward autumn and the air was brisk. The horses responded to that with good spirit and we made excellent time.

We spent our first night beyond the coastal refuge house, but before the turn in the coastline. We intended to remain hidden. It promised to be a chilly night, but we did not like the idea of a fire so near the road above us. We pulled the horses into a tight line behind a stand of large boulders on the beach, near the cliffs. Their shared body heat and blankets would keep them warm. The boulders would conceal us from view on the water side. The cliff above us domed sharply so anyone above us would be too far off the edge of the cliff to look down on us. Andreas and I took a shelter under an outcropping just above the horses. We snuggled together for warmth and got a reasonable night's sleep.

It was moon light as we prepared ourselves and the horses for travel. We walked them not wanting to risk their footing among the rocks. Andreas looked for and found a path he remembered from his trip along the road with the troops. It rose at an easy angle up off the beach to the cliff tops very near the road. We were a days travel west of Calibe.

The road was empty so we crossed and pushed into the woods. For that day and part of the next we navigated the game trails keeping our heading toward Kelton. We camped below the trees at night and moved slowly by day. We were not so far away from Breen .Our crossbows were always cocked and loaded. Any encounter was unacceptable, but Harald's men could spell disaster for us.

We were fortunate though and mid morning of the fourth day we road into Kelton. Kelton was an agricultural kingdom situated at a point nearly central to the other six kingdoms. The city was surrounded by far flung farms and close in it was surrounded by broken and repaired walls. Workmen labored constantly to repair what was cumulative damage from years of defense. Many skirmishes had fallen upon her. Even if the kingdom was not directly at war her people were called upon to defend against two opposing forces on their lands. The city took their damage and the skirmish would move over them. Now the walls had been repaired so many times that they had become weak. Any repairs were temporary so even in peacetime the walls fell to disrepair. A wooden palisade was being erected to surround the fallen wall. The logs were the dense grey timbers of the Iron Wood Trees. The wood was dense, but not impenetrable. The stone surrounded by the wood would make a solid solution to their problem.

Andreas had gone through the town when the troop had gone to Kirsh. He knew his way to Thome Kelt's estate. The palisade here was weathered and older than the one going up around the original outer walls. The gate was open and we were not stopped as we rode in. It was easy to see why once we passed through the palisade. Soldiers filled the yard before the house. They were training and Thome himself was leading the exercises and shouting encouragements.

He saw us and began coming toward us but he did not stop the training or his shouting. When we came together on a path worn in the grass from the gate to the house he called for the men to rest.

"I have been expecting someone to come officially from Frahn. I thought it would be sooner though. We know about Tanath and Elys from your march through here weeks ago."

"Representatives from Calibe and Kirsh went to Nagrom to meet with Frahn. That took time. Can we speak somewhere in private?"

"Of course. Come down from your mounts."

He called across the yard to two young men wrestling on the ground. They brushed themselves off and ran over to take the horses. He called to one of the soldiers to resume the training and led us into the house.

The house was a long log and stone structure with a wide covered porch and great open rooms. He led us to a warm fireside with upholstered chairs situated comfortably around it. A flagon of mead sat open on a low table beside his chair. He took steins from the mantel and poured out three glasses.

"Tell me then, what news?" he said as he sat across from us.

Andreas told him the details of the attack upon the kings as they returned home and of his trip as part of the escort to bring their bodies home. Of course their people were enraged, but Andreas had successfully appealed to them to send representatives to meet with Frahn who had his own pressing matters at home. I told about the two spies, their secret conversation, the subsequent captures of both and what I had read in the communiques found in Tige's foot locker.

"All of this leads us to now." Andreas drew out the leather roll of letters and undid it. He presented Thome Kelt with one. "This is the result of the meeting between Frahn and the men from Calibe and Kirsh."

We waited for Thome Kelt to read the letter. When he looked up Andreas continued with the points that the representatives had declared we tell him. "Kirsh and Calibe are already preparing defenses as we see that you are as well. They asked that we tell you that they are prepared to move against Harald if he moves before the war council can meet. Harald has committed an act of war and they will retaliate. They see the council as a courtesy only, but they are anxious to know your mind in this. We ride to Hoarfrost and Yer. We are to ask all the kings to travel as quickly as they can to Nagrom, or to send a trusted representative. Also they say, and we heartily agree that you trust no one but your closest family and advisors. With Lily Gebha back in play we feel that none of us are truly safe until she is permanently out of the picture."

"Will you go, Sir?" I asked.

"No. I have too much to see to here, but I will send my historian and my son."

"That is good news. Now we will be on our way again and find our way to Hoarfrost. Can you tell us of any incursions by Harald? Is there a good way for us to go that will keep us off the road, but near it in case we need to run from him?"

Thome did give us information on an encampment of Harald's men strategically located at an equal distance between Yer, Hoarfrost, and Kelton. If we travelled east toward Kirsh and kept the foothills there between us and the road and travelled north west through them we would come to Hoarfrost and with luck we would avoid all contact with Harald's camp. He advised us to ask August for a way around on our trip to Yer. No word of any forays by Harald's men on either of those cities, if there were any, had reached him yet.

We thanked him and left. Our horses had been fed and watered and were ready for a run. We knotted the leads of the pack horses around their necks and trusted them to follow. We crossed the road that ran north and south outside of the palisade and we let the horses run. The Iron Woods filled the land North toward Hoarfrost, south to the coast and all the way to the Black Mountains that were the kingdom of Kirsh. The trees grew wide and their needles covered the ground in a soft blanket that muffled our passing. The space between the trees was often wide enough to ride side by side. The pack horses stayed with us passing through the grand forest with ease.

We made the rocky foothills at dusk and nestled into a bowled valley amongst them. We went without a fire again. Thome's report of an encampment kept us wary. We had no way of knowing for sure, but if we were Harald we would be keeping a close eye on Kirsh and Calibe. We tended to the horses, slept a few hours, ate stale bread and fruit, drank water and led the horses through the hills toward Hoarfrost and away from the road that wound up into Kirsh. We kept crossbows ready again and moved as quickly as moving quietly would allow.

On our second day in the foothills we were less than half half way to Hoarfrost. Hiding four horses and the two of us while trying to remain quiet took a great deal of effort and slowed us considerably. We had been successful until the late afternoon of that day. We came around a great shoulder of granite jutting out from an old rock fall and came face to face with three men with longbows drawn and aimed at us.

"Hold! Declare yourselves."

"I am Andy and this is my woman Sade. We are travelling to Hoarfrost."

"Why do you skulk through these hills and not take the road more directly?"

"We had hoped to avoid encounters such as this."

I had been scanning the uniforms of these men and saw nothing that indicated whose men they were. I hoped that so close to Kirsh they would be Elys's men.

"So you are spies then."

"What? No."

"Why do you travel to Hoarfrost?" Each soldier participated in the interrogation as a question came to them. There was no apparent leader. They were equals.

"Why do you need to know?" Andreas shot back.

"You are on royal land."

"I don't give a royal crap!" Andreas shouted. I sighed and put my finger on the trigger of my cross bow. "I am off the road to avoid the troops camped to the west. I had hoped we would be safe in Elys's territory."

At the mention of troops to the west the soldiers attitudes changed. By the looks on their faces this was news to them.

"Will you come with us?" One said.

"Where?"

"We *are* Elys's men. May the Gods rest his soul. I will take you to Kirsh."

"Why?"

"To tell Elys's queen about these troops."

"We have pressing business in Hoarfrost, but for the queen we will comply."

We were led over the foothills and high into the mountains. It was nearly dark when a great iron wood gate opened to us and we passed under a natural bridge between two cliffs.

The city of Elys was situated in and around a box canyon. Caves dotted the cliff sides and were lit up with the fires and torches of those who resided there. Homes and shops dotted the canyon floor and were built of stone and iron wood. At the back of the canyon a stone structure, both natural and man made rose up the side of the cliff. This was the home of Elys. Now ruled by his queen, Andra.

We dismounted and led our horses as we ourselves were led to the entrance of the cliff side castle. A stone wall formed a half circle around the entrance and a gate house pierced the wall near the center. At this point our horses were taken and led to watering troughs outside the wall. The gate was opened by order of our escort and we passed through.

Andreas tried to whisper something to me but the soldier leading us said, "No talking!"

He led us under an entry arch and through a tall iron wood door that was heavy for him to open. A vestibule lined with benches was just inside the door. "Sit," the soldier said and we did. He went out through another tall door and the guard on the other side came in and posted himself as our guard.

Andreas took my hand and leaned in to whisper to me again.

"No talking," The guard said.

"I only wish to comfort my woman."

The soldier looked me up and down. He saw my weapons and armor, "No talking," he repeated.

Our escort returned shortly with an empty chest that he set at our feet and opened. "Put your weapons in here."

We sat and did not move.

"If you wish to see the queen you will do as you are told."

"It was your wish that we see the queen. We wanted to continue on our travels."

"Alright let me put it this way. If you wish to continue on your travels you will put your weapons in the chest."

"Well since you put it so nicely," I said, and began dropping weapons into the chest. I did not relinquish the dagger I always carried in the sash beneath my belt. That is to say I did not relinquish it until Escort patted me down and found it himself. His look was pure contempt. I shrugged and gave him my most innocent look; "Well, I have so many," I said. Andreas gave up all but the dagger in his boot and that they did not find.

"Don't worry, Dear," Andreas said. "We will have them back and be on our way shortly."

Our escort humphed and said, "No talking."

We were lead straight down a hall with many doors. The hall intersected with another hall that was carved from the stone of the mountain. Before us stood two ironwood doors that swung in when pushed by two of the four guards flanking them on either side. Inside was a half round domed room, a natural cavern within the mountain. A stout woman about my height was just moving into the room from a door behind a dais near the straight, far wall. She moved onto the dais and took a seat on the larger of two thrones there.

Our guard had stopped us at the door until the queen took her seat.

"Come," she said in the thick tongue of her people.

We moved forward. The guard bowed and was about to speak his purpose for bringing us when the queen recognized Andreas.

"Andreas! I did not think I would see you again so soon. And who is this? Saeede?"

Andreas nodded.

The guard was baffled.

"Gorm, these people are our friends. Bring their weapons to them."

Gorm bowed again and hurried to the door, but stopped when the queen called to him. "Gorm?" The soldier turned. "Good job." He bowed and backed out of the room.

"Come sit with me here and tell me why you have come. Are my people safe?"

We relayed all that we knew and told her of our mission to deliver the war council letters. "...Frahn bears a great deal of this upon himself." Andreas was saying when Gorm returned with our weaponry and the queen asked him to stay. "Although he pleads for peace he has put support of money and supplies behind you if you call for it. Your own people are bringing the message to you. They should be here on the morrow. They will have the details about that."

"Frahn is not much more than a boy. His father died much too soon. I do not blame him for the murders, only the circumstances that led to it and for that I hope the hell it has created is punishment enough," Andra responded.

"It has been lesson enough, at least for a young, unwise king. I have had opportunity to be of some counsel to Frahn. I can tell you that he feels great remorse," I said.

"And so he should. His act without blessing of council caused the deaths of two kings. Now council is called to wage war."

"Frahn had conversations with all of the kings about the matter of treaty. They were all indifferent to him. He had no blessing, which is true. But there was no damnation either. His heart wants peace and prosperity for Ahnges."

"A good king leads with heart, but that must be weighed with intelligence and wisdom."

"That is so true, Lady Andra. Frahn knew that, but he had not the experience to gain the type of intelligence and wisdom a king needs. His hope was to find it with the other kings and they did not care enough to turn their minds to the fancies of a fledgling king. Frahn

207

seeks unity. That flew in the face of an old but comfortable autonomy."

"Andreas told me you could be very direct in the right surroundings. I am glad that you are comfortable here, but I caution you to watch your tongue. Elys was a kind and good king. Our people have survived much under him."

"I know that. But I have seen now how each kingdom merely survives, scratching out an existence. Why do you not trade openly as friends rather than fight and smuggle over needed goods?"

"It has always been the way," those words came from Andra rather sadly.

"It is that way Frahn wanted to change. With reluctance from his fellow kings here he sought elsewhere to show an example of what could be done. Harald knew it and saw it as a threat, and a way to undo Frahn and gain power for himself. So, he had the effort sabotaged with Esporanza's death."

Andreas joined, "It now seems that Harald seeks to control all of Ahnges, by discrediting Frahn and usurping the power of the dead kings. You already blame Frahn for your husbands demise."

"Only the circumstances that he created that led to it, as I've said."

"Even after what Saeede has just told you?"

"I can see that he may have had good intentions."

"What then of Harald. What if he came seeking retaliation on Frahn? Would you give the man that ordered your husband's death allegiance against a man who sought your husband's friendship?"

Queen Andra was quiet. Her eyes met ours and she studied us as she considered Andreas's questions.

When at last she spoke there was a tremble in her voice. "I see now that my anger has been prejudiced. Much of my perception of Frahn comes from what Elys has told me. He saw him as no more than a social climber. A boy trying to impress his elders with new untried ideas. Elys was a good king, but he did not always see the good in people either," she swallowed hard, and when she continued the tremble was gone. "To answer your questions, I am glad that you came to me before Harald. I might have been blinded by my contempt for Frahn had he come. I could have let Harald deal with Frahn and then I could deal with Harald on my own terms. Now I must consider well all that you have told me about this fledgling. I will weigh it against what my envoy tells me on their return. I may attend this council myself."

"That is good news! We will feel better about our own mission with your goodwill behind us."

"Well then, you will stay here safe and warm until morning to sample our goodwill. We can have you out again as early as you like. You can go your own way by stealth on a more direct route or I can give you escort to Hoarfrost indirectly by our ways through the mountains. You should arrive in about the same time either way."

"We would be very appreciative of the escort. They must be only your most trusted guides though. We had hoped to avoid being seen at all except by those we were to contact."

"Oh I see. Gorm is one of my most trusted. This task will fall to you alone, Gorm.

"I see this will not allow me to entertain you as I would like, but I will have you to dinner in my apartment. I would like very much to know the woman who has captured the heart of this noble man."

I think I actually blushed.

"Gorm will you see to that, and join us?"

"As you wish Lady Andra."

Gorm left and Andra took us to her apartment.

Her apartment was modestly, yet comfortably furnished. She removed the robe that was her queenly mantel and we saw that she was stout only because she wore studded leather armor and carried a mace tucked into the belt at her back. She placed the mace beside her chair and went to a side cabinet. She pulled out a silver tray. Upon the tray were a crystal flagon and several crystal glasses. She poured a dark red wine for each of us and sat. We sat then and she graciously asked about me.

"Saeede, I only got to know Andreas a little bit, but that bit was mostly about you. After the initial shock of my husband's murder Andreas came to me to check on my well being. I asked him then if he had ever been in love. *'Only once'*, he said. Then he spoke about you so fondly that I hoped I would meet you someday. It did not seem to be likely at the time."

I did not respond directly to Andra, "Only once?" I said and looked at Andreas.

"Other women were only a dalliance until you came around."

I kept my head down until my face cooled and then I looked to the queen. Why did I keep going red in the face? That was not like me.

"Where do I begin?"

"Where ever you like, dear."

I took a sip of the thick fruity wine and thought. "Did he tell you how we met?"

"A little, but he told me more about how you struggled with your feelings about being abandoned by your father and the loss of your good mother."

I trusted he had not told her my father's true nature. "Yes, those things made me reluctant to share my feelings with anyone, but Andreas became a trusted friend. He probably knows me better than anyone. He never really shared either though, just innuendos here and there." To Andreas I said, "You couldn't just go with how we met?"

"It was weighing on me," he shrugged.

I turned back to Andra. "We first met in a small hamlet. I was playing my mandolin on a low wall near a pub at the edge of a market square. I had arranged my simple instruments along the wall with my tip hat at the far end. I remember that I began to play a lament on mandolin. That is when Andreas strolled into the market with his carpetbag in hand and stood a moment to listen. He watched me, and I him, and we exchanged smiles. He sat on the ground right there across the square from me and pulled his elegant harp out of the carpetbag and joined me. His harp is a master crafted piece. A carved lion rests atop the pillar. I knew then that he must be wealthy and still I knew from the way he played that I would like him. I know it is odd to say that we made beautiful music together, but we did. I fell in love with him first for that, no first his beauty, then that. My hat was full by the nights end, and he would not take a copper for himself. So I bought him dinner and we exchanged histories and stories of our adventures. I fell in love with him several times during those tellings. I often wondered if he felt the same. I was enthralled."

"You never told me that," Andreas said.

"I didn't want to ruin a friendship or our working relationship. We had a good thing going."

"So what changed your mind?" Andra asked.

"Well, that remains a mystery still," I teased.

We spent a restful evening over dinner and found that Gorm was actually Andra's nephew on Elys's side of the family. He was very serious and didn't seem to get any of our humor. He laughed when we all did, but it never seemed spontaneous. It bothered me, but he was young and awkward so I discounted it. He was genuinely affectionate to Andra so my suspicions of him were quieted.

Gorm requested that we play for her. "It would do her well to have some beauty in her life right now," he said. Our things had been brought to a room for us and Gorm went to retrieve the carpetbag.

We played several light songs, but the hour was getting late and we wanted an early start. We said our thanks and goodnights. Gorm agreed to wake us at the fourth hour and we all retired to our beds.

Gorm was good to his word and came to our door at the fourth hour with a breakfast tray for us. He did not stay and went to see to the horses while we ate and dressed.

We went down to the main hall to look for Andra but she was still in bed. Gorm met us at the gate with our four horses and mounted on his own. We mounted up and he led us out the way we had come in the day before. Once through the gate our route quickly changed and he took us up a rough path that led higher into the mountains and further east before turning north again.

Gorm was an excellent guide but a lousy conversationalist. We spent most of the next three days in silence. He only spoke when spoken to or if he needed to point out the path or an obstacle. Meals were quiet and awkward, but we bedded down early so it wasn't for long.

On the third day we came to a valley head. Below us a glacier melted into a lake. From that lake a stream flowed. The stream fell over a fall in the distance splashing over eroded boulders, deposited by the glacier, on its way to be coming a river. The river meandered through a sloping plain of sparse trees and snow covered grassland and emptied into the North Sea. On a high bank of the river and a cliff above the sea, near the river delta was Hoarfrost.

Gorm pointed out a thin path along the low side of a mountain spur that ran along the glacier side. We would not be seen approaching the city until we came out of the thinning woods above the floodplain of the river. From there we could run the horses. If anyone intended us harm from there we would soon be in the protection of Hoarfrost's walls.

Gorm would not take us any further. We thanked him and he wished us well. We watched him ride back up the trail and out of sight before leading our horses along the valley head to the trail he had indicated. The temperature dropped as we moved closer to the rough, churning sea of the north. The seasons were changing toward autumn to the south, but here it was coming on winter.

The place was locked up tight, but our letter of introduction presented at the gate opened the city to us. As soon as we passed through the barbican the portcullis dropped behind us. Our weapons were not stripped at the gate and our horses were courteously taken from us and lead away to nearby stalls. We were taken directly to the king's villa. We entered the rotunda and stood with two sentries while another went to take our letter to August.

We waited a long time and I began to worry that they had not trusted the letter and were preparing a prison for us. Our fears were unwarranted though and a young woman came to greet us.

"Welcome, Andreas and Saeede. My apologies for the wait. I am Yolan. My father and mother await you." She bowed and swept her arm aside to motion us to join her.

We did and she led us along the main hall to a short flight of stairs up. The landing opened into a lounge and there sat August, propped up on a couch and his wife beside him in a dainty little chair.

August recognized us immediately. "Oh good, good. It is you. I worried about a letter coming so soon from Nagrom. I hoped it was not a forgery from Harald. Some way to sic his assassins on us."

"We understand," I said. "Are you well, August? You look grey?"

"I am recovering. We were attacked on the road during our return trip by bandits. It was obvious their intent, they sought to capture and perhaps ransom me and my boy. They had my son and I marked from the very beginning. We battled them back and lost most of my

213

entourage before we fled. My son took a deadly blow but we got him back here before he died. I lost my son because he battled to save me." The words caught in August's throat and his wife could not stop a whimper. He took her hand but she excused herself and left the room through a side door followed by her daughter.

"I am sorry for that. Hearten was a noble lad. He loved us all deeply and we him. The sorrow is so fresh."

"You need not apologize for that, Sir. We are aggrieved with you."

"They are a well organized band of bandits."

"Those were no bandits, Sir. That is why we have come; to relay news that has bearing on that."

We again relayed our experiences since the council of kings. When we told him of the button found at the massacre of Tanath and Elys he could not confirm that the bandits that attacked him had any mark of Harald's, but when we finished our story he was convinced of Harald's deceptions.

"Frahn was a fool to entertain that treaty without support of the council. If he had the support, Harald would not be undermining him now. The knowledge that he had the kings' support would have stayed him."

"You may be right, Sir, but the facts are that he is acting against all of you now. He will certainly continue. My personal believe is that he seeks to be the high king at least if not the only king of Ahnges," I said

"We have a document penned by Frahn, but dictated by envoys of Elys's and Tanath. It is a call to war council." Andreas pulled the rolled satchel from within his shirt and produced the document.

August sighed and leaned forward to take the document. He read it, rolled it up, and tucked it into his own shirt. "I will be there," he said and fell back against his pillows.

"Are you well enough? Perhaps you should see to things here and send a trusted fellow."

"I would have sent my son. I will not send my wife or daughter out with this madman on the loose. If I had an army strong enough I would go after him myself. His guerilla tactics took some of my best men. I will go to the council myself to hear what is said. I cannot spare men here if he moves against us. I will go alone. When do you head back? You have some fame even in this backland. Will you escort me?"

This was not anything we planned on. We looked to each other for some hint of reaction. We knew each other well enough to know that this was not anything we wanted or felt prepared to do.

Andreas began to speak without taking his eyes from mine. "We still have to travel to Yer and deliver this news to Narhan. Lord August, from what we have learned of these attacks I doubt that even our experience would serve to save you if we were set upon. You are a king. You deserve better than what we can offer." I nodded my agreement.

We turned to hear August's response.

"No. I want you. I have felt since we met that you are more than you seem. Frahn maybe an untried king, but he is of good heart. And these men from Kirsh and Calibe have trust in you as well. Three can move more quickly than a troop. We will look like vagabonds. They will not suspect us even if they see me. I will change my appearance. No, I want you. My army could not protect me. Perhaps secrecy will be a better way."

"It is ill advised, Sir," I said.

"If we fail to protect you?" Andreas asked.

"I will tell my good wife that I accept full responsibility. If you fail then Hoarfrost will be led by a good queen."

215

Andreas and I looked to each other, resigned and speechless. We just wanted to go home.

"I suppose he lends credence to our visit with Narhan," Andreas said.

"You must take orders from us, Sir. You must agree to that at least, for your own protection, of course." I said.

"Of course, I will."

"We had planned to leave in the morning. Will you be able? We really should not delay."

"Will you allow me a small cart? I don't know that I could sit a horse for an entire day. I am sure we will be pushing on hard."

I sighed. Andreas sighed. We could not hide our regret, but if it was to be, a cart would probably be better for him.

"As long as it is a small cart pulled by a fast horse," Andreas said.

"Excellent, excellent." He pulled himself up from the couch and took a cane from underneath it. "Follow me. If you are there when I tell the queen, she will not beat me to a pulp." He laughed. He actually seemed excited about the trip. We were grim about it.

The queen and daughter did not take the news well. The daughter rushed from the room and slammed the door behind her. We stood awkwardly for some long minutes just inside the door to the queen's private rooms. She was still tender from the loss of her son and now her husband the King was going off on an ill-advised journey to leave her to see to the defenses. She cried and protested at him and raged at us for allowing it. Then she raged at him and cried and protested to us. The woman seemed in no way capable of standing up to the stress of running a kingdom in the face of a possible war.

When it was certain that August would not yield to her pleas she stood up from the bed where she had thrown herself in exhaustion. "What would you have me do then in your absence?"

"For now I would have you get a hold of yourself. I will be making other arrangements. Kier will be in charge of the guards and the soldiers. He will advise you of that. Make no negotiations with anyone while we face this war. Other than that run the house as you always do. The business of the people will call on your sense of fairness. Use it well and you will be fine. I will have Kier report to you each evening. Do not be afraid to ask if you have questions. You are the queen. You have the right to know. If you have suggestions, make them. Kier is a fair and intelligent man. He will help you to understand it all.

"We gave the name Hearten to our son to give him traits to embody. I ask you now to hearten yourself in his memory and for my sake. You are a good and strong woman. Be my good and strong queen."

"Oh, August, please forgive me. If I was not so torn apart by this great loss. Oh Hearten."

"I know my, love. Of course I forgive you. Forgive me for leaving you so soon."

"I do of course."

"We will talk more tonight. Now I must go and make arrangements. Please see to our guests?"

"Yes, she said." He kissed her forehead and lingered there as she caught her breath. "I'm fine now." He kissed her then on the lips and went out through the door by which his daughter had fled.

"I am so sorry, good people. That was not me, not usually."

"These are difficult times for everyone," I said. "I am sorry that August brought us to you with his news when you have so much to worry you already."

"You will keep my display to yourselves," she said in a commanding tone.

"Absolutely," I said.

"Goes without saying," Andreas added.

"Good, then let me show you what Queen Tovah is really like."

She led us from the room. Her bearing was regal, but as she ordered her household to their extra tasks for our stay she was kind and they in turn were eager to please her. That she was so loved and lovely eased my concern for her ability to govern.

She ate with us in the kitchen and then escorted us to our rooms. All of our necessary gear had been brought in. "It will be a chill night," she said, and lit the firewood that was laid in the hearth. "I will see that you have more wood and some brandy. Is there anything else I can do for you?"

Andreas and I looked to each other but neither of us was in need of more. "No, Lady," Andreas said. "Will you be there in the morning to see us off?"

"Of course I will."

"Then we will see you then."

"Goodnight," she said, and left the room.

A short time later a girl arrived with brandy followed by a boy with a pail full of wood.

We were tired, but the day had presented a new worry. We discussed it at some length, but there was no real strategy for such things. We would have to be even more cautious. The country could not afford the death of another king.

Andreas fell to sleep quickly, but I could not. I felt chilled. A panic that my malady had returned gripped me, but I was quickly rational and rose to add a log to the fire. The chill still did not leave me. This gave me a dark mood and sleep eluded me for most of the night.

I felt Andreas rise in the morning and the sun shone across our bed. I pulled the furs over my head and grasped at broken sleep while

Andreas washed and dressed. He came to the bedside then and tugged gently at the covers.

"Rise and shine, Wonderful."

"Ugh."

"Come now, the sun is already risen and we have a king to protect."

"Ugh."

I knew I had to get moving but the chill was still in me. "Warm clothes," I ordered. Andreas was nice enough to comply and he soon had my clothes laid out upon the bed. I pulled them in under the covers and did not come out until I was fully dressed.

We gathered our things and carried them through the rotunda hall in search of the royal family. A young squire who had come in search of us took us to the main hall where the royal family sat already eating the morning meal. We sat and ate breakfast with them.

August was much changed. His white hair and beard had been dyed a rusty brown and his clothes were those of a tinker. He informed us of his new identity, Joestine. He had arranged for tools of the trade of a tinker and household utensils to be loaded into his small cart.

"So if we are stopped I can prove I am a tinker. I actually do have some skill at it. I do have a house to run as well as a kingdom you know."

"That is very well, Sir. How will we explain that you are escorted by two minstrel's?"

"Well I thought that would be for you to decide. To find a tale you are comfortable with."

"That should be easy enough but sometimes the circumstances decide the story. For now, remember that you will always be tinker Joestine from Hoarfrost, even in our story, should we need one."

We finished our meal and said our goodbyes to the queen and princess. They made us promise to take care of August several times. "We will do our best," was our answer every time.

Outside our horses waited and we loaded them ourselves. August's—Joestein's cart was a two wheeled make with a small leather seat above a storage box and a small tailgate behind that was covered with oil cloth. August said his farewell to his family and led the way out of his city. His cargo jangled as we went. That was unacceptable. We stopped at the gates and transferred some of our gear to the wagon and packed his things in tight.

Staying off the road offered us no advantage. The forest was thin and the coast gave us little protection, and August's cart was off kilter off the road. I tied my horse and one of the pack horses to August's cart and ran up ahead on foot to act as scout. At mid-day I waited for them to catch up. I had seen no one and Andreas who was watching the rear reported the same. We made lunch of cold ham and cheese sandwiches along the side of the road, but ate as we traveled.

The chill stayed in me even as the sun rose and warmed the day enough that Andreas and August shed their heavy travel cloaks. I did not. Andreas inquired about that. "Just a chill," I said.

"A chill, or the chill?" he asked.

I feared the latter but could not yet be certain. My response was a non-committal shrug.

That night moved slowly into the thin woods and pulled far off the road to camp along the coast. We decided against a fire. The light could call our position to the enemy somewhere in the woods to our south. I curled up close to Andreas for the warmth of his body. Perhaps it was that my body responded more acutely to cold climates since the chill had taken me. He wrapped himself tight around me and we breathed under our blankets to create warmth. He slept at last, but I was miserable. The morning came and I labored through it. My lack of sleep kept me from functioning at a high level. When it was time to leave our camp Andreas took the scout position. I tied my horse to the cart and August was in charge of sighting our rear.

I dosed off and on in the saddle. When I woke again we were moving through a dense thicket of Cypress. We were on the coast side of the road but I could not see the road. The trees had thickened much there. Those trees that were closest to the water were irregular and flat-topped from the constant battering of the strong salty winds. The trees further inland suffered the deformity less and less. The foliage overlapped our surroundings with dense sprays of bright green. Andreas found us a good spot to rest. At this point we could risk a fire.

We made a small cook fire from the fallen limbs in the area. It was fast, hot burning, and sparky firewood, but we made a quick stew and a hot brew of Nagrom's kaffee. Andreas gave me some time to warm by the fire, but when it died down we buried it and went on our way.

We stayed within the dense trees for the rest of our trip as the road curved away from the rough coast giving us a wider breadth of land to navigate. The way was slow going to accommodate August's wagon, but we were well hidden from the road.

I slept that night with my face to a well banked bed of coals. I laid my back close to Andreas's warmth and at my head was a pile of logs that I could feed the fire with throughout the night. August pitched a tent across from us with the flap open to the fires warmth. August and Andreas slept well. I slept in snatches between bouts of chill as the fire grew cold and times of not so chill after I fed the flames from the pile of logs.

The next day I functioned fairly well and took up my task of scouting ahead. I battled the chill, but my time honed skill of repressing it had me feeling rather well. The day went well but we were approached during our afternoon rest. The men were skilled at moving through the woods and we were surrounded before we knew it.

They emerged from the woods in near silence. Only the slightest sound called our attention away from our tasks and then it was too late. They did not appear to be bandits or brigands as the attackers of the kings had been described. These men were liveried soldiers. We scanned them for Harald's mark but saw none.

They wore heavy coats of dyed red wool that came to their knees. The coats were lined with white fur that spilled out and folded back at collar and cuffs and accented the trim of the bottom hem and shoulder cowl. Chain mail hoods covered their heads and they pulled yellow fur lined caps down over the hoods to cover their ears and foreheads. Thick pants bloused out between the bottom of their coats and their fur lined knee high boots of grey leather. Gloves of the same material as their boots covered their hands. Their hands gripped great curved swords and battle axes. Bows were slung at their backs and large quivers hung on their belts.

As we sized them up they sized us. No words were spoken for a long tense time. Finally one man from our flank moved forward and we turned with our hands upon our weapons. August who was nearest me put a hand upon my arm and whispered, "These are Narhan's men."

"Hold strangers. There is no need to fear us if you are law abiding."

"Who are you?" Andreas demanded.

"We are men of Yer. We patrol this area to keep it safe for travelers."

"Well then well met," Andreas said. "We are on our way to Yer. We have only stopped for a mid-day meal. Will you warm yourselves at our fire?"

"Why do you stay so far from the road?"

"We have heard tell of bandits. We are no match for a band of thugs."

"What is your business in Yer?" The man was moving closer and eyeing August's cart and the horses. "You do not travel light. Are you on an expedition?"

The line of questioning was that which we feared.

"Expedition? No," Andreas gave a laugh. "We are just met, really. My wife and I are musicians. We travel about looking for a place to call home. Joestein is a tinker from Hoarfrost who we met upon the road. We performed for King August and Queen Tovah just the other night. We are making our way back around to the south. These northlands are too severe for my woman, though I find them rather refreshing."

"There are more direct ways south from Hoarfrost."

"Yes but we have played them only recently. We have found that fresh audiences give more coin. If we play again too soon they don't feel as obligated to throw into the hat."

"And what about you tinker? What brings you out? You are too late for the trade season."

Andreas and I held our breath waiting for August's story. He stammered a bit, but recovered and said, "Is it illegal for a man to travel these days? If you must know, though I don't see it is any of your business or concern; my wife threw me out. I guess I had it coming, too much drinkin' and carousin'. My work suffered from it and we had only her small income from the making of candles to support us. She only makes enough for one and I drank a part of that too, so she had enough of me. I have brought my small shop with me. I hope to find work in Yer."

It was a good story and Andreas and I breathed easier. The soldier looked around at us once more. "Why do musicians need such weaponry?" He asked nodding his head toward Andreas and me.

"We are not new to the life of travelers, sir . We have accumulated weapons over time from necessity, for our own protection, that is all."

The soldier scanned the circle of his men and nodded. My hand flinched upon my weapon, but the men took two giant steps backwards and were lost to the woods again.

"I will let the authorities at Yer know you are coming."

"Thank you," Andreas said.

The soldier nodded then he took one last look around the camp before turning and running into the woods. We heard them move away but the sound was like that of a wind moving across the tree tops.

August wanted to talk about what had just happened but we silenced him with a finger to our lips.

"They seemed very nice," I said. "So nice of him to let someone know we are coming."

"Yes. I wonder; do you think that we are close enough now, that with these able men guarding the way we could travel upon the road? We would make better time. Perhaps we could make Yer by nightfall," Andreas said.

We were speaking for the benefit of any soldier who may have been left behind to scrutinize us.

"I would be for that; a warm bed," I said. "Perhaps a kind inn keeper would let us sit by a warm fire and put out our hat while we play for their guests."

"Perhaps tomorrow night. Tonight I will be happy just to have a warm bed."

"Do you think I could buy a coat like they have?"

"We'll see," Andreas said. Then to August he said; "What do you think, Joestein? Would you like to risk the road with us, or will you stay amongst the trees?"

August rubbed his chin, not fully understanding why we would ask that. Our plan had been to stay to the trees all the way to Yer.

"Do you really think it will be safe?"

"I trust those men are not bandits. They wore like garb, they looked like soldiers, they moved well through the woods and that would take some training. Yes, I trust they are not bandits, but if you feel safer in the woods then we will stay with you."

August was confused and replied, "I will throw in with whatever you decide."

"Good then, we will risk the road and ride as fast as your cart will allow and hope that those soldiers are as good at guarding the road as we think," Andreas declared.

"I have made some broth from the ham bone. Let's drink this and have a bit of kaffee and be on the road. I long for a warm place," I said.

We had our lunch and buried the fire. The road was several miles through the trees, but the trees thinned as we moved south toward it. We saw no sign of the soldiers and when we got to the road we urged the horses to a gallop. August and his cart kept pace with us well.

Yer was in view for a long distance as the road sloped gradually down toward the western coast upon which it was situated. The city was inside a wall roughly round in its configuration. A central tower was the Narhan residence and the city buildings spiraled around that. Only one gatehouse allowed access into the city wall, but it was a series of three gates. Each gate was manned by four soldiers in similar garb as those we had encountered in the woods. We were questioned briefly at each gate in such a manner that it was easy to believe the woodland soldier had announced our coming. He must have had a swift horse somewhere. There was no way he could have beaten us on foot.

We were allowed to move into the city and went directly to a stable to see to the horses. From there we went to the tower in the center of the city. Whatever Narhan's soldiers thought of that did not matter now. We produced a letter of introduction and August announced himself. The tower soldier needed a bit of convincing about that but in the end a messenger was dispatched to announce us. We waited a long time to be received. It was odd for a king to leave another king and still another king's messengers waiting, even more oddly, he kept us waiting outside in the cold. That damn cold. It seeped into my vulnerable bones like a plague.

When at last we were invited in we were asked to wait in a small antechamber. There were only hard wood stools and no hearth to warm the place. We waited again. When finally Narhan came to us he was impatient.

"What news? I have much to attend to in these times of strife between the kingdoms. What brings you here and with August in tow?"

August was insulted by Narhan's tone. "Don't speak of me as if I am someone's burden, Narhan. I have come as an ally and to lend credence to the news that these two have travelled far to deliver."

"Calm yourself, August I will hear them."

This did not seem like the Narhan we had met in Nagrom during the Council of Kings. He was self-serving yes, but he had not been patronizing before this. His etiquette toward August was inappropriate to say the least.

We told our story as we had related it to August and Thome Kelt. He listened and did not interject at all during the telling. August told of his encounter with bandits that we believed were Harald's men in disguise. When Andreas delivered the war council letter he scanned it then tossed it on a side table. He looked at each of us but said nothing for a long moment.

When he finally spoke his face was tight and his words clearly enunciated. "Tell Frahn I will not attend. I have my own intelligence and I am well aware of Harald's movements. I will move my troops as I see fit. Do as you will August, as you always have. I will see to my interests here. There is a matter of trust among the kings now. I will trust myself and see what transpires."

August stood as if to confront Narhan. He opened his mouth to speak twice. Both times Narhan tilted his head as if to listen, but the contemptuous look on Narhan's face stayed his words both times. August turned to leave and hastened out of the room. We stood to follow.

"Don't expect to sample my hospitality this day. There is no room for you here as you have come unannounced."

"We would not think of staying," we said together.

"Good then I have business that needs my attention," he said, and pushed passed us to leave the room.

Andreas and I looked to each other for some feeling on Narhan's mood, but saw nothing but bewilderment in the other's eyes.

We left the room and caught up with August at the front door. Two soldiers flanked him. Two more had come up behind us to be sure we left the tower. No one spoke until we were away from the tower and out of earshot of any guards there.

"What was that?" Andreas asked of no one in particular.

"I don't know," August said. "Narhan has always looked at himself as a sovereign king in this realm. To trust no one now may have some merit. Our timeworn history is not one of dependence. He is closest in proximity to Harald, perhaps he feels that being so close the best defense is a good offense. He has a good army and strong walls. He could probably outlast Harald. Still if he needs help and has isolated himself away from the rest of us…" August let the thought trail off. "It makes no sense to me. He has been reasonable in time past. Our lands have not warred upon each other for two generations now. Our resources are so similar we have no need of what the other has. We do well without their Paradise Seed in our markets and they don't need for our Ecauldron. Neither he or Harald make any sense to me right now."

"I don't feel good about this," I said, "He acts like a man with his back to the wall. You don't think Harald could have gotten to him do you? He did chastise Frahn for moving ahead with the treaty plans even after it seemed he gave his blessing."

Andreas said. "I don't know. I no longer feel safe in his city after that cold reception, especially after what you have just suggested, but I don't like our odds outside at night so close to his realm. We should share a room at an inn near the gate. We will set guards tonight and be gone early in the morning."

"I agree, but I am not leaving here without one of those fur lined coats." I pointed to a shop across the road. In the window was a beautiful coat in a similar style as those worn by Narhan's soldiers, but this one was not dyed. The color came from the intricate embroidery that embellished every panel of hide.

We crossed the street together and did not leave the shop until we had each made a purchase of a fine warm coat. August purchased two, one each for his wife and daughter. The coat he wore suited him just fine he said and so he only purchased the two. The shop keeper was very friendly and directed us to an inn not far from the stable where the gate guard had taken our horses.

At the inn we arranged our rooms. Andreas being thoughtful of my cold directed me to see to the rooms and see a fire was started. August went with him to tote our needed bags from the stable and check on the horses. The stable was privately owned though so our fears of losing them to Narhan's mysterious ways were alleviated. When they returned I was snuggled into my coat with my feet up upon the hearth and my body slumped into a large upholstered chair.

"Are you unwell?" August asked.

"I fear I have taken a chill, Sir. A good night of rest and a hot meal should fix me up."

"I will order dinner sent to our rooms," Andreas said. "You can stay by the fire all the night if you need to. August and I have agreed to split the watch. " He looked at me inquiringly as he spoke.

I had no answer for him. The chill did seem as if it had returned. I had not felt it that deeply for nearly a year. It remained to be seen if I was just susceptible to the climate or if my brief reprieve had just been a fluke. I was more anxious than ever to be home to the more temperate climate of Mareese just to find that out.

Andreas ordered a feast of fine hot soups and stews, with freshly baked bread and hot tea and cider. We ate all of what was enough for six people. August pulled brandy from his luggage and poured it into our empty tea cups. The warmth of that inside me and the warmth around me allowed me to slip off to sleep.

I did stay all the night in that chair. Andreas covered me with extra blankets and I slept well for the first time since leaving Nagrom. He woke me before the first sun rose. August was already awake and dressed. He wore a three quarter of plate armor, leaving the lower legs unprotected. Andreas and I suited likewise in our own armor as we had since leaving Nagrom. We ate breakfast from our packs until we were well satisfied. Since we had paid the innkeeper in advance we left our key in the room and went out into the street. Our new coats covered our armor well.

The streets were empty, but at the stable a lantern was lit and our horses were nearly ready when we arrived. Andreas had paid for the early time and he must have paid well because the stable master and his boy were eager to get us out on time. I helped August load his gear under his seat while Andreas helped load the horses. Together we checked the saddles and harnesses.

"Have safe travels. Not many people are as hearty as you to travel at this time of year."

"Thank you, sir. We head south where it is warmer." Andreas spoke for us.

"Well, good speed then. Be well."

"And you."

The gate was still closed, but the men on shift were still those from the night before. "Change of plans?"

"Yes," Andreas lied. "Truth be told, we just don't like it here. No offense. My wife complains constantly of the cold and Joestein there, well he has grown fond of us and dislikes the cold almost as much as she does. I am indifferent, but two complaining is more than I can take."

The gatekeeper laughed and called ahead to the other gates; "Let them through."

"Thank you, sir. Have a good day," Andreas said cheerfully.

"And you."

We took the Breen Road south out of Yer only for as long as we were in sight of Yer then we crossed into the woods and swept slowly south east. It was a great risk knowing what Thome Kelt had told us about an encampment of Harald's men. Our plan was to split the distance between the road to Breen and the approximate location of the camp until we were south of it and could turn east. We would travel southeast as close as we dared to the road that connected Breen and Kelton. We would cross somewhere in the middle and then head due south. When we found the road that connected Nagrom and Calibe we would cross it and return along the beach strand we had taken when leaving Nagrom.

That was the plan. I was ahead scouting in the first hours after turning off the Breen Road when I came upon a camp of men. They were much further west than we had estimated. They were not Narhan's liveried soldiers. They did not appear to be soldiers at all, but they were well armed and two wagons held enough supplies to keep them for several weeks. I ran back to Andreas and August and we turned south again to give a wide berth for a few miles before turning east again into denser woods.

We pushed on, forgoing a scout in favor of speed. We rode on all day and through the night until we made the Breen to Kelton road. We made it safely across a clear road in search of a place to rest awhile before pushing on south. Our search never began in earnest. We were set upon by a band of twelve almost as soon as we crossed. They targeted August from the trees with their arrows. I jumped from my horse and ran to him as Andreas spun his around and appeared to flee the area.

When the arrows failed to penetrate their mark. Twelve came at us from all sides. They appeared to be bandits, but we knew better. We were surrounded. I stood back to back with August in the front of his cart. The bandits could not come at us all at once this way and we had the advantage of height. We each did battle with two while three moved to release the horse. Two more scrambled over the loose cargo in the tailgate. Their footing was unsure and we paid them no immediate attention. No others could reach us yet.

A blast of heat came at us from the side of the tailgate and the two who had been climbing there fell off in flames. The nervous stamping of the horse made fighting from the cart difficult as the bandits moved in on him. I dispatched the two I was engaged with and jumped down on the two who moved to take their places. They fell to the ground and we wrestled until Andreas sent in another ball of fire. They leapt from me to roll out the flames. I rolled away from them to escape and to extinguish those flames that had caught on the fur of my coat.

"Little close," I yelled.

I got no response from Andreas and did not expect one. He was moving about in the cover of the woods to make himself a difficult target. Away from the cart I now had more range of motion and drew my second sword. I ran screaming into the three that sought to cut August's horse loose from the cart. They attacked with gusto and I soon regretted my actions. August was involved with three bandits now and had slain one of his first two. One of the two that had retreated in flames was moving in to take August from behind. The remaining three were coming to join me. I saw the one moving to August step up on the cart and called a warning just as the man was launched off the cart and slammed into a tree by some invisible force controlled by Andreas. The three that had been moving to me altered their plan and turned their backs to my fight to spread out in search of Andreas. I took as many blows as I delivered, from the three I was facing, but at three to one I wasn't doing too badly. One soldier bandit began to swoon from lose of blood and I kicked him away. The other two came at me with renewed strength. I fought on, but I was tiring. I looked to August who was still on his feet and doing well against one last attacker. I could not spare a look around for Andreas and did not see him or the other three bandits again.

August came to my aid and together we slew the last of them.

"Tend your wounds and see to the horses," I said, as I plunged into the woods where I had last glimpsed Andreas. There was no sound of battle but I heard the sound of horses moving away toward the road that was now just to our north.

I stopped. "Andy!" I heard no return call. My heart skipped as I thought that they might be riding away with him; captured. "Andy!" I yelled again with every ounce of my strength. Again no response, but

I reeled around at the sound of motion through the woods. I t was him staggering toward me. An arrow stuck deep in his throat. I ran and caught him as he fell.

"August! Bring Andreas's horse!"

August was quick to respond. I found the medical kit quickly and rolled it open beside Andreas. "Do I extract it?" I asked Andreas.

His eyes went big and he turned his head slowly to indicate no.

"Can I break it off and then stabilize it?"

Slow nodding yes.

"Wait. I have a tool. It will be less pressure." August ran off and I heard him rattle through the cargo in the back of the cart. He rode the cart back to us.

He threw me a nipper and it cut the arrow with a quick snap.

"Should I use unguent?"

Slow nodding no.

I wrapped strips of muslin around the shaft and his neck in a cross hatching pattern. "There are no bubbles in the blood. They didn't hit your windpipe." His expression relaxed a bit but every swallow brought him great pain. "You need a skilled physician. Without your instructions I could not do it; even with them I doubt I could. The arrow is deep."

"Help me lift him," I said, and August lifted his feet while I lifted him under his arms. "We'll put him in the cart."

I went up first with Andreas in my arms. I kicked pots and kitchen utensils out of the cart as I pulled Andreas in. "Get our bed rolls." August went off and I threw the rest of the cargo, except our packs and the tools, from the cart. August brought the horses to us and then unlashed our bed rolls and tossed them to me. I covered Andreas who was going into shock with all of our blankets and surrounded him with as many bundles as I could to minimize his motion during travel. I placed the carpet bag in his lap and wrapped his hands around the handle. I leaned in and kissed him. "I will bring your unguents. We will get you safely home. I promise you." He nodded.

I told August; "Take it easy to the road. Head southeast until you find it. When you do take the road and fly. We are closer to Calibe than Nagrom right now so go there. Stop for nothing until you are safely there. When we get to Calibe you are Joestein the tinker until we know it is safe to reveal you. I will gather up our things here and be right behind you." I did not have to tell him twice.

I grabbed up our discarded gear and repacked the important things, taking special care with Andreas's med kit. The unguents were an old tried and true recipe of Andreas's mixed by Mam. They would speed his healing after an experienced physician removed the shaft and head.

Anything we did not need for survival I did not care about. I was in a hurry.

With the packs resituated and secured I took time to search the dead. I hoped for another identifier, a button, or signet with Harald's mark upon it. What I found was even better; a note on a goatskin parchment. *August is on the roads. Secure all roads that lead to Hoarfrost and Nagrom.* T here was no signature or seal. I took it and placed it securely against my breast.

I gathered the horses to me and knotted the long leads of the pack horses to the packs and knotted the reins of Andreas's mount to the saddle. I led them all out carefully through the woods while watching for an attack. When I made it to the road unscathed I mounted my horse quickly and herded the others before me. I rode hard, constantly watching the side of the road for signs of ambush and ahead to find Andreas and August. The horses ran together filling the width of the road.

The chill was in me as it had been for several days now, but it increased suddenly and I felt my strength sapped from me. I urged the horses for more speed, but they were giving me all they had. We crested a hill and on the road below us I saw August and his cart in the valley charging onward toward the next rise. I would catch them on that rise.

Suddenly arrows flew from the trees flanking them. August snapped the reins and the horse lunged, but he too was giving all he had. Six horse men crashed through the woods and ran beside them, three on each side. Two sought to wrestle the reins from August. Two swung at him with swords and two swung at Andreas who had only the carpet bag to defend with.

I had not been seen yet, but I would never reach them in time. All was lost. My anguish overwhelmed me and an un-natural roar burst from my throat. My vision went red from an intense pressure behind my eyes. The chill burned at me and though I tried to fight it, I blacked out.

It could have only been a moment before I regained consciousness. I don't think it was long at all. I was slumped backwards in my saddle and the horse tromped nervously beneath me. I remembered our situation instantly and shot upright. I was dizzy, but I could see the cart ahead. Andreas was still in the back but he was leaning back against the packs his arms flung wide. The carpet bag was on the road, thrown from him a good fifty feet. I did not see August, but there were six soldiers and seven horses sprawled upon the ground. Our other three horses were behind me grazing the grass on the roadside.

I prodded my mount gently with my heels, but he shied and would not move forward. I dismounted and ran a jagged dizzy path to the cart.

I was sure that whatever evil had emitted from me had killed them all. "No, no, no, no, no!" I repeated as I came closer and nothing moved. I went to Andreas first and my cold heart warmed as I saw his jagged breath. August was there. He had been hidden from me where he was slumped over the dash rail. He was alive as well. The horse though suffered not one but two broken legs in the fall forward. The bandit-soldiers were alive as well. I only had moments to react and get us out of there before they woke and attacked anew.

I ran back and gathered our four horses. They were skittish, but with gentle talk and some pulling I got them down the hill to the cart. Two soldiers began to wake. I hoped to take at least one alive so I kicked them in the head before they became aware and out they went again. I roused August who was wounded, but assured me he was okay. He helped me to unharness the fallen horse. I said a prayer and shot a crossbow between its eyes to end its suffering. The soldiers' horses began to wake and stand, but did not leave the area. I went to one and it let me remove the saddle. There I saw Harald's brand on the left rump. I led her to the front of the cart and August fit the harness to her.

Andreas was still lying back in the cart. I went to him and made him comfortable. The bandages held, but they were a bloody mess. He had defensive wounds on his hands and arms that needed tending, but they could wait until we got to Calibe. I ran for the carpetbag and brought it back to him. There wasn't much left of it or the contents, but I placed his arms around it, and tucked him in tight.

The cart was ready. I went to one of the soldiers that I had not kicked and pulled him up. August came to help and together we slung him over one of their own horses and tied his hands and feet together under the horse's belly.

August took his seat on the cart and gathered the reins. I herded our horses and three more of the soldiers' mounts together on the road. "Go," I said, and August had the fresh horse at a swift pace instantly. It took me a moment to get all six of those I had moving together but I did and we were off again on the road to Calibe.

It was late in the day when we arrived at last. "Bandits attacked us on the road," was all August had to say; that, and one look at us got us entry.

"We a need a physician now!" I shouted and a man dispatched himself at a run.

Our arrival had been followed by a great deal of commotion. Shouts and runners went back and forth. A young man no older than myself soon joined us.

"I am Xatar, son of Tanath. Please bring your fallen man. My physician prepares inside her home.

August and I lifted Andreas from the cart and carried him gently. Xatar ushered us into a lodge and up a short hall to a room equipped for medical treatment. A tall work bench was in the center of the room. The old woman who met us there instructed us to lay Andreas there and we did.

I pried the carpetbag from his arms. He was only partially aware and held tight to it. "It's okay Andy. We are safe now. We have brought you to Calibe and the physician here. Let me take it now. You know I will care for it."

His gaze was unfocused, but he heard me and let go.

"I have unguents," I told the physician. "I will get them. They are his," I said indicating Andreas with a nod of my head. "He has some talent in the healing arts himself. They are amazing. You must slather them on as you sew him up and then again after."

The physician was busy examining the wound but glanced up at me with a dubious look.

"I'll get them, you'll see," I said, and ran out. I passed August and Xatar in the hall. They were close together in a quiet conversation. Xatar looked very concerned and August was doing the talking. I believed that August had revealed himself to Xatar. I hoped he knew what he was doing. Upon my return they were gone.

The physician was cutting skillfully into the flesh around the wound. I could see that she was making a path for the barbed head of the arrowhead to travel without doing further damage on the way out. She placed the fingers of one hand around the wound and pulled the arrow out in one swift motion with the other hand. Blood pooled up in the wound and she inserted a tube of pig gut into it. She sucked on the other end until the blood flowed through. She spit and placed the end in a large pail. The blood cleared the wound.

"He is very lucky. He has lost a great deal of blood, but nothing vital was severed. The artery was nicked but I am sewing that now. The arrow went deep. It is a miracle it did not hit his spine. When do I apply that magic unguent of yours?"

"Anytime now," I said, and unrolled the kit on the table next to Andreas. I found a jar of unguent and opened it for her.

"Any special instructions?" She asked.

"Apply liberally," I said.

She smiled and said, "Well then do you have more than one jar?"

"Several," I replied.

She dipped two fingers in and slapped a dollop into the portion of the wound she was about to sew. I gathered four more jars in a line and set aside the rest of Andreas's medical kit.

The physician worked quickly and used two more of the four unguents. I helped her to clean up and we introduced ourselves.

"Thank you. Oh, I am so thankful." I took her hand and then found myself hugging her.

She laughed and said, "That thank you makes you most welcome. He needs to rest. When I know how well he is we will move him to a bed."

"Can I stay with him?"

"I'll have a chair brought in," she said, and left, closing the door behind her.

I stood looking down at him and took his hand in mine. It was cold. At that moment I realized the chill was gone from me again. I thought back to the last I remembered it being with me. I was certain it had left me at the moment I had released that insane roar. A shiver went down my spine. A shiver not of cold, but of fear. What was this chill and that roar? Was it the curse or the evil that was in my blood by birth? What was I?

The chair was brought in and I slumped into it; a wholly distraught creature.

·~·Chapter Ten·~·

Andreas slept and Etain, the physician, was there to check on him several times in an hour. When she was sure there was no internal bleeding she had him moved to another room in the lodge. She ushered the two men, who carried him, into the room. I followed and stood in the door as they put him in bed and covered him. Etain tucked the blankets in tight around him and pulled an additional sheepskin cover up over him.

"I will be back soon. It does seem as if that unguent is working well. I will have to ask him what is in it. I gave him a bit of narcotic to help him rest, but he should wake soon. Let yours be the first face he sees. It will help him to orient."

I just stood there staring at her. The realization of what I was had brought me to the awful conclusion that I could not marry Andreas. I could never marry. At that moment I almost wished he would die, the pain of his loss would be easier to take than knowing he was in my world and I could not have him.

Etain spoke to me of his survival and I wished that one of us would die. Me— I must die I thought. How? Could I kill myself, or would I have to throw myself into a losing battle? I stared. lost in my dark thinking.

"My dear, you look absolutely worn. Come sit. I will get you a tonic."

I heard her but I didn't move or respond. She came and led me to a chair near a window. I stood at the chair as if I could not comprehend its purpose and she had to put me in it.

"Oh dear," she said.

I looked at her and she wiped a tear as it trickled down my cheek, but I never felt it there. She met my eyes and held my gaze, but it was as if I looked through her, beyond her to somewhere else; anywhere else.

"Tsk, tsk," she said, and ran from the room.

Some time went by before she returned and forced me to drink something. I did not taste it, but after a time it heated me and I felt areas of my brain crackle as if they were being brought to life. I say that is what actually happened. I came out of my stupor and was myself , as far as I would ever be again. I looked across the room at Andreas still sleeping peacefully.

Etain was at my side and watched me as my shoulders slumped at the sight of him. "He will be alright dear, I assure you."

"I know it isn't that."

"What then? I was certain you had gone into some kind of delayed shock."

"Some kind," I said, and snatching my coat from our pile of gear I went out of the room, leaving her there.

I went out of the lodge and into the city. I wandered in search of a temple. Any temple would not do. I wanted the head god, the King of all. I found it by asking. It was outside the walls in a grove upon a hill. *Good*, I thought. If the god could not help me, or found me lacking and killed me I wouldn't have to find a way. If the bandits found me that was all the better and I could die a hero at least. The weather had turned and a rain shower fell across the land. I pulled the collar of my coat up around my neck, bent my head and went on my way.

The temple was surrounded by great trees of all kinds, but the largest of these were massive iron woods, gnarly in their age. The structure was of split iron wood and the roof was wood and slate.

There was no door just a lintel between two upright posts. I walked into a room; barren except for a long low table along the back wall. Upon the table were various offerings brought by the people of Calibe to convince their god that they were worthy. A pile of stone; smooth and round from the shore, a bracelet of jute and colored beads, a flask of wine, a bird feather, a branch of twigs so twisted as to seem braided. Meager gifts for a god.

I touched the things and felt no power from them. Perhaps the power was in the giving. I looked up as I had seen others do when caught in prayer. "Hello?" Nothing. I took a breath and began to speak. I pled, I begged, I promised and cried. No, I sobbed out my frustrations there in the temple of the All God. I had said many prayers in my life, like those I had said before putting August's horse to rest. Ritual prayers said more from protocol than any depth of feeling. This prayer tore me apart. I must have said a thousand words, but in the end all it meant was; why me? What do you want? No light emanated from the heavens to shine on me, the ground did not shake, and no angels came to sooth my pain or slap me right.

I took the wine and left the temple. I took shelter from the rain below an iron wood and drank myself numb. When I finished the wine I threw the flask upon the ground. "Bah," I said, and staggered back to find the home of the prince, Tanath's son, the newest fledgling king.

The city of Calibe was a jumble of huts and lodges. Lodges were constructed of stone and log while the huts were daub and wattle. One lodge house was situated centrally to the others and it was the largest. I took a chance based on experience and went to announce myself there.

"You have been expected," the sentry said and threw open the door to allow me entrance.

243

I entered immediately into a large room that filled the center of the lodge from front to back. An enormous stone fireplace filled the center and served as kitchen. Rooms lined the main room on either side. August was in conversation with Xatar and several other men. Of those, I recognized three, and one of them I knew to be Tanath's captain. He was healed of his wounds from the attack that killed his king. They stood when they saw me as men do when ladies enter a room. I found that ironic, I felt anything but ladylike at that moment.

Xatar came forward to greet me and I attempted not to stagger into him.

"Whoa now woman, what have you gotten into?"

"The sacramental wine," I replied. "And yet, here I still am."

"How is Andreas?"

"When I left he was sleeping peacefully."

Xatar lead me to the others and I attempted a curtsey, but I staggered and Xatar steadied me. "Is she like this often?" he asked August.

"I don't know her that well, but she has had a rough time of it. Perhaps we overlook this behavior this once?"

"Overlook it!" I cheered, and spun into a seat at the table near the fire with the rest of them. "You should overlook it," I said, aiming down my index finger at Xatar.

"So what are you all discussing?" I asked.

August brought me up to speed. I comprehended that they now knew who he was and that we would be escorted back to Nagrom. He went on and on, blahbitty this and blahbitty that. I had to focus to keep my eyes on his as he talked, but I kept drifting to his big blahbitty mouth.

When he was through I stood up, swayed, but kept my feet under me. "You know what I think?" I asked. They must of thought it was a rhetorical question because no one answered. "Well, anybody know?"

"What do you think?" Xatar asked with a wide smile across his face.

"I think, you think too much. Councils and strategies; Just go burn Harald out, starve him, beat him, pound him out. Then just for fun go get Narhan and do the same."

"Why Narhan?" Xatar asked.

I fished for the parchment I had taken from our first attackers. It was tucked in at my breast and I saw the men raise their eyebrows as I dug for it.

"Ha!" I said as I pulled it out. "This is why." I tossed the sheet to Xatar.

He read but did not see how it pointed to Narhan so I explained. "Both times that we were attacked August was their primary target. Harald did not know that August was on the roads. No king knew, but Narhan did. We spent the night in Yer, and though we left early, Narhan had plenty of time to get a message out ahead of us."

"Good God, she's right!" August said.

"No, not Narhan. He was for the treaty. You heard him yourself at the kings' council," the captain said.

"Was he for the treaty or for Frahn's pursuit of it?" I asked. At that moment the question even surprised me. It is odd how clarity can come from an inebriated mind. "Think about it. He encourages Frahn to pursue it so that he can convince the other kings of its worth, but he knows that they will be offended. So he convinces Harald to act against him and then all of you so that he might be high king. Of course he has taken time to groom Harald into believing that they are allies. Maybe he even said he would represent him at the kings' council. Now he sits; his position is strategic. He acts as if he is neutral and will protect himself if attacked, but he sends that message and shows his hand."

The room went quiet. The implications were staggering. When we had thought that Harald was acting alone it seemed insane. Now considering that Narhan might be behind it all seemed genius—evil, but genius none the less.

Then the room was full of chaotic conversation. Several at once. I was beginning to succumb to the wine and the air inside was stifling. "Gentlemen," I said, bringing them all to silence at once. "My work here is done. I must away." I staggered from the table to the door and in the morning I found myself lying at the foot of Andreas's bed, not remembering how I had gotten from the lodge to there.

I stretched and my head pounded. I steadied it with one hand in front and one in back as I let my body slide from the bed to sit on the floor.

"What's wrong beautiful?" Andreas's voice was weak and scratchy.

"Too much feeling sorry for myself. I'll tell you all about it when you feel better."

"I do feel better. Etain has been amazed by the power of the unguent. She plans to remove the cat gut stitches tomorrow. The internals will just be absorbed."

"No, it can wait for now. Let's worry about you for now. I'm fine."

"If you are sure. I'd really like to sit up if you don't mind helping me to the chair. I do feel a little weak."

I helped him and then went to pour a pitcher of water over my head.

"Better?"

"Some."

"How is the devil's cold?"

"Gone for now. I don't understand the changes."

"What the hell was that on the road?"

"I don't know. The devil's cold itself maybe."

"I've been lying here thinking about it. The roar has only happened twice now right?"

"Yes."

"The first time when you found and were protecting Mam, and the second time when you had found and were protecting me and August."

"That's right but I thought we were just going to worry about you."

"There is nothing to worry about me. I'm going to be fine."

I moved from the basin stand to sit on the bed. "Could we worry later then? I really need to sleep some of this off."

"Sure, but think about this. What if the devil's chill is actually coming under your control? What if it is a precursor to danger?"

I was curling up under the blankets, my eyes were already closed, but when he said that they popped open and I met his gaze. It was resolute. To Andreas his theory was fact. I did not feel like I controlled the chill in any way except to block it out so I could carry on. He read the doubt in my eyes.

"Well, just think about it."

I closed my eyes without another word, but sleep did not come easily. The devil's chill occupied my thoughts. The devil's chill and how I would tell Andreas that we could not be married. The hangover mercifully brought me some sleep; thready as it was. I was glad of it; to be taken away from my gloom was a blessing.

When I woke Andreas was not in the room. I rose and gathered fresh clothes from our bags and went in search of a bath. It was during this search that I realized Etain had a family. Andreas had joined Etain and her two young children at the hearthside. They were having tea and watching the children play. They were happy to see me. In my state of mind that annoyed me, but I smiled and went to stand beside Andreas.

"If it's not too much bother, I could really use a bath."

"Of course dear, if you don't mind helping."

"I don't mind."

"Follow me then."

The bath was in a public building outside not far from the lodge house. No one else was there at the time. It was built over a natural spring. A contraption of split logs hollowed at the center and joined together with leather protruded from the floor in the center of the room. Several tall copper tubs lined the walls of the room. Each basin was covered with a copper lid. Etain ordered me to uncover a tub; as I did she swung the logs around to a position over that tub. Next she removed a copper plate from a slot between the joining of a wooden trough and the center contraption. Cold clear water rose up and trickled down the trough into the tub.

Fresh wood had been set in under the tub. I looked for and found tallow candles. Lit one and set it into the fine tinder beneath the logs. The fire started nicely and warmed the water as it filled the tub.

"You will find shams in that closet over there. The heat will last you about two hundred counts. There are oils there on the floor on that side of the tub. Enjoy. I'll send my boy in to rebuild the logs later, don't you worry about it. I'll have lunch and tea for you when you're through."

I smiled half-heartedly, nodded, and she left.

I spent most of the bath with my head underwater. I had heard about people drowning in tubs. They must have been invalids. I could not do it. I inhaled water once but it hurt intensely. I shot up out of the water coughing so hard I thought I would expel the lungs with the water, so I gave up. I sat in the warm water, sampled the oils

Etain had offered me, and washed. The smells turned my sour stomach and my dark mood even darker.

I had not felt this way for a long time. Settling in Mareese had made me happy. The chill had a hold on me, but I had always handled it and pushed on. Maybe Andreas was right about it. Could it be some sort of precursor? It had come on me during perhaps the darkest time in my life. Was it a seed laid by the temporary possession of a demon? Or could it be it had always been in me—dormant until the rage at my friend Wallace's murder brought it life? As the spawn of a devil could it be a congenital part of me? The priest in Dinar had not been able to exorcise it, even for all the pain his attempts had given me.

I sat contemplating this new idea until the water cooled. Then I dried and wrapped myself in a sham. I did not want to be around people, but it was inevitable. The longer I stayed in the bathhouse the longer I could delay. But there was a point at which this became unreasonable so I dressed and went into the house.

Etain was good to her word and had a large bowl of soup and a mug of tea staying warm on the hearth side for me.

"I was beginning to think you'd drowned," she said, as she moved the lunch to a table.

No such luck. I thought, but I said, "No, someone gave me something to think about this morning. I needed time."

"I see. You look much better," she said.

"I wish I felt it."

"Well the soup will nourish you and the tea will right your head."

"Thanks, Etain. You have been very kind."

"It's what I do, dear." Etain said, then went to tend to her children.

Andreas came over and sat across from me. "What's up, Sade? I know you. I haven't felt you this dark since Wallace."

"Since Wallace? You say it like it was a place, some non-event, some point in time of little consequence."

"How should I say it, Sade? I meant to ease into it, not hit you over the head with it. God's Sade I know how much it hurts you. You remember me right? I was there."

"Sorry," I said, but I didn't mean it.

Andreas went quiet and watched me as I ate. I avoided looking at him. When I had pushed my bowl aside and taken up the tea he started again.

"Sade?"

"Andy?"

"I'm concerned is all. You said someone gave you something to think about this morning. I know you meant me. You didn't see anyone else. I'm glad you took the time to consider my thoughts. So…?"

"What?"

"What do you think about it?"

I gave him an uncertain shrug as a way of response.

"Come on Sade, you have to talk about it. Something is eating you. What else could it be?"

"You don't want to know right now, Andreas. Just drop it please. I will tell you in good time. I have to tell you. I'm just not ready yet."

"Oh, Sade, not that."

"Not what?" My anger was growing and I had to lower my voice. "How can you possibly know what I have to say to you. I haven't even put it together fully myself yet."

"It sounds like you want to brush me off. You *have* to tell me? Unless you are pregnant, and we haven't been together long enough for that yet. What else could it be?"

I shouted at him, "I think I'm destroyed. There, that is what I think. Happy, now? Couldn't leave it alone could you? Couldn't wait until I was ready to talk about it. Gods Andreas you think you know me, but you have no idea what this is like."

I turned from him, tipping over my stool as I stormed out.

"I do know you, Sade, and I love you still," I heard him say behind me. For a split second I wanted to run to him, but I could not let our love continue.

I went back to the room for my coat, intending to go out and walk off my anger, but something within me made me stop. I fell upon the bed and wept. I loved Andreas, but how could I have him with evil churning around inside of me? What life would he have? He would only leave me for someone sane.

He came into the room then and seeing me there fell on the bed beside me and held me with such tender might that I could not regain my composure and I sobbed until I fell asleep from exhaustion. When I woke he was beside me still.

"You can't get rid of me Sade."

"I don't want to, but…"

"But what Sade, tell me what so I can help you."

"I don't think you can."

"Of course, you know that because?..."

I sat quietly, gathering words, and strength, and my love for him. He waited. I gathered.

"Yesterday and this morning I wanted to die, I wanted to kill myself or have you die."

I expected some response, and though his look was one of shock he said nothing.

"I went up to the temple of The All God. I prayed. Mam never taught me about God or religion, just nature and survival. But, I prayed; long and hard. Nothing happened. I felt no presence, no epiphany, nothing but loneliness. I actually stole an offering of wine from the alter. Drank the whole thing. I wanted someone to tell me why I ever lived. Why the spawn of a devil lived. I wanted Him to take it all away. To take me away. It would be okay then, death would be so much easier to face than living without you, so I wanted one of us to die. I actually did try to drown in the tub today. I don't think it can be done."

"Why do you think you have to live without me?

"Come on Andy. This is going to wear on me. Someday I will go mad from it. I know it. I'm appalled at myself right now. I'm a suicidal, depressed, sacramental wine stealin' drunken mess. I'm better than this Andy. But when the cold gains hold on me, my thoughts go dark. I go dark.

"You got me thinking though that the chill is not a curse that might someday be removed, but a part of me. I think it and it feels right that the chill and that awful roar lay dormant in me until the rage at Wallace's murder triggered it. The priest in Dinar with Father Gan to assist him was not able to remove it, even for all the pain it gave me. I am the child of a devil. Could it be a congenital part of me? I think you might be right about the chill being a precursor to danger. I have thought that it came to me *during* my killing of Wallace, but under the minion's control I was not aware of it coming into the dream. Do you remember the storm? The cold wind and the snow? Do you think that could have been a manifestation from me and not the demon minion? Could I have been trying to protect Wallace and save us both and not knowing how left myself with this chill?"

Andreas opened his mouth to speak but he couldn't find the words, so I went on.

"Settling in Mareese made me happy and the chill was subsiding. When I was without you I had time to reflect and realized I could no longer go on in denial of my feelings for you. A load had been lifted from me. I felt joy; if I know what joy is. The chill left me for days, until Hoarfrost. It got worse as we went to Yer. When we left, it subsided again until there was danger again. I was catching up with you on the road to Calibe. When I saw you under attack it was as if the fear and anger exploded within me and escaped in that roar. It overcame me so hard that I could barely stay on my horse. The roar causes me excruciating pain. Every nerve and blood vessel sears like fire. It is so excruciating that I blacked out, not for long I think. I did not pass out when I used it to keep Malisgalar from Mam, but it was painful, and though I love her it is not with the intensity that I feel love for you."

"So you still love me then."

"Yes. I am afraid so."

"Then do not let me go. I will make you happy. We can live away from danger. The chill will leave you and you will be fine."

"You know we can never have children."

"But…What? How do we?…"

"We don't. Not unless Mam can concoct some way that one of us would be sterile."

"I always thought I'd like a child someday," It hurt him to say that. "What if…"

"I am already? Then I will abort it." I heard myself say it, but I instantly doubted that I could. Still, I continued my thought, but in a hushed tone, "I won't bring another person into the world to face what I do every day. Another of devil's blood." I said no more, to let him think.

The silence between us was heavy. I went to the window and looked out at the village around us. I wished I hadn't done that as I saw Etain and her children run across the yard to welcome her husband home from his chores. Still, I could not take my eyes from them.

I too had often thought of having a child someday, when the right man came along. The right man—I turned and looked at him. He was gorgeous, so beautiful inside and out.

We stayed in sad silence a long time, until Etain came to remove the cat gut stitches from Andreas's neck. The scar it left looked like a star. That seemed somehow appropriate for him.

"You will have to send me some of that unguent. It is simply amazing."

"I will give you the recipe. I will even show you how to make it if you can get the ingredients."

"And if there is time. A messenger waits to take the two of you to Xatar."

***

The main room of Xatar's lodge was set for dinner. The tables had been pulled into a circle around the fireplace. A hog roasted on the fire spit all day and the savory aroma filled the room. Loud talk and laughter stopped when we entered and Xatar proclaimed in a loud voice: "Here they are, our honored guests. Come sit. I have saved you seats by me." He patted the open spaces on either side of him and ordered a serving maid to fill our plates and cups. We moved through the room and were met with handshakes and pats on the back.

We took our seats. I sat between Xatar and his historian. Andreas sat between Xatar and August. Xatar introduced himself to Andreas who asked Xatar; "What is this all about?"

Xatar laughed. "Of course you do not know." Then he addressed the crowd of guests. "Andreas here does not understand why we celebrate." He turned to Andreas, but spoke so all could hear. Well, first you saved a king." August grasped Andreas by the shoulder and shook him in the affectionate way of men. "Then you saved him again. Your command of the elements is renowned. As soon as August told me the story I knew it was you."

"But it was not..." Andreas looked across Xatar to me. I shook my head slightly to say no. "It was not such a big deal. It is what we do," he finished.

"We? Oh, yes, of course. His lady Saeede, gentlemen. It is she that recovered Narhan's note."

A cheer went up from the guests. Andreas looked at me again, and gave an apologetic shrug. I smiled and returned the shrug. Then I laughed, a great robust laugh. Women never get the credit they are due with these arrogant royal types. If only they knew what I could do if they made me angry enough.

Xatar went back to his meal and Andreas caught my attention, he mouthed the words; "What note?"

"Sorry, forgot to tell you," I mouthed back. This time his shrug was more confused; not so apologetic.

After the plates from dinner were removed and fresh casks of ale rolled in and tapped Xatar turned the talk to his plans for the war council. He was leaving the matters of the village to Varga, the historian and his mother. He would go himself to Nagrom with twenty five men and we would travel with them, along with August. We would leave the morning of the following day.

Xatar was adamant that his father be avenged and wanted Narhan to answer for his involvement as well. If it meant war then he and his people would meet it. He was fiery. I hoped he was also smart. The war council promised to be interesting. Frahn would have a lot to do to stop this war if all the royals were like Xatar.

The conversation became intense and we realized that we had been invited to sit in on a plan of campaign, as Xatar called it. Our attendance wasn't really necessary but we wanted to know how we were travelling and with who. All manner of formations and scouting contingents were discussed. Each had merit and in the end the choice was a good one. We would ride in the middle of a six row column, four abreast. August would take his wagon. Andreas and I would flank him on two of the horses we had claimed from the bandit soldiers. We made up the third of five rows. Xatar and his captain would be just in front of us in the second row. Four scouts would span out on foot one mile ahead of us. If they needed fast transport they would sit in the back of two wagons at the rear of the line. Archers flanked each side of the column five to a side, on horseback. The horses that Frahn had lent us would all be used for packing supplies now and would be tied to the backs of the supply wagons.

As we met, outside the village bustled with activity. Wagons were being loaded and horses shod for the earth packed road to Nagrom. Men sharpened swords and axes, pikes and daggers. Women mended cloaks and britches while smithies restored armor. Xatar had a citizen army, but they were proud and wanted to look their best.

We left the meeting still in progress to see to our own gear. It was a mess. Our armor needed mending, and the weapons we trusted and had been wearing were in need of sharpening. The worst of things was what we had carried in the carpet bag. Many of our weapons were bent and beyond sharpening. Our instruments were almost all beyond hope. Only the flute from Malisgalar's lair, Mam's journal, and Eindal's ledger had survived the hacking that would have killed Andreas had he not had the bag to protect himself. The ledger and journal would need repair and the bag itself was not worth keeping.

Etain told us where to take our armor and weapons. We went together with our armor and only our dearest weapons. We were told to come back in the morning and all would be done. We put the carpet bag in the back of August's wagon and went to bed.

We ate breakfast with Etain and her family who would not accept our help with cooking. We enjoyed their company very much. Her husband would be joining us in the march to Nagrom. He was a pike man and would be at the front of the column. She was worried, as well she should. We promised to watch out for him the best we could.

We went to gather our gear from the smithy as the lines began to form for our march. We assisted each other with our armor and weapons and found our place in line. A page boy held our horses and we mounted. When all was ready Xatar gave a whoop and the march moved forward. Cries and cheers went up among the watching crowd. When we passed through the city gates Xatar called us to a gallop and we were off.

There was some tension on the road on our first day out. We were approached from the rear of the column by armed men riding swiftly, but they were Queen Andra's men. We recognized Gorm near the front and told Xatar. Still no one knew who could be trusted. Xatar ordered his men into a defense and we waited. When the approaching troop closed the distance they too moved into a defense, but three mounted men broke off and rode toward us. Xatar ordered his captain and two others to ride out and meet them. It was not long before each trio returned to their troops. They asked to join and bring strength to numbers. Xatar agreed and the captain rode out again to the center. When he did Andra's troop moved slowly forward.

The two troops joined together and Xatar met them properly, without threat. One rider led them in, followed by Grom and another captain. That rider reached a hand to Grom in greeting and removed their helmet. There sat Andra, proud upon her mount. She moved into the row with Xatar and her troops moved into rows between ours. We were not accosted on our way to Nagrom. Etain's worries for her husband's safety were unwarranted as it turned out.

It took four days to reach Nagrom. We presented our letter of entrance to the soldiers at the gate. After a short wait we were allowed to enter and when we did the place seemed to bulge from our presence. The troops were forced to make camp in the hills outside the city walls. Thome Kelt's son and historian had not yet arrived. Andra's troop had not seen or communicated with them, but they had swept wide of the cities. Rooms were made ready at the castle for Xatar and Andra, and their closest advisors.

Two more days passed without a sign of Thome Kelt's emissaries. We spent much of that time briefing Frahn on the events of our mission. He was shocked at the accusation that Narhan was the mastermind behind Harald's actions.

"The letter is not signed," he complained. "How can we prove it was him?"

"I tell you, Sir, the man was unkind to us and disrespectful to August even when he knew who he was. He may as well have thrown us out of the city for the lack of courtesy he showed. He was annoyed that we had come at all. The note is handwritten surely someone must recognize his hand."

Frahn looked again. His sigh said it all, we did not need to hear his words, but he said; "It does look like his writing."

"It could be a forgery," I offered.

"Possible, but difficult to prove," Andreas said. "If you have some documents that we could compare."

"Excellent idea. Come."

He rose and crossed the floor of his private chamber to another door. It was locked and he opened it with a key hung from a chain around his neck. Inside was a dusty store of books, scrolls, and documents. He lit a lantern that sat on a central table. We could see that although the room was dusty there were bare spots on the table between piles of documents. Frahn had been at work here already. He informed us that he had been reviewing old treaties, most of them broken, and protocols for a war council. He began going through the piles on the table as he ordered us to sit.

He pushed a few documents toward us. "Compare these," he said. "I have something more."

"Are these written by Narhan?" I asked after looking them over.

"I don't believe those are, why?"

"He is not a signatory."

Frahn stopped his paper shuffling. He had acquired another small stack. He picked them up and looked for Narhan's signature on them. "Here he is," he said, and handed over four more documents.

"And has he written any of these?"

"I need Pinkert, my historian to determine that. I will send for him but first I must tell you, I read all of the letters in Tige's locker. There are a few that are signed only with an N. Could that be Narhan?"

"It could be if the Ns match the N in these signatures," Andreas said.

"I have them here." He moved to a table across the room and produced a locked box. He opened it with another key on the chain around his neck. After some shuffling he produced three letters. The Ns did indeed match that of Narhan's signature. Frahn went to fetch his historian. While he was gone we spent the time examining and comparing documents. We compared Tige's letters to the treaties, and the treaties to the note I had gained from the body of one of Harald's men. Then we compared again, this time in reverse order.

Frahn was gone a very short time but when he returned we were sure we could identify several letters within the note as being in Narhan's handwriting. Pinkert joined us immediately and he agreed. He and Frahn looked for specific documents that Pinkert could recall had been in Narhan's hand and so had more than just his signature.

They gathered four. All four regarded land disputes; one with Harald, one with August, and one with Thome. The fourth declared his right of sovereignty and demanded that all the kings respect his borders. All four treaties were written before Frahn became king. The other kings disputed the boundaries, but it was Narhan who infringed on the borders that he had claimed. He hunted and foraged on the land of others or fished in their waters. The connection between Narhan and Harald was even more confusing knowing that.

It was all very interesting, but what was most interesting was the matching of the handwriting. Frahn bundled the treaties and letters together with the note off the bandit soldier and tied them with a bit of twine.

The four of us returned to Frahn's room and listened as Pinkert gave us all a history lesson of Narhan's politics. Even Pinkert learned from it in the telling and the placing of missing pieces. It was early morning when we all retired much enlightened by it.

Early on the fourth day since our return to Nagrom, Thome's son and historian arrived with forty well trained men. The council began that same day at breakfast. All of the royals present were in favor of pushing back at Harald. The evidence against him was very good. We had Lily's confession that she had killed Esporanza and that she had done it for her king. We had the letters from Harald to Tige, and Tige's tabard with Harald's symbol on it. There was the button Tanath's man had found after the attack that killed Tanath and Elys. We had horses with his brand on them from the attack on us on our way back to Nagrom from Yer. Xatar had questioned the captured man from the attack on the road, but he got no useful information. The man was more afraid to talk than he was to face imprisonment. Xatar had him killed for that. No doubt it was his first act of reprisal for his father's death.

It was Narhan who had them baffled now. When Narhan attended the council of kings he seemed to be interested in pursuing a treaty with Crystalier. The royals now had to face many questions. When we met with Narhan in his tower in Yer he had been outwardly rude to August. Both times that we were attacked were after we left Yer. Both times August was their primary target. Narhan could not have gotten word to Harald in Breen, but there was time to get word to Harald's men in the field. Did Harald know that his men were being commanded by Narhan? Did Harald's men believe their orders came from their king, or did they follow Narhan? Were they actually Harald's men? Were the two kings together in a conspiracy?

Was Narhan for the treaty or for Frahn's pursuit of it? Did Narhan manipulate Frahn, encouraging him to pursue it knowing that the other kings would be offended? Was he manipulating Harald as well; to act against Frahn? Where did Lily fit in all this? What was his end game? Would he have Harald fight his war and then send in Lily to finish off the rest of them so that he could have Ahnges to himself as high king? Of course that meant he controlled Lily and had taken time to groom Harald into believing that they are allies. Was Harald absent from council because Narhan had offered to represent him?

Narhan's location was strategic and well defended and he declared he would move his army as he saw fit. He made his statements as if he meant to be neutral, but his demeanor was antagonistic.

The debate now was how to proceed against two kingdoms at once. Which king was the more eminent threat? Harald's men had killed two kings. One king was surely guilty, but the other could be a victim of intrigue launched against him by the other. Which one was which? Both kings had much to answer for.

Andreas and I stayed out of it, but conferred our own thoughts to each other, throughout the day.

A battle plan began to emerge, but Frahn remained firm on his stand for peace. "A war on two fronts even with five armies will deplete resources that our people need to survive."

"We have all been seeing to our stores for ages, Frahn. I yearn for peace, perhaps more than any of you," Thome said gently. "My homeland lies in the middle of every foray that has ever been on Ahnges. We are not unreasonable, but it is time that this stop. Your idea of a trade treaty has made me think long and hard. I am for it. Still, it will never happen if Harald and Narhan are allowed to go on harassing us so that we cannot move ahead with negotiations."

"There is another way," Andreas whispered to me.

"What?" I asked.

"Let the people solve it. Let the Breens seize Harald's power and force him to abdicate. Then get Harald to tell us about Narhan."

"That could take years."

"I don't think so. Do you trust me?"

"God help me I know I will regret this, but yes. I trust you."

Andreas stood and shouted out above the voices of the debate, "There is another way."

All voices stopped and all eyes turned to Andreas. Our part in all of this was well enough known now that no one questioned his right to speak.

"Let the people solve it. Let the Breens seize Harald's power and force him to abdicate. Then get Harald to tell about Narhan."

The consensus agreed with me that it could take a very long time.

"Not if we isolate Harald from his resources, and from his only possible aid—Narhan."

"How do you propose we do that?" Frahn asked most interested.

"Saeede and I have been to Breen. We know a few people there. Once they understand what Harald has done and the word is spread, it won't take long. Some small faction there already is wary of Harald. The farmers in the area are neutral, but if Thome could offer them commerce and protection in a conflict, I believe they could be swayed to support him. Harald could be taken with very little if any bloodshed."

"Why have you not mentioned this before?" Frahn asked.

"I suppose we did leave out some details, but it was unintentional I assure you, our task was to bring you Lily, not bring down a king. I though of it now; I am telling you now."

For a moment the room went quite, but then it took up again with enthusiastic talk.

Thome suggested that we go and bring Harald out in much the same way that we had with Lily. "When the citizens are screaming for his removal you could be there to do it," he said. The idea was met with overwhelming enthusiasm.

"No! No. We are going home. Our part in this was over weeks ago. You have the evidence you need. We will give you the back way in. This is your responsibility. We have done more than we ever intended to do here. This is not our war. This is not our country and we want to go home to ours."

We were offered money and titles to stay. At one point someone suggested they give us Breen. Even though we tried to tell them no, they voted anyway. The vote was unanimous. That was quite an offer. To have our own holdings was a magnificent thing. We would be expected to act as royalty though and we were anything but. Still, we considered it, perhaps our way of rule would be more altruistic, especially with Frahn's treaty gaining support. Of course there was Mam and now Mya to consider. Breen did not have an apothecary, perhaps she would relish the idea of starting new. We would miss Mareese, but a bit of Mareese in Ahnges would be an example to the other kings.

As the conversation went on we reminded them that Lily was still out there somewhere, in allegiance to Harald, or Narhan, or both, and that Frahn still held two spies who might hold information on Narhan.

These kings had been raised on a more traditional style of war. Narhan had recognized that weakness and used it against all of them— including Harald. We could see that our experience would be valuable to them. We couldn't stand it if we had set them on the path and then they got lost because we had not stayed to guide them. We decided to stay and help.

We spent a few more nights under Frahn's roof to aid all the kings present to formulate a plan. Queen Andra and Thome Kelt arranged for certain goods to be sent to the smithies in Breen. Arrangements were made for our return to Breen. Too much time had passed for us to return in the smithies' good graces, but Frahn saw to it that needed tools and supplies were sent with us as a gesture of good faith. The wagon we had taken from Breen had been returned to the smithies by other means when our mission had taken us to alert the kings of a war council. That act was as much honorable as it was diplomatic. To send more supplies now was as much to get the smithies to listen to us as it was to help them prepare for an insurrection. Andreas went over final arrangements with two of Frahn's men about the packing of goods. There was no letter to be sent this time. We could not afford for it to fall into the hands of Harald's or Narhan's bandits.

When all was agreed on and our wagon was ready we made arrangements for a ship to sail out on the evening tide. We spent the day socializing with the soldiers of the three visiting troops. We paid special attention to Etain's husband and gave him Andreas's handwritten recipe for his unguent. In the afternoon we went to retrieve our bags and say our farewells to the kings. We were sent off with hugs and invitations to visit the kings in their own kingdoms when this was all over.

The ship was a ruse to throw off any spies that Harald might still have within the castle or the city. Two people were dressed in our clothes and sent in our stead. They were messengers with letters hand written by us to Diony and Mam, and by Frahn to his Queen, Sion.

We dressed as Sig and Helm. I slipped back into that persona, again for the benefit of anyone who might be in bed with Harald. I sat beside Andreas and he drove us through the postern gate and through the city streets to the Northern Gate.

·~·Chapter Eleven·~·

Once outside of the city Andreas put the horses to the test. Our load was heavy. We really should have had four horses, but we were trying to look as much like the Breen Smithy lackeys as we could. We made decent time and spent the night at the hostel barn with the wagon and horses pulled inside. No one else came to spend the night and we were glad we would not have to carry on small talk with strangers.

We were loaded with anvils, hammers tongs, and other tools that a smithy could use. Gifts of ore and Iron Wood from Queen Andra and Thome Kelt would arrive within a few days of our return. None of this would be cause for suspicion as it all fell within the realm of a smithy's needs.

Our return to Breen had to seem as normal as possible to the citizens and to Harald especially.   We could not afford to be questioned by the authorities. We knew the smithies were not fond of Harald. Of the three smithies Simo had been the most kind to us. We would take Simo aside and reveal ourselves to him.   He was scratching out an existence under Harald's reign. Our hope was that his kindness would hold at least long enough to hear us out.   We suspected from his whispered conversations with the other smiths that his kindness would extend to sympathy for our cause.

We rose early and after leaving a few coins in the money box we went on our way. We made it to Breen late in the evening of the next day.   The guards at the gate questioned us, but Andreas lied wonderfully and the gates were opened for us. We entered and pulled the wagon up in front of Simo's house.

267

Andreas knocked and Nia came to the door.

"By the god's," she whispered.

Simo came up behind her then. "Lads. I never expected to see you again. You abandoned us."

"Yes, but for good cause. I trust your wagon was returned to you," Andreas replied.

"It was. What brings you here now then?"

"I will tell you, but not here on your door step."

Simo hesitated a moment, but then he opened the door wide and he and Nia stood aside to allow us to enter.

We stood in the doorway for an awkward moment until Nia suggested we sit at the table. We moved to it but remained standing as they took their seats.

"We have news, but before we take of your hospitality we have something to tell you about ourselves," Andreas began. He took a deep breath before he continued. "We are not who we seem to be."

"Oh?" Simo said, and leaned forward.

We had agreed that Andreas would talk for us initially, but he was silent for a long moment. We had deceived Simo, and this was proving hard for Andreas to admit and then convey our regrets.

When at last he spoke he was emotional. "I am not Sig and this is not my little brother Helm," he said, and put his arm around me to draw me closer. We are greatly sorry that we deceived you, but as I tell you our news you will see it was necessary."

"So who are you then?" Simo's tone was angry.

"I am called Andy and this is Sade," I took the cap from my head and raised my face to the light.

"We are so very sorry to have had to deceive you. You were most kind to us," I said.

"A women," Nia whispered.

"What gives? Tell us your news before I throw you out of here."

"What we have to say weighs heavily for the people of Breen. We will discuss it after the telling but you must swear to hear us out first and what we say cannot leave this room for now." Simo and Nia shared a long look. She touched Simo's hand and he returned his gaze to us. After a long look into our eyes he at last nodded once to affirm his agreement.

"Is that a nod of agreement, sir?" Andreas asked.

"It is." Simo said.

We told him everything that had transpired since the night of Esporanza's death. The conversation went long into the night. Simo and his wife had many questions after the telling. We answered all that we could and promised answers to those we couldn't. We told them of the tools that Frahn had sent with us and the ore and Iron Wood that was to come from Kelt and Kirsh to be used to make weapons for the citizens. We would of course assist and help them to hide them away until the time was right.

We learned that Vance and Coop would be agreeable and that there were others who could be convinced to take action if that action meant the ousting of Harald and was supported by the other kings. He was sure that the majority of people would be behind our mission, even if they did not outwardly support it.

Lily had not been seen for weeks and so it was assumed that the bandits that had attacked Elys and Tanath had taken her to Narhan, probably at her request.

We slept a few hours on the floor of Simo's home until he woke us early to take the wagon into the Smithy barn. He had us wait in the loft then until he could talk to Vance and Coop. When they came in we put our ears to the loft floor and listened. Simo relayed our story well and with very little embellishment. Coop became nervous while Vance was excited about us.

"At last," Vance said. "Harald has played a cheaters hand and been caught. Where are they now? I'd like to thank them."

Simo raised his voice enough for us to hear him clearly. "Come down," he said and we did.

Vance came right over; "Simo tells us a wonderful story about you," he said and hugged Andreas. Then he came to me and held me at arm's length. He looked at me a long time. "You are beautiful," he said at last. "How is that you had us so fooled? We must be blind men."

"I thank you for the compliment. I believe you bought the story that Andreas was selling. I just acted the part he gave me."

"A fine story for a fine actress, I say. It will take me sometime to think of you as other than Sig and Frog."

"Do not try too hard. We need to enter those personas again and it will not do to have you tripping over names."

Coop was next to us shaking Andreas's hand. "No it will not do," he said to Vance. To all of us he said, "This whole thing has me on edge." He took my hand and kissed it. "There has been a heightened presence of soldiers since your attack on Harald's fortress. It did not go un-noticed when you did not return. Thankfully, Vance here is a quick thinker and he said that you were conscripted into Frahn's army. What do we say now that you have returned?"

"That is a twist." Andreas said.

"We will simply say that you escaped and came home out of loyalty to Harald." Vance proclaimed.

"No," Andreas asserted. "We must not give Harald reason to conscript us here, especially as Saeede would find it very difficult to disguise herself in a battalion of men for long.

"I can say that I was wounded and sent back" He did not point out the star shaped scar on his neck, still pink. I have scars that I can show as well. Our time away from you was not a vacation. We'll say that Saeede, as Helm is too stupid to remain without me and so we made our way here. Taking the money we earned from our duties to buy tools for our beloved caretakers, the smithies of Breen."

The smithies looked at each other for some common agreement.

Vance was the first to speak. "I can work with that."

Simo nodded his agreement, and Coop shrugged, more resigned than dedicated, but we would take it for now.

"Where do you come up with these things?" I whispered to Andreas as the smithies were deciding.

"Wits," was all he said.

"I save mine for battle," I said.

"Battles come in many forms."

"So they do."

***

We stayed in the barn talking for quite sometime, answering their questions and asking our own. We needed to know the level of discord among the citizens, and of those dissatisfied how many would stand and fight?"

Vance assured us that he could raise enough people to take the city guards out of the conflict if we could assure support from the five good kings. He even thought that that there would be men among the guard that would join us. "Once things get going I expect there will be more who will join in. There are many old folks and women and children who will be afraid to fight. Many of them may influence their male family members not to be involved for whatever reasons they hold dear. When things turn their way though..." He let his thought trail off.

The smithies would go about motivating the citizens while we coordinated with the other kings. The first step in our co-ordination had already gone rather well. We had the smithies on our side as we thought we would. Next we would assimilate ourselves back into the daily life of Breen. That seemed to be the part of our scheme that held the most risk. When the ore and Iron Wood arrived from Kirsh and Kelton we would send word of our progress back to the kings through them and they in turn would tell us what plans had been made on their part. The smithies were advised of this and it seemed then that there was no more to be said.

The smithies opened their shops. We took on our personas as Frog and Sig and went to work unloading the wagon. When that was done we pulled the wagon behind the barn and left the horses in the paddock behind Vance's shop with the other horses waiting to be shoed.

271

That day passed normally, without any visit from the kings men. The next day was not so normal. We were asleep in the loft when a loud banging came upon the barn door early in the morning.

We could see two fortress guards through the small windows on either side of the loft doors. There was nothing for us to do but answer it. They knew we were back in town. If we did not answer hat would seem suspicious. Andreas went down first. He would try to keep them from seeing me. We did not know what they wanted, though we could guess and be right. I laid low against the window to where I could just see out and watched as Andreas opened the door.

"What goes, sirs?" Andreas said.

"We could ask the same of you, Sig, is it?"

"Aye, that's right, but what do you mean?"

"You went away for quite some time. Conscripted to serve Frahn we were told. What brings you back here now to Harald's city? How is it that you are released from service? There is a move by Frahn against Harald. How do you declare your loyalty now and where is that little brother of yours?"

"My brother sleeps in the loft, that is if we have not disturbed him. I am released from service because I was wounded and they found my ability to fight wanting after that. He showed them the scars that were riddled across his torso from the beating he took while vulnerable in the back of August's wagon. He did not call attention to the wound at his neck because that wound might identify him. My brother was released with me, because he is too weak minded to continue without me and he could not comprehend his orders without further instruction from me. Even Frahn's captains could see he would be useless to them without me. We returned here because we have no where else. The smithies of Breen have become our family. They were beloved caretakers when they sent us to Nagrom for trade. While there we were conscripted. Once released it seemed natural to come here."

"What of your own family? Do they not need you to help on the farm."

This questioning could be dangerous. If they had checked on our family they would know now that there was none. Andreas's response would have to be very good to convince them of our identity now.

"We lost the farm. It was inevitable. Trying to maintain a place through conflict after conflict. Mother died years ago. As the farm came closer and closer to failing father sent us off one or two at a time to make our way in the cities. He split us up in hopes that some of us would survive conflict. Helm and I were the last to leave. We buried father and left."

"This is not the story that you told when you first came to Breen."

"No, it's not. Father thought that it was best if we not present as paupers and orphans. Give no cause for sympathy, he said. We were taught to seek respect; hard work would be the way to that. He pointed us to Breen and the smithies had work, so here we are."

"Where is this farm of yours then? Certainly it must still exist."

"Well of course it does. Father sold it to a young family with grand ambitions. It lies east and north toward Hoarfrost but west of the Hoarfrost road. It falls within Kelt's realm."

The soldier went quiet assessing Andreas's demeanor. "Alright, then. If I have further questions I will send for you. If I do bring your brother with you."

"Yes, Sir."

The soldiers left and Andreas shut the door. The one who had said nothing looked back over his shoulder at the loft windows. I let him see me through the dirty window to support Andreas's story of my existence.

Back in the loft we did not sleep again that night. The late night visit of Harald's men was nerve wracking. We would have to put a fire under Vance's efforts to unite the citizens against Harald's subterfuge with Narhan against the other kings. There was nothing else we could do but push ahead with our clandestine manufacture of weapons and wait for a delivery from Kelton or Kirsh.

273

When the smithies arrived for work in the morning we told them of the late night visit. The full realization of what their underground activities might garner filled them with apprehension. We went on with our plan. We always had someone in the front yard working while they watched. Those of us inside worked to construct a secret hold under the the floor where the new anvil and forge would be built.

It took us three days to complete. We were left alone by Harald, but we all noticed a more alert guard contingent throughout the city. We also became aware of one man who seemed to be spending a lot of time on the porch of the pub down the street. He was hosting a game of Lucky Guzzler most days. Other days he seemed to be just carousing with the old men who spent their days there, but he always kept an eye towards the smithy.

We kept my chores to the back paddock and inside the barn as much as possible. I did most of the digging and mixed the dirt we removed from below the floor in with the manure when I cleaned the paddock. Day three we constructed a sliding floor. It supported the anvil and still rolled back and forth on wheels and runners Vance had made. We were well pleased that it still looked like the original wood floor.

On day four Vance and Andreas went outside of town to gather stones suitable for the new forge. While they were gone a wagon of ore came in from Kirsh. Gorm drove the horses and another unknown man sat beside him in the wagon. They looked like miners in leather pants and soiled tunics. I sent Simo out to greet them and pull the wagon in. We unloaded the ore into the bins along the barn walls while we talked and planned. Coop sat in the yard shaping a copper disk on a dapping block with a sinking hammer. He sat where he could watch the man on the pub porch.

A few hours later the ore was unloaded and Gorm had a good idea of our status. I told him that we needed a farm to back up Andreas's story to Harald's man. He thought he knew a place in about the right location. It was in Kelt's territory, but he would stop and make arrangements with Kelt on his way back to report to Queen Andra.

He assured me that all would be ready when we were. We established a signal to let the kings know when we would be making our move. We would send Simo and Nia on a wagon full of wares toward Kelton. This would trigger our part in the conspiracy. Andreas and I would lead a party of insurgents. through Lily's secret way into Harald's fortress. Once Simo and Nia passed the front of the Five Kings Army the army would move on Breen and Yer.

The kings reasoned that they could not move on Breen alone without risking Harald's escape to Yer. Small patrols of united troops were busy rounding up Harald and Narhan's men and moving people into safe areas around both cities. The main force would remain in their home cities until the word was given to move out to a unified front.

We would continue our efforts to bring the people together against Harald and to supply them with arms and armor. When the Iron Wood arrived we would have to know our final strategy and when we would be expected to be ready.

Gorm left and Vance and Andreas returned that evening with a load of stone. When they did the man on the pub porch left and walked up to the fortress.

"We need to meet your people, Vance." I told him. "Where and how soon can this be done? Do you know yet who will serve us and who won't?"

"I have fifteen men, including the three of us. Two are in the city guard. I have a small shed behind my house we can meet there. If they come one or two at a time we should avoid detection."

"I wouldn't be so sure," Andreas said. We know of one man who is watching the shop. What if they are watching your homes as well?

"No, I'm sorry to disagree, Sade, but I think we need a message chain. We will decide what each person is to do. Vance you will help us to know by describing their strengths and weaknesses. We will need most of them to go with us through the back way. We will make a plan and when we know it is solid we will plug in the people and let them know there part in it. No one but us will know the full plan, or the other players in it. That way if any of them is caught and questioned they cannot give up the entire thing. Those who are to enter the fortress with us will know only a meeting a place; that sort of thing, but if we are careful and thorough it will come together smoothly in the end."

"That does seem safer," Coop said.

"Buck up, Coop, try not to be so nervous. You might give us a way." Vance said. "

Coop was embarrassed, but he knew it was true. He gave no response, but a resigned shrug.

"We will need boats. Do we have any of the fisher folks with us?" I said.

"Only one." Vance replied.

"See what he can do to get boats as close to the southern wall as possible."

"What about the farmers?" Andreas added. " I know there hasn't been much time. Have you been able to speak with any of them?"

"I have two horses to shod and return tomorrow. I will feel the owners out then." Vance said.

"I'll go with you," Coop offered. "I have some pots to deliver down on the quayside. I have heard some grumbling down there as well. Harald wants to tax their boats. I'll take you to the right people and we can talk to them ourselves."

"Great!" Vance said. Vance was emerging as the obvious leader, at least of the three smithy's he was the most enthusiastic.

"Will the two city guards be able to get the gate open, do you think?" Simo asked.

"We talked about it." Vance said, "but it seems unlikely. They are wall guards; not likely to be assigned to the gates anytime soon."

"How much time do you think we have to pull this all together?" Simo wanted to know.

"With Harald already suspicious of us, it's hard to say. No more than a week—less than a day."

No one had anything to say to that.

"How many do you think we will need to take out the king?" I asked Andreas.

"Well I expect Harald to be more wary now, and so more guarded. I wish I knew if Lily was still in play. If she is not in her room then it's likely someone will be. It is possible that Harald knows of the passage by now and has it guarded. You and I should go and check that out tonight.

"Alright we all know what we have to do. Get it done, and fast We had better get back to the business of smithing for now." Andreas said.

Vance fired up his forge and took Andreas over to show him how to smelt the ore for bar stock. He would need plenty of bars for the forging of swords. When Andreas was working on his own Vance went to see to the foundation of the new forge. I assisted Andreas. By closing time we had ten bars of stock poured and filtered the slag through the sand box out back. The colorful, glassy, fluid filtered through to a trough where the water could be collected and reused. The solid material remained on the surface and could be chipped away to be ground into powder. Vance sold this to the potter to add to her glazes for use in ceramics. Vance had the foundation stones for the forge in place and the mortar could now rest and dry over night. Simo and Coop went about their normal tasks. We worried about Harald's man who had been watching us, but when we rehashed the day we were confident that it could all be explained away. Nothing had happened outwardly that wasn't just like a normal day to anyone else; though it had not been so to us.

We closed up shop and Simo pulled out a jug of hard cider and we went to sit in the front yard. Nothing wrong with workmates having a drink together. I stayed just inside the barn and leaned against the jamb. This helped to obscure me while still seeming like part of the group. Coop drank his cup and left. Vance had another and when he saw the city guard change he left and intercepted one of his men. They looked jovial as they talked, but we knew Vance was giving him an update. Vance went home and the guard went to the barracks to check in before going to the pub. We stayed in the yard until Nia came home. Simo invited us to dinner but we declined and went instead to the small pub down the street.

The place was small. Only four tables filled one side of the room. They were separated from the bar and kitchen by a thin walkway. There wasn't even enough room for stools at the bar. One old fellow stood talking to the bartender and his wife. Two more sat at a table near the door enjoying the evening breeze. Vance's guard man sat at a table with one of his mates. He gave an acknowledging nod as we walked in. We nodded as if to say hello, but we did not speak to him or sit with him. I went to the last table and took a seat in the corner. The window there let in a beam of light across the table. When I sat behind it the bright light served to hide my face. Andreas went to the barkeeps wife and asked about a meal then came to sit across from me, to further block sight of me.

Our meal came along with some mead. We partook slowly and waited for the place to fill up with the evening crowd. As the suns went down my corner fell more into shadow and I began to relax.

The small pub was filling to capacity mostly with guards, both city and fortress. It wasn't long before four came to take the other chairs at our table; the last ones in the place. One was friendly and soon he and Andreas were sharing stories, most of what Andreas said was a lie, but he held up and by the end of the evening Sig and Frog had a friend inside the fortress. What good that would do was yet to be seen. We would have to check him out with Vance. What was valuable was that Andreas had managed to confirm; by the use of his story about marrying a noble woman, that Lily had not been seen since her disappearance. No one seemed to know where she was.

Andreas bought a round for our new friends and we left. "A smithy's day starts early. Nice meeting you all." He said as he guided me out.

We went up to the loft gathered what gear we needed to scout out the secret passage and waited for the moons to pass. We waited for a guard rotation and began our count as we went over the western wall just as we had the night we kidnapped Lily. We ran along the west wall and stopped under the bridge buttress, to catch our breath, and wait for another rotation before running to the trees near the end of the inlet that divided the fortress from the city.

We had seen no sentries or bandits in the area. Everything went well and we were soon climbing down to the passage entrance. The entrance was empty as well and there was no sign that it had been discovered. Whatever Lily meant to Harald she had not seen fit to warn him of a vulnerability. We did not risk a look inside for fear of revealing ourselves too soon. Andreas bent the elements once more to hide the passage from discovery and we left.

We were back in our loft before anyone knew any better.

We woke to the sounds of Vance building the walls of the new forge. He wanted to get them up early to let the mortar have all day and night to set up. He planned to fire it up the next day. We helped him to place the stones and Andreas told him about our new friend of the fortress guard. He promised to look into it. The forge was built before Coop and Simo arrived for the days work.

When Coop arrived he placed the pots he had made and repaired for some fishermen into a large sack and slung them over his pony. Vance asked me to fetch the two horses he had shod for the farmer and his own horse from the paddock. I brought them all around to the front yard and saddled his horse for him. The two smiths went off together.

We waited anxiously for their return. We knew they would be gone a long time, but the longer they were away the more we worried they had been discovered and captured. They did return though and they had covered their tracks well. They gained us two more fisherman and a farmer. One fisherman gave Coop some pots and Vance had to buy a horse from the farmer to look as if they had drummed up business while they were out. Vance didn't like the man personally, but he knew the location fit our plan well. Vance felt the man was genuinely disgruntled at Harald's actions. He bought the horse to secure the man's loyalty.

Vance had chosen the farmer specifically for his location. He had the homestead closest to the southern wall and his barn was situated close to the water. He arranged to have the fishermen row two boats down the shore and tie them against the shore just below the barn. From the there the boats would be hidden from the city guard by a the rise of land at the shore. The fortress guards likewise would not see the boats as they were hidden from there view by a short peninsula We knew the place. It had to be the one that we had hidden by waiting for our chance to return over the wall the night we had kidnapped Lily. The barn would serve as a staging point for those who were chosen to join us on our return to take the fortress; this time we would kidnap a king.

We congratulated them both on a job well done.

Andreas and I had spent the day smelting more ore into bars for the forge. Vance was well pleased with our work and promised to show us how to work metal. That seemed exciting, until he told us we would be making the horseshoes and doing the daily work of repairing gates and things while he worked on the new forge hammering the bars into swords. We had to keep the smithy running smoothly and agreed to his wisdom without argument. By days end we could both make a shoe and weld a crack in metal.

The man from the fortress returned to the pub porch again. Whatever his purpose was it did not sit well with us, but as long as he was there we felt that we were safe from capture. What ever he was watching for we had not given him to see or he would not be there. We would worry more if he was gone.

The day ended and we went our separate ways. We spent another evening at the pub and took a place standing at the bar, to have more contact with the other patrons. Our friends did not show.

We heard some grumbling about the tension at the palace. The men were not happy with Harald's reclusive behavior. Word of attacks on his men in the wilderness had reached them and it angered them that he led from the confines of his own apartment. He was pulling his men back into the city but he did nothing to add to her defenses. Narhan was to send aid, but when one of Narhan's captain's paid a visit the meeting was short. That was weeks ago and there was no word, or men to come from Yer.

There wasn't much there that we didn't already know, except that it confirmed Harald was in the fortress, confined to his chambers. What was interesting was that he was so afraid and pulling his men back and that Narhan seemed to have abandoned him. This was all good news for us. We ate our meal and returned to the loft for a good night's sleep.

In the morning we told the smithy's our news. It was time to finalize a plan and give each man their assignment. We all worked in the barn that day as much as possible and discussed things. The man at the pub was still there.

At the end of the day we had all of our details worked out. Vance had worked fluidly as we talked and had hammered out eight sword blades. We only needed the delivery of Iron Wood from Kelton now to complete the swords and give our plan to that messenger.

We were heartened when that came early the next day. Vance estimated that he could have twenty more swords tanged to their hilts in three days. We told the messenger to have the kings ready in four. He said they were ready now and just awaiting our signal. We told him then that we would bring Harald to Nagrom as quickly as possible. The kings should plan to convene council soon after the day of attack. If we did not appear with Harald and had not sent a message saying why, then we were lost or captured and they should look for us. He would relay that message too.

·~·Chapter Twelve·~·

Vance hammered blades by day and Andreas and I fit them to pommels by night. Vance's instructions had been concise and two days after the Iron Wood had been delivered we had a surplus of swords and few daggers for anyone who joined our fight as the insurrection unfolded.

Our planning went on almost without stopping. Vance found no more people he felt he could trust our plan to but in the end we had twenty six including ourselves and the smithy's.

Our plans were conveyed through the grape vine and on the third day after the Iron Wood delivery we were ready. On the fourth day several merchants left Breen on tasks needed to support their wares. Vance took his new horse, newly shod and rode out as if to return it to the farmer. The potters husband took his mule, a shovel and a burlap sack, as he always did when digging clay. The pub keeper left his wife to tend the pub while he went out with a bushel basket to gather apples for cider. The candle makers son went out to tend the bees in a clearing in the woods. There were more. Some were hands on the nearby farms. None of them had intent of carrying out their normal errands that day. At the Smithy we went about our usual tasks.

Eventually the assigned merchants, farmers and fishermen made their way to the barn by the southern wall. Our two men from the city guard had managed to position themselves there that day. Towards evening one of them spread his blue cloak across the top of the wall and sat upon it. That was the signal that our ten designated men had entered the barn. Simo had arranged for his wife to join him on this day and they took the wagon Frahn had given us. If asked he was to say he didn't need to wagons and was off to sell it to the miners in

Kirsh. Andreas and I joined them riding in the back of the wagon. Coop stayed behind to keep the shop open until things began to happen. He was in charge of ten others when it did and their job was to get the East Gate open and to supply arms to any who joined us.

When Simo had driven us out of sight of Breen he pulled off to have a picnic with his wife and to give us time to do what we must. Andreas and I jumped out and ran through the woods to make our way to the barn.

If all of our timing came together as we hoped, The Five Kings' Army would be through the gates by nightfall, we would have Harald by morning. And Breen would fall to the council of kings until we could take our place there.

We arrived at the barn and waited for the first sun to kiss the horizon. The farmer stepped out and waited for the signal from our men on the walls. When he had it he whistled one short note and Andreas and five other men ran to the first boat. Three man hid below the net while the others fished. They maneuvered the boat to the ocean side of the fortress to work the shore until they came to a place the fishermen knew. That place would bring them near the trees north of the fortress. Once there they would pull the boat out and after a short uphill climb they would move into the trees until dark fell.

When the second sun kissed the horizon I went with Vance and four more men to the second boat. It was nearly dark now and the fisherman in our boat, maneuvered the boat along the shore and into the inlet as I fished and the others hid below the nets. We slipped in and the fortress guards paid us no mind. The cold of the perpetually dark inlet chilled us, but I was glad of it. I knew we were in utter darkness then.

The fisherman, who's name was Poe held the boat as I climbed out and then up the cliff to the passage opening. It was my job to secure the passage and drop ropes to the others below.

I felt vulnerable. There had not been a guard when Andreas and I had been there last. That did little to cure my apprehension. I made the mouth of the passage and pulled myself in. I saw and heard no one. I secured two ropes to the root that I had tied Lily to and let the lengths down over the cliff. I sat then with my arms around the ropes and my feet braced against the passage entrance as an extra precaution for the men climbing up.

Soon a rope came threading down from the cliff above. I saw no one at first, until the first man all dressed in black let himself over the edge and made his way quickly to the opening. Each man came as quickly and quietly as he could. They bottle necked at the entrance as they climbed over me. When all of the men from below were up we pulled up those ropes. There were still three more to make it from Andreas's group and they did it without incident. Andreas let go of the rope from above and climbed without aid, as he was familiar with the climb. A man coiled that rope and when Andreas was safely inside we grouped into a single file line.

I was first, with Andreas behind me and Vance next. Vance would be a good in a fight. He was strong and smart. The others with us were reasonably fit and untested, but Vance vouched for their willingness and strength.

We went slow and quiet. When we came to the backside of Lily's secret portal we stopped. We had arrived without incident. All of this seemed too easy. That made me very apprehensive. I listened, but I heard only the breathing of the men with me. Andreas could not be sure his elemental illusion had held. I checked the portal for traps and found none.

I had never planned to return this way and so I was not sure now how the door would open from that side. I checked around, but finding no apparent mechanism I took my chances and stepped on the pressure plate that had closed it before. That worked and the hearth popped open just a bit toward the stairwell.

I drew my swords and those who hadn't already, followed my lead. I took a deep breath and peeking through the gap pulled on the secret entrance. The room was empty and looked as if it had not been disturbed since we had left it. I listened again and heard nothing. I motioned the others in and moved across the room. As I checked the entry door they each pushed by the hearth door and filed into the room. The last one through pulled it closed.

The door was locked. I whispered to Andreas to put us under silence and he did. I went about unlocking it and pushed it open just enough to peer through a slim opening. I saw three people in the room. There was a guard posted at the door that led to the inner court yard. Two more were lounging on the furniture, I did not see Harald, but I did see the man from the pub porch. We knew he had to be one of the guard, but to be here now in Harald's apartment meant he was in the inner circle of Harald's schemes. I did not know who the third person was I could not see the whole room, but I suspected there would be at least another a guard at Harald's room and one at the door that led to the rest of the house.

I signaled to the others that I could see three and pointed out what direction they were in. When I opened that door we were in it. I mouthed the words, "Perhaps two more." And held up two fingers, "Ready?" and waited for each man to nod agreement.

I pulled the door open with a jerk and jumped in ready for attack. All four were armed one of them was Harald, but the cowards ran. There was no guard at Harald's door, just one more at the door to the inner house. We had to pursue. Three went into the inner hall while the fourth went out to the balcony overlooking the inner court yard and called an alarm.

"We are breeched! Save the King!" he yelled, twice, before I could get to him. There was no time to grapple with him so I made a hasty decision and ran full at him to heave him over the rail. It was the quickest thing I could do. He landed with a snap of his neck and back— dead. I always regret the taking of life, but for the better good it is sometimes necessary.

Andreas took everyone else and they entered into Harald's house. I saw guards running to our location. I could not possibly fend them off alone. I ran back into the room shut and locked the door and barricaded it as quickly as I could with as much furniture as I could move before the pile began to budge. I moved then to the door that Andreas and the others had taken and went out into the hall. I could hear a clash of battle from somewhere just below me. I closed the door, locked it and set a simple percussive trap. There would be a small explosion, which would singe the first men through the door and create a loud clap to deafen and disorient them. It would also let us know when it was time to watch for attack from this direction. I had better traps, but no time to set them. This would have to do.

I picked my swords up off the floor and ran to the sounds of battle. Andreas, Vance, and our ten compatriots, faced off with sixteen trained soldiers. Andreas remained protected and was about to unleash some elemental force. I hoped it wasn't fire. The area was too contained for that. I ran ahead and with a flurry of blades turned three soldiers from their attention on three of our untrained citizens. The citizens rejoined with renewed fury and the three soldiers fell quickly. Vance had engaged with two and I started to move toward him when Andreas's incant released upon the soldiers.

A force of air detonated just behind them and they were thrown into our line. We were ready for that. Andreas had prepared us for it if such a situation presented itself. We soon had ten dead soldiers and six laid out unconscious. Andreas and Vance assisted the others to tie up and gag the six while I checked for the best way to continue. There was a hall and two doors. One door surely opened onto the inner courtyard. "Barricade that door," I said and pointed to it. Three men quickly had two trestle tables stacked one atop the other and piled with benches and settees. The hall was short and turned in either direction at the end. It appeared that it would travel along the outer wall of the fortress house. On the other side of the wall would be the outer hall that ran completely around the house.

I went to the door that had to lead to another room. I pressed my ear to it and I could hear muffled speech. I tested the latch; it was locked. Another listen told me that they had gone quiet. Who ever was there was waiting for us. I checked but found no traps upon the door.

At that moment the explosion from my door trap upstairs went off. Andreas knew what that meant and sent Vance and three of our least wounded men to block and defend the stair well. He strode then, with purpose, to position himself equal distance from and with view of the door I was about to open, the stairwell, the hall, and the door to the inner courtyard. Four men took up positions to surround and protect him. That left me with four to enter the room with.

I didn't like our odds. But I knew Andreas had command of his elements and of the men who had come with us. We shared a look and he nodded just as the soldiers came into view at the top of the stairs.

This time Andreas shot a blast of fire over our men to hit the first soldiers in the belly. They went down in a heap. The first two were toppled by the tangle of men behind them and fell in a broken heap at Vance's feet. He and another man quickly moved their broken bodies aside. Four soldiers scrambled for cover around the corner at the top of the stairs. Our men remained ready and waited.

I unlocked the door, but was startled as the door to the inner courtyard was suddenly battered hard from the outside. Another glance at Andreas and I saw that he was watching all points of attack. I shoved hard on the door expecting it to also be barricaded, but it was not. My momentum carried me halfway into the room. I was face to face with two of the men from Harald's apartment and eight other very strong and capable looking soldiers. Behind them all stood the man from the porch and Harald.

My four citizen soldiers followed me in. We were out numbered two to one. My men did not falter, but I backed away. Andreas had no view of my opponents, and I needed to draw them out. "Go back," I said and my men backed through the door behind me.

My plan worked and the eight soldiers moved to the door. I moved forward again, blocking their exit so they could only fight two at at time.

The room in which we stood was loud. The courtyard door was being rammed, Vance and his men still battled at the stairs, and I and my men clashed with the soldiers as they came to us through the door. Andreas sent a fire blast searing through the door just above our heads. It detonated amidst the soldiers between us and Lily and Harald. They screamed from the pain but Lily quickly took up a rug a smothered the flames that caught on their clothing. They were hurt, but not badly.

I went over the events of our entrance into the fortress. Suddenly I knew that we had been expected. The retreat of the four from upstairs had seemed cowardly at first, but now as I stood in a door way fighting feverishly with an onslaught of soldiers I felt very trapped. I risked a look at the man from the pub porch and at Harald. Close up now I knew the man from the pub.

I needed Andreas to know also, so I said, "Lily Gebha, as I live and breathe."

"Not for long worm," she said through clenched teeth. Then; "Now!" she shrieked.

From both branches at the end of the hall a mass of soldiers came at a run and ready for battle. Andreas threw a blast of fire at them and took out the first five men, but the others surged over them and we were engaged.

I sent three men to join with Andreas. Vance sent two of his men to join. Andreas sent another blast of fire to explode at the back of the men advancing from the hall and then drew the staff sword form his back and ran to that fight. His blast took out several more, but that seemed insignificant. We were over run.

Lily continued to taunt me as I fought on at the door with one of my men. "You did not think you could be rid of us so easily did you?" she laughed. You could learn from me. I could teach you so much. Too bad that you are on the wrong side of this. You have so much potential, but you are careless. You are not aware of things and people around you. I knew it was you when I heard the smithy's workers had returned, but I had to see for myself. When Andreas came to the smithy's door that night and you watched from the loft window I confirmed it. From then on I watched you from the pub porch. I knew you were raising an insurrection. At night Harald and planned with his captains. You see you are no match for us. We will outsmart you every time."

The man fighting beside me faltered and fell to one knee. He defended, and I got an arm under him to help him up while I defended with my other. We fought on. Four men fell to me and my partner before he too fell. I faced six more alone as Lily taunted and laughed from behind them.

At some point I became aware that the fight behind me at the stairwell was subsiding. Had Vance held them or was he about to fall. I had no way of knowing.

The battle was long and exhausting. We were taking hard hits and had it not been for being able to minimize attacks by virtue of narrow doors and stairways we would have been lost. I was using one sword as a shield and could only attack with one. I was still hit several times, but my armor was holding and no wound was life threatening. My fatigue was what would cause my end.

I wondered if our citizens soldiers would break and run, or surrender. Sounds of battle went on all around me, but I dared not look to check on my meager band. I tried to measure the battle by the sounds of it. It was then that I realized the banging at the courtyard door had stopped. What was more, I realized it had been so for some time. I cast my hearing that way and I heard the sounds of battle in the distance.

The Five Kings' men had arrived! I looked right at Lily Gebha as I fended a blow from one of her four men still standing against me. "The Five Kings' Army has arrived. I hear them at the gates!" I shouted so my comrades could hear me. I watched as Lily's sneer at me changed to a look of fear.

"Curse you foreigner!" Harald yelled. Then he turned and left through a side door. Lily followed close behind him.

"Dammit, they are away!" I yelled for all to hear; "Lily and Harald Flee!" I gathered what strength I could and increased my attacks, no longer using my second sword as a shield and pushed forward. My renewed assault killed one of the four before me and a lucky blow finished another quickly. I fought wild and enraged and beat the two men backwards. Then suddenly Vance was with me and we finished the last two men quickly.

Without a word I motioned to Vance and we ran in pursuit of Lily and Harald.

They had gone down a hall way with doors on either side. I did not think they would put their backs against the wall again so we continued down the hall. It intersected with another and we could hear the battle Andreas and the others fought in the other hall. To our left the hall ended, but there was one more door that would lead back again into the fortress. To our right the hall intersected with the hall where Andreas and the others continued to fight. Beyond that it mirrored the hall in which we stood. Lily and Harald were no where in sight.

I motioned Vance to the door at the end of the hall while I ran into the hall where Andreas fought. If he had seen Lily flee he would indicate that to me. He was preoccupied of course, but his line of sight to the hall was good. I had to shout over the battle; "Did Lily come this way?"

"No," He shouted back. I ran back to Vance who took the cue and kicked open the door. Before I even arrived he was through and halfway up a flight of stairs. I followed and we turned left. That was our only option, but it was also back in the direction of Harald's apartment and Lily's escape passage. We ran until we came to an intersecting hall. Fallen fortress guards told us this led to the stairway that Vance had defended from below. We turned in and found the door to Harald's apartment wide open.

What we saw when we entered was a heartwarming sight. I recognized Gorm and a captain of Tanath's along with about twenty of The Five Kings Army. They had Lily and Harald on their knees and were binding their hands behind their backs.

I did not take time to relish the moment. Instead I said, "I need men." We were given fifteen. We lead them at a run back the way we had come, down the stairs and came up behind the battle with Andreas and our few remaining citizen soldiers. It was not long before we turned the battle and those who had not fallen laid down their swords in surrender.

In the end we lost five of our citizen soldiers. The others, including Vance had all taken injuries. Three were serious. Our reinforcements of Elys and Calibe soldiers watched over us as we gathered our dead and tended our wounded. After some rest we removed the barricade over the courtyard door and ventured outside.

A clash of swords and shouting could be heard here and there but we saw no one in the yard. Andreas and I volunteered to find a safe way through the fighting so we could get our men the aid they needed.

It was not a difficult task. We joined in on three more small skirmishes, but The Five Kings' Army was in the process of rounding up Harald's men and assuring the citizens that his self serving reign was over. The way to the city was clear. We returned and saw Gorm's group bring Lily and Harald out. "They are rightfully yours," Gorm called down to us.

"Will you see to our people then?" I called back. "Your men watch over them now."

"We will be happy to." They brought our prisoners to us where we waited.

"Right through that door. Many thanks."

Gorm went to see to his soldiers and ours. Tanath's captain and five men stayed with us and escorted us out of the fortress. I held tight to Lily and Andreas held on to Harald. They did not struggle until we entered the bridge that connected fortress to city. It was obvious that they feared the citizens now. Served them right after plotting against them. Our plan to kidnap Harald and sneak him out of the city had gone awry, but I was glad of it. Having him face the wrath of people he had not considered in his plan seemed poetic. Having Lily "Porch Man" Gebha turn up to face the same ridicule was just a bonus.

The city was a mess. Bodies of three armies filled the courtyard. We learned from one of our compatriots from the city battle that Coop was among them. I said a prayer for him. He was not a strong man but he had made up for it with courage.

As we passed through the city we were pelted by the splatter of debris thrown at our captives. We marched them out of the city and into the camp of The Five Kings' Army. Our prisoners were taken to an enclosed wagon with thin windows up high for circulation. The door was locked tight with a bar and chains wrapped around that and locked with three heavy locks. The kings had prepared for every possible outcome.

We were taken then to the command tent. There sat Queen Andra, King Thome Kelt and Tanath's son, soon to be king, Xatar. King Frahn paced the floor with his head down. He had been an naïve key player in the events that had led to that the night. What that caused weighed heavily on him.

It was clear that they had all seen battle but had been well protected. Even Frahn who had pledged only monetary support saw in the end that he must, for that sake of his integrity, join the battle. He led the assault on Breen's gates himself. When the battle swayed our way they retired to command from behind. August had taken the surrender of Yer and stayed behind with a contingent of men there to initiate a transition.

When we entered they all stood. No one said a word. They looked to us and Andreas said, "It is done. They sit in your prison wagon now."

"They?" Frahn asked.

"Yes, Lily decided to return for the fun. She was disguised again, this time as a fortress guard. Harald was well aware of her identity though. They knew we were coming. We did not know who Lily was until the end. She had watched us from the pub porch, comfortable in a new identity."

"She was smug, and thought they had outsmarted us. She was shocked to learn the kings had joined together. That frightened them well. That is when they ran. I chased them, along with the leader of the rebels. They ran right into Gorm and Tanath's captain, whose name I do not know," I said.

"Mackey was with Gorm," Xatar joined. "I am happy that a troop from Calibe was able to assist in such a great manner." The prince beamed. He was as proud as his late father.

Queen Andra came forward and said, "You must be exhausted, and I can see you are hurt. Let me take you to be tended to. There will be plenty of time to tell us your story at the Kings' council."

The good Queen escorted us from the command tent to one right next to it. Inside men of all three armies laid on cots or pallets on the ground. Healers went about seeing to their needs.

There was no where to lie so Andra went to a pile of blankets and made pallets for us herself. As we waited to stretch out for a much needed rest, a familiar voice came to us from the far end of the tent. Etain called out to us and made her way through the commotion and came to see to us herself. She made quite a fuss and praised the merits of Andreas's ointment as she slathered it on our wounds and bandaged them. "Many men have been saved today thanks to your unguent," she said.

"I can't take all the credit. Saeede's mam improved upon my original concoction," Andreas said.

"Thank her for us, Saeede," I heard her say, but the aroma of the unguent, the hum of the noise ,and my deep weariness was sending me to a deep sleep.

When I woke the chill was gone from me again. It was warm in the tent from the suns high in the sky beating down on it, but the chill itself had subsided to just a whisper deep down in me. Andreas still slept beside me. I found my hand was in his and I felt good about it. I raised his and kissed it before slipping mine from his sleepy grasp.

I sat up with some difficulty. My wounds were healing, but tight, and my muscles ached from the relentless fighting we had endured in the fortress. Andreas muttered sleepily beside me, but did not wake. I stood, stretched, and went out into the camp. Hungry, I went in search of food. I found it at the campfires of the different armies. They made me welcome at each and fed me until I could eat no more.

Andreas found me sitting with Andra's men. He had one hand full of bacon and an apple in the other as he approached and sat on the ground beside me.

"I saw Frahn," he announced. "He is preparing his men to leave today. He would like us to go with him."

"We need to get our things from the smithy."

"I told him that. He sent a man for it. I didn't think you'd mind."

"No, as long as we have the ledger and Mam's journal. There isn't much else there worth keeping."

·~·Chapter Thirteen·~·

As we rode Frahn told us how the battle had gone for them. We learned more about the surrender of Yer. Narhan had fled and his generals surrendered immediately when faced with five armies led by August. They did it to save the city and her people. Under questioning they admitted that Narhan had fooled even them. Narhan had fled with his historian and the captain of his personal guard. It was the personal guard that had been sent out into the woods to wreak havoc.

When it came to the attack on Breen there had been an initial resistance, and the city guard fought well. There was a small uprising from the citizens within the wall and it grew steadily until the men at the gates were faced with slaying their own families and friends. From there the advance to the fortress was easy. But the battle for the gate went hard. Many fell on both sides. Frahn was pierced in the side and the ride on horseback pained him greatly, but he wanted to ride home amongst his men. When the gate was breeched he was forced back and his captains persuaded him to return to camp. He did so reluctantly, but conceded his command to them.

We rode into Nagrom the next afternoon, having ridden all through the day and night and the next morning. Pinkert, the historian met us at the stronghold porch. He had been in charge of the city while Frahn was gone.

We would rest a few days. Then as planned the other kings would arrive and hold council to decide what to do about Yer and who would see to things in Breen until we were ready to take possession of it.

We took full advantage of the time to rest, and drink, to discuss our future, and to get to know Frahn even more After all we were going to be neighbors someday.

The Council of Kings did not start out well. The caravan that was to bring Lily and Harald to appear and face judgment arrived on schedule, but with alarming news. Lily had managed to escape. Her binds were cut and she had slipped through the little roof hatch through which meals and water were lowered. When they had gone to let the prisoners out for their morning ablutions; Lily was gone and Harald lay dead on the floor of the wagon. His neck had been snapped.

So our triumph was short lived. We would learn nothing of Narhan's involvement in all of this, but it was certain that he had been. How Lily had eluded an army of men was not hard to imagine. To her disguise was as much an expression, a purse of the lips, a tilt of the head, or squint of the eyes as it was a certain gait, or roll of the shoulders. She was still dressed as the man from the pub porch. I imagined she strolled right through camp as if she belonged.

It was a concern to all the kings to have an assassin on the loose. They spoke at length of new laws and practices that would help to keep them safe. I have little faith in anything they proposed. Lily was cunning and insidious. I wondered if I wanted to move to Breen after all, but I realized that she knew more about me in Mareese and I didn't have an army to protect me there. I was convinced that when Lily decided she wanted me dead that she would make it so.

After a time the kings came to realize that too. They would be more careful and vigilant of strangers from now on. It was time to move on and address the healing of an emerging nation of states. Time to set aside the city state mentality. The council turned to more immediate matters.

We suggested, and it was agreed that Pinkert look after Breen until we could take over. His knowledge of the area would help reestablish order and see to the proper steps to rebuild the city. We trusted him to protect our interest so that when we came to stay the transition would be smooth and more importantly accepted by the citizens there.

Queen Andra had taken a tour of Breen and found the people to be resilient. They mourned their loses but every citizen that she spoke to had conveyed their thanks for the Kings taking down a charlatan. They were excited that the kings had finally acted together and looked forward to better days ahead. Before she left Andra ordered her holy woman to stay behind to see to the needs of the grieving.

August had done the same in Yer. Yer was in a state of shock. They had not suffered the physical pain of War, but they were betrayed by a leader they thought loved them. They would recover and August offered them any help they needed. They chose the merchant guild master to see to the business of the city. What he found was not good. The coffers had been greatly depleted by Narhan before he fled. He could not possibly have taken it all but it would be a burden on the people to replenish what was needed to maintain that great city.

Frahn volunteered to look at his own books and send what he could to the people of Yer. He did sit in the prime shipping spot of Ahnges and his people had prospered from it and so had the coffers.

Charity was growing in the Kings and Queen of Ahnges. Talk turned to open trade amongst the cities and from there to trade with the cities of Crystalier. We invited them to come to Crystalier and see her wonders for themselves. Arrangements were tentatively made but in the end they all agreed to go.

For us; our work was done. We had much to do to settle affairs in Mareese and bring them across the sea to Breen. We had much to discuss about marriage. We stayed until the council was adjourned, but after that we stayed only long enough to arrange a ship home.

Frahn hosted a farewell party for us on our last day. It was nice to be part of the party for once and not the entertainment.

***

Let us know how this plays out," Andreas told Frahn. "Although we leave you to it we do care what happens here. It is just that there are still things that need smoothing out at home."

"We do understand. All of us Kings and Queen Andra are grateful. I dare say we owe you a debt."

"Be careful," Andreas said. "You never know when we will come to collect. Take care of Breen until then."

We all laughed.

"Go, knowing that you have done well here. I will be in touch. I have a letter for my wife." He handed us a sealed parchment. I took it and tucked it into our bundle.

"Good luck Frahn."

"Yes," was all he said in return.

We bowed and left his court.

The ship was a large merchanteer. Strange how Frahn could see the advantage of such trade, but the others had been blind to it. We hoped when we saw them again the treaty would be discussed openly and at length. We boarded the ship with time to spare and were directed to a small berth.

On the bed of the berth was a brand new carpet bag. It bulged from the contents inside it. We opened it together to find it packed with brand new instruments and a note with Frahn's seal.

"Many thanks. I expect to hear you play when the kings meet with Crystalier to determine the treaty. I hope all Kings and Queen Andra will be able to go together!

God speed.

Your friend, Frahn."

Andreas picked out a melon bowled mandolin and tuned it. I went straight for a silver flute and tested the fingering. We played until the shouts to get underway came to our ears.

I found my root and chewed some before placing another to dissolve below my tongue. We went up to the deck and sat upon the taffrail to play as the sailors took us out of port and turned us toward Mareese.

Home! We were going home at last.

·~·Chapter Fourteen·~·

Mareese looked more beautiful than I remembered it. We approached the wharf in the morning light. Her white walls played the colors of the suns' rising back at us. I was happy to be back here to my life and my city. My city—how odd that I, who had always hated cities, would call a city home. I longed for the place while we were away and now that we were here I couldn't wait to walk her streets again. Could we make Breen as attractive a place? At least it had the ocean views and forest land, great big wonderful miles of forest.

I recalled the telling of Lily jumping from the ship she had stowed away on to Nagrom. I imagined myself doing the same and running straight home to Mam. Of course I had too much dignity for such things and when we were at last ready to disembark I walked down the plank to the dock. Andreas was the one who jumped from the ship, as if he had read my mind. He landed gracefully, jumped to his feet and took my hand, as a gentleman does for his lady.

"Please Andreas, you are making a spectacle of us," I said, as I knelt to kiss the boards of the dock.

I stood and took our bundle and Andreas took the new carpet bag from the pile of cargo being unloaded to the dock. We went arm and arm into the city.

"You know there is still the matter of our marriage, Sade."

"Yes, Andy," I sighed.

"I wish you didn't make it sound so terrible."

"I am sorry. I do want to marry you. So much I can't even tell you, but I must resolve this thing within me first. We have waited so long to declare our love. Can you not wait a while longer to let me make myself right for us?"

"We have waited long; it is just that which has me anxious. I want you now."

"I should have never given you a taste of me. I should have known the chill would come back and ruin this."

"It is not ruined yet. Oh sweet Sade, can you not see you are not ruined by this. We will get answers and Mareese is the place to do it. We will talk to Diony. She has pull at the Seers Academy. Someone there will be able to help you get rid of it or failing that to control it. You will marry me Sade. I will hold you to your promise."

"Yes, you are right as always. I will be more positive from now on. Maybe I'll even learn to read your mind. Yes, what an idea! You are brilliant, Andy."

"Ugh."

***

Mam and Mya were happy to see us. They had bonded well and made a good team in the shop. Communication was still an issue but if they remained patient they were well on their way. I gave Mya a few pointers and she was happy to have them. She was very excited to know that we had brought her treasured things with us and that they would be delivered the next day. We returned Mam's journal to her. It was tattered from the attack on Andreas while in the cart, but it was salvageable.

After the initial merriment of our return calmed down we sat Mam and Mya down and announced our plan to marry.

"Aou ie!" Mam said and clasped her hands above her head.

"What do you mean, about time? We only just agreed last month."

"I ew ih."

"Yes, well so did we apparently, but knowing, and admitting are two very different things."

Mam came to me then and put her hands to my face. "Ah ir; Ohay oo ee ha-ee."

"Yes, Mam I am happy. I will try not to be a sad girl any longer."

She went to Andreas and hugged him. When she came away she wiped a happy tear from her eye.

"Where will you live?" Mya asked.

"Well, I will move in with Andy eventually, but I have some things to resolve before there can be a wedding. When I do we will need a lot of help arranging things. So I'd like to stay here awhile longer, then Mya, if you would assist us with arrangements it will be much easier."

"Of course!" she squealed.

"Do you think we should let Mam help too?"

Mam shook her fist at me.

"I think if you don't you will be very sorry."

We breeched the topic of moving to Breen and settling into the fortress house there. The idea excited Mya. She had lived in Frahn's stronghold most of her life but had never really been accepted there. She longed to live with some status and comfort. We would have to watch her carefully to be sure she kept a respectful head toward others. Mam was harder. She had her shop and loved Mareese and the people there. She too had been an outcast and in Mareese she was loved and respected. We promised her a shop and a chance to be a positive influence on what we hoped would be a thriving, creative, and cultural influence to the rest of Ahnges. She promised to think about it.

Mam kept the shop closed that day and we all sat in the warm kitchen discussing our plans. Andreas went to his apartment late that night, but was back in the morning so we could report to Diony and Ray Vin Wholfe.

We delivered Frahn's letter to Queen Sion first and then went to knock on the door of Diony's office. Brynal answered. "So it is true, you have returned. Come in," he said, and stepped aside for us to enter.

Diony was coming around the desk and hugged us both. "Welcome back."

"Good to be back," we said together.

"Please sit. Tell us everything. We have one letter from Frahn and we know why you stayed behind, but it took so long. What a mess. Sorry you became so involved, but at least the assassin is dealt with.

"Well…" and so began our telling of how she had gotten away and two kings murdered. We told her about Narhan emerging as the mastermind behind Harald's actions and in the end how the kings united in an action not so much of war but of shadow diplomacy.

We told her how we had created an insurgence against Harald and had planned to kidnap him and bring him before the Kings' Council to answer for his crimes against them.

"Lily surfaced again there, and although we failed at our plan it was good enough and Harald and Lily were captured." Andreas interjected.

"Oh good, so you got her again!" Diony said.

"No, she managed to escape again from the caravan that was transporting them to the council. She was gone and before she slipped away she snapped Harald's neck and left him dead on the prison wagon floor."

"We must find a way to deal with her."

I said, "We must, but there is more. Narhan fled his city. King August reported that even his own citizens and men were fooled by him. We were there. Everyone was very friendly to us, but he had men within the ranks that were loyal and took their orders to attack us. Many of them fell or were captured as The Five Kings Army spread out to rid the land of them. How an entire population could be fooled eludes me."

Andreas concluded, "Frahn acted alone on the treaty. He took bad advice from Narhan who he viewed as a friend. Five kings are now in agreement to meet and author a treaty together. First they must have this convoluted mess that Narhan has created cleared up. We asked Frahn to keep us informed. I believe that he will. In the beginning he was alone in finding a peaceful solution to the strife there. When we gave the solution to all of the five remaining rulers they were doubtful at first, but as they talked it through they became enthusiastic. In the end they are united to making Ahnges a peaceful place They gave us a holding if we agreed to help them take Harald and Narhan down and were successful,"

"What is next for the two of you then? Will you be leaving us?"

"We have left it open, but if we could create a stronghold loyal to Crystalier and Mareese then the treaty would go better. We think that if we use Mareese as an example; on a much smaller scale, that we could be a catalyst for a better Ahnges." I said.

"But there are other things we must see to before we can seriously take that on…" and so began my telling of the recurring ebb and flow of the chill. I had to achieve control of it at least if I could not be rid of it.

"I will speak with Eble. Can I send him around to speak with you?"

"I'd rather go there. I don't want Mam to overhear and worry."

"Sure. When can I tell him to expect you?"

"As soon as possible."

"Call on him tomorrow. He walks the yard outside the buildings every morning at mid-day."

"I will. Thank you."

"And what about you Andreas? How will you occupy your time while Saeede is busy."

He thought a moment deciding not to reveal our marriage plans publically just yet. "I do have a ledger to repair that was torn up during one of our skirmishes. I think I will rewrite the important parts of it."

***

Six months passed while I studied under Eble. As Chief Elder at the Academy he was more administrator than teacher and was able to devote a great deal of time to me. He agreed with the theory that the chill was a warning. Without the chill present he could not teach me to suppress it any more than I already knew. It impressed him that I had been able to do so. He told me that if I could suppress it I could call upon it. I was leery of that, afraid that I might call it and never be rid of it. He reasoned and cajoled me until I relented and gave it a try. All the while he spoke softly his instructions. I concentrated on all that I had ever done in my mind to suppress the icy chill. Then I worked backwards until the chill was in me. He forced me to let it intensify to where I could barely stand it and I was near convulsions when he softly encouraged me to control it again. It was all we did that day. I went home utterly exhausted.

The next day I did it twice, and three times on the third day, and so on until I could do it at will and not be tired. Next I mastered a meditation that might; and he emphasized might, help me to see the danger it predicted. So we had nothing more to do but concentrate on the roar. Both times I ever used the roar it had surprised me. Both times I had feared the loss of a loved one. I got to where I could generate anger from past events and memories. My loss of Wallace, more my guilt at having killed him was the best one to use. Eventually I could channel that into the roar and then I learned to control the force the roar would have. When Eble was through with me I could do this even without the chill in me. It would be a formidable weapon, but only in dire circumstances. Even though I could stop myself from swooning after the great energy passed through me it still left me momentarily dizzy and wobbly. Eble assured me that my control would become refined each time I used it. Knowing that I could control the thing gave me the confidence to pursue my relationship with Andreas whole heartedly.

Throughout the winter there had been no sign or indication that Lily had returned to Mareese. That made us no less wary; in fact as spring approached we became more alert for her. Travel in the winter was often difficult. Two people in exile could gain passage on a ship more easily in spring and summer when captains were less worried about risk to their ships. Wherever she and Narhan had retreated to they would be wary of detection from Ahngesian and Mareesian spies. It would be difficult for them to move about, until they had secured other identities. That delay would not deter them for long though with Lily in the mix. One autumn to winter change would have been ample time for them to put on new identities. We were on our guard.

In the last days of a harsh winter I talked with Mam about my fears of having a child that might still carry the devil's blood. She understood. She had tried to abort me more than once from fear of what I might be. She had pursued further research on the matter without my knowing in case the day ever came that I would ask her about it.

"I don't want to have to abort, Mam. I really don't think I could. I want to never become pregnant. What does your research tell you about that?"

She paged through her notes to one page and pointed a determined finger at it.

The ingredients would certainly render a woman unable to conceive, but the side effects were awful. If I survived the pain, and fever then I would always be barren. It was the remedy I was seeking, sad as that was.

I thanked her and went to discuss it with Brynal. He was saddened by it, but not surprised that I had pursued it. He knew that I would. He understood the risks to me and to a child if I bore one that was more devil than human. He feared more the remedy that would prevent it. Still in the end we decided to never have children of our own.

The next day Mam and I made arrangements to proceed. She brewed her potion and I drank it down with a willow milk chaser. Andreas came to be with me. I was fine all day, but at night I woke in severe pain and the fever followed soon after. My life-giving ovaries were shriveling up and would die inside me. Three days it took — three gory, painful days. I slept nearly two afterwards. When I felt well enough I went downstairs. Andreas was there. It was very late at night or early morning. Mam and Mya were asleep.

I went to him and stood behind him with my hands upon his shoulders. His mood was dark and I felt it too. I leaned over to put my head next to his. "I'm sorry Andy."

He wrapped an arm around me. "I know Sade. It will be alright. We will be alright. I love you."

Spring came. Word arrived from Frahn at last. Lily and Narhan continued to elude them. Neither of them had been sighted anywhere on Ahnges, but that was no surprise knowing Lily's skills. It was assumed that he and Lily were together somewhere now but there was no way of knowing where. That information put us very anxious. If the two of them had plans of taking out four more kings and a queen so that they could steal an entire country; what would stop them from taking us out in revenge for ruining those plans?

Frahn's queen, Sion, prepared to go home as soon as the weather broke and the waters were safe to sail again. A send off party would have been appropriate, but with Lily on the loose Diony hosted a private dinner in her apartment. Only Diony, Brynal, Sion, Andreas and I were present. Ray Vin Wholfe was busy seeing to our safety. Sion had become a friend during her stay with us and we would miss her. When the dinner was over we played a tune we had written for her as a going away gift. We called it simply: Sion's Song. She was appreciative and we promised to play it when the treaty council met at last. Sion sailed with the morning's first tide on one of Diony's own naval ships. She was accompanied by an additional team of trained men for her protection. When Sion was safely home the ship and men would return to Mareese. Diony sent a letter of congratulations and encouraged Frahn to remain vigilant for Lily.

***

We spent the summer making plans for our wedding and a move to Breen. Mam had agreed; after some influence and assurance from Diony that she would find a suitable replacement to purchase the shop. Mam would have her own money then to purchase or build a place in Breen. We promised to introduce to Etain and informed her she would be the only apothecary on the whole continent.

We were married one crisp autumn afternoon and moved into Andreas's apartment. Our covenant was rejoiced by not just our friends but by those in Mareese who had come to know us by our music. So joyful was the occasion that the covenant was rejoiced for three days. The revelers were not so joyful after. We really should have thought ahead and had Mam mix an extra-large batch of hangover cure.

Life returned to normal and we passed another winter. We had been away from Breen for over a year, if we were to take it as our own we would have to do so soon. We wrote to Pinkert and he responded to assure us all was well and the people were well aware of our situation. He kept us apprised of his decisions and we were happy with every one.

Andreas and I suffered from wander lust after. Settling down was harder than we imagined. We wanted to travel, one last time before settling down in Breen. We wanted to go where no one knew us; somewhere neither of us had never been before. Then one after noon Andreas surprised me by saying: "I have a wedding present for you."

"A little late isn't it, Andy. Besides, we promised we wouldn't."

"It's okay this belonged to both of us already anyway." He produced a leather sleeve in which was a meticulously scribed dossier.

"Eindal's ledger. The ancient arcane fully transcribed?"

"Yes. Read it while I pour us some strong alcohol to celebrate. Brandy?"

"Please."

Eindal had been a purveyor of rare and wondrous items. The transcribed ledger did not disappoint. The first item in what we now call Andy's Ledger was listed as God's Iris.

"God's Iris; is it a flower?" I asked.

"No. I think it means more literally; God's Eye. See here? He pointed out some specific text and spent the afternoon educating me on what he had transcribed.

What I learned was certainly fit for an adventure.

We wrote to Pinkert to alert him that we would be delayed on a matter of dire importance.

Finis

About the Author

Nance Bulow Morgan has been a photojournalist and worked in the print industry for three decades. A native of Northern Illinois, Bulow Morgan now resides in the Sandhills of North Carolina.

She has published a book of prose and a fantasy novel, Legend Destiny, which became the spring board for The Minstrels' Tale Mysteries. Minstrels' Covenant is the second book in that series!

Other Books by Nance Bulow-Morgan
Legend Destiny
Voyage: A Book of Prose
Minstrels' Gambit: Book 1 of the Minstrels' Tale Mysteries

Current Projects
Minstrels' Prize: Book 3 of the Minstrels' Tale Mysteries

www.ingramcontent.com/pod-product-compliance
Lightning Source LLC
Chambersburg PA
CBHW051237260626

47162CB00002B/482